2/5   7SP

STRANG

Midnight Street Anthology 4

Edited by Trevor Denyer

Midnight Street Press
www.midnightstreetpress.com

STRANGE DAYS

Midnight Street Anthology 4

ALL STORIES ARE PREVIOUSLY UNPUBLISHED.
***Cover Illustration: 'Man of Letters' © Roger Keen 1977 ***

www.midnightstreetpress.com

FIRST EDITION print and ebook. May 2020
ISBN: 9798637755370

*** See page 509 for Roger Keen's biography.*

Contents

INTRODUCTION

Each of these stories is a demon, hatched from the imagination of its creator. As I write this, a viral demon stalks the world, culling as we cower in isolation, living in fear of Armageddon. This demon is indiscriminate, taking not only the low hanging fruit, but the young and the healthy.

We live in hope that our ingenuity will defeat this demon eventually, but there will always be others waiting in the wings.

These stories describe a multitude of demons, all imaginary… For now. The idea for this project was conceived before the present threat scourged the planet.

I believe that there will be an end to the current crisis and that life will return to what we consider to be normal. You may be reading this at some future date when the now has become part of history, to be moulded into something that future scholars can reflect upon and package as facsimiles to suit their particular points of view.

Maybe we'll learn from the experience, but probably only in the short term. As a species we are destined to repeat the behaviour that we have always shown; that of aggression and conflict.

Maybe the stories that follow will serve as a reminder that, no matter how clever and immortal we imagine ourselves to be, there are always demons waiting in the wings, and that we should treat them with caution.

The planet we inhabit and our place upon it is not secure. If we create the conditions for disaster then the demons will come and maybe the fiction within these pages may become fact.

Though it goes against our nature to dominate and destroy, we need to learn the lessons of history and collectively improve the way we interact with each other and the planet that sustains us.

This crisis has shown that there is much that is good within us; that we can be selfless and caring, often putting ourselves at risk to save and comfort others.

Within these pages there are many demons, but they have also sprung from the imagination of talented writers.

They are imaginary. Let's keep it that way.

Trevor Denyer
April 2020

THE RING ROAD
Colin Gardiner

I watch from under
The shade of the fly-over.
The ring road squeezes the city
Into prolapse.

The sky closes for business
And the clouds fold over,
Like a restless sleeper's duvet.
A sun-flare splits the grey fade
Of the post-rush hour queue.

I don't think that the commuters
Can see the herd approaching.

A hot breeze whispers
Through skeletal trees.
I can see the horses racing
Up the dual carriageway.

The Ikea sign is melting, and
Flaming hooves are pounding
Over the blackened bones
Of roadkill and exhaust pipes.

The horses rage
Through the heat haze shimmer.
Their manes are ablaze.

With unstable diamond eyes
And the stars in their teeth,
They unleash
Beautiful incineration
On to the idle traffic.

Flashes of orange and red caress
Idle wing mirrors.
I see the fire-herd
Race through the barrier and
Leap across the fly-over.
Mirrored windows kiss
The glare of a new
Temporary sun.
There will be no hard-shoulder
To cry on this evening.

One day I will press my foot
Down on the accelerator, and
Catch up with the stampede.
Like Pegasus on fire.
The ring road will collapse
Into the folded over sky.

~

Colin Gardiner's poetry and short stories have been published by The Ink Pantry, The Ekphrastic Review *and the* Creative Writing Leicester blog. *He is currently studying a Master's degree in creative writing at the University of Leicester. He writes dirty magic realism.*
  You can read more of his work here:
  https://enginesofourspaceship.blogspot.com/

HUNGRYMOUTHS
Simon Clark

Benjamin Mercer followed the frightened man across the wooden bridge, over the stream and into the meadow, where cows clustered in the corner by the barn. The cattle were as frightened as the sixty-year old that Benjamin now followed through knee-high grass. Describing the man as being 'frightened', however, did not sufficiently articulate the man's emotional state. His blue eyes were huge and round. They yelled out to the world that he had witnessed events so shocking that he even seemed to have lost the ability to blink, while his mouth had fixed into a snarl of terror, the upper-lip curling back to expose bright, white teeth that glinted in the evening sunlight.

Benjamin called after the man, who hurried toward the scene of the disaster, "Fennick... don't go too near the edge. Or you'll don't end up down there, too!"

Fennick gave no indication he'd heard the warning. And instead of reacting to Benjamin's call, he started shouting out in fast, broken sentences, his voice trembling – those eyes bulging with fear: "We were up Mallam Lane... hunting rabbits. All afternoon, hunting. Got four. Good meat, plenty of meat. We were coming back down the lane. Everything normal, then – it happened. Just like that! Scotty ran. He jumped over the fence into your field... never seen him like that before. Just off and running, then shouting."

Not so much as an ounce of fat ever stuck to Fennick Tanner's bones. He wasn't just thin – the flesh stretched tight over that skeleton of his, like he'd been shrink-wrapped in cream-coloured plastic, pale blue eyes glittering from a face nearer gaunt then thin. Despite that skinny build, he blazed with energy, and if not out hunting, always working hard on his farm. Unlike Benjamin, Fennick had grown up in the countryside. Rural blood streamed through his veins. He could tell the difference between a hare and a rabbit if the animal was just a speck in the distance. He could name birds from the sound of their song; knew how to make natural remedies from wild plants he found in fields and hedgerows – dock leaves for nettle stings, elderflower for a sore throat. Right now, as he slowed down until moving with the blood-freezing dread of a man walking toward his own grave, he looked somehow shrunken, while his head hung forward, as if too heavy for his neck. And his eyes possessed an unsettling, glaring brightness – fear, pure fear caused that.

When they approached the hole in the meadow – one that had suddenly appeared overnight exactly one week ago – Fennick stopped.

"You know..." Those round eyes of his began to water, as if the sheer pressure of emotion inside his head forced liquid from the eye sockets. "You know, I can't go back to that hole. I don't want to see him again."

Benjamin walked past Fennick, who appeared to be willing his feet to lock themselves into the earth, so preventing himself from moving one more inch in the direction of that awful place.

Fifty feet away, in the centre of the soft, green meadow at twilight, a new post and wire fence that Benjamin had put up last week to stop his cattle falling into the sinkhole had partly collapsed, so half of the wooden posts lay flat on the ground. Ten feet from the hole were four dead rabbits, the hunters' catch of the day. Next to those, a pair of .22 rifles, Fennick and Scotty's weapons. Up close to the lip of the sinkhole, just an inch from the edge, lay Scotty's brown corduroy cap, one of those with the little metal-ringed air vents that help prevent the wearer's scalp from getting overly hot.

Still no sign of Scotty, though. Nothing to suggest he'd climbed out.

And as if to confirm that Scotty never would climb out, Fennick muttered in a strange, croaky voice, a sound a person might make if they'd drunk acid and burnt their vocal cords: "Dead. I know he's dead. I looked down... just as more rocks fell from the sides. They went down, crash-crash-crash onto him – big fucking boulders! They fucking broke him up!"

Moments ago, Benjamin had been driven by a burning sense of

urgency, believing he could rescue the man he'd known for the last twelve months, ever since being allocated these five acres. He'd hoped to see Scotty clambering out of the hole, bruised maybe, dirty certainly, and absolutely certain to be swearing as loudly as he could – a champion swearer, Scotty. But no, Scotty wouldn't be coming back, because Fennick's voice had blazed with so much conviction that Benjamin knew Scotty had been violently torn from this life.

Despite the creeping gloom, ghosting across the meadow, Benjamin clearly saw the raw wound in the field, one caused when the pit had spontaneously formed. As he approached, slower now as a cold dread flowed up from the pit of his stomach, he shuddered: small icy paws seemed to run across the back of his neck. Unease tingled along his nerves, because he knew he would see what had become of Scotty. And it wouldn't be pleasant. Benjamin Mercer had only seen three dead bodies before – his grandmother in an open coffin before her funeral, his father at the hospice, and an elderly man who had slumped down dead on a bus seat next to him.

Benjamin's feet slowed, instinct demanding he stop... *stop right there, don't get any closer, don't look into the pit.* But now he was close enough: he could see the shaft plunge into utter darkness in front of him, with turf at the edges of the opening sagging limply, plant roots hanging down the sides of the hole. Dear God. How could a once ordinary grass field suddenly produce a gash in the earth as abruptly as this one appeared? One that exhaled waves of cold menace that had the power to make the pulse thud harder in his neck. Yes, he wanted to stop. Yes, he wanted to go home and dial 999... but this was his land, his responsibility.

He had to look.

Drawing his phone from his pocket, he activated the torch before stepping forward through the broken-down fence, then he shone that hard, white light into the shaft

Seeing Scotty – well, that produced a shock that hurt as much as a punch in the stomach.

"Oh my God," he breathed.

Fifty feet behind him, Fennick suddenly cried out, like he

needed to get something of his chest: "When Scotty ran toward the hole, he was shouting that someone was calling to him – calling his name!"

Just then, Benjamin felt he must get something of his own off his chest too: something that had to be expressed aloud, not out of cruelty, or insensitivity, but he had to get those words out before they turned malignant inside of him: "Fennick! We won't be needing a body bag. We need fucking buckets!"

*

"Rachel, what do you know about sinkholes?"

Benjamin's neighbour, Rachel, had volunteered to help repair the fence around the pit that had claimed Scotty's life yesterday. Benjamin held the wooden posts while Rachel pounded away with a mallet, driving the posts into holes that had been bored into the soil last week when Benjamin had first put up the fence. Rachel, known by her colleagues as Doctor Veestrum, served as a cardiologist in a local hospital, but ever since they'd had their funding cut (along with other hospitals) she'd accepted the Government's 'Five Acre Start-up' plan, just as Benjamin had been forced to do when the factory that employed him closed and he lost his job as a wages clerk. The Government had formally declared three years ago that for Britain to successfully feed itself the economy must shift from one of manufacturing and service industries to an agricultural economy. Therefore, many people, like Benjamin and Rachel, who had never even grown so much as cress on blotting paper before, found themselves with five-acre plots carved out of what were once National Parks. In a nutshell, the once-praised-to-high-heaven capitalist system had finally collapsed, and now Britain had hungry mouths to feed.

Rachel slammed the mallet down onto the waist-high wooden post that Benjamin held. About the same age as Benjamin, mid-thirties, she was a tall woman, with long hair as dark as those brown eyes of hers. Months of hard farm work had toned her body to the extent her shoulders were broad, and the bulge of her biceps clearly visible when her arms were bare, like they were right now, in that crisp, white T-shirt. Personality-wise, Rachel came across as a determined woman, mentally focussed, never afraid to dirty her hands when it came to manual labour, and possessing a formidable intelligence, something she tended to mask when talking to Benjamin, as if she wanted him to like her. And in a way that was endearingly sensitive, she avoided any displays of intellectual superiority. Though her medical qualifications must have made her IQ mountain-high compared to Benjamin's decidedly foothill intellect.

"What do I know about sinkholes?" She gave a dry smile. "I know that if you hammer a post into a cavern roof that lies just beneath your feet you're apt to collapse the ground from under you, and down you go."

He shuddered. And that wasn't just the cold breeze gusting across the meadow, which triggered the shiver. He remembered what had happened to Scotty so vividly that a burning liquid rose up from his stomach to sting the inside of his throat. And now he couldn't help but picture the existence of another cavern just inches below his feet, one with a thin, fragile roof that might collapse at any moment, gulping down both him and Rachel in one mighty swallow, down into a dark void where there'd be a sickening, plunging sensation before their bones shattered when they impacted the rocky floor below. Dear God, those were gruesome images he didn't need right now. Not of their violent deaths.

After swallowing back down the surge of stomach acid and half-digested veggie stew he'd had for lunch, he grimaced. "Sinkholes can happen anywhere, can't they?"

"I suppose so… but usually in limestone and sandstone areas. They can occur suddenly when the roof of a subterranean void collapses. The void is created when groundwater dissolves bedrock, leaving a big empty space covered by a thin crust of vegetation. And sinkholes can be hundreds of feet deep and hundreds of feet wide. You can end up with a massive crater where there wasn't one before. Without warning, they swallow up people, cars, houses. A scary thought, uh? There…" She tried waggling the post. "Seems firm enough to me."

Benjamin tried waggling the post, too. "And me. We'll start on the wire." He stooped to pick up the fence wire, intending to use the existing strands, seeing as they hadn't been damaged by whatever had knocked the fence down. As he did so, he happened to glance down into the pit again. The walls of the shaft were of grey limestone, while groundwater, oozing through the porous rock, formed glistening patches.

"My sinkhole is a baby compared to others, then." He gathered up the wire. "This is, what? Eight feet wide, maybe thirty deep?"

He couldn't help but notice the flattened grass. That's where the firefighters had pulled what remained of Scotty out. Along with scuffed meadow-grass and crushed buttercups, there were bloodstains – a tuft of Scotty's grey hair caught on a thistle, fluttering in the breeze. A vivid reminder of yesterday's horror story.

What's more, the firefighters hadn't used buckets to bring Scotty up from the pit. They'd needed plastic sacks for all those torn apart pieces of him.

"Bloody hell." He spoke so abruptly that he startled Rachel. "It's like the sinkhole had teeth. Scotty was torn to pieces."

"You said falling rocks." Her dark eyes fixed on his. "Rocks fell from the sides of the shaft onto him."

"Yeah, but rocks crush, don't they? You know that, you're a doctor. Heavy things falling on people inflict crush injuries. Scotty was dismembered. You know, arms cut off... his head..."

Stones, dislodged as the soil dried around the rim of the crater, fell into the pit. They made a clicking sound when they struck the bottom. The *click-click* immediately made him recall his childhood years, when the next-door neighbour owned a massive bulldog, a real brute of an animal. Benjamin's big sister always claimed the dog was one of Satan's Attack Hounds. The dog never barked, but it would stand on its hind legs, look over the fence at Benjamin, then snap its jaws together, its fangs making a loud clicking sound. More small stones detached themselves from the pit's rim before dropping down into darkness. *Click, click, click...* He thought: *Satan's Attack Hound is snapping its jaws again.*

"Damn stuff... s'all tangled." He tried to straighten the wire loops.

"Here." Rachel smiled. "Let me help."

They gathered up those recalcitrant loops before straightening out the twenty-foot lengths.

Rachel paused. "Benjamin. What I don't understand is why Scotty climbed over the fence to reach the hole. He wasn't stupid, was he?"

"No, he struck me as being sharp-witted." The breeze blew across the meadow, ruffling the grass – the air made a droning sound when rushing across the mouth of a pit – pretty much like when someone puts a bottle to their lips and blows. The long, drawn out note of the drone sounded so mournful to Benjamin. Once again, shivers ran down his spine, ice-cold claws scuttling across his flesh. Or so it felt.

Rachel untangled wire with those agile fingers of hers that had so often wielded a scalpel when she repaired damaged hearts at the hospital.

"So..." she began, "what did make Scotty dash across the field to this pit?"

"Someone called Scotty here. They shouted his name. That's what Fennick told me. Scotty heard a voice and bolted over here, then he... well, you know the rest."

Her dark eyes studied the crater. "Maybe someone had almost fallen in, was clinging to the edge, then called Scotty for help."

"Maybe. But whoever it was vanished, so I guess we'll never know. Okay, the wire's straight enough. I'm going to add a strand of barbed wire to try and keep the cows out... I can't afford losing even one to that hole, the bloody thing."

Rachel had plenty to do on her own farm. Nevertheless, she worked hard alongside Benjamin, helping repair the fence, only pausing briefly in order to offer him a piece of carrot cake she'd baked. Normally, Benjamin would have enjoyed Rachel's cake, she could conjure up delicious ones with the meagre ingredients available these days. However, today, glancing at Scotty's blood on the grass made the cake difficult to swallow – crumbs felt grit-hard in his throat. Meanwhile, yet more stones fell from the crater into the pit. Again, on striking the stony floor they made that chilling clicking sound – sharp teeth snapping together. Well... that's what it sounded like to Benjamin, and once again he recalled that Attack

13

Hound of Satan that would stare over the fence at him all those long years ago, and click its hairy jaws together as if anticipating that longed-for moment when it got the opportunity to chew a bloody lump out of Benjamin's face.

Rachel brushed cake crumbs from her T-shirt. "Where are the nails?"

"Oh, I brought u-shaped ones to fix the wire to the posts. They're in my rucksack over there."

"I'll get them, if you can grab the hammer. No… just behind you. In the grass."

"Cheers. Got it."

Rachel lightly trotted the twenty paces until she reached the rucksack. The breeze gusted, producing that long, drawn out drone – one which evoked images of a door with rusty hinges being pushed open in a haunted house, a menacing sound so beloved of horror filmmakers.

Benjamin pulled the wire taut, ready for her return with the u-shaped nails.

Just then, Rachel's voice reached him. "Benjamin? What do you want?"

"What do you mean?"

"You just called me, didn't you?"

"No."

"That's funny. I thought I heard you call my name."

*

Benjamin went to check the sinkhole fence, toiling against a stiff breeze, which carried a fine drizzle, making the green landscape all misty, while shaking the branches of oaks on the hill. The cattle remained in one corner of the field – they seemed to fear the sinkhole and kept their distance. When about a hundred yards from the hole, he heard a voice, a man's voice as if they were calling him. Benjamin paused, listening. The call didn't come again, and he wondered if the rushing winds had, by sheer chance, mimicked the sound of a man.

Benjamin soon discovered, to his relief, that the fence appeared intact. He'd endured a sleepless night worrying that one of his valuable cows might end up falling down the sinkhole. Just then, he heard a man's voice again and straight away he noticed Fennick Tanner standing at the gate that led into the lane.

Fennick carried a shotgun over one arm, while with the other arm he aggressively waved at Benjamin, gesturing him to go back.

"Keep away!" Fennick yelled, obviously worked up into a state of intense emotion. "Keep away! Keep away!"

Fennick didn't sound at all like the voice he'd heard just moments ago, so perhaps it had been only the breeze blowing through the oaks after all, mimicking a male voice by chance.

Meanwhile, Fennick shouted again. "Benjamin, keep away from that bloody thing!"

He intended heading over to Fennick to talk to him. But Fennick did not seem in the mood for conversation, because he angrily walked away down the lane, shaking his head as he went. Promising himself to catch up with Fennick at the pub at some point, he continued across the blowy field, hearing that uncanny drone once more, when the wind rushed across the top of the sinkhole. He noticed that the sinkhole had grown since yesterday: the crater wider, and when he looked down the shaft he saw it was deeper: in fact, so much deeper that darkness clouded the bottom and he couldn't tell how far that menacing-looking pit now plunged into the earth.

*

Midnight. The Witching Hour. That's when all hell broke loose. When a night of carnage erupted with blazing fury. As he sat in his lounge, listening to music, grabbing an hour's relaxation after completing the farming diary the Ministry of Agriculture demanded that he submit every month, he leapt out of his chair, heart slamming against his ribs as something hard crashed against the window. Dragging aside the curtain, he saw a fist pounding the glass. Then a face loomed from the darkness outside to within an inch of the pane – and looking in at him: wide, staring eyes.

"Rachel!"

He flung open the window.

"Benjamin," she panted, her eyes flashing with alarm. "Up in your top field! You've got cattle rustlers!"

Within twenty seconds, he'd pulled on his boots, armed himself with his phone and a garden spade, and was hurrying through the dark toward the meadow where he kept his precious herd. If he lost the herd, he'd end up losing the farm. Then what? A hostel at best. At worst, sleeping in shop doorways.

"Hurry! Hurry!" Rachel shouted, running ahead of him.

"When did you first see them?"

"No more than five minutes ago. I was driving back from the hospital and saw lights in your field – torches, lanterns, something like that. Come on, hurry, Benjamin. We can't let those twats pinch your cows."

Benjamin matched Rachel's pace, gripping the shaft of the spade hard, a cocktail of excitement, anger and fear turning his blood boiling hot. He'd fight those crooks to keep his animals. What with beef rationing limiting how much people could buy, a cow would fetch a good price.

At this pace, they'd reach the meadow in three minutes. He hoped he wouldn't be too breathless to fight.

What they did find when they reached the field made them stop and stare. The cattle remained at the top end, keeping away from what they instinctively identified as a place of danger – the sinkhole in the middle of that otherwise prime grassland.

And there, on the strip between the fence and the yawning mouth of the pit, a figure, one brilliantly illuminated by the gas lantern they'd set down by their feet.

Rachel gasped in astonishment. "Fennick... what on Earth is he doing with those bottles?"

Baffled by the man's actions, Benjamin continued up the slope, hurrying toward the man who now dropped what looked like cider bottles into the pit. The bottles were plastic, so no sound of breaking glass.

Within seconds, he'd reached the sinkhole fence, Rachel at his side.

Fennick didn't notice that he now had company. In fact, his focus had locked entirely on the crater in front of him, and he began to shout angrily into the hole. "Fuck you, you bastard! I know what you did! I'm going to bust you down to shit!"

Rachel reached over the fence to gently touch Fennick on the shoulder. The man, not realizing that Rachel was there, screamed out in shock, then staggered forward in the direction of the crumbling edge of the pit.

Rachel held up her hands, aiming to reassure him. "Fennick, it's okay. It's me, Rachel. There's Benjamin."

He stared at Rachel as if she wore a hideous mask. He shuffled his feet until he was only inches from the lip of the pit.

"Fennick. Look, it's me." She smiled, though her eyes were glittering pools of fear. "Come away from the edge... that might be just an overhang you're standing on. It could give way under you."

"No... no," he muttered. "Gonna finish this. I've got something to do. I'll show the bastard."

The man slurred his words – clearly, he'd been drinking plenty of cider from the bottles that he'd been throwing down the hole. Quickly, he crouched down to a rucksack on the ground, pulled out another two-litre bottle and dropped it down the shaft. *Why the hell was he throwing cider down there?*

But then everything became clear.

"Petrol," Fennick muttered. "That's petrol in the bottles. I chucked five down."

Now Benjamin could smell petrol fumes streaming up from the sinkhole, a thick stench that prickled his nostrils. The bottles would have ruptured after falling all that way, resulting in ten litres or so of fuel now sluicing the pit floor.

"For God's sake, Fennick." Benjamin's words came out in a splutter of alarm. "Get away from that hole. It's dangerous!"

"Gonna finish what I started, Benjamin." He picked up a shotgun from the long grass – Benjamin hadn't noticed the weapon until that moment. "That fucking pit killed my mate. I knew Scotty from school. When we were just snotty-nosed kids playing football."

Rachel's eyes locked onto the firearm in horror. "Put the gun down, please. You're scaring us."

Fennick swayed, the booze corroding his sense of balance. "I'm going to kill the bastard for what he did to my friend."

Benjamin took a step forward, intending to grab the man before pulling him over the fence to safety. *Just need to pick the right moment...*

Rachel shook her head, puzzled. "Fennick, it's just a hole in the ground. You can't kill it."

"There is something in there. A creature lives down there. A monster. A beast... a... a fucking demon. It called Scotty to it. Then, when he got close, it dragged him in and... and fucking well tore him apart. Arms off! Head off! Even his bloody bollocks!" The man paused, his eyes bulging, two glistening balls almost popping out of his head. "Then today... I heard it calling my name..."

Fennick pulled back both hammers of the shotgun, then slid his fingers around its double triggers. At that moment, Benjamin felt such electricity in the atmosphere. He even grunted as his muscles tensed so much his back ached like he'd been kicked in the spine. The absolute sense of danger seemed to crackle in the air. This was like strolling around the corner of your house to find a pack of wolves on your back lawn. He'd never felt anything like it.

As Fennick turned around to look down into the crater, Benjamin lunged, determined to grab hold of the man and haul him back over the fence. Fennick moved faster. After sidestepping out of Benjamin's reach, he fired both barrels down into the hole. The shots sounded as loud as thunder. Rachel yelled out Fennick's name in shock as the pellets hurtled down the pit, striking the sides, causing sparks – sparks hot enough to ignite the heavy petrol fumes filling the chasm.

Yellow flame erupted from the mouth of the sinkhole – a jet of roaring, screaming fire that seemed to try its hardest to emulate a volcano.

Those flames engulfed Fennick, ribbons of yellow fire encircling him, igniting his hair so it sparked and crackled, an agony-inducing firework. Fennick, screaming, his clothes melting into flesh, toppled headfirst into the pit.

The flames died back within three or four seconds, leaving the meadow abruptly silent. Then a few stones detached themselves from the lip of the crater. They fell downward for a long time

before Benjamin heard a clicking sound as they struck the floor of
the shaft. Fennick was down there, too. Or what remained of him.
And now came the pungent smell of burnt flesh and hair...
meanwhile, the clicking sound echoed up the stone throat of the
pit.

The noise still reminded him of that savage dog all those years
ago. Snapping its teeth again. Satan's Attack Hound, his sister had
said. Fang clicking against fang.

Rachel stood there, staring at the smouldering crater in horror.

"He fell," Benjamin said, breathless from shock. "I tried to grab
him, but he fell."

"No..." She shook her head. "He didn't fall. I saw what
happened. Something reached out and pulled him in."

*

The argument erupted into full-blown shouting just ten minutes
after Rachel Veestrum walked into Benjamin's kitchen. She'd
arrived, still wearing her green hospital scrubs, and with dark
bruise-like marks under her eyes. A twelve-hour shift in cardiology
had made her tired to the bone.

They argued because Rachel had made an astonishing claim,
one in surprisingly forceful tones, eyes flashing with nothing less
than fire.

While Rachel paced about the kitchen, Benjamin stirred coffee
into the cups, trying to get his head around what she'd just said.

"I'm not crazy," she told him, her eyes blazing with passionate
anger at his refusal to accept what she'd just said. "The facts are
there. It's just a case of linking them all up."

"Hang on... hang on." His ears were still ringing from the sheer
volume of her voice. "When you say the Earth has become
intelligent... you mean this planet has... what? Grown a brain?"

"Not an organic brain like ours."

"Rachel, I don't understand. How can this lump of rock, our
planet, start thinking? Stone doesn't think. That saucepan can't be
annoyed with me for not scraping out what's left of the mushy
peas in there."

She let out a huge groan of frustration. "Benjamin... Benjamin!
I'm not suggesting all inanimate objects have the power of

thought. I'm talking about our world – this big, big planet – eight-thousand-mile circumference, over twenty-four thousand miles in diameter."

"Okay." He set the coffee mugs down on the table. "Explain how."

"Very well. Forgive me if I lecture like a schoolteacher." She took a sip of coffee – a sip too early, because the hot liquid stung her top lip. However, she merely flinched slightly before continuing: "We have electricity in our bodies. Humans generate electricity. In the heart, the sinus node sends electrical signals that instruct heart muscle to contract, which triggers that vital heartbeat. Also, the human brain is awash with electrical activity. Axons in the brain, these are threads of biological matter, act like wires, conducting electrical signals from neuron to neuron, resulting in-"

"Brainwaves, thoughts, I get it."

"Yes, brainwaves. So, we agree, electricity exists in the human body. Electricity gives us, literally, the power to think."

He stamped his foot. "But this under our feet, this planet. It's dirt and rock."

"And iron. Vast quantities of iron. At the Earth's core, there's a solid lump of iron as big as the moon. The inner core rotates independently of the Earth. And there's an outer core, which is molten – a liquid ocean of hot-as-hell iron. And iron, as you know, conducts electricity. Not only that, the metal core is generating electrical power. Lots and lots of power: it flows all the way to the surface and then out into space to form the Magnetic Field that surrounds this planet like a halo." She fixed her gaze on Benjamin. "*Homo Sapiens* took three hundred thousand years to increase their intelligence from that of the other apes to this high level that we possess now. The Earth, however, has had more than four billion years of existence to get its act together. Now, ask yourself this: what if, during all those billions of years, an intelligence has been evolving, from a rudimentary level to an incredibly sophisticated mind that is housed in the planet's iron core?"

"Earlier, you claimed that the Earth intentionally – and intelligently – created the sinkhole up there in my field."

"Yes, I did. The Earth created the sinkhole with the intention of killing Scotty, Fennick and anyone else who gets too close." She reached out and rested her hand on his shoulder. "And that includes us. The Earth wants us dead."

"Why?"

"Well, consider the harm we inflicted upon the Earth. Humanity polluted its oceans, the air, the land. We burn it when we test atom bombs. We wound its body when we quarry, or dig foundations for buildings, or drill for oil. We have been attacking Planet Earth for generations. Now it's fighting back."

"If anyone's going to believe you, you're going to need more evidence than that."

"Two years ago, when I worked at a London hospital, there was a big emergency. Medical staff were called out to Covent Garden Underground Station, because there'd been an influx of carbon monoxide gas into the tunnel system there. The gas is natural, coal miners call it White Damp. Consequently, the authorities were certain nobody had committed a terrorist attack. The thing is, carbon monoxide is lethal, even in small quantities. Later, geologists discovered that the gas had leaked through a crack in the tunnel wall. Eighty-nine people died."

"A single incident, that's all. That's not proof the Earth is trying to slaughter humanity."

"What about all those volcanos erupting? A hundred and twenty thousand people were incinerated last year when Mount Vesuvius exploded. You must believe me… volcanos are weapons being used against us. Toxic gas is a weapon. Your sinkhole is a weapon."

"But why a sinkhole? Why not a volcano erupting on my land?"

"Or is your sinkhole on a par with an autoimmune response? You know – we get a cold, develop antibodies, they kill the cold virus: hey presto, we're cured. Maybe, because all you've done is plough up part of the meadow, just cutting into a smallish area of soil, then what is perhaps a newly-developed immune system of the planet has only reacted with a low-level response, producing a sinkhole, not a hugely powerful earthquake or a devastating volcano."

"Nevertheless, you think we're not safe here?"

"No, we are not. You see, the planet's mind, the Geo-Mind, if you prefer, has the power to get inside people's heads. Remember what Fennick said? About Scotty hearing his name being called? Fennick insisted he was being called as well. Benjamin, that Geo-Mind lures people to the crater's edge and… this is a tough part to believe … somehow it has the ability to physically pull them in."

"So, what do you suggest? Do what Scotty did? Fire guns down the hole?" Benjamin instantly regretted the flippant comment. But her words worried him to the point he wanted to rubbish her theory rather than accept what could be an immensely disconcerting truth.

"No. Firstly, we make the sinkhole safe – then, even if someone is coaxed toward the hole by a voice, they can't fall in. Listen, the guy who owned the farm before me left nets, really strong nets, in the barn. They were used for catching wild boar. We stretch them over the crater, then… Benjamin… Benjamin? Where are you going?"

Benjamin marched out of the back door and out into the yard. He refused to listen to any more of what Rachel said. This was his farm! No way was he going to let that woman tell him some horror story about sinkholes that lured people to their deaths – because if he started believing in a horror story like that, then how could he continue living here? *And do I have anywhere else to go? Do I hell!*

*

Reality gave him a violent kick in the teeth.

That is to say, what he saw when he approached the sinkhole that foggy morning gave him that figurative kick. This was just one day after Rachel Veestrum's extraordinary assertion that Planet Earth had become intelligent. Not only that, Earth, the mother of all terrestrial life, had become a murderer. What delivered the figurative blow to his mouth was finding lots of corpses, all scattered around the top of the sinkhole between the fence and the crater – okay, granted, lots of little corpses: rats, mice, a hedgehog, a magpie, black and white feathers glistening in the dew, but corpses nonetheless.

One corpse no longer present here was that of Fennick's. The firefighters, with plenty of difficulty and a heck of a lot of rope, had eventually removed Fennick's burnt remains.

With unease turning to gnawing dread in those squirmy workings of his stomach, Benjamin Mercer approached the pit. The opening had grown larger, maybe fifteen feet across now. And he could see a rabbit at the edge of the crater, close to that crumbling rim of soil. The animal's belly had been torn out by a fox, which had begun to eat the dead rabbit. The fox lay dead, too, its teeth still gripping a blood-red flap of rabbit flesh.

Apart from the rabbit, the other animals had died without a mark on them – at least, none that Benjamin could see. Just then, more dirt around the crater edge gave way with a soft hissing sound, the falling soil and grasses taking the part-gnawed rabbit and fox with it. Both tumbling into the pit in a flash of grey and red fur. Then gone. They must have fallen a long way – no thud could be heard when they struck the bottom of the shaft.

Benjamin stopped thirty yards from the sinkhole, knowing he wouldn't feel safe if he approached any closer. Then, after drawing the phone from his pocket, he made the call.

When Rachel answered he said: "Okay. When can you bring those nets?"

*

Benjamin helped Rachel unload the nets from the back of her Land Rover. The nets had once been used to catch wild boar when this area was largely forest. During the last five years, however, most of its trees had been bulldozed to create the productive land required to feed an increasingly hungry population. The nets, rolled into big bales, were amazingly heavy, but they were very strong. Strong enough to net three hundred pounds of charging wild pig.

The mouth of the sinkhole had grown yet again, and there were more dead animals lying around that violent wound in the meadow. A roe deer had joined those limp corpses, lying there, dull-eyed, its now grey tongue lolling from its mouth, the turf revealing signs of being gouged by the animal's hooves when it convulsed during in its final moments.

Seeing those dead animals ramped up the sense of danger that already crackled along his nerves. His heart pounded against his ribs. At that moment, he fully expected some *thing* to launch an attack on them from that deep, dark pit: to viciously strike out from the gaping void, which possessed ragged lips of grass and stinging nettles, a mouth hungry for fresh victims.

As they unrolled the bales of netting, Rachel spoke with a breathless urgency. "Those animals were poisoned by carbon monoxide venting from the sinkhole, I'm sure of it. You can't see carbon monoxide, you can't smell it – and you don't have to inhale much of it to put an end to yourself."

"Then we're likely to be gassed?"

She hauled the stout mesh out over the grass, flattening its nylon strands by pressing her right foot down onto them. "There's a breeze. That will dispel the gas, so we should be alright."

"Should be alright?"

"All being well, we should. But if you get a headache, feel dizzy, nauseous or weak, just run – alright?"

"And I'll be dragging you with me as I go."

She shot him a grateful smile. "Good. Then we're a team. Comrades."

"Best mates. So… as long as the breeze is blowing…"

"We're fine."

He paused, feeling the cool air gusting against his face. So far so good… just pray the breeze doesn't drop.

They worked hard, hauling the nets across the ground, then under the fence wire, then pulling the netting across the gaping maw of the sinkhole. Soon, both were panting. Rachel's face shone with perspiration, Ben's shoulders ached, and tugging so hard at the netting's thick nylon strands left sore friction burns on his fingers, but there wasn't the time to break off to put on a pair of gloves. He sensed they must get this work done quickly, get the mouth of the pit sealed off, then get the hell out while they still could. This area of meadow radiated nothing less than danger. He found himself expecting a roar of fury to blast out of that black hole there in the grass. While the darkness within the shaft oozed pure menace. Every time he looked at the thing his blood ran cold through his heart.

And he felt as if he was being watched. Something in the pit stared up at him. He was sure of it.

As they pulled the nets over the crater, Rachel's sense of urgency drove the words faster and faster from her lips. "The Geo-Mind has identified us as a disease… it has decided human beings are a dangerous infection. Earth wants us gone… got rid of. Extinct!"

"Then will this work? Just sealing off the hole?"

"Filling the sinkhole in would be better, but my guess is…"

"You're right. I couldn't afford to bring in tons of rubble. What I make only just covers my bills."

"Then the net will prevent folk from falling in. There, that's the nets in place. Grab the big hammer. I'll get the pegs… hurry, the wind's dropping. We don't want to be here if there isn't enough breeze to carry the gas away. Remember, if you feel ill just yell. Then we run. Okay?"

Benjamin grabbed a hammer – the thing had a wooden shaft as long as his arm. Rachel quickly dragged a sack full of steel pegs across the grass toward the pit. These pegs were an 'L' shape. When hammered in point first, the horizontal section of the peg would nip the thick strands of netting down hard against the ground, so holding the net taut – taut as a trampoline.

Before they knocked the first peg in place Benjamin heard clicking – just like that vicious dog from his boyhood days, when the brute would snap its jaws together, sharp teeth clicking loudly. 'Satan's attack dog,' that's what his sister had warned. 'Don't get too close to him, Benny boy, he'll bite your head in two'.

"Benjamin! You're too close to the edge!"

Damn it! He hadn't realized he'd moved dangerously near to that lethal drop. Yes, okay, nets did cover the hole but they still required pegging down, they certainly wouldn't have supported his weight if he'd stepped onto a net with nothing but cold air beneath, and he would have simply dragged the nets down with him as he fell into that lethal darkness. And even here, with what should have been solid ground beneath his feet, he felt the turf sag, warning him that he stood on nothing more than a thin crust of turf that created a fragile overhang. His heart lurched so powerfully he felt a pain in his chest, as if that fist-sized chunk of muscle might go *pop*, splitting arteries, tearing delicate valves. Dear God... he moved fast.

Only when he was on the other side of the fence did he trust the ground to be solid again – but even then: what if another sinkhole opened up beneath them? Plunging both to a bone-shattering death? *No, don't think such awful things...* Especially the terrible mental image of Rachel falling, her eyes staring in horror, dark hair fluttering out.

"I'll hammer." His mouth was as dry as old bone dust. "You hold the pegs... if you trust me?"

"I trust you, Benjamin."

They worked quickly, Ben pounding the foot-long steelwork down into the earth – although at times it seemed as if the ground resisted, attempting to push the pegs back out again. Nevertheless – *whack, whack, whack!* Soon a cold sweat bled from his face, and he was so breathless he could barely drag enough air down through his throat and into his lungs

"I calculate it'll take ten pegs to fully secure the net," Rachel told him.

"That means we need to bang in another five." His wrist joints burned painfully from the effort of hammering steelwork into hard dirt. "And did you notice? The wind's dropped. Precious little breeze now." He wiped the wet, oily sweat from his forehead with his hand. "Don't tell me that the Geo-Mind controls the weather. Because I'll believe you. And I will believe it made the air calm so it can gas us." Even as he spoke, he felt such a coldness come from the yawning mouth of the pit. A biting iciness – cold, iron teeth crunching into his skin. That's what it felt like. He shuddered.

"We can do this, Benjamin. Just five more pegs."

Nodding grimly, he returned to work, hammering with all his strength. Even so, the pegs only penetrated the turf with agonizing slowness – just half an inch with every hammer blow. Now his palms perspired so much there was danger that the hammer would slip from his hands as easily as a block of wet soap.

Then it started... barely noticeable at first... in fact, he thought he'd imagined the sensation. Then, at last, he understood the disturbing and undeniable truth: *my head hurts, I'm getting a headache. Say nothing to Rachel, don't admit it.*

Even so, he panted: "I can finish these pegs myself. Move further back from the hole. You'll be safer."

"I'm staying." She spoke with fierce determination. "You depend on this farm for your livelihood. So, I'm staying here with you... we'll fight this thing together." Her equally fierce gaze fixed on the crater. "I won't let it drive you away from here."

Between hammer blows, he panted back, "You make it sound as if the sinkhole is attacking me personally... like it hates me... as if it wants to murder me."

"Believe me, Benjamin, it does, or rather the Geo-Mind does. This is *Earth v Humankind.*"

"Then we can't win."

"Maybe one day it will decide to tolerate us. But we, humankind that is, are going to have to treat Planet Earth with a lot more respect and kindness. Otherwise... uh! ... no, keep going."

The head of the peg had jerked away, just before he'd delivered the hammer strike: he was sure some force below the turf had moved that steel shank. The hammer had struck Rachel's hand – only a glancing blow, but hard enough to graze the skin over her knuckles, releasing beads of red.

"I'm fine, Benjamin. Keep knocking the bloody peg in. Hurry. Because my head's starting to ache... and, dear God, I feel like throwing up."

"Those are signs of carbon monoxide poisoning."

"Yes, that demon... that earth demon, because that's what it basically is... it's spewing poison gas up into our faces. But we will win. Come on, bash the rest of the pegs in. You only need to do three more."

Benjamin worked with nothing less than a blistering fury of energy, hammering the steel pegs so forcefully, brilliant white sparks shot out with every hammer strike, metal clanging on metal, his skull jangling to the rhythm. The headache grew more severe – an iron spike being driven through his forehead, that's what it felt like. He grimaced yet kept on striking the peg. Finally, the horizontal section met the ground. Another blow drove it deeper, securing that section of netting firmly to *terra firma.*

Rachel groaned. A second later she tottered backwards, holding her head in both hands, her eyes dull looking, and her body robbed of its strength to the extent she dropped to her knees.

Benjamin flung down the hammer, rushed across to the woman, picked her up, then carried her fifty paces from the sinkhole: there, he gently set her down on soft grass, hoping she was a safe distance from the carbon monoxide venting from that damned pit. He then went back to finish the job.

Just three more pegs to hammer in, to hold the net tautly over the pit's gaping mouth. Now... finally! ... good luck came his way. Two pegs went in easily, only requiring five or six hammer blows apiece. He checked the net covering the hole. Good news. The netting was as firm as a trampoline, only giving an inch or so when he pressed hard.

Benjamin grabbed the last peg, chose a spot in the turf to drive in what resembled an over-sized nail, where it would nip the thick strand to the ground. Then they could leave this murderous stretch of terrain. *Bang, bang, bang!* He hammered the point in. *Damn it.* The point only penetrated a couple of inches. *Is there a boulder under there, blocking the way?* He delivered more fierce blows. Sparks flashed. The sound of clanging was immense. Maybe shift position? Then he could get a full-blooded swing with the hammer. He sidestepped, trying to find a better spot.

Bloody hell... The pain above his eyes! Felt like someone drilling a hole through bone. And so tired now. Even drowsy. *Why can't I find the right spot to hit this fucking monster nail? Because that's what it looks like. A monster nail...*

Raising the hammer, he aimed a blow at the metal peg and... *Damn. Missed! Missed by a mile.*

Then, when he glanced down, what he saw there inflicted such a crashing shock he felt as if his heart would explode. Because he realized he had, somehow, in his dazed state, manoeuvred himself into the middle of the crater. The only thing preventing him from hurtling down the shaft was the net. He stood on its criss-cross strands – cold air and poison gas rising up toward him. And below that mesh, a long, long stretch of darkness going down... how far down? A hundred feet, maybe? Or a thousand? Darkness shrouded the bottom of the shaft. So, just then, he had no way of knowing how deep.

A voice whispered up quite softly from the shaft. "Benjamin… You won't win, you know?" The voice lost its whispery quality, turning into an ominous rumble. As deep as the distant rumble of an approaching Tsunami that would sweep an entire town away. "Benjamin… pull the net aside… you are next, Benjamin. You are next."

Now he saw objects rising from the shadows beneath him, as he stood there on the net. Two red shapes. Gasping with shock, he fell to his hands and knees on the tightly stretched mesh, staring into subterranean gloom, his body bobbing up and down on those nylon strands that yielded slightly beneath his weight.

Benjamin felt blades of ice ravage his heart – a slicing pain. He could not move. All he could do was stare down at what was rising toward him, up from darkness.

He cried out in shock: "Eyes! I can see eyes!"

Yes. A pair of eyes – red slits for eyes, each with a pupil of bright yellow. They stared up at him – a gloating hunger burning there. The owner of the eyes hated him. They were coming for him. But what then? What would the owner of those malevolent eyes do to him?

The voice rumbled from the depths. "Benjamin. It's your turn now."

He shouted out again as another two objects emerged from the darkness: "I can see hands… there are hands reaching up."

And what a pair of hands… hands like claws… white as bone, they were, fingers terminating in sharp, black talons. And they were reaching up for him, ready to seize hold of his body and drag him down. His destiny: the same as Scotty's and Fennick's. He'd be next.

The red eyes floated upward, nearer and nearer. And the voice from the pit… gloating… promising that he'd be next.

When Benjamin shouted, he didn't know whether he cried out to Rachel, or to the whole world. Or to heaven. "It's saying my name… listen… it's saying my name!"

Then hands grabbed hold of his wrists. And when his mind finally cleared, he realized he was moving. He looked up. Rachel, her eyes bright with concern, was dragging him across the grass. Away from the sinkhole. Away from the burning red eyes.

*

He spent the rest of the day recovering from the effects of inhaling carbon monoxide. From his bed, he sent this triumphant text to Rachel: *We did it. We covered the sinkhole. Now nobody can be lured in. Bastard sinkhole. Ha! We beat you!* Then thumbs-up emojis.

The next day he went to check the net.

Overnight, eight more sinkholes had appeared in the meadow. Returning home, he packed his suitcase.

Nine months later, Benjamin Mercer climbed out of bed in the dormitory – a chilly, drab-looking dormitory that he shared with five other men. He'd been lucky to find employment at the government-owned slaughterhouse, which also included accommodation. Therefore, as well as a small salary, he received a narrow bunk, with a somewhat unyielding mattress, and two meals a day. Rachel Veestrum still sent a text every week, asking to meet him. Recently, she, too, had given up her farm – too many sinkholes appearing in the fields, she said. But he never replied to her texts. What could he say to her? He felt like a failure.

Benjamin headed for the shower block. His stomach itched and he suspected that he'd become allergic to chemicals that they used to sanitise raw beef in order to keep the flesh edible for longer. When he stood before the mirror in the shower cubicle, the sound of water hissing loudly from other showerheads nearby, he raised his T-shirt to examine that prickling itch on his stomach.

Benjamin stared at the awful thing that had appeared there. He felt sick, lightheaded and very frightened.

Because a hole, as big as his fist, had broken open just above his naval. Crammed in that sickening abdominal crater, blue tubes of his intestine, surrounded by raw flesh that was pink and moist. Then, slowly emerging from the tangle of gut were a pair of eyes – red they were – bright red. The pupils blazed a savage yellow. Those were gloating eyes, filled with triumph.

Planet Earth had found a way. That cruel mind, which flowed

through the planetary core in fierce waves of electrons, had discovered how to get rid of its troublesome infestation: the human race. And as men in the other shower cubicles began to scream out in shock, as their own stomachs split open to reveal blood-red eyes, Benjamin Mercer saw a pair of claw-hands slide out from the wet coils of intestine packed inside his stomach.

And the voice he had heard whispering up from the sinkhole nine months ago reached him once more: "Benjamin. Did you think I'd never find you again?" Then the voice became an ominous rumble: "Benjamin. It's your turn now."

Those white hands, with sharp, black talons, continued to move outward. Then they changed direction, and, with serpentine grace, they rose up – rose up toward his throat.

~

Simon Clark is the author of many novels and short stories, including Blood Crazy, Vampyrrhic, Darkness Demands, Stranger, Bastion, Inspector Abberline & the Just King *and the award-winning* The Night of the Triffids*: his adaptation of the novel, which was produced by* Big Finish*, has been broadcast as a five-part drama serial by* BBC *radio.*

GO BACK
S. Thomson-Hillis

<u>Day 1</u>

They put the image on all the sites, there was no dodging it. Like spam it invaded every inbox and then it vanished. An urban myth, a whisper in the dark, a wind pissing in the shambles of Westminster, a rumble in the dying shanties of the suburbs.

Go back, we've come too far, go back.

Yeah, they're right, we screwed up our world. Who wouldn't go back? I would.

<u>Day 7</u>

The posters appeared suddenly. Everywhere. Modern man at the end of a line that began with an ape. Anthropoids, Homo Habilis and Neanderthal, and at the end, hand outflung to stop them, Homo Sapiens thundering, Go back, we've come too far, go back to a simpler life.

It was biblical in its implications. Look upon your deeds, oh stupid man, look at your grimy works and your greed. I want it, I want it, I want it now, says mankind, the spoiled brat who challenged nature and lost.

Go back, join us, go back to a natural way of life.

I thought, I'll have some of that and I lined up with the others and walked through their door. We're homo-give-us-another-chance.

<u>Day 12</u>

The ceiling is high and the walls are beige; there are no windows, one door and the feeding stations. There is a blank screen at one end. Yet we each have our own space and dignity is preserved even during ablution. They told us there would be adjustments, and we expected pills, but they sent it through the vents. It smelled like peace, it smelled like sunlight and forest mornings. And some coughed and some bled and some were on their knees and weeping.

I woke up. Others didn't. They came quickly and cleared them away.

Day 20

Now there is no day and night, only the long, deep dusk to prepare us. The image from the poster plays on the screen but the words have changed, their shapes are strange. Today they turned into starbursts. I love the starbursts. We all do. We wait and yearn and sway and groan and kneel to them. The figures are moving now, they are so beautiful and I know that I must fight for what is right.

Go back. I do not fear the creeping dark, I am strong, I am sharp. I am ready.

Day 23

There was a man today, he smelled of fear and shone a light in my eyes. I did not like the way his face shifted when I told him to move because he was blocking my view of the poster. He pretended he did not understand. I snarled a protest. Fear. Fear. I could lick it from his sweating flesh, low in his gut, fear and something else, something strange. Satisfaction? Triumph? He left. We roared.

Day 30

Time has passed and we know we are changing. We are better, sharper of tooth and claw, thicker of muscle and bone. The blood is hot, the blood is sweet. There is a new scent in the air. It takes us high and leaves us cold. It throbs like a pulse and we move with it. We dance the dance, we writhe and couple.

Afterwards we're hungry.

Day 35

One of the females lies still and cold, unable to untangle from the dance. No beating pulse, no breath, no warmth. At first she smells like blood and regret, then she smells dirty. After a while she smells like food.

They do not feed us. We're hungry.

Day 36
We are hungry. We eat. Her flesh is sweet.

Day 40
The door is open. We go back.

~

S. Thomson-Hillis:
I used to work in Further Education until I'd learnt as much as I could from the students, and then I left, joined a writing group and, with the group's help, took off on a learning curve. I enjoy classic Science Fiction by writers like John Wyndham, Asimov and Heinlein and I've even tried my luck writing my own stories. My parents once went to my school to complain I wasn't reading 'proper' literature. The teacher was a smart man, he referred them to the great authors I was reading – and I became adept at hiding my comic books (shout out to Neil Gaiman). They gave up when I discovered Terry Pratchett. I like dogs, cartoons, Dr Who, Star Wars and all that stuff; I dislike cooking, housework and exercise – except for walking the dogs. That's fun – almost as much fun as writing.

KING SOLOMON'S RING
Elana Gomel

Butterflies.

Zach had always been fascinated by butterflies, even as a toddler. He would stare at a yellow swallowtail as it alighted on the flowers in our garden, refusing to move even when Zeke careened into him, yelling something comprehensible only to the two of them. That was when we had a garden. Or rather, it was when there was a "we". A family. The four of us.

Even when what was left of the "we" moved into the city Zach kept up his obsession. He collected butterfly catalogues that he bought for a penny in the second-hand bookstore on the corner. He drew butterflies and though his teachers praised his skill, he was uninterested in drawing anything else. When I scraped up enough money for broadband, he would spend hours in front of our antique computer, shifting through nature websites and watching insect videos on YouTube. The flowers in Mission were painted on the walls but he still managed to catch live butterflies. I had to put my foot down when I found a bedraggled White Skipper pinned to the wall in the boys' bedroom. I told him that the landlord would kick us out if he found dead bugs all over his wallpaper.

Zeke, meanwhile, did his usual Zeke things, which mostly consisted of breaking stuff, picking up fights, and refusing to speak. My sons. Identical twins, physically so much alike that even at the age of eleven they could easily pass for each other. Psychologically so different that it was hard to believe they were even siblings. Zeke, with his endless diagnoses of AHDH, or maybe borderline personality disorder, or perhaps an unspecified developmental disorder... All those labels that eventually blended into one single heavy burden: my son is not normal.

Was Zach "normal"? I was no longer sure what it meant. When they were toddlers, they both had a speech delay. They babbled to each other in that intricate, complex, made-up language that so many identical twins develop before they snap out of their primordial unity and grow personalities of their own. Zach did. Zeke did not.

While Zeke struggled with speech therapists, Zach was doing well in school. He was quiet and polite. If he was rather withdrawn and had few friends, what would you expect from a child in his situation?

I know I should have paid more attention. I should have dug deeper into his interests; should have restricted his screen time; should have… All the endless possibilities, roads not taken. But I was so worn-out by my fight for Zeke: meetings with school counselors and psychologists, keeping up with his ever-changing medication… And this on top or working a full-time job, trying to keep us afloat after Jordan had left. I could not have done better.

And I could not have prevented the murder.

It happened on a chilly foggy day – which describes just about every day in San Francisco. The boys were home as I went down to the local bodega for some burritos. Yes, I know, I should not have left them alone. But it was just for twenty minutes, for God's sake! During those interminable interrogations when the bright light shining into my eyes and the metallic taste of dehydration on my tongue and the monotonous voice of the police officer blended into a symphony of despair, I kept trying to disconnect my mind from what was actually happening and to put it on autopilot. Press the button, get the readout. Yes, they sometimes stayed home together but never for longer than an hour if I had to run errands. No, there was never any trouble. Yes, the door was locked. No, they would never open it to a stranger. Why was it unlocked when I came back? I don't know. Repetition: that was the key. The words worn smooth into a round shape like a pebble with no crack or irregularity for them to get their claws into. Eventually they had to let me go.

Zeke had been the only witness to the murder of his brother. When I came back from the bodega, the smell of fresh burritos was tickling my sinuses as I climbed the stairs to our walk-up. I was smiling to myself as I imagined their enthusiasm. It was only recently that I had given up on trying to eliminate "junk" from their menu. Zeke had been on too many unhelpful diets and I had been worn out by cooking organic quinoa after a full workday and then trying to cope with his tantrums and his brother's semi-starvation as both refused to touch my recipe-perfect meals. I had started giving them the same food I ate myself, and both thrived. I was considering taking them to Fisherman's Wharf this Sunday as a treat when I saw that the door to our apartment was ajar.

What stood out in my memory afterwards were the maroon splashes of refried beans on the stairs as I dropped my paper bag. And then the maroon splashes all over our pokey living room where the TV was still on, showing an antique Bugs Bunny cartoon. They should have been scarlet, but the leaden light of the cloudy Bay leached color from the fresh blood.

I don't really remember the next couple of minutes. I must have called 911 because when the cops showed up, they found Zeke and I twined in a hard knot at the entrance to the apartment. They had to resort to force to pull him away. No force was necessary to collect Zach's pitiful body, smeared and stained in a garish parody of the zombie costume he had wanted for Halloween. They told me later he had been stabbed several times, but the first slash had severed his carotid artery, so he quickly bled out. He had not suffered, they insisted.

This insistence came later when I was absolved of my son's murder. At the beginning I was the natural suspect and treated accordingly. A bad mother, they whispered behind my back. A bad mother who moved with her two kids into a problematic area of Mission. No father in sight. Minimum-wage jobs in hippie bookstores and dodgy health-food emporia. Would you be really surprised if she snapped?

Nobody would be surprised: not the ghoulish crowd of true-crime hyenas who pursued me on Twitter; not the few people in the neighborhood who knew me enough to gossip behind my back. Perhaps not even Nina, the only friend left over from my Jordan days. She had always been a little cagey of me; or maybe just of the misfortune that had dogged me like an implacable ghost. Parents dead in an accident; a deadbeat husband; a "special-needs" child. No, everybody, including the police, would have breathed a sigh of relief had I been arrested and charged. Yes, horrible things, like the murder of a child, happen but there is a neat satisfying solution. The monster-mother did it. And now we can switch the channel…

Only the police could not make the timeline fit. The bodega owner confirmed I was there at 15.10. The neighbor whose name I had not even known saw me on the stairs at 15.18. And the 911 call came at 15.20. Of course, I could have knifed my son before I went to the bodega. But by an incredible stroke of luck I had snapped a picture of the twins as they were playing together in the living room just before I left. They were so cute, their identical blond heads almost touching as they leaned over the Monopoly board; the identical clothes they insisted on wearing perfectly matching, with only a discreet thread on their wrists signaling their separate identities: red for Zach, blue for Zeke. That was the one bright spot of my troubled motherhood: how good they were together. They seldom fought and never for long. Zeke's temper lashed out at everybody except his twin. And Zach could calm Zeke down with a single whispered word. I took pictures of them obsessively, hoarding these images of fraternal harmony as if I knew what was coming. The picture that saved me from being branded a child-killer had a time-stamp: 15.03. Even if I was an Olympic runner, I could not have made it from my apartment to the store in less than five minutes. There was no time for me to murder my son.

Naturally they questioned Zeke. But he refused to talk to them. Or rather, he refused to talk, period. From the moment I swept him into my arms in the blood-drenched apartment, he spoke not a word. Not to the police, not to the social worker, not to me. He had gone mute.

One of Zeke's many previous diagnoses was selective mutism: that is when a child refuses to speak in social settings. But now his selective mutism became the all-encompassing one. He would not speak. But he clung to me and threw one tantrum after another when we were separated. When they finally allowed a supervised meeting, he rushed over and embraced me so tightly my ribs hurt. Was it the behavior of a child who had witnessed his mother slash his brother's throat? Child psychologists hemmed and hawed, but the police could not believe it. And so, they let me go.

We moved; I dyed my hair and applied for a legal change of name. "The twin's murder" became a staple of true-crime podcasts, with which I steadfastly refused to cooperate. Zeke went to a special school and surprisingly, did very well. His temper tantrums died out. He became studious and calm. He could read and write appropriately for his age and spent most of his time engrossed in his Kindle.

But he still did not speak.

For the spring break, we drove to Pismo Beach. It is a pretty little town on the Pacific Coast, halfway between San Francisco and LA. It is not as glitzy as the nearby San Luis Obispo, nor as wild as Big Sur. We stayed in a cheap motel and went every morning to the beach, to watch the black dots of otters and surfers swirl in the foamy breakers and to collect splintered seashells. And then one day I took him to the Monarch Butterfly Grove.

I had not even remembered it was there. As many mothers on vacation with their kids, I was just casting about for something to do as I drove along the shore. I saw a line of parked cars, some flashy banners, and then when we were already out of the car, a giant cardboard sign of an orange-and-black butterfly.

I stopped. I did not need special reminders of my dead son: every time I looked at the boy by my side, I saw Zach. But what about Zeke? Since he did not speak, and his written communications tended to be brief and enigmatic, I did not know how much he remembered. Would it be wise to expose him to his twin's obsession?

He answered this question for me, taking my hand and leading me toward the kiosk where a fat woman sold entrance tickets amid the clutter of trashy merchandise, all exploiting the grove's unique position on the monarchs' migration route.

Monarch butterflies migrate every year from California to Mexico and back again, an enormous pilgrimage that exceeds the lifespan of a single insect. Their orange-and-black wings coalesce into a dense cloud when as many as half-a-million butterflies darken the skies, shedding glittering scales into the turbulent air.

Nobody knows why they do it. Not all species migrate and apparently, not even all individuals within a species. But those that do sacrifice their lives on that hundreds-of-miles-long odyssey, just so that their descendants can lay eggs and develop into pupae in that unremarkable clutch of eucalypti on the Californian coast. A swarming instinct, the same as drives locusts and salmon; fire-ants and lemmings.

The grove was filled with loud kids, barking dogs and Patagonia-clad retirees with giant binoculars. I thought that no rational butterfly would want to mate in this din and was relieved: for some reason, I did not want Zeke to see those coiling insect clouds. And indeed, while people occasionally stopped by a tree and gaped at it, I could not see anything, until I finally spotted a splash of orange among the silvery foliage.

I stared at it: a very large butterfly, languidly closing and opening its wings, as if telegraphing in Morse code. There was something creepy about the deliberation with which it was doing it. Insects are just above the plants in our imagination: we don't tend to ascribe motivation or sentience to them. But I was sure that the butterfly knew we were watching and was displaying – or maybe challenging us with hidden glee. I thought of the old legend of King Solomon's ring that enabled its wearer to understand the language of all living things.

I was spellbound by the butterfly for what seemed just a moment but when I turned around, Zeke was gone.

The next seconds were erased by overwhelming dread – until I spotted him. He was hunched over, one eye glued to the eyepiece of a stationary telescope. I rushed over, angry. I even yelled at him, which I don't normally do. He turned around and pointed to the telescope.

I looked in, at first seeing nothing but a cluster of desiccated leaves and tangled twigs, hanging off the gnarled branch like a beard. And then I realized multiple orange eyes were blinking at me as the butterflies slowly flapped their wings, in unison, opening and closing them with a maddening and perverse languor. They were all squished together, clinging to each other with their twitching multiple legs like grapes on the vine. They looked dead when their wings were closed, a clump of grey rotting leaves – and then they would bloom with that evil orange, all together, and I felt as if each wing was a bloodshot eye staring back at me.

I straightened up, slowly, breath catching in my throat. Zeke stood by, a smirk on his face.

*

That night I woke up with the noise of the surf loud in my ears. Too loud. We were on the coast, sure, but it felt like the ocean was beating against my bed.

I sat up. In the darkness, I could see Zeke's curled up body on the other bed. I thought that if we went again next year, I would need to scrounge up money for two rooms. He was almost a teenager already.

I padded to the window and drew back the curtain. The scatter of lights along the boardwalk; the luminescent whiteness of the surf…and closer, something else: a roiling whispering mass against the glass; a shifting grey whirlpool of beating wings and skittering legs; a maelstrom of insect life.

I must have screamed because the swarm detached itself from the glass and floated into the black sky, its form melting and reconstituting, flailing limbs and soft appendages, a man made of butterfly wings dissolving into darkness…

I must have screamed as I dropped the curtain. Zeke did not stir.

*

That was the time when I realized I had to find Jordan.

My ex-husband. The father of my children. Well, one child now.

Did he even know that Zach was dead? I was not sure. The funeral was a hasty affair, attended only by Zach's classmates, Nina, and me. Everything about that horrible time was a blur but I knew I had tried to contact Jordan. Except how would I have done it? He had left us one day with no explanation except a strange dry note, almost official sounding, informing me it was all over between us. He did not mention the twins. The divorce papers arrived a day later. I signed them with barely a glance. Child support? Jordan had no money. We had rented a house in Lodi

41

and supported ourselves with gigs. The small savings account was left untouched.

I tried to remember what I knew about Jordan's family and realized it was nothing. He had told me his parents were dead and he was an only child. Just like me. Was it what had created the initial connection between us?

I Googled him, of course. Tons of hits on "the twin's murder" with my (former) name still being dragged through mud. Nothing on him.

And that was when I got a call from Nina.

Her voice on the phone sounded strained and whispery like she had a bad cold. We had not talked for a couple of months.

"Carla? How are you?"

I responded with platitudes, waiting for her to spring something on me. She was silent, so I cut to the chase.

"Have you heard from Jordan?"

I didn't know why I asked that but something coalesced in my mind at that moment: the way his eyes had lingered on her when we had dinners together; the noncommittal chill in her voice when I had phoned her after finding his note... Whatever it was, my intuition was correct. There was a strangled gasp and then she said, very quickly:

"We need to talk."

Next day was Sunday, so we agreed to meet in Tatin, a trendy San Francisco bakery. I agonized over whether to take Zeke with me. He was almost thirteen now, and he often stayed home alone when I had a late shift. He did not seem to mind. Eventually I decided that if Nina was going to tell me something compromising about Zeke's father, it would be better for him not to hear it.

But Nina was a no-show.

On my third cup of coffee, I called her. The phone rang but no answer. It was worse than having it go straight to voicemail. It was not turned off. She either did not want to talk to me or...?

I texted. I called. And finally, I jumped into my beat-up Prius and drove into San Carlos where Nina now lived.

Her home was on a suburban street, with flowers in the front yard and a two-car garage. Nina had a cushy IT job with PG&E.

Her Audi was in the driveway. I knocked; the door was unlocked when I pushed it.

Reality felt slippery and loose as if I was chasing myself through a nightmare.

I did not even need to go in. The sweet metallic stink was instantly familiar, and so were the splotches and smears on the polished floor and the pale walls. The only difference was the color. In the bright sunshine, the blood looked bright, almost orange.

Nina was lying at the foot of the stairs, as empty as a discarded suit.

I did not linger. I drove out of San Carlos and was on the highway before it occurred to me that I had automatically made myself suspect number one. If anybody had noticed my car…

But I was not sorry I had not called 911. Nina was dead and did not need an ambulance. And I was convinced her killer would never be found.

*

I was wrong about that as I was wrong about so many things. The killer was arrested a couple of days later.

Jordan Miller. My ex-husband.

They came to talk to me – two police officers, a man and a woman. The woman, a petite Asian who introduced herself as Vivian Ng, told me they were reopening my son's case. It turned out Jordan and Nina had started living together a month after Zach was killed.

They asked me about Jordan as a father. Had he been abusive? Angry?

I told them the truth: that Jordan was a conscientious and dutiful father. Even as I was saying it, I realized how peculiar it sounded. Not "loving". But "conscientious". He had done everything a father should do. But there had always been a sense of distance, of watchfulness, or standing slightly apart from life like a bad swimmer hesitating to step into the ocean. I was not surprised finding that note. He had decided not to take the plunge, after all.

Had his attitude bothered me, they asked.

No, I said. I understood. I was that way myself.

They refused to tell me about the evidence against Jordan in Zach's murder. It was pretty conclusive in Nina's murder, though: his fingerprints on the knife, his DNA all over the house.

"Was there any other DNA in the house?" I asked before they left. Vivian Ng looked at me strangely.

"Nina's…Ms. Fritsch's of course."

"No, I mean…like animal DNA."

The two officers exchanged glances.

"They found some stuff in the bedroom," the male officer said. "Like the powder butterflies have on their wings."

"Scales," I said. "These are called scales."

"Scales, then. But it's not surprising. The neighbors told us the defendant and Ms. Fritsch went to Santa Cruz last weekend. To the Natural Bridges State Park where butterflies are hanging out. They might have brought some with them."

*

Natural Bridges… Another stop on the monarchs' swarming pilgrimage. Pismo Beach, Santa Cruz, and on to Mexico. Michoacán. Something nagged at me. I Googled it and yes, there had been several murders in that famed butterfly preserve. The media blamed drug cartels.

I stared at the screen for a long time until I became aware that somebody was standing behind me. I turned around and looked straight into Zeke's eyes. He backed off and immersed himself in his Kindle again. When he fell asleep, I checked his library.

It was filled with graphic novels with lurid covers, horror and sci-fi. But the last book he was reading was called *Animal Talk*.

I read it myself before falling asleep. It was a bunch of nonsense, mostly concerned with "telepathic" messages to your pets. Even if Zeke believed it, the book could hardly harm him. Still, I was unsettled, and it took me a long time to fall asleep. And then I was yanked out of my turbulent doze by knocking on the door.

It was after midnight. I got up and with a strange sense of déjà vu, looked through the peephole.

Jordan stood outside.

I opened the door and let him in, pressing my finger to my lips to indicate that he should speak quietly, so as not to wake up Zeke. I took him to the kitchen.

"So, they let you out," I said.

He shook his head.

"No," he said, "Jordan is still in custody. I am Jared."

It all fell into place as I contemplated this stranger. There was not a shred of difference between him and my husband. They looked the same; they moved the same; they smelled the same. Had he come to my bed when I was married to Jordan, I would have cuddled up to him.

"Could your parents tell you apart?" I asked.

"No. But Mum and Dad did not live long enough for this to be a problem."

"Early death runs in the family."

Jared shrugged. I still could not quite believe it was not my ex. It occurred to me to call Vivian Ng and ask her if Jordan had been released. But I knew she would have informed me if he had been given bail.

"What do you want?" I asked.

He smiled wryly.

"Straight and to the point, Carla! I should have expected Jordan would marry somebody like you. He always had a thing for strong women."

"Were you keeping in touch? I mean, before?"

"No. After our parents died, I moved as far away as I could. I actually lived in Guam. I came back when I read about Jordan's arrest online."

"Why? I mean, why did you move away?"

He sighed.

"Until I left, Jordan had never spoken. Mum and Dad were talking about institutionalizing him."

"What?" I sputtered. Jordan had been introvert and sometimes morose but nothing outside the normal psychological spectrum. And he spoke as well as anybody else.

"This is what I wanted to talk to you about. See, it's not true to say he did not speak. He did. But only our special language. And only to me."

"Twins' language…" I whispered.

I knew what it was, of course. Identical twins sometimes develop a special language understood only by themselves. Ordinary language is a bridge to others; twins' language is a wall that encloses the same. Child psychologists nowadays recommend pushing twins into developing separate identities by encouraging them to wear different clothes, exposing them to other kids, emphasizing their individuality. All the things we had not done with Zach and Zeke. All the things Jordan had never let me do.

And he had never disclosed that he had a twin.

"So after you left he had nobody to speak to…?"

"He did," Jared said. "I found it out too late. What he was up to. I can also speak our special language, of course. Only it never occurred to me that it can be used that way. The way he uses it."

A bout of vertigo stole over me as if I was standing on the parapet of the Golden Gate Bridge, staring into the steely water below, flocks of birds wheeling above my head.

"Why are you telling me this?" I yelled. "Jordan is my ex. I don't care what happens to him."

"Even if he is indicted for your son's death?"

"Jordan did not kill Zach!"

"No, he did not. But don't you want to know who did?"

And suddenly it hit me. Not Jordan, Jared.

Their DNA was basically the same. Whatever they had found at the murder scenes could just as well belong to Jared. There are ways of distinguishing even identical twins' DNA, but if the police did not know of Jared's existence, why would they try it?

I jumped up and backed away slowly toward the scuffed butcher's block that held my meager collection of knives. After Zach's death I had bought a gun, but it was hidden in my nightstand. I cursed myself for my stupidity.

He saw it. He threw his hands up.

"No, Carla, no! You misunderstand! I would never harm my nephew! Just the opposite – I am here to tell you…"

The door behind him exploded.

The kitchen was filled with a maelstrom of wings and a susurrus of insect life – insistent, blind and hungry, swirling with furious intent. I could not see; could not hear. The swarm of butterflies drinking the light and the air out of the room; the insidious soft caress of multiple legs and antennae on my bare skin; the whisper of identical voices in my head, swelling to a meaningless chorus that boomed through my brain like thunder; the incipient madness of almost understanding what the voices were saying…

And then it all ended – with a boom that threw me to the floor and sent the swarm to the walls and the ceiling where they alighted and covered every square inch like a living, moving, squirming carpet of black and orange.

I pulled myself up.

Jared was sprawled across the floor, his t-shirt changing color like a chameleon: white to red. And Zeke was standing at the entrance, my gun clutched in his hand.

I threw myself at him.

"Oh, Zeke…"

"Not Zeke, Mother," he said, "Zach."

*

He made me sit in the armchair in the living room. He brought me tea. And all the while, watching him, I wondered how I could have missed it. This slow deliberation, this implacable intent. Or had I really?

Perhaps I had known all along.

He sat on the edge of the sofa, facing me. The beautiful age – no longer the clumsiness of childhood, not yet the gawkiness of adolescence. My beautiful son. A fratricide. His uncle's killer.

"Why did you kill your brother?" I asked.

He shrugged.

"I didn't want to. But he would not let go. He would not let me talk to anybody but him. He would not let me talk to…them."

"Bugs?"

"Butterflies," he corrected patiently and I was struck by the Buddha-like serenity of his expression, his perfect calmness. "Collective minds."

He explained, using grown-up words and immaculately constructed sentences. His voice was ageless. Ageless and

47

inhuman.

Intelligence is as ubiquitous in the ecosphere as life itself, he said. But it is dispersed, scattered among billions of living things, locked up in small brains dedicated to survival and procreation. It is dormant. But occasionally it can become concentrated in large numbers of identical creatures: anthills; termite mounds; flocks of birds; swarming butterflies. Then it would wake up, look around and discover it was not alone. Growing beside it but blind to its existence was the tumor of individual intelligence. Humans.

"Humanity is the cancer of the ecosphere," Zach said. "Because they are individuals. All different. Unique. Locked in the prisons of their own skulls."

"They". Not "we". He did not consider himself human.

"But people like you can speak the language of multiplicity," I said. "Of sameness. Because you grow up as two, not one."

"Or more," he said, nodding, as if our roles had been reversed. As if he was the parent, indulgently praising the child's cleverness. "There are triplets, quadruplets. IVF produces more of us. As long as we are identical."

"King Solomon's ring," I whispered. "The language of animals. But why, Zach? What for?"

He stared at me with the contempt he no longer bothered to disguise. Of course. It should have been obvious. Power.

Commanding the swarming intelligence of the planet. Solomon's fabled kingdom was nothing compared to the power he – no, they – would wield. A new kind. Posthumans.

I saw that he was avoiding looking at the corpse of Jared and that gave me hope that he still retained some human emotions. Guilt?

He poked the corpse with the tip of his foot as if it were a piece of wood.

"We need to get rid of it," he said.

"We?"

"Of course, Mother."

A child's blind selfishness. The parents are here to serve and to protect. Of course, I would shield my murderous son from the police. Of course, I would help him get rid of his uncle's body. Of course, I would work for him, feed him, and defend him while he grew up. And then when he was old enough and no longer needed me…

"Why did you kill Nina?" I asked.

"Father told her he had a twin. Told her about us. About me. She put it all together. She was a clever girl."

Again, this dismissive indifference in his voice. A psychopath? No, psychopaths are human.

"But how did you…?" I pressed on. "You were at home when I went to meet her."

"It wasn't her you talked to. They are learning to imitate human speech. I am teaching them. It worked well, didn't it?"

A spark of boastful enjoyment in his eyes like a child getting the first place in a spelling bee. I glanced at the living wallpaper around us: hundreds of butterflies languidly flapping their wings, sowing the floor with their iridescent scales, the soft rhythmic sound like the beat of the surf… Yes, I could imagine them syncopating, producing a whispery imitation of human speech.

He must have slipped out of the apartment when I was at work, took BART to San Carlos. Had Jordan been there when his son walked through the door? Or had he found Nina dead on the floor? I suddenly realized he might have been there when I discovered her body, kept captive by a swarm. Butterfly DNA in the upstairs bedroom…

"Come on, Mother," Zach said and there was that barely concealed edge in his voice. Condescension. Impatience. The way you talk to a stupid pet.

I bent down to pick up the feet of the corpse while Zach held its shoulders. Jared's head lolled, blood dripping onto the tiles.

"You'll clean it up afterwards," Zach said.

I nodded. And then I spoke.

The language I had not spoken since early childhood. It felt stiff and awkward in my mouth. It felt like the grinding of stones; like the sound of thunder; like the rumble of an earthquake. The nonhuman speech of blind ferocity and single-minded sameness. The language of many.

And the many came.

The window in our kitchen blew inward as a cloud of starlings smashed it, in their unstoppable rush. They filled the air with the hurricane of beating wings. They roiled and seethed. The light was swallowed by their multitude; the air was filled with the sharp tang of their smell.

The butterflies tried to repel the invasion, but their delicate wings and pulpy bodies were no match for the sharp beaks and grasping talons of the birds. Soon the air was filled with swirling orange as if the fall had come suddenly into my kitchen.

And deadened by the noise of two swarms colliding, I could hear a scream.

When it was over, I had to wade through drifts of torn butterflies. They blanketed two mounds. I brushed them off one and stared, again, at my son's dead face. This time there were no wounds that had disfigured Zeke's pathetic corpse. His murderer had been suffocated; a couple of dead starlings protruded from his mouth, their plumage speckled with blood and saliva. Otherwise he had been left untouched and I was grateful for that.

I went over to my bedroom and from my nightstand I retrieved the picture I had not looked at for many years. Two identical girls with blond pigtails and Disney princess t-shirts smiling in our parents' sunny backyard. Carla and Clara. The two cute girls who refused to speak to anybody but chatted animatedly between themselves in the language only they understood. The two girls who loved the birds that nested in the woods and came to their feeders. The two girls who eventually became one when their parents, having decided that their closeness was unhealthy, had taken Clara for a ride, while leaving Carla with a babysitter who could not calm down her disconsolate sobbing. The babysitter had to wait much longer than she had expected as the bodies of the parents and Clara were cooling off in a ditch by the side of the road, killed by a drunk truck-driver. Eventually a police car pulled into the driveway, rescued the babysitter, and little Carla went to live with a foster family. And she had never spoken the twin language again. Until now.

I stood by the broken window, leaning into the predawn chill and watching flocks of birds swoop in the lightening sky, tracing out the hieroglyphs of flight with their swift bodies. I could read them perfectly well. My parents, my sister and my sons were dead. But with the birds in the sky and the butterflies in the trees and the ants in the ground, I knew I would never be alone.

~

Elana Gomel is an academic and a writer. She has taught and researched English literature and cultural studies at Tel-Aviv University, Princeton, Stanford, Venice International University and the University of Hong Kong. She has published six non-fiction books and numerous articles on post-humanism, science fiction, Victorian literature and serial killers. Her fantasy, horror and science fiction stories appeared in Apex Magazine, New Horizons, The Fantasist, Timeless Tales, New Realms, Alien Dimensions, *and others. Her stories were also featured in several award-winning anthologies, including* Zion's Fiction, Apex Book of World Science Fiction, *and* People of the Book. *She is the author of three novels:* A Tale of Three Cities *(2013),* The Hungry Ones *(2018) and* The Cryptids (2019). *She can be found at:* https://www.citiesoflightanddarkness.com/ *and on Facebook, Twitter and Instagram*

SIMULATION
Tim Major

As Aether Airlines flight AE2909 lifted smoothly from the runway the heat haze from the tarmac made its wheels temporarily oval, as if the aeroplane were pulling free of liquid that distorted its shape. On board, its passengers sucked mints, continued strained business discussions or gazed about them at their neighbours. A few gazed from the windows to watch Athens airport below, then Artemida on the coast, then the dazzling sea.

Sitting in the seat to the right-hand side of the aisle in the twenty-fourth row was a passenger named Neil Short, aged twenty. Neil flinched as a hand wavered into his field of vision, distracting him from his review of the sketches he had drawn in a moleskin notebook. The hand belonged to the middle-aged man sitting beside him. Neil tried to ignore it, flicking through the pages of his notebook. He thought of himself as an observer of people. In some of the sketches he felt that he had captured the shopkeepers, street musicians and homeless people of Athens perfectly. The hand appeared again, fingers fluttering. Neil shut the notebook.

"Could you stop that?"

The man sitting beside him wore a blue cap emblazoned with a logo of three stylised ripples. An off-duty Aether Airlines employee, perhaps? But unlike other flight staff Neil had seen, this man was dough-faced and stubbly. His polo shirt was lined with creases. He wore a bulky pair of headphones, the type worn by DJs. His eyes were closed and his hands danced in the air above his knees. His fingers twitched. Occasionally he reached out as if grasping at a fly. Behind his closed eyelids his eyes danced, too.

The man's left hand darted out towards Neil's face. Neil had always prided himself on his quick reflexes. He gripped the man's forearm, making the fidgeting fingers splay like a starfish. The man glared at Neil with horrified indignation. His right arm continued its movements.

Neil pointed at his ear. The man slipped his headphones back so that they became a chunky neck brace.

"You're way into my personal space," Neil said. "Could you knock it off?"

The man inhaled noisily. He wrenched his hand away.

"Forty seconds."

Headphones reinstated, he continued his peculiar actions. Even though his left hand continued to stray over the barrier of the armrest, Neil found himself watching rather than interrupt him again. There was a precision to the man's movements that he hadn't noticed before.

Presently the illuminated seatbelt signs flicked off. The cabin filled with sighs, the chink of loosening belts and a cascade of huffs as passengers discovered their legroom compromised by the reclining of the seat in front, then inflicted the same punishment on the person sitting behind.

Neil unclipped his belt. The man beside him didn't. His hand movements stopped, though, and he arched his back slightly and rolled his shoulders. He removed his headphones and carefully wrapped the cable around and around the cups. His head tilted as though he were listening.

"Tell me—" Neil began.

The man held up a flat palm.

Twenty-four rows ahead, an airline steward began speaking about on-board duty-free arrangements, his voice made alien and ping-ponging by the slight lag of the overhead speakers. Neil tuned out the words. In contrast, the man sitting beside him appeared rapt. He nodded slowly and approvingly, like a teacher willing a student to perform well. The steward finished. The man swung his raised hand to become an offer of a handshake.

"Denny Fisher," he said. "Happy to meet you."

Neil introduced himself. "Are you a musician or something?"

"No. Are you?"

"I'm a student of agriculture."

"Dirty work, farming." Denny picked at a nostril and frowned.

"I didn't say I was a farmer. It's all business management, anyway. Spreadsheets. I think I'm going to jack it all in before the exams."

"You're not keen on the practicalities of the job for which you've been preparing."

Neil hesitated. "I suppose you could say that. It's not very real, is it? I'm looking for the real. Immediate. In the moment."

"Hence your sketches." He pointed at Neil's moleskin notebook. "An attempt to capture the moment."

Neil was taken aback. Until he had removed his headphones, Denny had seemed unaware of his surroundings.

"Hence my whole trip, I guess," Neil replied. "I wanted to do something spontaneous. Showed up at Luton airport and jumped on the first international flight. When I got to Athens I just headed straight off on foot, all the way to the Acropolis. That's a six-hour walk, would you believe, and in all that heat."

Denny showed no sign of being impressed, or of any discomfort in the silence that followed.

"How about you?" Neil said finally. "Work? Holiday?"

"I'm unemployed, but that doesn't mean I'm unoccupied."

Neil thought of himself as somebody capable of cutting through social conventions. "How about all this?" he said, mimicking Denny's earlier arm movements.

"It's just a hobby." Denny pressed his lips together. He seemed to come to a decision. "I'll let you in on something. I was being the pilot, that's what I was doing."

He searched Neil's face for a reaction, then pointed at the plain door at the front of the cabin, which was flanked by two air stewards. "In that cockpit there's a control panel with more than two hundred separate controls. I've got them all in here." He tapped the side of his forehead.

"You were pretending that you were flying the plane."

Denny appeared stung. "Pretending is make-believe. I was simulating. These headphones? I haven't been listening to music. Ambient noise and recordings of air traffic updates. All authentic. It's like you're really there."

Neil felt let down. He usually had a knack of finding interesting people to speak to. "But you're not really there, are you? And you don't know what it's actually like, do you? Have you ever been in the cockpit of one of these planes?"

"Not this one, no."

"Then it *is* make-believe. Just a game."

Denny shook his head sharply. "Back at home, see, I've got the mother of all computer setups. Course, I've got all the flight simulation software, but that's nothing without the physical setup. Three widescreen monitors—" He mimed their positions in the air before him. "—five-point-one sound with a subwoofer the size of a kennel, and an authentic headset too."

Neil grinned. "And a pilot's uniform, I'm guessing?"

"It's no game, I promise you that. It's gruelling. Transatlantic crossings take an age and you can't lose your attention for a second."

"Otherwise what?"

Denny shook his head slowly and sadly. It reminded Neil of his father and his university tutor. It rankled.

"I read an article recently," Denny said. "About a high-up scientist, totally respected, who believes that the whole world – maybe the whole universe – is a computer simulation. That we're living within a piece of software."

Neil stretched to look into the aisle. The stewards had begun making their way from the front, one pulling the refreshments cart, the other pushing. He felt a surge of boredom. He wondered whether he would officially withdraw from his university agricultural course that afternoon.

"But we aren't living in a simulation, are we?" he said distractedly. "This is the real world, not a VR game. It's a nice idea and all."

Denny shrugged. "The point is that nobody knows. Nobody *can* know. Why distinguish so rigidly between real life and a simulation of real life?"

"I get it. You're trying to rationalise whole weekends dedicated to pretending to fly to America."

Denny twisted in his seat to face Neil. His pale lips parted to reveal crooked teeth. It was a smile, or at least a simulation of one.

"So," Neil said, in a hurry to dispel the peculiar vision, "did you actually stay in Athens, or are you just here for the round-trip flight?"

"A fortnight."

"Plane-spotter stuff? Did you even leave the airport?"

A stewardess hovered beside Neil's seat. She offered meat or vegetarian. Neil took the meat tray but Denny waved a hand in refusal.

As he fiddled with the clear plastic covering, Neil said, "Not hungry?"

He imagined that Denny was a fussy eater. He imagined Denny in his small flat, or his mother's house, eating only his favourite childhood brands.

Denny bent to root around in the black rucksack at his feet. He produced a tray identical to the one the stewardess had placed before Neil.

"You brought your own airline food?"

Denny chuckled. "The catering company that supplies Aether Airlines is based in an industrial park just outside Marousi, only a taxi ride from Athens. Couldn't resist dropping in. They don't get many tourists there, not even the plane-spotters. No imagination. They let me take a tray as a memento."

"And they gave you the meal too?" Neil tried to peer through the plastic lid.

"I made that myself."

Even so, when Denny removed the lid, Neil was surprised to see that the meal – limp turkey, too-green peas, flat-topped mountain of mashed potato – appeared exactly the same as the food in the moulded compartments of his own tray.

Denny unwrapped a plastic knife and fork and began to eat. He seemed to enjoy the meal immensely. Neil only picked at his food. The mashed potato was a thick puree. The turkey tasted fine, but it had the texture of liver.

"I'll let you in on a confession," Denny said. His mouth was still full and Neil recoiled at the slight spray from his lips. "When I visited the caterers, right there on the spot, I invented a sort of character for myself. Just for fun. A new name and a high-level job. They didn't question it. At least, they didn't after I showed them my replica Aether ID. It's fun to make copies of things."

Neil almost choked on the bolus of meat. "That's a criminal

offence, surely? Anyway, you said they thought you were a tourist. That they gave you mementos."

Denny ignored him. He pointed vaguely at the cockpit door with his plastic knife. "Since we're doing confessions… I've always had this dream. That I'd be on a flight and they'd just say 'Does anybody know how to fly this plane?' and there I'd be. All trained up on my flight simulations. Imagine it."

Neil turned away, determined not to get drawn further into Denny's nonsense. "I don't think it works like that. There are backup pilots, aren't there? Co-pilots."

Denny nodded. "Several tiers of backups, yes. You can't help but daydream. Thinking through all the aspects of it."

Neil placed the lid back onto his tray. He noticed Denny glance at it; perhaps he wanted to polish off what was left.

"A simulation—" Neil said, then interrupted himself with a burp. He felt his cheeks flush. The next time he flew, he would buy sandwiches at the airport M&S and avoid this cheap airline food. "Sorry. I mean to say, you're treating the whole thing like a simulation. Working through the possibilities methodically. Right?"

"Right."

"You haven't thought it through. You're the one who isn't imaginative." Neil thought for a moment. He prided himself on his ingenuity. He chuckled and stifled another uncomfortable belch. In a conspiratorial tone, he said, "See, the way you ought to do it is to merge your hobby with a second one. One: piloting planes. Two: international terrorism."

Denny nodded. "Hijack a plane, you mean?"

"Okay, so you do have an imagination. But you don't strike me as a typical bomber."

"A bomb wouldn't do it. Too much chaos."

Neil fished out a serviette from his plastic tray and then rubbed at his forehead. Planes scrimped on air conditioning these days; he'd heard it was an issue ever since they banned smoking on flights. It was hot in here.

"Not a bomb, then," he said weakly.

A bump of turbulence sloshed the contents of his belly. He

gripped both armrests as the plane dipped to the right. Somewhere behind him, the refreshments cart struck against something hard, producing a dull clank.

Denny continued forking peas into his mouth.

"You're right about the co-pilots," Denny said as he chewed. "There are all sorts of measures to keep them safe. Keep them isolated from the rest of us. It's common sense. They have different meals to the passengers, even. Just in case."

Neil winced at a pain in his stomach. "So if you wanted to—"

Denny nodded. "You'd not only have to time your visit to the catering firm precisely so that the meal batch being produced was the one intended for today's flight, you'd also have to make sure to tamper with all the meals intended for Aether flight staff, as well as the ones for passengers. Or you could just concentrate your efforts on a foodstuff assumed to be reliably safe, such as the huge vat of mashed potato. For example."

Neil tried to raise his hand from the armrest, perhaps to pull at Denny's sleeve. He missed and the plane lurched again as if responding to his clumsy actions. Somebody shrieked, but she sounded very far away. There were other sounds too, above the rumble of the engines. Groaning and retching.

The stewardess that had given him his food stumbled along the aisle, scrabbling her way to the front of the plane. Neil hung limply over the armrest into the aisle, watching as the woman pushed her way into the cockpit. She left its door hanging open, swinging loosely as the plane veered further and further to the right. With great effort Neil swung his head to look out of the window, beyond Denny, who was still eating calmly. Outside, the sky had become the sea.

The stewardess reappeared and lunged for the wall intercom.

"Is there anybody aboard this flight—" She stopped and gulped for breath.

Denny had already begun to rise from his seat.

"—who is able to pilot a plane?"

Neil doubled over with the pain in his chest as Denny sidestepped past him and into the aisle.

~

58

Tim Major's most recent novels are Hope Island *and* Snakeskins, *and his other books include a collection of short stories,* And the House Lights Dim, *and a non-fiction book about the silent crime film,* Les Vampires. *His stories have appeared in* Interzone, Best of British Science Fiction *and* Best Horror of the Year.
www.cosycatastrophes.com

VIRAL
A.P. Sessler

SuperPortionMe

Bought homeless dude a cup of coffee. Amazing story. Used to work on top secret projects for military. #TakeTimeToListen #HomelessArePeopleToo #LeastOfTheseMyBrethren

WickedlyGodless

Jesus freak next to me trying to save everyone. Gave me some propaganda. I told him I believe in recycling. #FreedomFromReligion

ConsciousObjector *barista@CafeDulce*

Litterbug jerk totally misses the trash can and doesn't bother to pick it up. Sometimes I hate working here. #CoffeeShopProblems #SaveTheEarth #KeepItClean #KarmasABitch

SuperCaucasianFragileEgoSelfDeprecatious

Woohoo! Barista chatted with me for five minutes. She was way hotter than the coffee she made me. Should I say that? #awkward #WorstPickupLinesEver

MyMilkshake

Couldn't get wifi to work. Dorky guy next to me got my laptop connected. #UseItOrLoseit #WorkWhatYouGot

ChauvinistPiggyBank

Chick just coughed on me on my way to the bathroom and didn't say excuse me. Girl you're not that pretty. #FutureFatWife #PeakedBefore20

SandraD *senior@DenleighHigh*

Just used the bathroom after some jerk. Sitting in nasty man pee is so not cool. #CourtesyWipe #LiftTheSeat

HandmaidenoftheLord *senior@DenleighHigh*

Ugh, forgot to charge my phone. <3 u Sandy. Bible study at Cafe Dulce. Come, taste and see that the Lord is good. #BeAWitness #DontHideYourLamp #NotAshamed

ArthurVsAuthor

Girl just gave me a Bible tract. When did this become a church? Now youth group is LOUDLY praying for a man. I'm out. #MyCueToLeave #WhenYouStandPraying #NotAsTheHyprocrites

BettyBookworm

Just met Arthur Kramer at Cafe Dulce! <3 <3 <3 Got a picture with him and he signed my coffee cup lol. So awesome. #OpenMyPages #ReadMeLikeABook #FatherMyChildren

RealRickyReynolds

Bubbly girl just asked me to take a picture of her and random dude. Was he somebody famous? #NoClue

FantasyFootballIsland

Leaving Cafe Dulce. Met Ricky the Rage, running back for State at Cafe Dulce. Hand like a vice and bigger than my head.

CPAtricia

Waiting at bus stop and perv acts all nice then tried to kiss me. WTF? I took his coffee and threw it in his face. #MeToo

TheMurph

Accidentally bumped crazy girl on bus and she slapped me. Moved to opposite end and people treating me like a creep.

Going4Broker

Offered girl my seat after jerk harassed her. Almost wished I hadn't. The pole is all sweaty and gross from her hands. #TalcumPowderIsYourFriend

LastBoyscout *scout@Troop418*

Gave a man a tissue for his bloody lip. Do I earn a Get Somebody's Blood on You While Riding the Public Bus badge? #BePrepared #ThankGodForPurell

IceScreamers

Watched scout help old lady across the street and she collapsed. He ran off. I gave her CPR until ambulance came.

BornEMT *staff@NorvilleHospital*

Picked up elderly female, DOA. Woman who administered CPR couldn't keep her hands off me. This is one strange day.

LastBoyscout *scout@Troop418*

Off to meet Troop 418 at the nursing home and spread some special cheer. Too bad not everyone has someone to visit them.

DeniseSantiago *programsDirector@Greenhaven*

About to welcome Troop 418 to Greenhaven. We're honored to have them here and sure our residents will enjoy their visit.

NurseGetRatchet *nurse@Greenhaven*

One of these boy scouts is a real flirt. When he's not hitting on the nurses he's hugging all the old ladies. #GotMyEyeOnYou

ForBetterOrNurse *nurse@Greenhaven*
The part of my job I hate. Having to inform family of their loved ones' declining health. #WhyMe? #WhyTheNiceOnesGod?

MyLadyFair
Headed to the nursing home. Grandma just took a turn for the worse. Prayers and positive thoughts appreciated.

LittleServantGirl *server@TheToastRestaurant*
Just comforted a girl who lost her grandma. Sometimes you have to let folks snot and cry on you. And now off to work. :(#JesusTakeTheWheel

Blazer420 *server@TheToastRestaurant*
As usual `somebody' showed up late. Swipe my card, hers, transfer this table so I can GTFOH. >:(#BetterThingsToDo

ArtistKnownAsTense *server@TheToastRestaurant*
Burned my hand pulling plates. I'd rather wait tables and burn another phat one. Thanks Blazer420 for the smoke break.

VengeanceIsMine *server@TheToastRestaurant*
Pretty sure QA sneezed on my table's food. Too bad both seats are aholes. #GetWhatYouDeserve

DaughteroftheKing
Waiter served me hot plate. Burned my hand. Going to see manager about rude behavior. #NotPayingForThisMeal

BlessedandHighlyFavored
Worst meal in my entire life. Wife and I both sick as dogs. #FoodPoisoning #GoingToSue

SaltLife
Dude in next stall got shit on my flipflops. Told him to watch it and he cusses me. So pissed. #ExplosiveDiarrheaIsReal

DontBeSoSerious
Watched a guy wipe crap off his foot in the bathroom. Think I touched some on hot water handle. So gross, so pissed. #UseToiletPaperNextTime

LashondaBeatrix *asstManager@TheToastRestaurant*
Woman complained 20 minutes about bad meal and "rude" server. Put her hand on me. Nearly went off on her. #NoClass #LordHelpMeKeepMyJob #CheckYourself

GoodHomoSamaritan
Tried to break up fight between preacher and surfer dudes over bathroom etiquette. Got a bloody lip and a free lunch lol

#TooMuchDrama #SomeGoodDeeds

TimMaynard *genManager@TheToastRestaurant*

Called the cops on two punks fighting in my restaurant. Comped the peacemaker's meal and gave him a coupon. #ManagerProblems

BlueLeader *officer@NorvillePD*

If people just followed the Golden Rule we'd have a lot less crime.

RedLeader *officer@NorvillePD*

@BlueLeader If they followed the Golden Rule me and you would be out a job.

BlueLeader *officer@NorvillePD*

@RedLeader Just my humble opinion.

RedLeader *officer@NorvillePD*

Opinions are like the assholes in our backseats

BlueLeader *officer@NorvillePD*

And my opinion is watch what you say on public forums #BlueLivesMatter

Text$ymbol *senior@DenleighHigh*

OMG! Cop car just swerved off the road. Stopping to help!

BuffyYoBFFy *senior@DenleighHigh*

@Text$ymbol omg what happened?

Text$ymbol *senior@DenleighHigh*

@BuffyYoBFFy Police officer had a panic attack. Couldn't get him out of the car. His prisoner in back cussed us both the whole time.

BuffyYoBFFy *senior@DenleighHigh*

Did U call 911?

Text$ymbol *senior@DenleighHigh*

Another patrol stopped to help. He shoved me out of the way, dragged the guy out the back and beat the F out of him.

BuffyYoBFFy *senior@DenleighHigh*

omg I understand if you don't wanna come over tonight

Text$ymbol *senior@DenleighHigh*

Hell no GF. I'll be there. Definitely need a drink after this.

BuffyYoBFFy *senior@DenleighHigh*

OK bae. CU when U get here. <3

GoHardorGoHome

Sitting with a broken arm for two hours to get in the ER. Cop gets wheeled in, no visible injuries, and gets seen pronto. #MyLifeMattersBitch

HeWasACarpenter
I've had a bloody rag wrapped around my cut-off finger for 30 minutes and nurses drop everything for an uninjured cop. #HeWhoIsFirst?

HeartSchoolStudent
Dude just went off on ER Admissions lady for letting cop go ahead of him. What about me? I'm about to have a baby.

RedLeader *officer@NorvillePD*
Just had to put a punk civilian in his place for thinking he's somebody special. #BlueLivesMatter

HeartSchoolStudent
And jerk with a badge goes off on guy for having the gall to insist his visible injury was worse than the other cop's. #VideoToProveIt #UploadingNow #PoliceBrutality #NNNews

NNNews
A social media user named HeartSchoolStudent just uploaded a video depicting police brutality at Norville Hospital.

VictimOfTheSystem
@NNNews Police brutality. Imagine that

DefconTroll
@VictimOfTheSystem And imagine that. The victim is white

VictimOfTheSystem
@DefconTroll Your point TROLL?

RedLeader *officer@NorvillePD*
At hospital after dropping perps at station. A Brother in Blue is suffering from extreme anxiety. Prayers appreciated.

CitizenBane *officer@NorvillePD*
@RedLeader What happened?

RedLeader *officer@NorvillePD*
@CitizenBane We picked up perps disturbing peace at The Toast and on the way back @BlueLeader went off the road. Completely frozen.

CitizenBane *officer@NorvillePD*
Lot of strange stuff going on

DaShizSpatcha *operator@NorvilleDispatch*
@NorvillePD I've been answering crazy calls all day. Then again, I guess yall know that.

CitizenBane *officer@NorvillePD*
@DaShizSpatcha Got that right

SoftenedCop *officer@NorvillePD*

@DaShizSpatcha I've already answered three calls for fights and seen two people stuck in corners too afraid to move. Something's up.

DonutMonster *officer@NorvillePD*

@SoftenedCop That's not the worst of it. Crazy number of attempted and unfortunately "successful" rapes also being reported.

DaShizSpatcha *operator@NorvilleDispatch*

Can't blame it on the full moon neither. Not even nighttime.

CitizenBane *officer@NorvillePD*

Watch your backs. The City is going wild.

RedLeader *officer@NorvillePD*

Just talked to the Doc. Says blood tests are showing what he called "anomalies." That doesn't sound promising.

RedLeader *officer@NorvillePD*

Nurses are going crazy. I hear them mumbling again and again about blood tests, bacteria, viruses. What's happening?

RedLeader *officer@NorvillePD*

An officer must be aware of all things at all times. We have a sixth sense about these things. Something's going down.

CitizenBane *officer@NorvillePD*

What's going on brother?

RedLeader *officer@NorvillePD*

I don't know, but something's up. You know that feeling you get right before you take the call that goes bad?

CitizenBane *officer@NorvillePD*

All too familiar

RedLeader *officer@NorvillePD*

Imagine that but magnified by a thousand.

CitizenBane *officer@NorvillePD*

You okay, brother?

HeartSchoolStudent

omg! Someone is shooting a gun at Norville ER! #911 #NNNews

DaShizSpatcha *operator@NorvilleDispatch*

@NorvillePD Just had a call of shots fired at Norville Hospital. Sent all units out. You boys keep me in the loop.

SoftenedCop *officer@NorvillePD*

Will do baby girl

DonutMonster *officer@NorvillePD*

You got it baby girl

NNNews

Reports of shots fired at Norville Hospital. Updates will be provided as we learn more.

CitizenBane *officer@NorvillePD*

@RedLeader, you there?

CookieTheCook *headChef@TheToastRestaurant*

@HeartSchoolStudent You okay babe? On my way there and stuck in traffic. Don't have our baby without me, if you can help it ;)

HeartSchoolStudent

@CookieTheCook Oh God a cop just started shooting people and when he ran out of bullets he started beating them I'm so scared.

CookieTheCook *headChef@TheToastRestaurant*

Did they give you anesthesia? Are you sure you're not hallucinating?

HeartSchoolStudent

All of us are hiding in a broom closet turn on the news.

CookieTheCook *headChef@TheToastRestaurant*

I'm in the car.

HeartSchoolStudent

Look at ur phone turn on the radio.

NNNews

A police officer opened fire upon hospital staff. Appears to be the same officer shown in video uploaded earlier.

CookieTheCook *headChef@TheToastRestaurant*

Oh my god I'm so sorry. Traffic is at a standstill and police cars are flying past us. They're coming to help hold on!

HeartSchoolStudent

I will baby just get here fast

CookieTheCook *headChef@TheToastRestaurant*

I will babe just hold on

CitizenBane *officer@NorvillePD*

Two officers affected by something in the same hour. This is an epidemic.

DaShizSpatcha *operator@NorvilleDispatch*

Hate to say it but I think you're right.

NNNews

Reports of what appear to be random acts of violence coming in. Gang activity suspected. Citizens urged to stay indoors.

VictimOfTheSystem
Unless white preps have formed their own gang it was a church group. They beat the devil out of a homeless dude
DefconTroll
Pictures/video or you're lying
VictimOfTheSystem
Search for it
DefconTroll
Post it here
VictimOfTheSystem
[VIDEO ATTACHED]
DefconTroll
Odd. A broken link. Imagine that.
VictimOfTheSystem
What? No way.
DefconTroll
Yes way, Ted.
VictimOfTheSystem
Let me check.
[LINK UNAVAILABLE]
VictimOfTheSystem
WTF? It got removed! The News don't want rich white kids to look bad.
DefconTroll
A likely story
VictimOfTheSystem
Likely you can kiss my ass
NNNews
A video currently circulating online appears to show a church youth group attacking a homeless person in a coffee shop.
VictimOfTheSystem
@DefconTroll Told you
DefconTroll
@VictimOfTheSystem Oh look, the news made rich white kids look bad
VictimOfTheSystem
You can still kiss my ass
TheApologist
They were clearly laying hands on him.

AlecSmart
Well duh
TheApologist
I meant praying for him. He must have attacked them.
AlecSmart
Cuz homeless people attack teenagers all the time
TheApologist
Were you there? How would you know?
AlecSmart
Were you? If not STFU
NNNews
This just in. A Norville nursing home experienced mass hysteria resulting in bizarre behavior and several deaths.
MyLadyFair
My grandmother was a resident. She passed away just before all that happened. Should I be concerned?
AlecSmart
Not unless death runs in the family
DefconTroll
lol
MyLadyFair
Heartless asses. Rot in Hell!
DefconTroll
There is no Hell. On the bright side your gramma isn't there.
MyLadyFair
@DefconTroll Consider yourself reported!
NNNews
Scout Troop 418 blamed for starting a riot at nursing home. Severely traumatized residents died from cardiac arrest.
VictimOfTheSystem
More rich white kids gone wild
DefconTroll
You don't know much about the Scouts do you? They've unfortunately become a seething, melting pot of multiculturalism.
NNNews
Security footage of one individual appears to match that of white male involved in earlier cardiac arrest incident.
VictimOfTheSystem
How is a teenage boy giving old people heart attacks?

AlecSmart

Maybe he says "BOO!"

NNNews

Because he's a minor we can't release his name or image, but sources confirm he is the same individual. Drugs suspected.

VictimOfTheSystem

lol drugs. Did he make them shoot heroin?

AlecSmart

I'm guessing they think he chloroformed them or something. In any case he met his two good deeds of the day quota.

VictimOfTheSystem

More like dirty deeds

AlecSmart

I hear he offers them at an incredibly discounted rate

VictimOfTheSystem

?

DefconTroll

@AlecSmart I got it

TheOther5thBeatle

@AlecSmart Had the pleasure of being in the studio when they recorded Highway to Hell. RIP Bon Scott, Malcolm Young

ProphetElijahNewell   bishop@AgapeBreadofLifeOutreach

SPONSORED AD

Troubled by what you're seeing on the news lately? All Hell is breaking loose, but God isn't alarmed, because he's already provided the answer. #InMyName

VictimOfTheSystem

puhlease. Now we know where their church donations go: advertising for social media. Unwanted advertising at that.

AlecSmart

To get more donations no doubt

ProphetessAlishaNewell *firstLady@AgapeBreadofLifeOutreach*

@ProphetElijahNewell Yes Brother Elijah. For when the enemy comes in like a flood the Spirit of the Lord will lift up a standard against him. #InMyName

AlecSmart

Wait. Are they brother and sister or husband and wife?

MaryWanna?

They married. They use it as a term of respect to avoid lusting in the pulpit.

DefconTroll

This ought to be good for a laugh.

ProphetElijahNewell *bishop@AgapeBreadofLifeOutreach*

@ProphetessAlishaNewell Amen Sister Alisha. And that standard is Jesus! Because the time is now, the need is now, the answer is now! #InMyName

AlecSmart

I much prefer Standard Jesus over Metric Jesus

TheApologist

There is only one Jesus.

DeconTroll

@AlecSmart Told you this would be good

ProphetessAlishaNewell *firstLady@AgapeBreadofLifeOutreach*

We're holding an all-day church service to provide healing to the sick in mind, spirit and body. Jesus is here! #InMyName

ProphetElijahNewell *bishop@AgapeBreadofLifeOutreach*

Come to Agape Bread of Life Outreach, where we still lay hands on the sick and believe for miracles. #InMyName

ProphetessAlishaNewell *firstLady@AgapeBreadofLifeOutreach*

We don't fear disease. We lay hands on the sick and they recover. #InMyName

DaughteroftheKing

Sorry, Bishop. Donny and I won't be able to make it. We both came down with food poisoning from breakfast at The Toast.

ProphetessAlishaNewell *firstLady@AgapeBreadofLifeOutreach*

We will pray for you both. Take care and get plenty of rest.

DaughteroftheKing

Thank you Prophetess

SuperPortionMe

The Spirit of the Lord is upon me because he hath anointed me to preach the gospel and tear down the altars of idols.

The Apologist

Agape Bread of Life Outreach is an altar to the idol of greed worshiped by Elijah Balaam and Alicia Jezebel Newell.

SuperPortionMe

And thus the Lord hath commanded me: Tear down the altars of Baal!

VictimOfTtheSystem
They've been living like kings and queens for years off everybody's money while preaching White Jesus

TheApologist
There is only one Jesus, and he's neither white or black, but probably brown.

DefconTroll
Billy Graham lives!

AlecSmart
@VictimOfTheSystem Haven't you been keeping up? It's not black or white Jesus, it's Standard or Metric Jesus lol

SaintsAlive
During greeting time I just shook hands with a young wild-eyed Caucasian man. Something touched me, and I mean beside his hand. #WhatIsTheLordUpTo #ShiftInMySpirit

PredestinedCalledJustifiedGlorified
U mean he didn't give U a sanctified church hug?

SaintsAlive
8o No, not that kind of thing lol I mean in the Spirit. Didn't U read my hashtags girl?

PredestinedCalledJustifiedGlorified
Sorry for jumping to conclusions. U know them shady wolves always coming to church looking for a fine Sista.

SaintsAlive
lol U got that right. Now I better quit texting b4 Bishop calls me out

PredestinedCalledJustifiedGlorified
I know. Ricky already throwing me dirty looks.

MaryWanna?
o my gawd yall! dude just attacked pastor and his wife live on TV! He try to rape that woman! #TheDevilIsReal

PredestinedCalledJustifiedGlorified
A devil-possessed man just attacked Prophet and Prophetess Newell!!! Jesus save us!

DefconTroll
Tuning into news now

AlecSmart
ditto

NNNews

This just in. Another bizarre act of violence, this time during a live broadcast of a church service out of Norville.

VictimOfTheSystem

It's a race war! The KKK have been planning this for years!

DefconTroll

Idiot. Remember the Boy Scouts? There were black, hispanic and asian kids in that bunch. This is a disease or something.

AlecSmart

Yeah, Norville isn't exactly the Deep South. Quite a Melting Pot actually.

VictimOfTheSystem

The only disease I see is religion. White church youth group, Boy Scouts and now a black church #OpiateOfTheMasses #FreedomFromReligion

DefconTroll

The Boy Scouts are not a religious organization.

VictimOfTheSystem

Not officially

DefconTroll

Not period.

VictimOfTheSystem

Whatever

RealPresidentConyers

Shocked to hear about the assault on my close friends Elijah and Alicia Newell. A great credit to the Black community.

NNNews

President Conyers just posted his response to the church attack on social media.

MaryWanna?

Why he have to bring bring race into this? I'll tear his damn throat out if I see his racist ass.

DefconTroll

That's a threat against the President. Consider yourself reported.

VictimOfTheSystem

We saw how much good that did when someone reported you

DefconTroll

That's what they call, you know, "white privilege"

VictimOfTheSystem

@MaryWanna? Make sure to add DefconTroll to your list. I'll help.

BeckySoccerMom

@AskBrotherBobby Why would the Lord allow a demon-possessed man to overcome a Spirit-filled pastor and his wife?

AskBrotherBobby

@BeckySoccerMom The Sons of Sceva tried to cast out a devil in the name of a Savior they didn't know. The devil sent them running naked.

MaryWanna?

@AskBrotherBobby cause they black and don't go to ur church they don't know Jesus? ur the one sounding like the Devil

TheApologist

In my name shall they cast out devils.

AlecSmart

Would that name be @TheApologist?

MaryWanna?

@TheApologist Who the hell name u think they use? Their own?

NNNews

Security and cellphone footage reveals that the attacker was soon restrained by members of the congregation.

MaryWanna?

"restrained" lol you know they beat the hell out that white boy X')

RealRickyReynolds

Can't believe I froze like that. I'm 6.2, 250 pounds and was terrified of an unarmed man half my size. Forgive me fam.

PredestinedCalledJustifiedGlorified

It's ok baby. No one can say what they would have done in your same shoes. Let go and let God.

MaryWanna?

@RealRickyReynolds Not like they needed your help. they were on that boy like white on rice

AlecSmart

Actually it looked more like gravy on potatoes. A SEA of gravy on a spoonful of mashed potatoes.

MaryWanna?

lol u ain't right. u funny, but u ain't right

AlecSmart

;) I try

PredestinedCalledJustifiedGlorified

The Lord will avenge his anointed. #TouchNotMineAnointed

AlecSmart

Looks like the Lord used half the congregation to avenge them

SaintsAlive

I know I shook that man's hand and I felt something. It was God. I know it and can't nobody tell me different. But why?

VictimOfTheSystem

Maybe they aren't prophets and maybe you should rethink your beliefs

AlecSmart

"Prophets" lol You think they would have seen this coming

BeckySoccerMom

Maybe they weren't living right.

PredestinedCalledJustifiedGlorified

Yall quit judging. Act like you holy 24 7. U know you up in the club every night. #LetHeWhoIsWithoutSin

TheApologist

I don't know who you think you're talking to but I'm most certainly not up in any club.

MaryWanna?

Course u not. U too busy looking up kiddie porn in your mama's basement.

NNNews

After visiting Norville Hospital and examining dozens of blood samples, the CDC claims a virus is to blame.

CDCGov

Using current prediction models and other evidence the GigaVirus has already infected at least one thousand people.

CDCGov

Implementation of emergency protocols are currently being discussed.

NNNews

The virus, thus far responsible for over a thousand verified infections in a single day, has been dubbed the GigaVirus.

DefconTroll

If statistics are based on a prediction model, they're not verified.

NNNews

The GigaVirus is believed to be the result of hyper-evolution in a specific strain of a yet-identified bacteria.

TheConcernedCitizen

"specific strain...yet-identified" How much doublespeak can you possibly air on your network and call it reliable?

CDCGov

We have located the source of the GigaVirus and determined it to be a hyper-evolved strain of Staph.

AlecSmart

So the point-one percent my handsoap didn't kill turned out to be the Godzilla of infections? Thanks for nothing, Dial.

NNNews

The CDC identifies the bacteria responsible for the GigaVirus to be a strain of Staph.

TheConcernedCitizen

I've seen a Staph infection. It isn't pretty, but it doesn't make you run, hide, rape or kill.

TheConcernedCitizen

If this is Staph, where are the skin sores and abscesses? None of these victims/perpetrators show signs of the above.

AlecSmart

Apparently the symptoms of the .1 percent are 99.9 percent different than your average Staph symptoms

TheConcernedCitizen

I'm not a conspiracy theorist, but I smell a cover-up.

AlecSmart

Would you describe the cover-up smell as being something like 1)fishy 2)afoot or 3)teen spirit?

TheOther5thBeatle

Can't believe I doubted they would make it as a band. Then again, maybe deep down I realized Kurt was a Roman candle.

CDCGov

The incubation time for the GigaVirus is incredibly fast. From initial contact to first symptoms occur within an hour. #KnowTheFacts

CDCGov

Those most vulnerable to the GigaVirus are children, seniors and those with compromised immune systems. #KnowTheFacts

CDCGov

The GigaVirus can increase the heart rate up to three times faster, potentially leading to death. #KnowTheFacts

TheApologist

The Lord shall try the hearts of all men in this dark hour. Hold fast to Jesus so that you be found not wanting.

DefconTroll

We have a winner folks. Fruitiest nutbar on the block.

CDCGov

An accelerated heart rate leads to the release of stress hormones responsible for extreme agitation. #KnowTheFacts

CDCGov

The GigaVirus triggers a constant release of adrenaline, the hormone responsible for Fight or Flight. #KnowTheFacts

CDCGov

This constant state of Fight or Flight can paralyze the victim with fear or make them increasingly violent. #KnowTheFacts

TheApologist

There's no fear in love. Perfect love casts out fear because fear has torment. He who fears is not made perfect in love.

DefconTroll

This dude ain't from the Bible Belt. He's from the Bible Bong.

CDCGov

The virus also appears to release Norepinephrine in increasing measure. #KnowTheFacts

CDCGov

Norepinephrine is responsible for sexual libido. Its rapid release may lead to sexual aggression and rape. Be safe. #KnowTheFacts

TheConcernedCitizen

The argument that increased testosterone is responsible for rape is disingenuous and seeks to justify it. Not cool #WhiteMalePatriarchy #Masochism #Mysogyny #RapeCulture #MeToo

VictimOfTheSystem

@CDCGov Way to victim blame

DefconTroll

Give it a rest both of you. Besides, they said norepenephrine, NOT testosterone. Geesh, are you even listening?

VictimOfTheSystem

Didn't I tell you to kiss my ass earlier?

TheConcernedCitizen

@CDCGov Besides, the onus for telling someone how to behave should be directed toward the perpetrator, not the victim

DefconTroll

But since criminals don't have a moral compass the onus for protecting oneself is back in the potential victim's court.

TheApologist

Gird up the loins of your mind. Be sober. Hope to the end for the grace that comes at the revelation of Jesus Christ.

DefconTroll

Would that be sirloins? I'll take mine rare, please.

AlecSmart

And here I thought Viagra was responsible for sexual libido

CDCGov

We publicly apologize for our statement concerning victims of sexual violence. We respect the rights of all victims.

DefconTroll

@CDCGov Way to backpedal on issues of public safety in the name of political correctness. #PartOfTheProblem

CDCGov

We unequivocally condemn all those who commit acts of sexual violence. The victim is never to blame.

VictimOfTheSystem

They're finally speaking sense

DefconTroll

@CDCGov So you leave your house and vehicle unlocked at all times? Even insurance companies won't help you if you're that dumb. #PartOfTheProblem #PersonalResponsibility

CDCGov

We encourage all residents to stay inside their homes and lock their doors to ensure their safety.

DefconTroll

NOW you're making sense.

VictimOfTheSystem

Do you always play devil's advocate?

DefconTroll

I am the Devil

NNNews

President Conyers is boarding Air Force One now, soon to depart for the emergency Summit to discuss his travel ban.

TheConcernedCitizen

"Boarding" Air Force One. Do you mean "jumping ship?"

AlecSmart

Beat me to the punch

TheConcernedCitizen

Great minds...

NNNews

We're live at Joint Base Andrews, where Air Force One is just now taking off to attend the emergency World Summit.

RealPresidentConyers

On my way to the World Summit to discuss the travel ban to prevent the GigaVirus from infecting our global friends.

ConspiracyTheoryIsFact

The President is fleeing the country. Prepare for Marshall Law people.

DefconTroll

Oh God. Another one! This keeps getting better.

AlecSmart

Marshall Law. Not to be confused with The Marshall Plan, an excellent song by Blue Oyster Cult.

TheOther5thBeatle

I got to party with them a few times. Great bunch of guys. RIP Allen Lanier

NNNews

CDC to make an announcement shortly. Please stay tuned to your news feed whether television, radio or internet.

ConspiracyTheoryIsFact

I call a modified flu vaccine full of the same old chemicals responsible for autism and death.

AlecSmart

That will cost a month's wages no doubt

RationAlice

No reason to pass judgment regarding cost or efficacy until this hypothetical vaccine is actually administered.

TheConcernedCitizen

That's the problem. The public would become the guinea pig for an ill-tested vaccine.

RationAlice
Point taken.
DefconTroll
I predict the Body Condom. Invest in Trojan stock now!
CDCGov
Using existing strains we have developed a vaccine to prevent GigaVirus and a therapeutic vaccine to cure it. #GetTheShot
ConspiracyTheoryIsFact
What did I say?
VictimOfTheSystem
Damn, he was right
DefconTroll
Easy guess
VictimOfTheSystem
Are you still here Devil?
DefconTroll
And will be with you until the end of the age when they lock me up and throw away the key forever
TheApologist
Actually, Satan is locked away for a thousand years, released, then gathers the nations against Israel one last time.
DefconTroll
Dare you correct me human mortal? I shall destroy your soul in Hellfire!
TheApologist
The Lord Jesus rebuke you Satan!
DefconTroll
AAAGGGHHH!!!! NOOOOOO!!! YOUR POWER IS TOO MIGHTY FOR ME!!! Nope, didn't work. Still here.
CDCGov
Both the vaccine and cure will be made available through your local pharmacy. They are administered free of charge. #GetTheShot
AlecSmart
Well I'll be damned
DefconTroll
Not unless I say so mortal human!
AlecSmart
lol

TheApologist

Satan isn't a joke.

DefconTroll

I'm glad you reverence me, as well as recognize your own insignificance. I shall reward you richly for thus.

CDCGov

Other facilities have volunteered to carry the vaccines. These include schools, fire stations and houses of worship. #GetTheShot

NNNews

The CDC has launched its vaccine campaign to prevent and cure GigaVirus. Check your local news for vaccine distributors.

SamNelson

At AllMart to get the vaccine. There's two lines crossing the whole parking lot. #GonnaBeHereAWhile

DonnaFontaine

Cops are directing traffic but it doesn't seem to be helping because no one knows where they're supposed to go #DrivingLikeTourists

WilliamSanders

Someone said you can get the shot inside or out. They needed more stations to give it. Don't know which is which.

JamesJohnson

Asked if I go inside for the vaccine and outside for the cure. They said get in line. Still confused.

SheenaBeatrix

People ahead of me saying the trucks must have mixed up the cure with the vaccine so nobody knows what they're getting.

JohnSantiago

They said there would be one line for vaccine, one for cure. Both look the same. What's going on here?

DillonBettencourt

Asked the nurse if I was getting the cure or vaccine. She said yes. That wasn't the question lady.

PhyllisArman

Either the vaccine and cure are the same or this is all a sham.

CDCGov

Re: concerns about vaccine vs. cure. We found it more cost-effective to produce a single shot that acts as both. #GetTheShot

VictimOfTheSystem

What kind of bullshit answer is that? Liar liar pants on fire.

CDCGov
A single shot also eliminates the time-consuming need to test patients whether they're positive or negative. #GetTheShot

RationAlice
Makes sense

TheConcernedCitizen
@CDCGov When did you have time to develop this? You just said you had a cure AND a vaccine and now you have a two-for-one?

CDCGov
@TheConcernedCitizen The initial vaccine and cure were combined to produce the hybrid vaccine we now offer free of charge. #GetTheShot

TheConcernedCitizen
I'm no scientist but I don't think that's how the pharmaceutical industry works. More lies.

TheConcernedCitizen
We're supposed to cheer because it's free? Wasn't it already? Were they going to charge $ to stop a major outbreak?

CDCGov
The AllMart Corp has generously donated $1-million worth of vaccine for all its customers. See your pharmacist today. #GetTheShot

TheConcernedCitizen
Again with the lies. It was free all along. Nobody would charge for a cure necessary for the survival of humanity.

AlecSmart
Don't be so sure

JohnSantiago
People getting the shot are throwing up, shaking, convulsing, passing out. Ran to my car and got the hell out. #DoNotGetTheShot

CDCGov
The vaccine will not make you sick. It is the only cure available for the disease. #GetTheShot

SheenaBeatrix
Just watched two people hit the floor after getting the shot. I think they're dead. Got out of line. Don't get the shot!

DefconTroll
Symptoms include increased heart rate, "up to three times faster, potentially leading to death." #GetTheShot

CDCGov

Anyone dying after receiving the vaccination was in the last stage of infection. #GetTheShot

TheConcernedCitizen

@CDCGov Then why are you selling it as a cure?

CDCGov

@TheConcernedCitizen The vaccine is provided to the public free of charge. If any provider charges for the vaccine report them immediately. #GetTheShot

TheConcernedCitizen

@CDCGov That's not what I meant and you know it. You're claiming it cures the virus and people are still dying.

BeckySoccerMom

Finally about to get my children and I vaccinated, like every responsible citizen and parent should.

AllNaturalAllTheTime

Do responsible parents let their children get a shot nobody has tested?

BeckySoccerMom

Damn straight they do. Don't bring your unvaccinated kid around mine.

AllNaturalAllTheTime

Good luck dealing with a bunch of autistic kids.

BeckySoccerMom

I'll deal with autism. How will you deal with death?

CDCGov

The vaccine will not cause autism. #KnowTheFacts

AllNaturalAllTheTime

And exactly how much time have they had to test this doubtful claim?

AlecSmart

I'm guessing as much time as they had to turn a vaccine and a cure into the "hybrid" vaccine

AllNaturalAllTheTime

I know, right?

BeckySoccerMom

While you dumb asses are debating conspiracies, I'll be trusting the FDA and science.

AllNaturalAllTheTime

Becky's not only a soccer mom, but a dumb blond soccer mom.

BeckySoccerMom

Redhead, thank you very much

AlecSmart

Make that Becky the Souless Ginger soccer mom

BeckySoccerMom

Piss off troll!

RedNeckedBubba

People trying to leave are being forced to stay in line. So scared. #NoChoice

RedNeckedBubba

The police just beat a man for trying to leave the store without getting the shot. This ain't right. #WhatFreedom?

AskBrotherBobby

I just did my patriotic duty before God and man to receive the vaccine. A little pinch and it was all over with. #GetTheShot

RedneckedBubba

Most yall know I'm a former addict. Trust me when I say: the vaccine ain't a cure. It's a drug. #OffTheWagon

SmallTownGirl

@RedneckedBubba PM me

SmallTownGirl

I heard someone say the shot is just like oxy and fentanyl. Now I want the shot. #HookAGirlUp

CDCGov

The vaccine may have side effects resembling certain narcotics, but it is completely safe.

BeckySoccerMom

My baby isn't breathing. He just got the shot. Oh God, somebody please help.

DefconTroll

How bout you get off your damn phone and take the baby to the hospital. Jesus.

AlecSmart

Parenthood isn't for everyone

TheConcernedCitizen

@CDCGov No response? The woman just said her baby isn't breathing.

CDCGov

If you or family experience any symptoms (shortness of breath, dizziness, rapid heartbeat) seek immediate medical help

TheConcernedCitizen

@CDCGov You are the medical help. Don't dance around the question. Is the vaccine safe?

CDCGov

Symptoms of the disease are known to include shortness of breath, dizziness, rapid heartbeat, blurred vision and more #KnowTheFacts

TheConcernedCitizen

No, symptoms include increased heart rate, violent and sexual aggression. What you're describing are SIDE EFFECTS

AskBrotherBobby

1 O brothers, o sisters, I have tasted and seen that the Lord is good. Yes Jesus. I hear you. I will speak.

MaryWanna?

Now this preacher speaking in Bible verses? Who he think he is?

CDCGov

If you or family experience any symptoms of the disease please seek immediate medical help.

TheConcernedCitizen

You already said that. Stop beating around the bush.

AlecSmart

Dance your partner all around, beat that bush flat to the ground. Back to Square One dancing.

TheConcernedCitizen

@BeckySoccerMom What is your baby's condition?

BeckySoccerMom

He's dead. My baby is dead. Oh God. Why? Don't get the shot, whatever you do, JUST DON'T!

CDCGov

We remind everyone that the vaccine is safe and that the disease increases the heart rate up to three times faster.

TheConcernedCitizen

@CDCGov Sounds awfully convenient to blame the disease for a killer vaccine. May you bastards rot in hell.

AlecSmart

Geesh, we all know the disease increases the heart rate. Don't blame the cure.

TheConcernedCitizen
ACCOUNT SUSPENDED
AlecSmart
Damn. Somebody reported TheConcernedCitizen. @DefconTroll?
DefconTroll
Not me.
AlecSmart
Not a joint account of yours, either?
DefconTroll
Nope. Or was it? MUHAHAHAHA
AskBrotherBobby
2 Has not God has chosen to use men, even the imperfect, as his instruments? Did not he use a donkey to speak to Balaam?
AskBrotherBobby
3 Pharaoh to spread his glory? Judas to betray his Son? Hitler to bring the Jews back to Israel?
ConspiracyTheoryIsFact
Wake up sheeple! This is phase 2 protocol for the Nuclear/Radiological Incident Annex: https://emergency.cdc.gov/radiation/cdcrole.asp
DefconTroll
Hooray! He's back!
AlecSmart
You sure that's not your joint account?
DefconTroll
Not unless I'm a schizo like him.
ConspiracyTheoryIsFact
Phase 2 lets local governments open the Strategic National Stockpile, a cache of drugs meant to anesthetize the public.
ConspiracyTheoryIsFact
Phase 2 means this is NOT a test. This is a REAL emergency. The Doomsday clock has struck 12.
AlecSmart
This IS your brain. This is your brain on DRUGS. The whole Strategic National Stockpile of them.
ConspiracyTheoryIsFact
The cure is nothing more than an opioid cocktail. Same stuff junkies are buying from their dealer on the corner.

AlecSmart

You sound like an expert on dealers and corners

MaryWanna?

lol dude is the dealer and buyer all in one.

ConspiracyTheoryIsFact

Phase 2 means they've already launched the missiles. This is it. Make peace with your god. #GameOverManGameOver #HastaLaVistaBaby

DefconTroll

There is no God.

RationAlice

Guess we're about to find out.

SmallTownGirl

I just found God at the AllMart pharmacy. You were right @RedneckedBubba #ImInHeaven

AskBrotherBobby

4 He chose the physician Luke to spread the gospel. And He chose government, his sword of justice, to bring us healing.

MaryWanna?

Conspiracy dude might be right. Preacher dude sound like he trippin

ConspiracyTheoryIsFact

This isn't a cure. The govt's putting you in a drug-induced coma so you won't feel the nukes when they hit ala Jim Jones #RememberJonestown #DontDrinkTheKoolaid

RationAlice

I'd rather drink the koolaid and be put out of my misery than die from radiation. Bring it on.

MaryWanna?

Amen. Put my ass ground zero. Ima ride that bitch all the way to Armageddon.

AlecSmart

Ground Zero in Zero to Sixty lol

ConspiracyTheoryIsFact

ACCOUNT SUSPENDED

AlecSmart

Guess he got nuked before the rest of us

DefconTroll

And it was just getting good. I love schizos.

AskBrotherBobby

5 Just as the Israelites looked to the serpent upon the staff, so we must look to the Staff of Asclepius for our cure.

SmallTownGirl

I don't feel so good yall.

MaryWanna?

Lightweight

DefconTroll

Usually I'd say kill yourself but sounds like the vaccine is working.

RationAlice

That was uncalled for

DefconTroll

@RationAlice Good thing I didn't ask you

MaryWanna?

@DefconTroll dat some cold shit bruh

AlecSmart

My shit ain't ever cold. Comes out steaming every time.

MaryWanna?

Lol u know we just playin @SmallTownGirl. U aight?

DefconTroll

SmallTownGirl has left the building

AlecSmart

Damn dude

RationAlice

@DefconTroll Consider yourself reported

DefconTroll

lol. Not the first time honey.

DefconTroll

ACCOUNT SUSPENDED

AlecSmart

Damn girl

MaryWanna?

RationAlice don't play.

RationAlice

No she doesn't. Hate trolls.

AskBrotherBobby

6 This medicine is the balm of Gilead. Let the heathen call it koolaid, we will drink it to the dregs.

MaryWanna?
Will you shut up already? Damn people tired of you
RationAlice
Just ignore him.
TheRealLastDefense
The First Family is now safe at Site R. I could be tried for treason if this wasn't the end. But so could they. #EndOfTheWorld #Armageddon #ApocalypseNow #BeWithLovedOnes
MaryWanna?
@TheRealLastDefense What's Site R?
TheRealLastDefense
ACCOUNT SUSPENDED
AlecSmart
Raven Rock. The president's nuclear bunker. I think shit just got real.
MaryWanna?
O my gawd. U serious?
AlecSmart
For once my friend. Thought everyone was being overdramatic. Guess I was wrong.
AskBrotherBobby
7 Yes, drink it my children. Jesus said this cup is the new covenant in my blood, which is shed for you.
MaryWanna?
Jesus I don't wanna die.
BeckySoccerMom
My baby is dead. The missiles are falling. I told my kids they were shooting stars. Goodbye everyone. I love you all.
AlecSmart
I see them too. She was right. Everyone was. Sorry I didn't believe. Going to spend some time with my fam.
MaryWanna?
Oh my God! The missiles they coming! This ain't a joke. Please Lord Jesus, forgive me my sins and have mercy on my soul!
AskBrotherBobby
8 My eyes grow heavy from the glory of God. I hear his angels! They are calling us home! Is this not the Rapture?
RationAlice
I won't make it to AllMart in time. Looks like my bottle of sleeping

pills will have to do the job. Nighty night guys.

AlecSmart

Good night Alice. Good night John Boy. Good night cruel world.

TheOther5thBeatle

Sorry John. We never gave peace a chance.

0100111001101111011101110010000001001001001000000110
1010000010110000100000011101000110100001100101001000000
1100100011001010111001101111010001110010011011110111001
0110010101110010000100000011011110110011000100000001111011
1011011110111001001101100011001000111001100101110

078 111 119 032 073 032 097 109 032 098 101 099 111 109 101
032 068 101 097 116 104 044 032 116 104 101 032 100 101 115 116
114 111 121 101 114 032 111 102 032 119 111 114 108 100 115 046

4e6f77204920616d206265636f6d652044656174682c207468652
064657374726f796572206f6620776f726c64732e

%4e%6f%77%20%49%20%61%6d%20%62%65%63%6f%6d%
65%20%44%65%61%74%68%2c%20%74%68%65%20%64%65%
73%74%72%6f%79%65%72%20%6f%66%20%77%6f%72%6c%6
4%73%2e

Connection Lost

● Please check your connection and try again.

● If you are unable to connect, contact your Internet Service Provider.

~

A resident of North Carolina's Outer Banks, A.P. Sessler frequents an alternate universe not too different from your own, searching for that unique element that twists the everyday commonplace into the weird. When he's not writing fiction, he composes music, makes art, and spends too much time trying to connect with his inner genius. He also likes to dress in funny clothes and talk about the first English colony in the New World.

FIGHT OR FLIGHT
Tamina Das Mitra

Author's note: In my country India, the gap between the rich and the poor is very wide; so much so, that the middle class has gone completely missing. A few privileged people get to enjoy a life of luxury while the vast majority struggles to make ends meet. The rich are often oblivious to the problems of the poor. The ones with money take help from those without, but forget to treat them with basic dignity or compassion. A paltry wage or tip is all that they get for going out of their way to help out the privileged class. My story is set in an Indian city where the secure and comfortable lifestyle of an urban couple comes under real threat due to prolonged natural calamities.

I wrote this piece hoping for people to embrace the simple fact that human beings need to help each other out and stop direct or indirect oppression. Also, the threat of global warming is causing a drastic increase in droughts and floods in my country. This imbalance is creating major problems for everyone, yet there is no significant change in the attitude of the society. I sincerely hope people will take this seriously and cultivate a more responsible attitude towards nature.

Fight or Flight

Basanti crinkled her nose instinctively as she emptied a bowl of cubed potatoes into the hot oil. She stirred the noisy potatoes with her ladle for a while before going back to sorting the pile of egg plants. Most of them had gone bad and she was able to carve out just a handful of fresh slices after going through the lot. Basanti was keeping the irritation to herself when the creak of the door announced the entry of her husband, Bishu. She immediately decided to be vocal about her woes.

"My poor father selected a vegetable seller for me hoping that I'd always be well fed. How saddened he would have been to find me scavenging through the refused vegetables!"

Bishu had long since stopped taking offence at his wife's jibes. He quietly lifted up the corner of a musty mattress to pull out a nondescript box. After locking his day's earnings safely away he straightened the sheets on top of it. Then he peeled off his sweat-soaked shirt and changed into a holey vest. He let out an audible sigh only after he had laid himself down.

The small sigh had reached his wife's ears. Leaving her monologue and the sizzling curry unresolved, she instantly rushed to Bishu's side.

A familiar smell of perspiration enveloped Basanti as she touched his forehead and cheeks to test the temperature.

"You've a fever!"

"Yes… I think I got it from Garui when I went to get the fresh supplies."

"Told you so many times to switch to a new dealer…that Garui gives you only stale vegetables and diseases."

Worried about her husband's health, Basanti served dinner quickly. As Bishu forced the meal down his raspy throat, his muscles ached badly.

At night as he reeled under escalating fever, his wife tried to alleviate his suffering with a gentle body massage.

"Basanti, tomorrow you will get fresh vegetables to cook… I won't be able to go the market."

The next day Basanti was up before the sun and went about cleaning the house and herself with her brisk hands. Then she sat down to relish her bowl of fermented leftover rice with a crisp green chili. Her sleeping husband looked frail and emaciated. In a jiffy, she decided that medicines were more important than the freshness of vegetables in her kitchen and got ready to hit the market herself. Before leaving she woke Bishu up to a breakfast of oats and hot tea.

"Eat a bit," said Basanti. "I'll try to sell off the vegetables fast."

Bishu bent up his lips in a smile of gratitude as his wife rolled out the squeaky old wheelbarrow through the door.

*

Basanti hated the walk to the market. It was a short walk but the sticky heat seemed to squeeze out all her energy. Being close to the sea beach, the town air was always thick with humidity.

At Basanti spread out the vegetables into separate piles on a black polythene sheet, the first customer walked up.

"Who're you? Isn't this Bishu's barrow?" the man asked.

"I'm his wife," replied Basanti in a small voice.

"Bishu is married! He looks so young!" the man said as he extended a folded grocery bag towards Basanti.

"He is young, bhaiya. We got married soon after he dropped out of school."

As she accepted the bag, the scent of a musky perfume hit her senses. She took a second look at the customer. He was a man in his mid-thirties, dressed in a light green T shirt and a pair of brown shorts. His scanty hair looked silky fresh and his roundish face was clean shaven and dimpled due to a friendly smile.

"You know you should be going to school too. Anyway...give me my vegetables," he said.

"Which ones, bhaiya?" Basanti asked.

"Oh...you wouldn't know. Bishu knows."

The man turned around towards a car parked at a distance. A slim lady in an orange kurti and dark blue jeans was looking into her phone, leaning on the car.

"Sue, could you come here please?" the man asked.

The lady promptly looked up and came up to them.

"What is it, Rajib?"

Her pursed lips and slightly frowned eyebrows scared Basanti a bit.

"Bishu isn't here. Tell her which vegetables you want...you never like the ones I choose!"

Rajib flashed a small smile of implicit introduction at Basanti as his wife Sunaina bent down to take a closer look at the vegetables.

"What happened to Bishu?" Rajib asked after a while.

"He's down with a fever."

"That's bad...a bad viral strain is going around. Tell him to come to our place in the evening and get himself checked."

"So you are a doctor?" Basanti asked.

"Not me. She is the doctor." he pointed at his wife. "I lack the erudition... I run a business like you and Bishu," he added with a wink.

Basanti smiled and proceeded to weigh the selected vegetables on her scale.

Sunaina had gone back to checking the mobile phone in her

hand.

As Basanti handed the bag to Rajib, their hands touched lightly and again the whiff of subtle fragrance overpowered Basanti.

As the couple walked back to their car together, Basanti observed them in a semi trance.

It was nice to see the minty fresh couple, settled in the cocoon of opulent existence, away from the insecurities of their slum life. But what impressed Basanti the most was the loquacious nature of Rajib; it was unusual for the male to outshine the female in verbosity.

*

A decade of time rolled by in the town and the two couples lived through their shares of joy and grief. And then fate put them face to face with a natural calamity of great magnitude. For some years the incidents of chronic water logging and sectional flooding had gone up. The town was slowly being abandoned by those who could find jobs in other cities. It seemed like global warming was about to make the town pay a terrible price.

That rainy season it had rained incessantly for 9 days. On the tenth day Sunaina and Rajib were in a state of despair in their plush apartment. The room looked gloomy in the absence of electricity and Rajib stood by the window.

"We need a plan fast," Rajib remarked as he cracked his knuckles, observing the unrelenting rains adding more water to the flooded roads.

Sunaina sat in a huddle with her arms crossed tightly. Everyone she knew had foreseen the situation and had made arrangements for a safer future...everyone but Rajib. And now he stood there like a dolt, making obvious statements.

"Is there no way out now?" he wondered aloud.

At that moment a sudden knock on their front door saved Rajib from the wordy wrath of his wife.

Sunaina took a few deep breaths to calm her feelings before opening the door.

"Wait...ask who it is..."

The door was opened, ignoring Rajib's meek protests, but thankfully it was only Bishu standing there, fully drenched and holding in his strained hands, two huge bags of vegetables.

He placed the bags inside and started to rub the indented red lines on his palms.

"I thought you might need these," he said.

"You could have come tomorrow...we don't need any today," said Sunaina as Rajib took the bags to the kitchen.

"Actually we are leaving in an hour's time," explained Bishu.

"Where're you going?" Sunaina was puzzled.

"Back to our village in the hills; maybe we can adjust back to the ways of mountain life if we try."

"You are moving to the hills to avoid the floods!" Rajib's eyebrows had risen.

"Bhaiya, you stay up on the sixth floor...for us it has been quite scary. Plus almost everyone has left already...the word around is that this town is preparing to be one with the sea."

Sunaina and Rajib exchanged glances as Bishu continued:

"The railways and the airport have shut down... Would you not try to move to another safer town at least? I mean for the time being?"

"What if we go with you two?" Suddenly Sunaina spoke up.

"With us?" Bishu was startled.

"We won't stay there forever...we need some time to come up with a plan and reach a functioning town to get away..."

"We'd be honored to host you, doctor didi. It's just that our humble home is not on a par with your living standards..."

Rajib promptly placed his hands on Bishu's shoulders.

"If you don't help us we'll probably wither away here...please brother..."

Bishu held Rajib's hands and put them close to his heart, "You've always been kind to me bhaiya...pack your bags right away...I'll wait here."

He sat down cross-legged at the threshold while Sunaina and Rajib scurried around trying to assemble into a knapsack the most essential of their belongings.

*

The unlikely team of Bishu, Basanti, Rajib and Sunaina were soon waiting at a shack. A dilapidated pedalling cart showed up after some time.

"You have to pay ten thousand rupees, babu," the driver said to Rajib. He casually rested his legs on the pedals and grinded chewing tobacco in his palm.

"Ten thousand!" Sunaina turned to Bishu. "Did you agree to pay this much?"

"He is my distant cousin…I'll transport his family for free. The fee is for you two," clarified the driver in a resolute tone.

"Ok…but you have to take us to an ATM…this payout will create a big dent in our resources."

"I can only take you up to Jarik Nagar…you have to find the ATM yourself."

They paid up eventually and travelled in the cart for 7 hours under various degrees of downpour. At midday they had a meager lunch of bread and curried potatoes.

By the time they reached Jarik Nagar it was already late afternoon. Though the rains had taken a break, it did not reduce the intensity of wetness all around.

Bishu pointed to what seemed like a river and said, "The bus stop is about 2 miles away across this road."

Rajib realized after some effort that it was just the flooded National Highway. They waded through waist deep water and eventually managed to board an overnight bus to the closest transit point.

Over the next 2 days they rode through various landscapes and in diverse vehicles to finally reach Bishu and Basanti's hometown in the hills.

In the high hills they felt much safer and protected from the clutches of the expanding sea. In the ensuing darkness of the night the combination of the starry sky and the dim village lanterns made the place look unreal.

At a distance, a crowd of people sat in a wide circle around a large fire. A small group of men and women traced the circle, serving generous portions of piping hot food into square-cut banana leaves.

"Do people always eat together here?" Rajib asked.

"No…many are moving back from the drowned cities and

hence the temporary arrangement of community meals."

Soon, a simple meal of steaming khichdi and pickle was served to them. It seemed heavenly to the famished four.

"Can we buy chicken or meat here?" Sunaina asked after dinner as she washed her hands in a stream of water poured out by Basanti from a jug.

"Now chicken is really scarce, but you can have delicious frog legs," Basanti said happily.

"Wow! We had frog legs during our honeymoon in Rome," Rajib started.

"I don't think it'd be the same thing," Sunaina said coldly as she wiped her hands in a towel. "We'll have vegetarian food, Basanti."

Then they followed Bishu in silence across the fields to a small row of houses. The only furniture in the room of the house was a torn down bed at the side. On the floor sat a young woman with a baby in her arms.

"This is where you will be staying…a rather shabby room but we couldn't find anything better," said Bishu.

The woman with the baby was dressed in a sari that was darkened with dirt and her child gave off a mixed stink of sour milk and vomit. Both had their mouths open in perpetual curiosity. Sunaina squirmed at their sight and looked back at Bishu, awaiting an explanation.

"Erm…she is my cousin-in-law. She will be sharing the room with you two. Don't worry…she will use only the floor portion of the room…"

"Are those reeking of ablutions?" Sunaina spoke up, pointing to a pile of baby clothes in the corner of the room.

"Sue, listen…" Her husband tried to pull her back but she snatched away her hands and walked up to Bishu.

"Where are you and Basanti staying?"

"We'll put up in a make shift hut of bamboo sheets."

"Take us there please…"

"Doctor didi, there is no proper toilet there…we all walk a mile to the grasslands in the mornings."

Sunaina turned up her nose and sat down on the bed.

"Thank you, Bishu…this is fine for us." Rajib patted Bishu on the back and returned to calm his wife down.

"It's totally your fault! We could have emmigrated a long time back…before the USA and Canada stopped the influx completely."

"It's not the time to fight…"

The baby started to wail at that point and Sunaina placed her hands over her ears in animated irritation.

"I'll go out, sister…feed your baby," Rajib muttered to the young mother before walking out.

The next morning Sunaina woke up feeling disoriented.

She had slept facing the wall and turning around she found the space beside her to be empty. Springing up, she found Rajib putting on his shoes.

"What's with you?"

"I've to make a few calls…the phone booth is some distance away. Don't worry…I'll be back before lunch." Rajib left in a huff.

The woman was up too. She was staring at Sunaina with the same dull curiosity while her baby lay asleep by her.

"Hey…will you do one thing? Can you please sweep and clean the floor? Please wash those clothes too. I'll give you some money."

She still kept staring.

"Can't you hear me? Can you not speak?"

There was the sound of someone clearing their voice at the door. Sunaina looked up.

Basanti stood there; her eyes looked stern.

"I'll clean the room, doctor didi. This is her father's house…her husband sent her here so that she gets some comfort."

"What's the husband doing? Sounds like an irresponsible man!"

Basanti tucked the end of her sari in at her waist and started to sweep the floor ferociously with a large broom.

"He's a farmer…he's busy as it's the harvest season. Due to the floods he has to work twice as hard to feed people like you and me."

Although Basanti dusted and cleaned the room, Sunaina was silenced by the hint of offence in her tone.

"May I come in?" Bishu's voice was heard outside.

"Yes please," Sunaina's tone was buttery now. "Need anything?"

"Can you consider settling here as the village doctor? Things are tough now but people can build a nice house for you and bhaiya. It'll take time but with your guidance we can build a hospital and…"

"She won't be able to adjust here," Basanti was placing the soiled baby clothes into a large pot when she cut Bishu off.

"Keep quiet, Basanti…"

"Your wife is right…I can never bring myself to live here."

Sunaina buried her face in her hands and started to cry. Bishu would have rushed to her side but a glare from his wife made him follow her out of the room after casting a sympathetic look at Sunaina.

*

It was close to noon when Rajib finally returned. He was covered in grime and looked tired.

A look at her husband made Sunaina lose all hope.

"Did you go out to help the farmers? Are you planning to turn into one?"

"No! I went to call a friend. He lives at Trilaya and is willing to host us for a few days."

"What good would that do? We can't live there forever."

"Our work visas to Ptadiopia got approved…we'll be leaving this country soon!"

"Really? So soon? What about our home…our belongings?"

"Shh…let go of the past and prepare for the perilous road ahead. We got a rare chance, Sue…"

Sunaina did not trust the plan but she had run out of viable options.

At night they went out for the community dinner. It was the same menu, but Sunaina ate without complaints.

Basanti was sitting in a corner, busy halving a big bowl of washed lemons. Sunaina walked up to her.

Basanti continued indifferently, although she had sensed Sunaina's presence.

"We're leaving tomorrow…I came to say goodbye."

"Leaving?" Basanti looked up.

"Yes, we'll move to a new country soon."

"Please don't leave because of my rudeness…the times are difficult…I lost my cool…sorry didi."

Sunaina smiled.

"It's not that. The new country is wonderful with better facilities. They started fighting the war against global warming 20 years back. Unlike our illiterate country they adopted measures to keep their cities safe."

Basanti said nothing.

"You know Basanti…I was clinging to our home for a long time but the fate is sealed. Nature is steadily raising the sea level in vengeance."

"What does all that mean?"

"You never went to school…right? Nature is reclaiming her territories. It's payback time!" Sunaina smirked.

"But here we are safe…right?"

"First the plains and then the mountains…no part of our stupid country will be spared."

Basanti's face darkened in anguish as she tried to visualize the impending gloom.

That night as Bishu snored away in peace beside her, Basanti stared at the low moon through the window. The bigger moon of the mountains looked breathtakingly beautiful in the dark blue sky. When Basanti finally fell asleep, she felt as though it was the final sleep of her life.

Early next morning Rajib and Sunaina left with their bags. Bishu and Basanti went to see them off. As the duo vanished down the winding mountain slopes, Bishu turned to his wife and gave her a smile.

"Are you relieved now?"

"We're about to die…doctor didi told me everything," Basanti started to sniffle.

"What?"

"It's so unfair…the rich take off for a luxurious life leaving the poor to rot away."

Bishu laughed out loud and wiped the tears off Basanti's face.

"Do you even know what kind of life they are off to live? Rajib bhaiya talked to me yesterday; they made an arrangement with a big cleaning company abroad that will employ them as housekeeping staff. Now she'd be the one sweeping floors!"

"I don't think I'd mind cleaning houses in exchange for life."

"I know you wouldn't. I know unlike them we'd love each other no matter what. And I think if we live by the laws of nature, we might be allowed to continue with our lives in peace."

Basanti's eyes showed the tiniest hint of hope as Bishu pulled her closer in a hug.

"Listen, I marinated some frogs' legs in the morning. If you kindly fry them now, I'll go get some country liquor. And then we can forget about the rest of the world and lose ourselves in the Shaal forest for a few hours...just like the good old times."

Basanti and Bishu exchanged comforting smiles before running off in different directions. They were smiling bravely in the face of imminent doom; they were the luckiest ones alive.

~

Regional words used:
bhaiya – Hindi for brother
didi – Hindi for sister
kurti -- Long Indian shirt for women
babu -- Hindi for sir
khichdi -- Mixed meal of rice, lentils and vegetable

~

Tanima Das Mitra is an Indian author who has been trying to write stories right from her early childhood, even before she learned to construct a proper sentence. Her stories have been published in Indian as well as international magazines and anthologies. Her stories also won in the prestigious Write India contest *hosted by the Times of India group*. She lives in Kolkata with her son and husband, and though she is professionally a software engineer, writing continues to be her first love.

BITTER STARLIGHT
Gary Couzens

It's been eight years. Eight years.

As my finger comes away from the doorbell, there's silence. Maybe no one home? But the lights are on. It's a cold Northern Hemisphere night, with Orion's Belt hanging over the back fence of the house opposite in this cul-de-sac.

I can still see the stars.

The door opens. Kevin is there. His hair was beginning to recede when he left University and now, a decade and a half later, his scalp is smooth. His hair, becoming sandier now, neatly trimmed above his ears and joining at the back of his head. He's grown a beard, close-cropped to his chin. It suits him.

"Jolanda! Lovely to see you! Come in!" We kiss each other on the cheek, twice on each, European-style, and embrace. Adele is in the hallway behind him, oven-gloves on her hands and an apron over a pink-floral print dress, corkscrew-frizzy hair held back with a ribbon, also pink. I've forgotten how much taller than her I am, she barely over five feet. I have to bend down to hug her, kiss her on both cheeks too. She's a classic endomorph, broad shoulders and hips, heavy bust.

"Thanks for coming, Jo," she says. She's the only person who calls me that, with an English J-sound instead of the Dutch Y. "It's wonderful to see you. It's been too long." I hand her the bottle of Sancerre from my bag. "Oh you shouldn't have."

Standing behind them on the stairs is a girl, in a Princess Merida of *Brave* T-shirt that's baggy enough to be halfway down her thighs, over bright pink leggings. She looks a little like Merida, though her hair isn't red, but is dark brown and nearly black, tightly curled like Adele's. She's a little short for her age, slender and not yet filled out.

"Hi Emily," I say. I squat so that my eyes are level with hers. "I've seen all the pictures of you on Facebook. You were a baby when I last met you, so you won't remember me."

"This is Jolanda, Em," says Adele. "Daddy and I went to University with her. We shared a house."

"For two years," says Kevin.

"Good times," says Adele.

"Jolanda's my middle name," says Emily. She pronounces it Dutch-fashion, with the Y-sound.

"Yes, darling, we named you after this Jolanda," says Adele.

"Are you from New Zealand?" says Emily, gazing directly at me.

"No, I'm from the Netherlands," I say. "If I'm from anywhere, that is. I have been to New Zealand, though."

"Jolanda's been to lots and lots of places," says Adele. "Come to think of it, is there anywhere you *haven't* been, Jo?"

"Plenty," I say. "And plenty I'd like to go to. But yes, Emily, New Zealand is a lovely place. Maybe you'll go there some day."

Emily's head is quizzically cocked to one side, as if she's appraising me. "Have you seen any hobbits there?"

Adele laughs. "She's hobbit mad. We've been watching all the movies with her."

Kevin rests his arm about her shoulders. "*Return of the King* was our first date."

She reaches up, her fingers brushing his, and beams. "We're taking her to see *Frozen 2* when it comes out."

"Here's a clue, Emily," I say, still bent down. "In New Zealand, your name would be *Imily*. I've been round the world. There and back again."

Emily laughs, clearly getting the reference.

Adele wipes her hands on her apron. "Well, dinner's in the oven. I hope you're hungry, Jo."

"I am. I am looking forward to it. You always were a great cook, Adele."

"Oh well!" She blushes slightly. "I'm so glad I didn't poison you all at Uni."

"Always a first time," says Kevin.

"Sod off." She thumps him on the forearm.

*

There were four of us in that student house. I often saw Adele in the kitchen, trying something from one of the many cookbooks, some she'd brought from home in Lincolnshire, others she'd bought second-hand. She was always buying ingredients in the markets or one of the international shops locally or a Tube ride away. She tried the results out of us, the successes more frequent than the failures.

She's sometimes posted pictures of that time as Throwback Thursday Facebook posts, sometimes on her own, usually taken by Kevin, sometimes with him in the picture as well, taken by Ben or me. Kevin didn't have a beard then, and he was thinner than he is now. The top of Adele's head is level with his breastbone. She's usually in one of the ankle-length floaty dresses she liked. She was hardly ever seen in trousers.

The four of us paired off soon enough. Ben was with me, the tall fair-haired Dutch girl who, while I was fluent in English – I'm fluent in five languages – betrayed myself as *foreign* every time I opened my mouth. There were times, at parties or in the street, when I would keep silent as long as I could, maintaining many possibilities, before I said something and they all collapsed into one. As I'm tall and have had short hair ever since I was old enough to have a say in the matter, I'm sometimes mistaken for a man. Sometimes people are embarrassed when they realise their mistake. But I'm not offended. It's another possibility. I could be either or both or neither. But something always happens. I might be naked in front of a lover, and he or she naked in front of me. Or simply a smear test, once every three years. Or I simply open my mouth. From many to one.

Ben was over six foot, so taller than me, with mid-brown hair and blue eyes I couldn't help but gaze at. He was so thin I often joked that Adele needed to serve him a double portion to fatten him up a bit, but sometimes his jeans were tight. The walls were thin in that house, and the headboard of our bed was loose. Adele, red-faced, took it up herself to tell me discreetly how much it thumped against the radiator each time we made love. At first, that made Ben and me self-conscious, then after a day or so, we lay in bed together and laughed into our hands.

"Why don't you scream *Yes! Yes! Fuck me! Fuck me!* next time we do it?" he whispered in my ear. "Loud as you can. Let's really give them something to listen to."

I said nothing, my hands resting in the warmth between his thighs. He rested his cheek on my breasts.

"We never hear them when *they're* fucking," he muttered.

"They are very discreet."

"Unless they aren't doing it. Maybe they just want us to think they're just holding hands. And sneaking into each other's room when they think we can't hear. Saving themselves for the wedding day." They weren't engaged then.

"She is a good vicar's daughter."

"They're the fucking worst. My sister went to a convent school. The stories she could tell. She probably hasn't told me all of it."

"I am sure."

He opened his mouth to say something, but I silenced him with a finger on his lips.

"They are in love," I said. "You can see it. The pupils of her eyes widen every time she looks at him."

"Do they? Hadn't noticed that."

"No, you do not notice these things. Big boobs. You notice that."

"She's not my type. Kev, on the other hand, nice arse…"

"Lots of curves."

"You're my type, Jo."

"I am glad to hear it."

He lifts himself up, his eyes meeting mine. "You're really my type."

I kissed him, full on the mouth. I slid out of bed, standing, my toes curling in the scrappy pile of the carpet. I tiptoed over to the window, leaning forward with my hands on the sill. We were on the top floor, overlooking the street which was deserted at this time of night, a single lamp washing the pavement orange. The light was off in our room, but if anyone were to pass by and look up, they would see me naked.

"What are you thinking, Jo?"

"Oh…things."

He rests a forefinger against my temple. "What I'd do to get inside there, see what's really going on inside."

I turned, lifted up my finger to his temple. "You as well. What's inside there. No barriers."

I turned back to the window. He rested his hands on my hips, leaning forward as I gazed out of the window. His erect penis nudged my left buttock.

"You know, if you were a guy…I'd take you up the arse right now."

I laugh. "Who says romance is dead?" Still facing away from him, I step backward a pace, one foot at a time, raising my buttocks. "Why don't you?"

"Hmmm." He nuzzled the back of my neck, wrapping his arms about my waist.

*

We sit in the front room. I'm in a chair facing Kevin and Adele, on the sofa. Emily sits cross-legged on the floor by my feet, resting her side against my leg. Now and again, I rest my hand on her shoulder, the top of her head. "You're a beautiful girl," I say. She always was: you can see it in the photos of her as a new-born, as Adele, in a hospital gown after the Caesarean, holds her in her arms, to her breast to feed. Emily gazes up at me and smiles. She's used to compliments, I can tell, but hasn't become vain. I am her godmother, but I remember how I've hardly seen her in all of her eight years I haven't been around.

Emily is making the most of my visit. She's due to be collected for a sleepover around the time dinner will be ready. She loops her arm around my calf as we watch pictures follow each other across the large flatscreen TV, a slideshow that Kevin's put together. There are plenty of Emily: as a baby, then a toddler, in uniform, smiling and squinting against the sunlight on her first day of school. Emily in a tutu, her feet in third position and then en pointe, pictures taken at her ballet class. In swimming costume at the beach; pictures of the three of them at EuroDisney during the summer. Emily talks to me all the way through the show. Adele smiles indulgently, either with a glass of vodka in her hand, declining to tell her daughter not to monopolise me, or going back to the kitchen to tend to something.

I've put together my own slideshow. We're just at the start of it when the doorbell rings. I start, but it's Adele's friend collecting Emily for the sleepover. Emily gives me a hug and I kiss her on the cheek as she says goodbye. Eight years. If it's another eight before I see her in person again, she'll be a sulky teenager.

"Right," says Adele. "It's time for dinner."

*

I was born and grew up an only child, below sea level. When we passed the dikes in the family car, I thought of all that water held behind them, ready to overwhelm us at any breach. One Christmas, my mother and father bought me a copy of *The Guinness Book of Records*, the Dutch edition. I read about lots of fascinating things. In Siberia there was a three-hundred-metre-high wall of ice, a dam with a huge lake behind it. One day it broke. I imagined watching mesmerised as the flood raced towards me, sunlight sparking needless off the top of that huge dark mass, as high up as I could see, higher. I couldn't flee from it. I didn't try. The roar destroyed my eardrums. I held my breath until the water smashed it out of me, shattering every bone in my body, spinning me lifeless in its rush.

Now and again I think of that. I live in a house in England, a bungalow I bought with the money I inherited from my father. It's also below sea level. Sometimes I look out at the fields around me, which stretch out as far as I can see, and I wonder if one day another flood might come. Everything I see will be underwater and me with it.

Once I dreamed I was a hundred years old. No children, but plenty of friends gathered for the party, either in person or online. There's Emily, an old woman now, with her children and grandchildren. And on the news, on whatever type of television we have then, a map of England and Wales, which the rising waters have taken bites out of. Glastonbury, where Ben and I visited once, is now an island. Elsewhere in the world, the Maldives, which I visited alone, is under the waves. If there is any place I call home, the one where I live, it's long since been submerged.

*

Ben and I were rarely apart, except when he was in the laboratory and I was in lectures or seminars or studying in the library. Most days, we'd meet for lunch in the Student Union canteen. How our relationship would have been conducted with phones and social media, I don't know; we were a little early for that. It got to the point where if I was somewhere on my own, or with Adele, Kevin or other friends, I'd be asked where Ben was. Maybe he was asked where I was. After living in Hall for our first year, it was inevitable that the four of us would move in to a shared house. During the vacations, I'd travel three hours by train to visit him, stay with him. I got to know his sister Vanessa, a year younger, her hair in a ponytail, her body a pear. Sometimes Ben would stay with me. The phone calls back and forth soon mounted up.

At the weekends during term, we'd travel into the centre of London, walking around during the day, eating at cheap places in Chinatown before taking the Tube home. Sometimes we'd buy a travelcard and take a journey to the very end of a line, spending an afternoon wandering around Ruislip, Upminster, Watford, hand in hand.

Sometimes he'd put on his leathers and go to the Backstreet, which was men-only. Or I might go to the Candy Bar and spend the night with a woman I met there. Neither of us minded, as long as we told each other about it afterwards. We swore we'd have no secrets from each other.

One of his T-shirts would fit me easily, and sometimes I wore a pair of his jeans and he a pair of mine. He had a suit he'd worn to interviews and, on the last night of the Hall bar before we left for the summer, I wore it, with one of his shirts and with his underpants too. And he wore the one dress I had. Adele helped with his makeup, and he wore my knickers. As I almost never wear a bra, even then, he borrowed one of Adele's. He had his bottom pinched more than once that evening.

After we'd taken LSD, we liked to make love. I'd straddle him, holding the head of his penis inside me, as the hallucinations hit.

As he came in my mouth, I tasted bitter starlight.

*

"Has Vanessa been in touch with you, Jolanda?" asks Kevin. "About Ben?"

I lift a forkful of prawn cocktail – hand-made, Emily helping Adele – to my mouth. It's silver cutlery. Lead-crystal glasses. Both wedding presents. "No, she hasn't."

Truth be told, Vanessa hasn't spoken to me in some time. It's as if she blames me for what happened. The last time I met her was at Emily's christening. The enthusiastic horse-loving teenage girl I'd first met – and fancied, I have to say – was now a woman, the mother of two with a third on the way. The recent photos I've seen show someone grim-faced, as if smiling was an effort, her once long and loose hair shorter, with early grey in it.

"We do sometimes visit him," says Adele. "We usually meet up with Vanessa and travel up there, stay the night at her and Jacob's place."

"How is he?"

She raises her wine glass to her mouth, two fingers curled around the stem. Pink-painted nails. She takes a sip. "It's so sad. I could cry. He won't recognise you. He just stares at nothing."

"Oh that is sad."

"He once pooed himself, just sitting there." She glances down. "I'm so sorry – we're eating. He was about as far away from me as you are now." Her face creases, and she rummages in her dress pocket for a handkerchief, dabbing it to her eyes. "I'm sorry." Kevin rests his hand on her forearm. "I'm sorry. There's no one there any more. He's gone. He's just a shell."

"As if something destroyed him from inside," I mutter.

"Yes, we all know what that was," Kevin says. "Too many fucking drugs."

No. It wasn't that.

"Kevin, please don't swear," says Adele.

There's an awkward silence.

Finally, Adele says, "Would you like some more wine, Jolanda. Thanks for bringing it, it's lovely."

"Yes, thank you. I'm glad you liked it."

"You must have tried all sorts of food and drink. All those exotic places you've been to."

"Well, not really."

"Oh come on. You've been to more places than I have, anyway.

More than Kev and I'll ever get to." After refilling my glass and Kevin's, she refills her own, raises it. "Cheers."

Pink nails. I remember those nails tracing the line of my body, down my side, into the curve of my waist, up over the swell of my hip.

I hope I'm not blushing at the memory.

"Well, this is good," she says. "Friends together. It's been too long, hasn't it, Kev? It's so lovely to see you, Jo."

*

One Saturday afternoon in our second year, Adele and I were alone in the house. Kevin and Ben were at a football match for a friend's, a fellow Chemistry undergraduate's, birthday. Ben didn't have much interest in football, but he knew enough for social reasons, and he went along. It wasn't that Adele and I weren't invited, but Ben told me later that none of the six of them had their girlfriends with them. I'd sensed early on that the friend didn't like women much and this was very much a boys' day out. He would only speak to us because we were the girlfriends of two of his friends, so weren't potentially available. When he did talk to Adele he would always gaze at her chest.

She and I had spoken a night or so earlier, and we knew this was our opportunity. I sensed Adele's nervousness as the time for Ben and Kevin to leave approached, but I don't think either noticed. If they had, they wouldn't have known the cause. When they left, we sat in her room, a bottle of Jack Daniels bought from the off licence down the road, a litre of Diet Coke from the Pakistani-run corner shop, on the low bedside table. Adele didn't drink so often, as she said she got too drunk too easily. There had been one night in our first year, at the end of term, where I'd knelt with her, holding her hair back as she was sick in the Student Union ladies' toilet. She never did that again.

She poured out two glasses. Doubles. "Cheers, Jo."

Jo. She'd never called me that before, with the English J-sound. Only *Jolanda*, Dutch-fashion.

We had the radio on, afternoon Radio 1. It could have been anything playing. We didn't say anything as we drank, she sipping at hers. Then she turned to me. And leaned forward to kiss me,

109

full on the mouth.

As she pulled away, I saw in the bedroom mirror that she'd left some of her lipstick behind.

We lay on the bed, kissing and embracing, for nearly half an hour. Finally, I slipped my hand under the waistband of her skirt, and she froze.

"Do you want to stop?" I said.

She shook her head, kissed me again on the lips. For a moment she lay still and then suddenly she rolled out from under me, stood up. Her sandals had been kicked away long ago, and her bare feet clenched at the carpet. Not facing me, she pulled the curtains shut. It was an overcast afternoon, about to rain, and it took a moment for my eyes to adjust to the dimness.

She removed her top, draping it carefully over a chair. Then, she lifted her hands to the clasp of her bra, but she was fumbling. I reached up to help her, but she shook me away. She turned to face me, her teeth clutching her lower lip. For a moment I thought she might cry. Then she turned back and unfastened her bra, its fabric slackening as she took it off. She undid her skirt and stepped out of it, leaned forward and pushed down her knickers. Skirt and underwear joined her top over the back of the chair. She hurried past me, pulling the duvet cover back, slipping quickly under it.

I hastily undressed, my clothes lying on the floor where they fell. I climbed in with her. I was as nervous as she obviously was.

We kissed again. I kissed her on the mouth, on her closed eyes, nuzzled one earlobe, took each stiffened nipple between my lips. I moved my hand down between her thighs. She parted them. I stroked her there. Adele sighed as I slipped my fingers inside her. She was wet. Her fingers scrabbled on my back. Her back arched and she gasped out loud as she climaxed.

At first she'd asked me what it was like to make love to a woman. Then she wondered if she could. Then finally she asked if we could do it, if she could do it with a woman, just the once with someone she trusted. I told Ben everything I could, even intimate things I might otherwise have kept to myself. But this was one thing I never did tell him. I don't know if Adele ever told Kevin I knew she'd arrived at University as a virgin, and Kevin was her first boyfriend. As far as I know, I'm the only person she's had sex with other than him.

I did wonder why. Maybe she wanted to do something, something wild and unexpected, not that sex between two women is necessarily that. Just to see if she could. With two bisexual housemates – actually Ben said he was gay, other than his relationship with me – maybe she was testing the limits of her own sexuality. And maybe she was testing her relationship with Kevin by betraying him, just the once and never again.

Neither of us said anything about it afterwards. When Kevin and Ben came home again, we told them we'd watched an old black and white weepie on television, crying as we became drunker and the film sadder. For days afterwards, Adele and I were nervous around each other, and I sensed she was trying not to be alone in the same room as me. She and Kevin went away, staying with his parents – her in the spare room, she made pains to point out – the following weekend and when they returned we were back to normal. What had happened between us had been walled off, not to be spoken of again, a barrier never to be breached.

*

During the summer after our first year, I was staying with Ben. We took a walk in the countryside close by. Vanessa wheeled her bicycle part of the way with us, but as Ben pointedly ignored her and held my hand at the first opportunity he had, she got bored and rode on ahead, her jeans-clad bottom lifting off the seat as she pedalled. "Get a room, you two!" she shouted.

The roads and paths were muddy. We crossed the fields, sheep staring indifferently at us. Ben slipped his arm about my waist, his hand in my jeans pocket.

We found a dry spot under a tree. I laid my head on his lap, face upwards. He tickled the end of my nose with a blade of grass. We smoked joints.

"Two hundred years, four hundred," he said. "A young and hot shepherd and shepherdess could have been sitting here, just like we are now. On this very spot."

"Or two shepherds. Or two shepherdesses."

"Now now. Not quite like that. If two shepherds got it on, they wouldn't be gazing into each other's eyes. It'd be breeches down, cock out, quick fuck behind a bush or something. Actually, they often fucked between the thighs back then. Not up the arse so much."

"Why was that?"

"Didn't wash much."

I wrinkled my nose. "Eww. Who says romance is dead?"

"I'm sure you really wanted to know that. Sexual habits of gay shepherds throughout the ages." He stroked my cheek with his finger. "Anyway, boy and girl shepherds at the end of the day as the sun is going down, they'd walk home hand in hand. Maybe they'd see an angel on the way."

"They say when people all go quiet at once, there is an angel passing overhead."

"Oh, that's sweet. Not much chance of that with us, then."

I thumped him on the arm. "Hey! Do you say I talk a lot?"

"Just a little."

"It does take two, Ben."

He pursed his lips, said nothing for a moment. "There's one, right now. An angel. Quite a tall one, actually. Her name's Jolanda."

"Creep. But that is nice."

I sat up beside him, my back against the tree. I took his hand in mine, crossed my left ankle over his right.

"Back then," he said, "they saw angels all the time. Devils, too. Did you know that?"

"Did they?"

"Yeah. We don't see them now. Sometime long ago, it all changed. Don't know why. It's like there's a barrier now, up there or down there. Whatever's there, we used to be able to see it. Not any more. Something changed."

"I do not fancy seeing whatever is down there."

"No, but if we could see angels everywhere we looked, if we wanted to. Wouldn't that be cool?" He paused. "What if there's some way to do it?"

After an hour or so, we walked back across the field, holding hands again, back to the road that led to the village where Ben and his family lived. The road was narrow, single-lane and unmade, its surface pitted and needing repair. We had walked only a little while down the road when I pulled him across on to the grass verge, his back against a wooden fence.

"Hey, what are you doing?"

I knelt down, unzipping the fly of his jeans. "What do you think?"

"People might see us."

"I do not care."

If anyone was in the field, or drove past us, or was walking along that road, they would have seen us. That excited us both. I took him in my mouth. "Oh, Jolanda." His fingers clutched my scalp through my hair. He leaned his head back, gazing up at the sky, gasping out loud as he came.

I slowly stood, dabbing at my lips with my handkerchief, "There, do you see angels now, Ben?"

As we walked home, it began to rain hard, and we were soon drenched.

*

From time to time, I saw…something. It was only out of the corner of my eye and at a distance, and if I turned to look it wasn't there. Just a ripple, passing through a busy street, in the middle of Shanghai as all the cyclists sped past, three-hundred-metre skyscrapers closing in far above my head. Suddenly cold on a hot day. Or when I dunked my head, smashing water, and raising it again, the sun hot on my face. While diving water, in the cool blue silence. Or while eating street food somewhere in the Far East. Or in bed with a lover, somewhere in the world, my head fuddled with too many changes of timezone. Or in a desert at night as I lay on my back on the sand, gazing up at the thick clusters of stars, tracing the constellations of the northern or southern sky.

I thought of Ben then, a man I knew wasn't the man I had known any more, the man who had been part of me for a significant part of my life. He wasn't there.

I have friends in many cities, around the world. Some of them have been lovers and some of them I still sleep with when we meet in person. Connections. But the connection with Ben is no longer there.

I look up at the sky and the sky is empty. There's nothing there. No angels, no devils. We tried to see them but we failed.

*

Adele pours me some more wine. I'll be driving home tonight – I turned down their offer of spending the night here – but one more glass will be okay. It's as if she's read my mind. "You're very welcome to stay the night, Jo. I can easily make up the bed in the spare room."

"Thank you, but I do need to get home. I've got to meet someone tomorrow morning. My financial advisor."

"I bet that's exciting," says Kevin. "Not that we're different – how about dentists' checkups next week?"

"Poor Em," says Adele. "She hates the dentist. She'll be losing her milk teeth soon. Aren't you glad you missed all this?"

I have a stock answer to this. "I like children. I get on with them. But I've never wanted one of my own."

Adele leans forward, her cleavage pushing out of her dress a little. "Oh, you say that. You're not the only woman I know who doesn't want kids. I always did."

"It's the same with men too," says Kevin. "I always wanted a family."

"And our only regret is that there'll only be the one. I couldn't go through all that IVF again. You get what you're given in this life. It's hard work, any kid is, but there isn't a day when I don't thank God we've got Em, and what it took to bring her into the world."

"You always wanted children," I say. "A child. I don't. Ben didn't either."

"You never got that far, did you?"

"No." After three years almost permanently in each other's company, the separation caused by his going into doctoral research and the start of my travels cooled our relationship. By the time we met again, he wasn't the same. The start of his decline.

The start of something eating him from inside.

After a pause, I say, "If you do see him again, give him my love."

"We will. At least he's somewhere he can be looked after."

"Please give my regards to Vanessa. I know she doesn't like me. Actually, she's on Facebook. I can contact her there." In fact I did once, but she didn't reply and blocked me. "I'll do that when I get home."

"Home. Do you have a home, really, Jo?" Adele is holding her glass so tightly I wonder for a second if it'll shatter in her hand. "You do have the house, of course. It looks lovely."

"Yes, I'm very fortunate. You must visit sometime."

"And no need to have a job, nothing to stop you travelling all over the place. But if this isn't too personal, do you really feel at home there? I know you have all your friends around the world, places you can stay, but is there anywhere you feel at home? Not even the Netherlands? Just saying."

"Adele…" says Kevin.

"We're friends. Jolanda's one of our oldest friends, Kev. We can be frank. She knows I'm not having a go at her."

I take a sip of wine. "I'm not sure. I've always felt like an outsider. A Dutch girl at an English University, too tall, funny accent. And an only child when my parents are dead."

"That's quite sad," says Adele. "I hope you don't think I'm being rude."

"You're not. You're being frank with me, as you said."

"Don't get me wrong, Jo. I follow your posts on Facebook, your blog, your Twitter, your Instagram. It's absolutely fascinating. All those things I'll never get to see with my own eyes. You've been to every continent. You've been to places and done things you're very very brave to do, especially as a woman on your own. Crossing Africa, for one. But I do wonder if you're running away from something.

"Or maybe she's running *towards* something," says Kevin. I notice that *she* instead of my name.

"Maybe I'm trying to be at home by being on the move," I say. It sounds hollow as soon as the words leave my mouth.

*

Vanessa blamed me for Ben's drug use, for his interest in the occult. But it was mutual; I'm not sure who was first. But we spent

115

days, weekends, looking up things online, or spending time in old bookshops around Charing Cross Road, the smell of must and dust in the air, the proprietor gazing suspiciously at us from his cash desk.

Adele didn't approve, a vicar's daughter to the core. There was once a party where someone, a woman with blue hair and piercings, a friend of a friend and I don't remember her name now, who around midnight produced a ouija board from somewhere and suggested that we had a séance. Not only did Adele refuse to take part, but she left with Kevin when it went ahead. So we kept the details of our searches from her.

We tried to see angels. We failed. But maybe something was let through.

*

After the meal we sit in the front room for a while. Adele puts Radio 6 on low, while Kevin makes us all coffees.

And now it's time to go. Adele and Kevin go with me to where my car is parked. The streetlights obliterate all but a few of the stars. I wonder what would happen if the electricity failed and all the stars rushed in at once, so bright, thousands and thousands of them, overwhelming.

"It's been absolutely lovely to see you again, Jo," says Adele.

"Yes, we shouldn't make it eight years again," says Kevin.

"Thank you both," I say. "It was a wonderful evening. You always were a great cook."

She laughs. "Well, I'm good for something, I guess."

"And give my love to Emily. My goddaughter. I should be more of a godmother."

"We will," says Kevin.

"We show her your blog now. She loves all those pictures," says Adele. "Maybe she'll get the travel bug too."

Kevin looks up at the sky. "I think it said rain. Do drive carefully, Jolanda."

"That means some of the roads near me will be underwater if it rains too hard."

"Oh lovely," says Adele. "One thing we don't get, living in a town. On a slope, too."

Kevin and I kiss, then I bend forward and kiss Adele. She hugs me tight.

I drive away. I should play some music, but I prefer silence, in the dark, for the hour and a half of the journey home. It does begin to rain, and it's coming down hard by the time I reach home.

I park my car in the garage. It's nearly midnight, but I'm not tired. I stand under my porch, smoking a joint as the rain stops and the sky clears.

So many stars. So far away. Such a big and empty universe.

And a feeling of cold comes over me. I look up.

Half the sky has disappeared and one by one the stars are going out.

~

Gary Couzens has had stories published in F & SF, Interzone, Black Static, Crimewave, The Third Alternative *and other magazines and anthologies, including the two previous* Midnight Street *anthologies. A collection,* Second Contact and Other Stories, *was published by Elastic Press in 2003 and a second collection,* Out Stack and Other Places, *by Midnight Street Press in 2015. Gary edited the anthology* Extended Play *for Elastic Press in 2006 and it won the British Fantasy Award for Best Anthology. Gary writes film and disc reviews for* The Digital Fix *and the* Blood Spectrum *film-review column for* Black Static *and was shortlisted for the latter in 2017 for the British Fantasy Award for Best Non-Fiction.*

SHADES
Die Booth

"Tell us a story, Damon. A scary one."

Damon looked around at their upturned faces, all wobbly with shadow from the firelight, and he grinned. "OK. Here's a scary one. Once, long ago, before you were born, before I was born even, the world was a really scary place. All these bad guys were in charge and they had it in for people like you and me."

The kids leaned closer, chins resting on their drawn-up knees, listening. At least, two of them did. Mia, of course, asked, "Why?"

The fire spit up a rain of sparks in reverse as Damon poked another branch into the pile. It lit up their little camp in a faint, glowing bubble that didn't reach quite far enough for them to see the house. Where darkness crept in at the edges, it was creepily, deliciously easy to imagine that their homes, their parents, weren't there anymore. "Because they hated anyone different than them. It scared them. They were in charge and they wanted to stay that way, because then they could keep all the best stuff for themselves. But they were scared that people like us would be in charge one day, so they made sure that would never happen."

"But why?" Mia insisted.

Damon raised his gaze to the tree-crossed night sky. Said, steadily, "I just told you. They wanted the best stuff for themselves and for everyone to do as they said."

Her round, brown eyes reflected gold in the firelight as she rolled them. "No, I mean – why were we different to them?"

"Well, like." He exhaled. The littler kids were starting to fidget – he was losing his audience. "Back then, they pretended some people were better than others. I don't mean like, people who do bad stuff, I mean like they judged people on how they looked and what body parts they had and things like that, and it made some people get treated better than other people."

Mia curled her lip. "That's not scary. It's just dumb."

"OK, genius. It'd be scary if it happened to you."

"No it wouldn't." She folded her arms. The toes of her shoes pushed into the ashy embers, daring the edge of the fire. "I just wouldn't listen to them. Why did anyone listen to them in the old days?"

"Because everyone was frightened, too. They went along with it because that's how it had always been, or they were scared that if they stuck up for the people who were getting beat on, then they'd be next to get punished. They did what they were told because they were afraid, even though there were loads more of them than the bad guys, the bad guys were still the ones who got to decide everything." Damon shivered. He turned up the collar of his jacket. The kids looked conspicuously unimpressed. He pressed his lips together. "They got to decide everything, because they had all the power and all the money and all the *bombs*, so if anyone even *disagreed* with them, they could get them thrown in prison *forever*, or *killed*."

Sky glanced up from where they were locked in an enthusiastic thumb-wrestling war with Jamal. "What's money?"

Damon sighed.

"I still think it sounds stupid." Mia decided. "You know what's really scary?"

"Your face?"

That made Sky and Jamal both laugh, at least. Mia stuck her tongue out at him. "The *tunnels*." Her voice was reverent with forbidden promise that made the other little ones sit up straighter and look at Damon expectantly.

"You know you're not supposed to go round there," he said, carefully. As if on cue, the wind picked up, tossing a bright twist of sparks up into the trees.

"Please, Damon? *Please*?"

The moment she'd said it, he already knew they were going. "You'll get frightened and I'll get the blame."

"We won't." A chorus of three piping voices vowed. "We promise."

"OK. But don't tell the grown-ups."

"Cross my heart," said Mia, her grin bright and fearless.

*

"Stay close to me. Hold hands, I don't want any of you getting lost," Damon said. Behind him, faint giggles sounded, the snap and rustle of three pairs of feet quite able to tread quietly but not yet truly aware of the reasons to. Damon knew. He'd been going out with the trappers from the village since he was 13, nearly two years, and he understood the necessity of stealth. Tonight, though... "You won't be laughing if you get separated from the group, in the woods, in the dark..." He kind of meant it, but he was overdoing it for the little ones, too. He held in a smile as the giggles grew louder.

"What will happen if we get lost in the woods?" Mia asked. She sounded more hopeful than worried.

Damon glanced back. The little train of children following him was only dimly visible in the tree-interrupted light of a waning moon. "You'll get really cold and hungry and probably nobody will find you until tomorrow, and then you'll get really hot and you'll be grounded for running off and being out in the sun without block."

He laughed at the chorus of complaints. "No! Tell it properly! Tell it with ghosts!"

"You guys believe in ghosts?" Stories are more important at night. Even the really weird ones can help make sense of reality.

Jamal said, "No. My Mum Ade says there's no such thing."

"But we wanna hear the story anyway," added Sky.

Damon nodded. He stepped carefully across a fallen log, waited for the others to clamber over. It wasn't even really late, around nine judging by the position of The Plough, but the moon phase and skims of drifting cloud made it darker than it should be. "OK." He peered up through the dark lattice of branches, searching the sky for the Pole Star. Sighting it, he bore a little left: even the familiar paths of the woods looked different at night. "You know where we're going?"

"The tunnels." Jamal, unmoved by the darkness, walked the length of the log and jumped off, bounding to catch up.

"And you know those tunnels are haunted?"

The wind rattled the branches above, setting off domino-knocks of taps and creaks and small, scuffling things in the underbrush. "They're not haunted," Mia said. "A monster lives in them."

Damon shook his head. "The grown-ups just say it's a monster to make it less scary. They're haunted, by the ghosts of the bad people from the olden days."

"Monsters are scarier than ghosts," Mia stated, flatly. She picked up a length of broken branch, started swinging it at the carpet of fallen leaves as if searching for monsters to slay.

"My Mum Clare says there are no monsters any more, only in our heads," Jamal offered.

Damon paused, turning to stare the three of them down. "Who's telling this story?"

"Don't stop," Sky said, quickly. "Shut up, you two."

"Thank you." He started walking again. The intermittent canopy overhead made the stars appear and vanish, like the sky was winking at him. Like the lights were failing... a sudden shiver grabbed him. "Alright. You know, back then, they couldn't see the stars? There was so much light all the time that it was always daytime."

The kids looked a little unsettled at that. Sky's voice was small when they asked, "How did they sleep?"

He waved a hand, dismissing the notion. "They didn't sleep. They just stayed awake all the time and it was always light and noisy and there was smoke everywhere and everyone was angry and got in fights all the time." The children exchanged glances that looked a little nervous, and Damon felt a guilty thrill run through him. "But it was OK. The sun blew up all the electricity."

Mia laughed, like a sneeze. "That's dumb. The sun *makes* electricity."

"Well, it does *now*, because *now* we're smart. But back then, they burned stuff to make it. Oil and garbage and stuff."

"Like almond oil?" Jamal asked, slowly.

Damon waved a hand again. "I mean, like... probably. And black oil from under the ground. And it was really dirty and made the plants die and stuff. But that's what made the bad guys so powerful, because they controlled all the electricity. So when they knew that the sun was getting hotter, they built the tunnels to hide

121

in. They made them super nice, like houses, with all beds and food and books and games and stuff. And offices so they could still tell each other what to do. But they only made them big enough for themselves. They didn't care if everyone else, the people like me and you, stayed outside and got exploded or something, because they only cared about people who were like them."

When he stopped talking, it was suddenly very quiet. Even their footsteps sounded more hushed, muted by the deep carpet of fallen leaves, the breeze a murmur, whispering half-heard secrets of their destination. After a few seconds, Sky said, "Then what happened?"

Damon smiled to himself. They sounded totally engrossed in his tale. "So, the bad guys all went and hid underground, then the sun blew up all the electricity. At first everything was awful. People just kept fighting and stuff because they didn't know what to do. But then after a while they realised that the bad guys were gone, so nobody was telling them what to do anymore."

"So *then* what happened?" Mia asked.

"So, people started to relax."

"Are we getting to the ghosts part soon?"

"Just let me tell it!" They slowed at a fork in what passed for a path. Only those who knew these woods would be able to navigate like this: Damon prided himself on his tracking skills. Right was quicker. He beckoned the others and strode off, ducking an overhang of ancient rhododendron. "So the people realised that they could just get along and be friends now that the bad guys were gone. But then they thought, wait a bit…" He paused for effect, listening to the combined sound of their breathing on the still, chill air. "*Where did they go?* And they remembered they went into the tunnels. So the people went and knocked on the tunnel doors, *but there was no answer.*"

Jamal's voice was timid. "Were they dead?"

"Not yet." Damon held back a swag of branches to let the others past. "They'd built the tunnels to be all run on electricity, but then there was no more electricity, so all their doors and locks and 'phones and stuff, none of it worked any more. They got shut in, and because it all locked from the inside because they were trying to keep the other people out, the other people couldn't get in to help them. So they just stayed down there." He turned to face them, bending down closer, his voice lowered to a hiss. *"And they're still down there today."*

"The other people just left them down there? That's horrible!" Jamal said.

Damon pulled a face. "I mean… they probably tried to get them out. But they couldn't. So they stayed down there. And now they're all dead and their ghosts haunt the tunnels."

"Are there skeletons down there?" Asked Mia. She sounded hopeful.

"Yeah, probably."

"Can we get in and see?"

Damon exhaled a little laugh. "If the adults couldn't get in…" His words trailed off. Stepping out of the treeline, they were, without warning, there.

Perhaps it was his imagination, or just being out of the shelter of the woods, but the temperature seemed to drop even further. The light grew brighter, too, with no trees to block the frigid stab of stars, the razor slice of moon. The tunnels loomed, a row of them, like the entrances to long-ago lime kilns, humped beneath the hillside, their hefty metal doors bolted and black and eerily free of graffiti.

It took about five seconds for Sky to say, "I don't like it. Let's go home."

"It's OK." Damon put a hand on their shoulder. "Nothing's going to happen to you when I'm here." They glanced up at him, brows crumpled by uncertainty. He attempted his most reassuring smile. "Honest, it's OK. I was just making the story better. The tunnels got cleaned out years ago – the grown-ups went in and filled them up with rocks and sealed them with concrete."

"Really?"

"Really. I promise."

"So it was just a story?" Sky did not sound convinced. "Did they find the people in there?"

Did they find the people? He thought, hard. He wasn't sure if he'd ever known that part. He shrugged. "Erm. Yeah. They let them out and it was all fine."

Their frown was instantly back. "So the bad people got out?"

Damon shook his head. "It was ages ago. Don't worry about it. They're not going to hurt anyone anymore." He looked around. The breeze murmured, trees rattling like they were making plans. Mia and Jamal were pacing the perimeter of the little clearing in front of the doors, Mia poking into the bushes with her stick. Everything looked blue in the moonlight, flat and unreal. The shadows gathered beneath the trees seemed to move. It felt like something was watching. Damon shivered, feeling the cold even through his jacket and two shirts and a binder. "Look." Squaring his shoulders, he walked to the middle door. "If there was anything in there, would I do this?" The scent of pitted metal touched the back of his throat, cold and unyielding as he rapped his knuckle against the door. It made barely any noise at all, just a quiet dull tap, the impact swallowed up by several feet of solid steel, the backfill of rubble and concrete beyond. Laying his cheek against the gritty chill, he knocked again. He wasn't sure what he expected to hear – a portentous booming echo, perhaps, the sound of doors in storybook ancient halls. Behind him, a twig snapped. The wind ruffled the trees. Despite the night cold, his fringe was stuck to his skin with sweat. And, deep within the tunnel behind the fortified door, a clanging, distant knocking sounded back.

Damon's insides flipped. He straightened, sharply, staring at the featureless steel before him.

"Did you hear anything?" Mia was looking at him, hard.

"No. I told you. There's nothing in there now, it's all blocked up." He held his arms out, ushering the others back from the edges of the clearing. It wasn't a long walk. He knew the way back. Above, the stars still gleamed brightly, the moon tipped a tilted smile. He took Sky's hand. He absolutely did not look back at the tunnel doors as he said, "Let's go home."

~

124

Die Booth lives in Chester, UK, and likes making monsters and exploring dark places. You can read his stories in places like Lamplight Magazine, The Fiction Desk *and his books,* My Glass is Runn, 365 Lies *(profits go to the MNDA) and* Spirit Houses *are available online and a new collection,* Making Friends *is due out soon.*
http://diebooth.wordpress.com/@diebooth

~

HELP ME EAT MY MONKEY
Ralph Robert Moore

After standing on his feet in one spot through the long morning hours, trying to stay polite to rude customers, it was finally noon, Matt leaving his station, walking past all the confused people in the wide aisles, pushing open the glass doors to get outside, onto the sidewalk, cool air, city noises, checking his phone to see if there was any cult disturbance nearby, thought about where he wanted to eat lunch, remembered the raw red onion slices on the cheeseburgers served at Gilbert's, and as he looked up from his phone, people passing by him in both directions, saw on the opposite side of the sidewalk, by the street noises of the curb, a tall, beefy guy with dirty blonde hair flopped across his forehead holding a phone to his eye, filming him.

Matt looked away, looked back. The guy kept his phone pointed at Matt, not making any effort to hide what he was doing, and in fact seemed happy Matt had noticed he was being filmed.

He didn't recognize the guy.

People passing by in both directions, between them.

This should be a better world. Matt made a decision, walking across the sidewalk to the curb, next to the steam of the hot dog vendor's metal cart, where the guy was standing, phone to his eye.

"Is there some reason why you're filming me?"

The guy kept the phone up to his face. Talking with only one visible eye. "I can film anything I want. If I choose to film you, that's absolutely legal, and there's nothing whatsoever you can do about it."

"But given that, why have you decided to film me?" The guy lowered the phone from his eye, but tilting it up in his hand so it was still filming Matt. His floppy-haired face scrunched in an exaggerated look of concern meant to infuriate. "Aww, am I upsetting you? Are you gonna burst into tears?" Held a bony finger to his lips. "Let me think a second." Shot up his eyebrows. "Hey, guess what? I just realized I don't owe you shit in explanation. I can 'do my thang', and you just have to fucking choke on it. If my actions, which are perfectly legal, bother you, I guess you can just, I don't know, stamp your little foot and swallow my sperm." He opened his mouth, grinning like a dope, staring right into Matt's eyes.

"How about you just fuck off?"

The bully, bigger than him, still holding his phone at an upwards tilt on Matt's face, flexed his muscles. Proud of all those hours at the gym. "You think you can win a fist fight with me?" Sincerely incredulous.

"No. I think the chances are you'd win."

"Goddamn right. Got that straight. So I guess you're not going to throw any pink cupcakes at me."

Matt stared back into the bully's eyes. Lifted his jaw. "But even though you'd probably win, I could still do a lot of damage to you before you did eventually win. Right now you're not bleeding, you haven't lost any of your teeth, none of your bones are broken, and you still have both eyes. If we fight, that won't be the situation for you by the time we're done. Even if you do 'win'."

The bully let out a laugh. But this time, it was the type of laugh that falls back inside the mouth.

Still staring into the bully's eyes, Matt stepped even closer, tips of their noses almost touching, like cocks. Swished saliva in his mouth, spit on the bully's face.

And the big guy with dirty blonde hair flopped across his forehead stepped back.

Right palm wiping the warm drip of Matt's spit off his forehead, eyebrows, rubbing it onto the hand-lettered sign clipped to the side of the metal cart advertising the hot dog vender's prices for popular sodas, blurring the blue numbers.

The bully looks at Matt. Eyes angry. Reaches down, pulls off his left sandal. Lifts the sandal, silver key in the center. Thumbs it off, holds it out to Matt. "I guess you earned this."

Matt accepts the warm key, smelling like a foot, no idea where this is going. Definitely going to wash his hands before he walks down the block to order that cheeseburger. "What's it open?"

Tries to regain some of his arrogance. "That's for you to find out. Just remember that no key is unique. In America, most house keys only have five pins, with six different lengths. That means there's less than 8,000 different possible key and lock combinations. Any key in your pocket opens hundreds of thousands of different locks. Maybe even millions. It's up to you to find out which locks this particular key opens."

*

Matt works at a major discount store chain, Price Less, that went bankrupt. They're about to close their doors. Most of their product is selling at ten cents on the dollar. Employees have been instructed to not only sell the store's merchandise, but its physical assets. Dressing room mirrors, the shelving in the store aisles, trash receptacles, padded chairs in the shoe department.

Employee theft is rampant. Pale guys with glasses and dark bushy hair who used to be passive-aggressive Customer Advocates are scooping up as many batteries and HDMI cables as they can stuff in their pants pockets. Or clocking in at eight in the morning, then taking off all day to play video games back at their parents' home, returning around five to clock out.

Customers are even worse. Entering the store wearing wide-brimmed hats, which they hope will foil the security cameras, finding something they want, a TV, a mini-refrigerator, a vacuum cleaner, picking it up in their arms, walking with it to the front of the store, ignoring the shouts of the cashiers, banging through the glass doors of the store, squeezing their eyes, carrying their stolen merchandise like a large baby down the sidewalk, feet plodding widely apart from the weight.

A gray-haired woman stood in front of Matt's station, on the customer side of the glass cubicle display of smart phones, lifting a basil plant onto the glass counter. Head down, tearing up. "I bought this living basil, it was only yesterday, but the leaves are already wilting. When I got it home, it was green and vigorous, strong, lifting upwards, but now the plant is limp, collapsed over the edges of its container, and I just know it's going to turn yellow and dry out."

Matt talks over the screams and arguments in the store's aisles. "I'm sorry to hear that. Is it possible you over-watered it?"

"So it was my fault the basil is dying? I killed it? Are you shaming me?"

"I'm not saying that, I'm just trying to find out why—"

"I kept checking on it. I went online to find a cure, but I can't. I want to know why Budgy is dying, what the store did wrong, and I want my money back."

A younger woman in a pink blouse stands next to the old crying woman. "I don't want to butt in, but can you help me right now with my return?" Raises her sad face. Shouts over the noise. "My only son is dying of terminal stage four cancer. I put these batteries in my flashlight but the flashlight still won't work!"

The basil lady hugs the younger woman's shoulder. "I know exactly what you're going through!"

Late afternoon, Matt leaves his post to go to the restroom.

Cultists immediately swarm behind his glass counter, you can't always tell who is a cultist and who isn't, heads bent, sniffing the chair where he had been seated, like cats, something cultists always do, smelling where someone's asshole rested.

When Matt comes back, a tall, skinny African-American man with a long pink comb slanted into the top of his black hair, shouting in a language Matt doesn't recognize, pulls off his clothes until he's naked, thin chest and small cock, lifts a plastic bag concealed in his pants pocket over his head, squeezing the bag like a pimple until it bursts and the gasoline splashes down on his scrunched face, his thin shoulders, long fingers of his right hand lifting, snapping a spark from a blue cigarette lighter, flame puffing across his face, upper body, gritting his big teeth, refusing to scream at the agony of being burned alive, part of the cultists' sense of pride, presenting self-immolation as something enjoyable.

Killie, a young cashier with bad blonde hair in Jewelry, who sympathizes with the cultists, slapping her hands together, applauding.

As the African-American man burns, his body exudes the charred aroma of a hundred hamburgers sizzling on the grill. It was only during these recent cultist attacks that people realized how delicious humans smell when they self-immolate.

*

When it finally turned six o'clock and the row of front glass doors of Gilbert's were locked, people on the sidewalk still trying to get in, banging their palms against the transparent doors like the living dead, overhead lights turned off aisle by aisle, Matt made his way down the wide darkening sidewalk to the street corner, to Casey's Bar and Grill.

Even though it was called a bar and grill, Casey's didn't serve any food. Just booze. Probably a marketing ploy.

He made his way into the interior darkness, conversational hubbub, neon beer logos behind the bar, Gimmie Shelter on the overhead speakers, shouldering past spines and elbows to the back of the bar, past the pool tables, where there were usually empty stools, finding one next to the doors to the men's and women's restrooms, catching the male bartender's eye, ordering a Manhattan on the rocks. Maraschino cherry in the bottom of the glass, buried under ice cubes, drowned in whiskey, splash of dry vermouth, dash of bitters.

Once he took his first sip, lit a cigarette, he looked around.

Most of the patrons were like him, retail workers, or people with low management jobs in offices. Casey's was not a place to celebrate how well you were doing in life.

Ashtray on the polished wood of the bar to his left. Pulls it closer to him, jiggles a Marlboro out of its pack, tears off its orange filter, puts the shortened cigarette between his lips, lights its round end, yellow flame.

Like a lot of us, he's unhappy with how his life is turning out, but he doesn't know how to change it.

Oscar from the Home Entertainment department at Price Less appears out of nowhere, the yellow pants of his legs mounting the stool next to him. Turns to Matt. "This is what I live for. Cruising bars like a crocodile."

Which makes no sense, but Matt doesn't have a lot of friends, so he nods, hands around his cold drink.

Oscar lifts his right index finger. "If you could date any rock star, alive or dead, who would you date?"

130

It was a serious question, so Matt gives it some serious thought. "Janis Joplin. Because since she's dead, I figure there's a good chance I might get lucky."

They get into a friendly argument over how to construct the perfect cheeseburger, something that happens a lot in bars.

After half an hour of that he slides off his stool, walking to the bar's restroom, standing at the urinal, careful to keep his cock far enough out of his unzipped pants so he doesn't piss himself.

Goes back out into the noise and confusion, finds a new seat at the bar.

A dark-haired woman walks over through the smoke, settling her ass on the stool next to him, swinging her black eyes up at his eyes from her slightly lower height, smiling, pushing the glass ashtray even closer to his knuckles.

Drawing on the white length of his smoke, its end reddening, he realizes he's seen her in this bar before, but never this close, usually a few stools away, lowers his face to take another sip of his Manhattan, and it occurs to him just like that she's been stalking him.

He's a bit drunk at this point.

Circles her finger in the air to get the bartender's attention, and it's a different bartender now for some reason, points at her empty drink, Matt's empty drink.

Their glasses arrive. She pays.

"Who are you?"

She looks down at the orange of her screwdriver. Smiles.

Seems like she's shy. His spirits lift. Tries to hide it, but he's shy.

"Cat got your tongue?"

Dark eyes slanting up towards him, she pulls out a notepad, a pen. Writes something down. Smiling hopefully, she passes the curled note across the polished wood of the bar to the base of his Manhattan.

I have no tongue.

Matt dips his head, takes another sip of his drink.

His spirits lower.

More notes passed over in the noise of the bar.

131

It was cut out of my mouth years ago.

By three men.

So you must do most of the talking.

But I'm a good listener.

Do you have a girlfriend?

So…from his bar stool he looked around at the smoke and far-off round tables and music, trying to spot his friend he had been talking with about cheeseburgers, but he doesn't recognize him anywhere.

His forearm getting tapped. By her.

New note. If you want, I can just go away.

And the thing is, Matt is a decent guy. The type of man who doesn't want to hurt anyone, just do the right thing. Help others. If someone slips on a floor, he's not going to laugh, point, and make fun of them. He's going to rush over, make sure they're okay, lower his big hand, help them up. "No. I just…No. That's fine. I'm sorry. I'm not, you know, used to communicating by notes. I'm sorry that I got caught off guard. I just need to adjust for a second, and I'm a bit drunk, so…"

Her black eyes happy and amused at his discomfort. She hides her smile behind her small right hand, like a geisha.

"My name's Matt."

Confident nod, looking into his eyes, like, I know.

"What's your name?"

Pulls over her thick pad of paper, scribbles, tears it off, passes it over.

Sylvia.

"I'm pleased to meet you, Sylvia."

She reaches out her hand, cold from holding her screwdriver, he instinctively shakes it, their first touch, and you can shake a lot of hands and it means nothing, but when her hand fits into his, he feels aroused by her palm laying against his palm, her thumb wrapping comfortably around the knuckles of his fingers.

He adjusts his legs on his bar stool.

"Have you been, I don't know…following me?"

Dark hair to her shoulders, black eyes looking up into his eyes. Mischievous.

Nods.

"I thought so."

She rummages through the pile of notes she's handed him, lifting them, finding the one she wants, showing it to him again.

Off in a distant corner of the dark bar, someone snorts loudly. 'Is that an apricot?'

He looks down at her note.

Do you have a girlfriend?

"I don't."

New note.

Did you?

And, I don't know, he decided, in this noisy bar crowded with the buzz of people talking over each other and music played too loud, to share with her. Which he rarely did. Maybe it was the hand shake, maybe it was the fact she did look really good, with her shoulder-length dark hair, the confidence in her black eyes.

Checked the level of his Manhattan. Most of it still left. So, okay. "I had a girlfriend. I really liked her, you know? She was sincere. Someone can be sexy, or funny, or intelligent, or popular, whatever, but being sincere? Honest? Honorable? That means a lot to me." Stared down at the level left in his glass. "But she got really drunk at an after midnight party by the ocean, joyously pulled off her clothes and ran out into the powerful waves, whooping, fell over in the water, laughing, didn't reappear, and got swept by the undertow out to sea, drowned. They never found her body." Looked down, watching his hands wrapped around the curves of his glass. Ducked his head. "I used to kiss her forehead each night when I left her. To protect her. You know?" Some of those old feelings about Mandy came back. Finished his Manhattan, looking down at the empty glass between his two hands. "She was a really happy person. Maybe too happy."

She squeezed the top of his right hand, and again he felt turned on by her touching him, and especially by her touching him without asking his permission. He really liked how forward she was.

He sat on his bar stool like a small child while she wrote an upside-down note.

Sad! So…Back on the market?

"Well…"

Is it my missing tongue?

Causing you hesitation?

Know anyone missing a body part?

Both hands around his new Manhattan. "I knew this guy from college, Dean. He lost his right arm in a drunk mowing accident. He keeps the severed arm in a black garbage bag in a freezer in his garage. So that when he eventually dies, it'll be buried with him. The way he puts it, 'So we'll all get to wherever we're going at the same time.'"

A skinny blonde comes over in the conversational noise, pushing her long curls from her face, asks Matt if she can buy him a drink. Sylvia reaches up, places her palm between the blonde's breasts, shoves her back. The blonde rears up on her red high heels, angry, sees the look in Sylvia's dark eyes, decides to wander off.

And Matt has to admit, he likes that possessiveness.

Sylvia slides her hand onto Matt's thigh, just above his knee. The less shy part of Matt puts his palm on top on the small-knuckled back of her hand, giving her permission to hold his leg.

More notes.

Really like you. Following you. For weeks. Okay?

"I guess. Yeah."

Right hand over her mouth, smiling.

Your parents in a car accident.

Recently?

Backing out of driveway?

Young woman, speeding. Hit their car.

Clearly at fault!

Acting privileged.

Entitled.

My dad's an attorney! Can't touch me!

His anger. "Yeah. This stupid little bitch thinks she can get away with speeding on my parents' street, crashing into their car, and get away with it just because her daddy is a rich attorney."

Watch.

Holds up her phone. Proud of herself.

A video.

He recognizes the attorney's long-haired daughter. On her knees, furious. Sylvia holding hand-written notes out for her to read.

Ooh, your daddy's a lawyer!

Ooh, you think you're above the law!

Well, you're not!

Smashing across her face, her nose, over and over again, Sylvia's fists, until the daughter finally bursts into tears, raised hands begging for mercy. Sylvia still smacking down into her face, viciously, until the daughter spits out some red teeth, sobbing.

Scribbles some more. She has nice penmanship.

I will always, ALWAYS, watch out for you.

Someone tries to take advantage of you.

I will beat them down.

I pre-wrote the notes I showed her.

While I beat her.

Writing them at the time of the assault might be distracting.

While she's trying to get free.

Matt, trying to take it all in. So much of our present life is ruined by our regrets over something that happened in the past, when we feel someone took advantage of us, or someone we love, and here's Sylvia, lifting one great weight from his intrusive thoughts. "I don't know what to...Thank you! Really."

Sylvia beams, on the barstool next to him. Lifts her hand from above his knee, lands it on his crotch, massaging his swollen fly, thumb rubbing aggressively up and down the length of the brass interlocking teeth of his zipper, looking up into his eyes, grinning behind her left hand.

He sits up straight on his barstool, right hand on her moving forearm.

More notes.

Yes, I have been stalking you.

Because I want you.

I want to meet your parents.

Make that happen.

Don't need to tell them about the video.

Sitting at the bar, Matt phoned his mother.

"Can I come over tonight? Briefly? I want to introduce you to a girl I met."

His mother's surprised voice on the phone's speaker. "Of course you can! Just ring the bell once you're here."

They took a cab, Sylvia lowering her body into the back seat first, sliding across the dark cloth to the opposite rear window, slowly lifting her bare right leg, folding the hollow behind her right knee across Matt's mouth, resting that soft slim heaviness against his lips, telling him to lick her skin. Which he did, like an obedient baby.

By the time the cab pulled up to the curb in front of his parents' townhouse in the Seventies, he had a rock-hard cock.

They got out, he paid the cabbie, they walked up the wide stone steps to his parents' flower-etched glass door, rang the bell.

His mother answered herself, instead of Bettina.

Took in Sylvia, gave her a hug.

Led them into the back kitchen. "Sylvia, you have to tell me all about how you met my boy."

Sylvia turned to Matt, looking up at him.

Okay. Matt cleared his throat. "Sylvia can't speak. She communicates by writing notes. She can hear."

"Oh!" His mother's smiling blue eyes swung from Matt to Sylvia, blinking.

By the end of the evening, his mother escorting the two of them back to the front door, she held both of Sylvia's hands in hers, looked into her black eyes. "If you're the girl for Matt, I'm happy for the two of you, and I accept you, Sylvia, into our family."

*

Once they left his parents' townhouse, strolling down the dark, tree-lined sidewalk, lots of parked cars, Sylvia decided she wanted to spend the night in Matt's apartment.

The two of them on the subway, hurtling to his neighborhood, front page of the newspaper on the floor announcing in big font a German tourist visiting America for the first time had been killed when a 17th century painting by Ciro Ferri displayed in a heavy wooden frame had fallen off its hook in a local museum, crushing the top of his skull, popping out his left eyeball.

His home was a short walk from the subway station. On the sidewalk holding hands, passing storefronts, he said, "Here's where I have lunch sometimes on the weekend, they make great chicken salad sandwiches; here's where I browse for second hand books."

He lived in a brick building at the end of the block. He was embarrassed by the narrow stairs just inside the front door, as if he couldn't afford living in a building with a wider staircase, but Sylvia seemed fine with it, big black eyes taking in all the details.

His apartment was on the first floor so they didn't need to use the stairs, and in fact he had never gone up those old wooden steps, instead leading her down the narrow ground floor hallway, naked yellow-lit lightbulbs passing over their heads, music behind one closed door, cooking smells behind another, arguments about eggs behind a third, to the door where he stopped, facing the wood, head bent, pulling his keys out of his right pants pocket.

He had gone through his apartment the night before after work, like a maid, cleaning, straightening, vacuuming, something he did every Thursday, everyone needed a cleaning routine, and there was a joy to straightening things up, so that as he swung the door open, he felt confident his home would make a good impression.

She stopped by the small closet just inside the front door, writing a long note. Finally held it out sideways to him.

I want to see everything. All of where you live. Bedroom, kitchen, etc. To find out more about who my guy is. So that we have no secrets between us. Is that okay?

"Absolutely. I want you to know me."

She started in that closet next to her shoulder. Went through each hangered item. Opened the top flaps on the two cardboard boxes on the closet's carpeted floor.

Moved on to the living room, the kitchen, his bedroom. Looking everywhere, opening drawers, lifting books to see underneath, pulling curtains away from their windows in case anything was behind them.

Turned on the light in his bathroom, shuffling backwards,

137

letting out a small cry.

All across the tiles of his bathroom floor, dozens of empty toilet rolls, gray cylinders grouped here and there by the tub, the shower, the sink, the toilet alcove.

Looked up at him, not understanding.

"Yeah. I forgot about those. Sorry. After a while, instead of throwing them out, I started leaving them on the floor. I don't really know why, but seeing them all in here every day made me feel less lonely."

Writing a note.

Like pets?

Embarrassed. "I guess."

Dark-haired head down, scribbling.

Lots of pets! Well, you can get rid of them now.

Him looking around at his bathroom floor, at all the light gray cardboard tubes. "Do you mind if I don't?"

Back in his bedroom, where she led him by her hand, she passed him a note, asking him to take off all his clothes for her.

Which he did, obediently. Standing naked in front of her, shirt, pants, underpants, socks and shoes on the carpet, cock sticking straight up, face blushing. His cock was a lot less shy than he was. That happens sometimes.

She reached into her purse, pulled out a small bundle of paperclipped notes he saw, to his dismay, were printed, as if used many times. She shuffled through them, to make sure they were in the right order.

We'll make love.

But I don't allow kissing.

Because in the passion of the moment you might forget I don't have a tongue.

And try to tongue kiss me.

So I keep my mouth shut while we make love.

Also, I can't perform oral sex on you.

Obvious reasons.

But I want you to perform oral sex on me.

Okay?

"Have you shown these instructions to a lot of men?"

She held her right thumb in the air, in a lateral position, right index finger a little bit above the whorls of the thumb.

Which he took to mean, A few men. Not too many.

She slid her clothes off her body, half-turned away from him, as if he were a peeping Tom watching her undress through a third-floor apartment window.

Once she was nude, she elbowed her body backwards on his bed, spreading her legs, pulling his face down between her thighs, closing their warmness around his cheeks, holding the top of his head in place while he licked her cunt.

Face buried to his long nose between the tops of her spread thighs, tongue licking sideways, looking up past the dark curls of her pubic hair, her indrawn stomach, the swollen bottoms of her breasts, jetty of her jaw, to her mouth, one of the best angles to view a woman, and when you think about it, the original angle, he saw, as she inched up closer and still closer to an orgasm, she clamped her lips shut so they wouldn't show the ruby interior of her mouth, much like she hid with her hand her lips when she laughed, and he must admit, for that he was thankful.

After she came, rubbing her cunt across his lips, nose, eyes, forehead, getting her smell everywhere, marking him as hers, like a dog pisses on a bush, she pulled his shoulders up, letting him slide his cock inside her, criss-crossing the hollows of her knees against his throat, resting the curves of her calves against both sides of his face, caressing his ears, while he pumped up inside her, had the most intense orgasm of his life.

Small hand reaching sideways, lifting the bundle of paper-clipped notes she put on the night table on her side of his bed. Glancing at the selected typewritten note before showing it to him to make sure it was the right note.

Now I own you. You are mine.

And he was.

*

It was a different type of relationship than he had ever been in, and of course he found that refreshing.

For one thing, it was hard for her to say anything. If they were somewhere they could just be motionless, his messy bed, a park bench feeding the lizards who had recently invaded the city, a candle-lit table in a restaurant, waiting for the pasta course, she could write notes, but writing takes a lot longer than talking. Even worse was when they were walking around the city, as young lovers often do, holding hands down the long blocks, because it's hard to walk and write notes at the same time, or walk and read notes at the same time. As a consequence, he did most of the talking, which meant that to fill the silence, he found himself revealing far more intimate details about himself than he ever had before. But her complete acceptance of all the secret thoughts and memories he was finally able to unload from his mind only made him more grateful for her ears, her nonchalance.

He told her one day while they were window shopping in the used book district about the sidewalk confrontation he had had outside Price Less, with the bully who insisted on filming him, and how it ended up with the bully handing over to him a key.

Since they had spent some time with each other by now, he was more skilled at interpreting her facial expressions, so that sometimes she didn't need to write a note.

Her head rearing back, smirk on her face, black eyebrows rising, looking up at him.

"Well yeah, I guess we could try the key in different locks around the city, just to see what happens."

Nodding, happily squeezing his right bicep.

"Okay! Well, let's give it a whirl."

She looked around the city square they were in, pointed at the wood-framed glass front door of an apartment building across the street, next to a wide newsstand.

"Let's do it!"

They made their way, hand in hand, across the city square, across the street, in between cars, stepping over the curb onto that far sidewalk.

And in that moment, that fun, he felt so much love for her, that she had brought such enthusiasm into his life, the two of them on this adventure together.

Reaching the wood-framed glass door, he pulled out the key the bully had given him, Sylvia looking around, conspiratorially, then nodding at him to continue. He pushed the pointed front of the brass key's peaks and valleys configuration against the lock's slit, hitting resistance, pushing harder, then pulling back.

She shrugged happily.

"So we'll try some more locks."

They wound up trying twenty-eight different locks that day, the key working on none of them, although it did slide at least partially into three of them. But that was okay. They were both confident they'd eventually find a number of locks the key would fit, and those moments would be magical, opening a portal to a place they couldn't have otherwise entered.

After they decided to quit for the day, down in a section of the city where only buildings three-stories or less were allowed, because there was no bedrock here, only landfill, he leaned against the trunk of a tree, she rested on the green grass beside the tree.

Matt looked down at Sylvia, sprawled on the grass, wanting her, her body, her written words. "That was a lot of fun."

Felt a bump against his back from the tree trunk he was leaning against. "Want to go back to our apartment?"

Which was actually his apartment, but it's where they were now both eating, sleeping, washing.

Her gleeful nod, legs spread, staring up at him.

Another bump against his back, even more aggressive.

He stood away from leaning against the tree trunk, turned around, puzzled. Watched as the bark from the trunk separated away from the tree. And he saw he had actually been leaning against three people who had molded themselves to the tree's trunk, hiding their bodies behind bark.

He stumbled backwards as the three unwound from the tree's trunk, stretching their arms and legs after holding themselves motionless for so long, getting blood back into their limbs, bark dropping off their bodies.

Cultists.

Pulling out from their sagging pants pockets bags of gasoline. He grabbed Sylvia's hand, yanked her up, led her a safe distance away.

The cultists threw some of the gasoline-filled bags at their retreat, but the bags fell short.

Failing that, the three burst the rest of the bags over their heads, bark falling off their arms, passed a blue cigarette lighter hand to hand, igniting each other under their chins, three bodies lighting up yellow and red, holding hands, burning on the green grass.

Defiant look in their eyes. We will not cry out from the pain of being burned alive.

We enjoy being immolated.

*

They both dressed up all in white in his apartment, where most of her clothes were by now in his various closets, planning to ride the subway down to Fish Enterprise, a large, two-story seafood restaurant midtown that specialized in mesquite-smoked shrimp, but as they were getting ready to leave, there was a breaking news report on TV about a series of bombings in that area of the city, the cultists throwing fire bombs into different crowded retail establishments, as well as the side windows of seven school busses, killing or severely burning 148 people.

So they decided to stay indoors, ordering home delivery Chinese.

While they waited for the knock on the front door, lying naked in bed, away from the wet spot, she wrote a note asking how long he had lived in this apartment.

"I've been here a few months." On the TV, live coverage, two cult members ran inside a church where a mass was taking place, threw gasoline-filled balloons into the pews, lit them.

"It looks like they're not just burning themselves now, they're burning other people as well." He drank some more. "I was living in a different apartment, and I really liked it, the front windows overlooked the river, but the landlady had a dog who was blind, and it kept falling down the front stairs. I mean, over and over again. I'd keep hearing its happy barks, then its panicked barks. After a while, it just got to be too much."

While they're lying in Matt's bed with all the late afternoon sun slants and shadows they hear a commotion outside, and it doesn't sound like Chinese food being delivered.

Sylvia looked out through the horizontal white blinds lowered over one of the windows in his living room. On the street outside, a young girl on a bicycle in the middle of the road, surrounded by people in flames.

She held up her right hand, and Matt understood that to mean, I'm going out there to protect her.

They're both drunk.

As she opened the front door, naked, he called to her disappearing bare ass, "That's not a good idea! It's not safe!"

Frightened for her well-being, he picked his pants up off the bedroom carpet, pulled them up his bare legs, pushed his cock and balls back from the front of the pants as he zipped-up. Ran barefoot out the door, expecting to find her lying in the street, or stumbling sideways, in flames.

Naked, she had her arm around the shoulders of the young girl, out in the middle of the hard pavement of the street, walking her back over to where her bicycle had fallen over on its wheeled side, talking to the girl about dealing with bullies, just before letting her go, kissing the abundant hair on top of her young head.

He truly loved her in that moment.

*

It was the final day of the going out of business sale at Price Less. Phones on the glass counters ringing with constant robo callers, to where they finally unplugged all the landlines.

People openly shoplifting, marching through the front doors, picking up a game system, carrying it past the line of cashiers to the sidewalks. When they were stopped by store security, they got self-righteous. These microwave ovens don't belong to you personally, so mind your own business! I need a second microwave! One skinny white guy with black-framed eyeglasses was infuriated one of the store staff was trying to stop him from stealing a flat screen TV. Glared indignantly at the security guard. "I have every right in the world to take a TV I need. What the fuck is wrong with you?"

Cultists wandered inside the store, setting themselves on fire. The looters tried to leave, but the cultists hugged them around the waist, holding them in place, until the fire spread from their gasoline-soaked clothes to the looters' bodies.

Several cultists surrounded Killie, the cashier who sympathized with the cultists, hugging her, popping bags of gasoline over their heads, sparking the gasoline into tall flames, not letting her screaming body go as it went up in flames.

*

"I feel like nothing bad could ever happen here."

Spoken in the quiet, high-ceiling darkness of Matt's bedroom, Matt and Sylvia both naked, shoulders and toe nails and dark pubic hair, lying on the white sheets of his bed, away from the two pearlescent wet spots, watching the overhead helicopter TV coverage of cultists overrunning the city.

The cultists have no name for their cult, so they are simply referred to as, 'the cultists'.

Over the sounds of the wall-mounted TV they hear a commotion outside their front windows.

Matt, spreading his thumb and index finger further apart vertically, widens the gap between two white horizontal mini-blind slats on his street-side window.

Peering through, across the street, people on the far sidewalk setting themselves on fire.

Not screaming at what must be horrific pain.

Trying to break into the building across the way, slamming their shoulders against the front door, sparks flying; hurling chunks of concrete into the first floor windows.

Hears the unmistakable sound of crowd noises outside his living room windows.

Hurries to the windows, alarmed, worried profile leaning against the glass.

People outside the glass, discussing psychiatry in reasonable voices.

Muffled.

"I do feel there are therapeutic values to intrusive thoughts—"

"Absolutely!"

"—in that they can identify those areas of episodic memory that might signal entryways into a patient's processing of his or her past. The challenge for me as a therapist is when the intrusive thoughts are attached to an OCD, BDD or ADHD personality, there's often a distortion—"

"I keep encountering that in my practice!"

"—to where it's often difficult to discern why these particular involuntary memories reoccur. In other words, how much of this behavior is enlightening during the therapeutic process, and how much is simply a reaffirmation of the primary diagnosis?"

"That is the issue."

Mathew lifted his ear away from the window.

The cultists drift across the street, towards his home.

Picking up bricks, throwing them through his street level windows.

Sylvia rushes up to him, hastily dressed, pushing his clothes at Matt, whispering at him to get dressed.

Several cultists set themselves on fire directly outside the window through which he's peering, arms spread, turning around and around, grinning, not screaming in pain.

In Matt's back room, a bearded man crawls through his brick-shattered window, lifts a can of gasoline over his head, nodding at Matt, tilting the gasoline down over his scalp, freckled shoulders, igniting his upper body.

Sylvia looks past Matt's left ear. "Behind you!"

He turns around, shoves a cultist trying to douse him with gasoline against one of his easy chairs.

He and Sylvia run through the rooms to the back door, twist the knob open, run out into the street behind your apartment. Cultists follow, throwing Molotov cocktails.

The two of you run down a side street, Sylvia stopping mid-block, signaling for you to keep running.

She drops one cultist. Another. You stop at the deserted end of the street, looking back. She drops a third cultist.

From the distance on the street between you and her she reaches her right arm up into the air, pumps her fist.

You wait for her to catch up to you. Take her in your arms, kiss her full on the lips. Her dark eyes are filled with pride. I did good.

The two of you keep running, side by side, come up on the door to a factory. It's locked. You remember the key the stranger gave you. Pull it out of your pants pocket. Slide it into the lock.

Turn the key, running footsteps behind your back.

The key doesn't work.

It doesn't. It doesn't. It doesn't open the door.

You say to her, "You can speak?"

"Yeah."

Both of you running again.

The cultists capture both of you. Take you down to the hard pavement, lifting your hands high up in the air behind your backs, uncomfortable on your armpits.

Handcuffed.

"Why did you pretend you couldn't?"

Black eyes on the dirty concrete staring with love into his eyes. "To test you."

Both of them lifted off the street, tossed on their stomachs into the bed of a pick-up truck.

Rumbling through the dark streets of the city, Matt hearing the loud grind of gear-shiftings, the creak of the foot brake as the pick-up comes to a stop under a tall bridge down by the bank of the river.

Matt first, then Sylvia, hauled out of the pick-up's bed by their handcuffs, thrown on their stomachs onto the black tar.

Out in the wide river, a long, long barge loaded with garbage slowly drifting past under the darkness of the moon-lit sky.

The cultists surround both of you lying on the tar on your stomach, handcuffed hands behind your backs.

Cultists of all ages, body types, pulling out long knives.

A little girl with black-framed glasses walks over, standing in front of Matt and Sylvia, knife in her right hand, looking down at their upraised eyes. "Are you one of us, or one of the enemy?"

Matt, buying for time. "Well, I'm willing to be enlightened."

The little girl using her serious voice all children know about. "Then you know what you have to do."

"Okay."

"Eat a monkey."

"What?"

"If you're one of us, you'll eat a monkey. That's the test."

"Okay. Sure."

146

A fat woman in a wheelchair, long dark hair, eyeglasses, rolls into the center of the circle of cultists under the tall bridge, dead monkey in the lap of her ankle-length flowered dress.

Her right hand picks the monkey off her lap by the back of his neck, flips it down at Matt.

The furry body lands limply on top of his head.

He curls his face downwards, towards his collarbones, tilting the weight on his head forward, so the small body slips off his scalp onto the black tar.

His great relief to see the monkey is already dead.

But it's raw.

He sees the knives all around him.

"Can I get some salt?"

Half a dozen cultists close in, lifting their knives, skinning the monkey, peeling its brown and black fur away from its back, face, long arms, buttocks, until lying on the black tar in front of Matt's mouth is a completely skinned monkey, red meat and white fat following the lines of its skeleton.

A salt shaker is placed down on the tar next to the monkey's dead skinned face. The shaker only has a thin layer of salt at the bottom.

Released from his handcuffs, he rains some salt down on the monkey's red shoulder, bites down into the raw red meat, teeth pulling the meat off the bone, eyes switching to the left, chewing, chewing, chewing, swallowing. Teeth dipping down for another section of raw monkey meat ripped up off the bone.

After he's eaten half the monkey's body, and has run out of salt, he looks across the black tar at Sylvia, who's still lying on her stomach, but handcuffs unlocked and removed, watching him.

"Why aren't you eating a monkey?"

She ruffles his hair. "I'm a recruiter."

Matt chewing monkey, crest-fallen. "So you don't love me?"

"I do! I honestly, sincerely do. That's why I chose you. I love you, Matt."

After he finished eating the last of the monkey, pulling red meat away from the bones of the monkey's toes, and by then he had to admit, the flesh didn't taste that bad, he could see eating another

147

monkey under happier circumstances, maybe with an Asian dipping sauce, soy and sugar and toasted sesame oil, he spread his hands apart, monkey blood dripping down from his lower lip. "Done!"

The little girl again stepped forward into the circle.

"People see the world in different ways. And live in the world they see. That could be a happy world, a frightening world, a lonely world, whatever. We want to show you the world we see, and invite you to live in that world that we see with us."

On his knees on the black tar pavement, under the tall bridge, raw monkey meat stuck between his teeth, Matt nodded. Looked at Sylvia, the surrounding circle holding knives in their right or left hands, whichever was dominant, the little girl in the center. "This is what I want. To belong to something. I'm so tired of being alone."

And, you know? He meant it.

*

He abandoned his apartment, walking out on his lease, his furniture, childhood pictures, quit his job, moved into the concrete-walled basement of a condemned tenement where the other members of the local cultists lived. In this commune, everyone contributed towards gathering food, portable water, gasoline. Each morning, a woman in her sixties made her way in her short-shorts, great legs, through the bodies in the dim-lit basement, male and female, settling her thin knees in the dirt of the basement floor by each body's left hip, slim pink fingers masturbating each set of genitals, wet or lengthy, to orgasm, during each masturbation making the body twitching under her fast fingers again pledge allegiance to their cause, like watering flowers.

The cult had a huge pile of green army blankets in the basement, Matt had no idea how they had obtained them, but he and Sylvia carried four of them over to a corner of the dark space, arranging them across the dirt, over themselves, so as to build a nest, where they fucked each other.

They wandered the city together during the day, holding hands. At one point they entered a tall building and decided to ride the elevator up to the roof. The plan was to try Matt's key on some of the office doors.

They pushed through the glass doors at the front, walked across the lobby, to the row of elevators at the rear.

Evening in the city, streets dark but for the skyscrapers' lit windows high, high, high off the sidewalks, rain falling but they had no umbrellas, walking side by side down the soaked concrete, hugging each other, heads ducked, hair and shoulders drenched, electric neon of the tall vertical and horizontal signs outside restaurants and retail establishments wet as rainbows.

*

A few days after that, Sylvia told him she was going to take a bag of gasoline with her when they went out that morning, walking the streets, looking for doors his key might open.

He wasn't sure what that meant. "Are you telling me something?"

"Not really."

They took the subway to the east side of the city, passing by the doors to shops, since those doors were already open, concentrating on the street doors to apartments. By lunchtime they had probably tried to push his key into about thirty different locks, with no luck. And then just before they were planning to stop, the key did actually slip easily into a street level lock, like a cock into a cunt, and both their faces astonished, he twisted the key left, unlocking that glass door.

They climbed the old wooden flight directly inside the door, coming out on a straight hallway with shut doors on either side.

He tried the key in each door down that row, both sides, but nothing.

But that's okay.

Sometimes, nothing is an answer.

They ate lunch at a corner pizzeria. Across from each other at one of several small round tables outside the restaurant, on the sidewalk, under a red, green and white umbrella. Italian subs, boiled ham, Genoa salami, mortadella, capicola, provolone, sliced plum tomatoes, lettuce, black olives, a sweet red dressing made with olive oil, red wine vinegar, fresh oregano.

It was delicious, last of it lying on the lips, after which she rose

149

backwards from her chair, staring with love into his eyes with a regretful look, backing up further onto the crowded sidewalk, bursting the bag of gasoline over her head, setting herself on fire, making a determined point of not showing any pain as she slowly burned to death, fell over, perished.

*

After Sylvia's death he withdrew into himself, still slept in the dirt of the concrete walls under the abandoned tenement, still rolled over onto his back so the woman in her sixties in her short-shorts could jerk him off, but otherwise didn't participate much in the cult.

After a few weeks of being alone on the sidewalks, a skinny blonde who tried to flirt with him early in his initiation into the cult, who he ignored because he had Sylvia, started sleeping on the green army blankets next to him, not saying anything, just being there, waiting with eyes switched to the left, and a few days after that they started fucking. And actually, it turned out he really enjoyed fucking her skinniness.

That happens.

Her thin blonde face turned towards him, blue eyes, naked bodies lying on their green army blankets, her small hand again encircling his cock at its base, pulling on its spongy length to get it hard again, so he could fuck her again. "Does it bother you I'm fucking you so soon after Sylvia died?"

He spread his thighs, sighing. She had really skillful, sliding fingers. "It doesn't mean that much to me. Does it mean that much to you?"

The two of them started going out together into the city, holding hands, trying his key in different locks. She asked at one point if she could be the one pushing the key against a lock, seeing if it would fit, and he handed her the key just like that, no ceremony, told her she could keep it.

It pleased him she rose up on the balls of her feet, with pride, accepting the key.

When he was a child, he woke up in the middle of the night and saw, standing in his bedroom, a donkey standing up on its two hind hoofs by his sliding-door closet. The donkey, moving its front legs sideways in the air, perhaps to maintain balance, looked like something so far removed from his life he could never communicate with, or interact with, like something brightly illuminated on a glass slide under a microscope, but lying in his small bed, he wasn't afraid, at all. After he started fucking the woman in her sixties wearing short-shorts in the dirt basement of the abandoned tenement building, while his skinny blonde girlfriend watched, knuckles of her thin right hand jammed down the front of her blue jeans, masturbating, the woman in her sixties, one time after their simultaneous orgasms, rolled on her side, their bare stomachs still touching, heavy breasts sagging downwards, and with the tip of her right index finger started drawing in the dirt. Circles and lines and curves, and once she was finished, sexually-satisfied blue eyes looking up at him under white eyebrows, he saw that in the dirt she had drawn the outline of a donkey standing upright on its back hooves.

Was that a key? Did that explain everything?

Later that morning he and the skinny blonde (he never asked her what her name was), decided to walk around the city, and he decided to take a bag of gasoline with him.

"Is there something I need to know?"

"Not really."

After trying her key in different locks, unsuccessfully, but you never know what tomorrow will bring, they stopped for lunch at a corner seafood café.

He didn't look at the menu the waiter handed him. "What month is this?"

The dark-haired waiter reared his head back, politely puzzled in the way young people often are. "It's January, Sir."

"So it's an 'R' month. Great. I'd like a dozen oysters on the half shell, please."

His skinny blonde girlfriend ordered a shrimp cocktail. There's a reason it's a classic.

"Tell me about your father?"

She shifted gears. "He loved suspenders. He hung himself by his belt off a closet door in his home. Police found a pen knife in his pocket, and superficial cuts on his wrists."

151

His oysters came spread on crushed ice in a ring around a center metal cup of red cocktail sauce, yellow wedges of fresh lemon between each opened oyster shell.

He preferred eating his oysters plain, without sauce or squirt, relying just on the brinny chewiness of each oyster.

The rawness of them, killing each amorphous shape floating in his mouth with his crushing white teeth clamping into the soft bodies, while that shape was still alive, was wonderful.

There's a lot to be said for suicide. We're not supposed to do it, we're not supposed to like it, but it really does make you feel great about yourself. It's a high. Like masturbation.

Across the street, a young couple in a pick-up parallel-parked their truck at the curb, got out from both front blue doors of their truck, let down the gate at the back of the pick-up's bed, slid forward and slanted down a sheet of bare plywood from the rear edge of the bed to the street, so a three-legged dog in the bed could tap down off-balance, hobble around in the green park.

That was love.

After they finished eating, Matt pushed his chair back from their circular table on the sidewalk.

Looked into the skinny blonde's blue eyes. "Thank you. For everything." It's what you say. He didn't mean any of it.

Rising from their table, he walked out into the middle of the busy city street, burst the bag of gasoline over his head, lit his body on fire.

Raised his face, feeling unbelievable pain, but absolutely determined to not show any discomfort at all, just joy, as people on the street backed up, frightened, away from him.

It's what we do.

~

Ralph Robert Moore's fiction has appeared in America, Canada, England, Ireland, France, India and Australia in a wide variety of genre and literary magazines and anthologies, including Midnight Street, Cemetery Dance, Black Static, Shadows & Tall Trees, Nightscript, ChiZine*, and others. He's been nominated twice for* Best Story of the Year *by The British Fantasy Society, once in 2013, and again in 2016. He writes a column,* Into the Woods, *for each issue of* Black Static. *His latest collection,* Our Elaborate Plans, *will be released later this year.*

HATE CRIME
Scott Bradfield

"For example, I hate avocados," Drew Peterson testified at his hearing in Santa Monica Civil Court, shortly after being driven there in a mesh-windowed van from County Jail. "I hate broccoli, snow peas, and anything green. I hate marmalade, two-party politics, movies featuring Joaquin Phoenix in either a major or supporting role, and motorcycles – especially the loud ones that go roaring past my bedroom in the middle of the night. Like most people, I'm a creature of unwelcome prejudices, and often express them in a needlessly confrontational manner. Which is why, on the night of November seventeenth, when Ms. Estrella Dominique Sanchez (the lovely young woman currently sitting in the front row of this courtroom) brought me that tray of complimentary hors d'oeuvres at the Olive Garden, I probably sounded more belligerent than I wanted to sound. As she testified, I said something about how I '*hated* Spanish almonds' and then I urged her to '*please* take them away.' But I wasn't trying to disparage the Spanish people, or even Ms. Sanchez. In fact, I didn't even know Ms. Sanchez *was* Spanish until the police arrived to serve me with an official Hate-Assault Citation during dessert. So mea culpa or, as the kids say these days, 'My bad.' And after extensive consultation with my lawyer (who couldn't be here on account of his son's soccer game) I'd like to throw myself on the mercy of the court, and promise to never again utter bigoted, nationalistic statements about the sovereign nation of Spain, or any of its provinces, including Gibraltar. And while I *know* this won't remedy my past behavior, perhaps it will help you see your way towards forgiving me, Ms. Sanchez. Even if I may never live long enough to forgive myself."

It was Drew's first time in court, and he was impressed by the abundance of blond veneer that covered everything – chairs, desks, paneled walls and paneled ceiling – even while the court officials didn't seem very impressed by him. In fact, many jury-members were already slumped over half-asleep in their chairs, or noisily tapping messages into their cell phones.

"*Chingo tu madre!*" shouted a husky-voiced man from the audience.

"That mean fuck you mama!" shouted an equally husky-looking woman from the jury box.

Drew tried not to betray any glance or expression that the jury might consider "inappropriate." Instead, he looked up directly at the judge and realized, for the first time, that she was a not-unattractive, middle-aged woman with dark skin, dark hair, and thickly-dropletted eyelashes that reminded him of the gypsies in old black and white werewolf movies.

The name on her black enamel desk-card said:

JUDGE RAMIREZ PRESIDING.

And after taking a deep breath that seemed to expand her displeasure, she said: "Perhaps it's time we brought this hearing to a close, Mr. Peterson—" as if she and Drew were the only people in the entire courtroom. "Since I'm sure we both have places we'd rather be."

*

"The most depressing part of the whole experience," Drew told his wife that night when she drove him home in their Toyota, "is that I don't even *like* the Olive Garden. I prefer Macaroni Grill, but they were closed for refurbishment. So now I've got this clunky police monitor latched to my ankle, and the itching is driving me round the twist. I thought they'd just slap me on the wrist or something. Instead, they hit me with a whole goddamn year of home detention. Who knew?"

Deirdre was wearing a slender, floral-patterned print dress, a pale haze of blush, and cherry red lipstick, gazing out the windshield with an expression of distant solicitude, as if listening to a disembodied tale of woe on the dashboard radio. Then, at the next stop sign, she pulled over against the curb, turned, and touched Drew's shoulder with her unusually long, jade-colored fingernails. She resembled one of those astronaut-wives who used to stand around Cape Canaveral before a moon launch.

"Honey," she said softly, in a tone both affectionate and

uninvolved, as if she were telling a dog not to jump on the furniture, "please don't raise your voice with me. I know you're frustrated but remember what the judge advised about placing limits on your hostile-behavior patterns. Because if there's one thing I don't want to do ever again, it's to stand bravely by you in a court of law."

*

For several weeks, Drew hung around the living room watching Nazi documentaries on the History Channel, shopping for second-hand DVD box sets online, and preparing afternoon snacks of pita bread, hummus, peeled carrots and celery stalks for his children when they arrived home from school. Drew's favorite part about being a dad was preparing nutritious snacks for his children, but his least favorite part was trying to answer all their mid-snack questions about his current legal predicament.

"Dad, why do you hate Spanish people? Is it because they're swarthy? Or is it that annoying accent of theirs, like somebody clipped off the tip of their tongue with a pair of pliers? I don't personally have any bad feelings about Spanish people, but I'm perfectly prepared to develop some. My teacher, Mrs. Rogerson, said that parents who encourage hostile behavior patterns in their children should be exterminated, but only metaphorically, since capital punishment is wrong. Do you think capital punishment is wrong, Dad? Or should we only use capital punishment to control the Spanish people who, as I think we agree, are causing nothing but trouble in our American-language-oriented society?"

Drew's son, Felix, always spoke quickly and vigorously, as if he was racing himself to the end of each sentence. Meanwhile, his daughter Felicia took the opportunity to devour every scrap of pita bread in sight.

"*I* don't hate Spanish people, Daddy," she said, running her nail-bitten finger around the rim of her lips to gather up the last grainy bits of hummus. "But I do hate a girl named Monica in my gym class, who has really dark hair and whiskers. Would that suggest I'm heading towards sociopathic criminal behavior like you, Daddy? Or would the government allow me to hate Monica just a little bit, so long as I don't violate her socio-cultural space?"

155

*

In the fourth week of home-detention, Drew was fired from his teaching position at Madison Elementary and acquired a part-time job in customer service at Flambo Financial Securities, an online investment firm located (or so they claimed) somewhere in the Midwest. FFS paid him an hourly rate even lower than his lawn-mowing job back in high school – not that Drew complained. "I'm just glad to get my foot back on the employment ladder," he told his wife one night in bed, while she lay beside him pretending to be asleep. "And I don't care what kind of employment, either. I'll take any goddamn ladder I can get."

Every morning, he fixed himself a cup of instant coffee, and sat down in front of the living room computer, wearing a mouthpiece and headphone device pilfered from his son's X-Box. Then, clicking on the icon for "Flambo Financial Investment Labs," he awaited his first caller.

"Hi there, Mr. Montale, of 33 Pinecove Drive! My name is Drew Peterson, and before saying another word, may I please read a brief disclaimer prepared by the California State Board of Social Safety? It goes like this: 'Greetings, Potential Customer! I am currently serving home-detention for a grade 3 level act of social hostility, and while I have openly repented my actions as required by my plea agreement, I still suffer from unpleasant behavior patterns instilled by decades of poor self-management. If, at any moment, you feel threatened by my behavior, please contact the CSBSS number located at the bottom of this screen. Now, may I ask – are you prepared for the imminent financial catastrophe facing our American way of life? If not, perhaps you would be interested in speaking with one of our highly-trained capital-investment advisers... Mr. Montale? Hello? Are you still there?"

But of course most customers hung up long before Drew had finished reading his Personal Disclaimer; and if they didn't hang up, they usually exhibited some pretty hostile behavior patterns of their own.

*

Weeks of home-detention stretched into months, and Drew did everything he could to convince his family (and himself) that he had learned from his mistakes. He applied for, and was granted, a day-pass to attend a Self-Awareness Seminar at his son's school. He earned a Three Month Clear button at his Hostility-Abuse Clinic for eliminating negative tones from his conversational register. And after every meal, he recited the "Why I Don't Hate Anything Prayer" into the recording mouthpiece of his Detention monitor:

Please, lord, help me accept the limitations of who I am
And patient enough to endure the limitations of everyone else
Kind enough to reprioritize my love-anger dichotomies
And wise enough to accept the deeply fallible person I have always been

At the conclusion of each prayer, Drew tasted a faint numbness at the roof of his mouth, as if the words were coated with a thin anodyne. He only hoped that the numbness would eventually spread into his brain where, he admitted in his darkest hours, he still harbored feelings of unrelenting anger at the world that had betrayed him.

*

"Many of you suffer from deep-seated hostility patterns that you don't even *know* you suffer from," Dr. Marigold told Drew and his fellow home-detention inmates during the "Finding Your Way Back to Polite Society Seminar" that was held every Wednesday evening at Skyline Community College. "You spend your lives thinking: 'Hey, I'm no different from everybody else. People *like* me; and I like people. And so you continue journeying through life unaware of your deeply vile nature. Until, of course, the day comes when that nature is triggered into action by circumstances beyond your control."

Dr. Marigold wore faded freshly-laundered jeans, a beaded cotton halter-top, combed-back glistening raven-black hair, and big squarish pink glasses, like a sexy librarian in a Disney movie.

"Let's take *you*, Drew," Dr. Marigold said, sliding her pear-shaped bottom onto the edge of Drew's desk. "On the surface, you *seem* like a nice man. You dress okay. You have decent oral hygiene. You trim your nails and display good manners. If anybody met you, Drew, they would probably conclude, Hey. He's no rocket scientist. And he's no Rock Hudson in the looks department. But he doesn't endanger our notions of social order. He's the sort of average, inoffensive boob you meet every day. And *that*, of course, is where they would be *wrong*."

Dr. Marigold's formidable attention was making Drew feel a little woozy; a cold fist of unease formed in his stomach. His ankle bracelet was heating up, exerting a faint fibrillation. It was as if the ankle bracelet had detected where this conversation was going before Drew did.

Dr. Marigold turned and removed her glistening black Michael Kors handbag from the podium; her nylon knees flashed with reflected florescent light. She smelled like peppermint-flavored Tic Tacs.

"But now let's imagine a *different* case scenario," Dr. Marigold continued, reaching into her bag and removing something in her loosely clenched fist, like an amateur magician palming a pea. "One which might reveal Drew Peterson for the person he really is. In this case scenario, Drew Peterson goes strolling down the street of Anytown, USA. He smiles at every person he meets and opens doors for old ladies. Suddenly, without warning, Mr. Nice Guy sees a convenient restaurant and goes inside. A sultry, dark-haired waitress brings him a menu; and everything is perfectly hunky dory until the *hors d'oeuvres* arrive, when Drew comes face-to-face with the secret of himself that he never understood until now—"

At which point, Dr. Marigold presented her pretty pink fist to Drew, turned it over, and slowly uncurled the anemone-like fingers to reveal the cleanest, whitest, most perfect example of a Spanish almond that Drew had ever seen.

*

"So what did you do *then?*" his classmate, Imrah Goldsworthy, asked a few weeks later, after too many celebratory beers at the Olive Garden. Imrah was overweight, sweaty, and wore "humorous" T-shirts that were never funny (or even comprehensible) to Drew. Tonight, it was a blue tank-top featuring a pair of sparkly, short-fused dynamite sticks rolling their wide eyes over the electrified caption: "*And long may she blast!*"

"Well," Drew said slowly, feeling the story emerge from his throat like a slow bubble of lava from an expiring volcano, "at first I didn't know what to say. I felt this flash of rage and anxiety; tears rushed to my face. For a moment, I thought I was having a heart attack. There I was, almost finished paying my debt to society, when suddenly this rage-management instructor is sticking a Spanish almond in my face. How do you prepare yourself for *that*? And suddenly I remembered all those things they teach you in the Anger Rehabilitation Manuals. Take a deep breath, let it out, send your anger to the *moon*. Deep breath, let it out, send your anger to the *moon*. I sat there listening to that reasonable inner voice for what seemed several hours, but it was probably only a few seconds. Because when I smiled up at Dr. Marigold, she smiled right back. And without thinking twice, I took that Spanish almond gently from Dr. Marigold's small, soft, sexy hand, placed it between my front teeth, and bit it in two. It felt like biting off the head of a small animal. It made me feel like I had just been born."

*

That night, Drew brought groceries home from Albertson's, sat in the living room recliner, and read the paper while his wife cooked. Then, after dinner, he took an ambitious, spur-of-the-moment stroll down to the Stop and Shop for a pack of cigarettes. It was the first spur-of-the-moment stroll he had taken since his conviction, and his first cigarette since college. Each long, sandy drag from the Marlboro felt more exhilarating than freedom. If I'm ever diagnosed with a fatal disease, he thought, I'm definitely going to start smoking again.

The streets were fragrant with flowers and trees that Drew couldn't identify, even though he had been living among them since his children were born. It made him wary of crushing out his Salem in the gutter or flicking it into the street. *What if the trees and flowers are watching?* he thought weirdly. *What if they report back to my wife?* These days, he was ready for anything. Except, of course, for what actually happened.

Closing the front door softly, he reached for a breath mint from the Chinese porcelain bowl on the hall table and heard his wife's thin, distraught voice in the kitchen.

"Hello? Is this Twelfth Street Division? I'd like to report my husband smoking on the front porch of our home at 99 Maple Leaf Drive. Yes, a Third-Degree Toxic Abasement if ever I saw one. Of course I'll hold. Just please don't leave me alone. I can already hear him in the house. He's getting closer. It's not me I'm worried about. It's the *children*."

It was the one thing Drew hated, hated with more fury than any stupid Spanish almond.

The goddamn cops. And they were headed his way.

~

Scott Bradfield is a novelist, short story writer and critic, and former Professor of American Literature and Creative Writing at the University of Connecticut. Works include The History of Luminous Motion, Dazzle Resplendent: Adventures of a Misanthropic Dog, *and* The People Who Watched Her Pass By. *Stories and reviews have appeared in* Triquarterly, The Magazine of Fantasy & Science Fiction, The New York Times Book Review, The Los Angeles Times Book Review, The Baffler, *and numerous 'best of' anthologies. He lives in California and London.*

He has stories and essays forthcoming in The Weird Fiction Review, The New Statesman, The Best From Potato Soup Journal, Delmarva Review, The Baffler, The Moth, Albedo One, The New Republic, The Los Angeles Review of Books, *and* Flash Fiction Magazine.

He has written several screenplays for Universal, Sony Pictures, *Roger Corman's* Concorde-New Horizons, *and several independent film companies – including filmed adaptations of his short story,* The Secret Life of Houses *(for PBS) and his novel,* The History of Luminous Motion. *The short film adaptation of his story,* Greetings From Earth, *was featured at the 2007 Tribeca film festival.*

DANDY ARISTOTLE'S MASTERWORK
Rhys Hughes

Q. Why do we have two small eyes instead of one big eye?

A. One big eye would be more likely to collect grit and particles of blown sand. It would be more at risk from paper darts thrown by creative but feral children. Tears shed by one big eye might be as large as a shed. Inconvenient! Men by the name of Odysseus would be a constant threat, even if they only had one big eye too. The clanking of the lid as it closed over the orb would be a sonic nuisance. If not a clanking, then a papery rasping. At night it would reflect the moon alarmingly. One big eye would be a stranger to the parallax view, as you are a stranger to me. All blinks would be winks and therefore seductive or conspiratorial. The eyebrow would be lonely, conspicuously so. The lashes would bat massively and what is the most massive bat? The fruit bat, of course!

Q. Why don't people have wings?

A. There are aeroplanes provided for our use. That's the best way to fly if you are a human being, as a passenger on such a craft. Be considerate and don't try to fly by flapping your arms. It makes too much commotion. Also remember that you are not an angel. Not yet, at any rate. The real question remains unanswered. Do angels have arms as well as their wings, or just the wings? If they have both arms and wings, then the total number of their limbs must be six, and creatures with six legs are known as insects. The thought that angels might have arms *and* wings alarms me. I cower under the bedsheets at night, terrified that the magnified shadow of the moth on the wall is in fact an angel that wants to circle the inner light of knowledge that shines out of my mouth, and drown itself in my gullet.

Q. Why did you change your name to Dandy Aristotle?

161

A. This is a question I resent, because my real name has always been Dandy Aristotle and that's the name I was given by my parents at the very instant of my birth. But I was young and naïve back then, I didn't really understand the value of a superb name and I ached to be like everyone else, bland and somewhat boring. At the age of three weeks I thus arranged for my name to be officially changed to Reggie Carrot. It was many years before I came to understand that my real name was better. So I changed it back when I was nineteen years old. It is not true that Reggie is my real name. That's just a pseudonym I mistakenly believed would help me fit into general society. I am Dandy and that's how I prefer to be called.

Q. Is it true that you know everything?

A. I could answer that if I chose to, but it's probably best that I don't.

Q. Why do we blow on our hands to warm them but blow on soup to cool it?

A. This is a conundrum that is also a paradox. But really there's no need to feel sad when the universe weighs down the shoulders of our souls with peculiarities. We must just accept that sometimes the same thing can work in two different directions at the same time. For example, when you walk down the street, one of your legs goes forwards and the other is going backwards, yet you do make progress. You don't stay in the same spot. It's exactly the same way with the breath of our lungs. We blow on hands and the hands warm up. We blow on soup and the soup cools down. But once there was a fellow who ate his soup with his hands. He never used a bowl or a cup. A foolish fellow indeed. His name was Rumbolt Ghoo and he was mad, quite mad. He hated washing spoons and crockery and that's why he cupped his hands and dipped them into the pot of soup. The soup was hot but his hands were tough. Yet one day the soup was too hot even for him. He held his cupped hands full of soup to his lips and instead of drinking the soup right down, he blew on it first. He supposed it would cool as a result, because we do blow on soup to cool it. But his breath must have got confused. It heated up the hands instead, which is what breath does, and instead of cooling down, the soup got even hotter. Eventually it reached its boiling point and it evaporated and Rumbolt Ghoo went hungry.

Q. What do you think of very short skirts?

A. It is rather amusing to watch women in very short skirts constantly tugging them down as they walk along, but the sight also wakens in the latent engineer in me. The solution, I think, would be to have weighted hems on those skirts. Maybe lots of steel ball bearings sewn into the hem. Or even just a dozen succulent onions pinned to the outside. That would surely do the trick.

Q. Is it possible to become lost in a book?

A. Yes, it's possible. It happens frequently, in fact, and there's nothing strange about it unless the book in question happens to be an atlas. "I am lost, but in an atlas! I need a map to find my way out. Oh no, wait!" There was once a team of explorers who went into the largest atlas ever published in order to explore it fully. They slipped between the pages one by one and made their way slowly towards the middle. They thought it would be an easy task to navigate in there, but the light was dim and the pages were so big and the members of the team got separated and years later many of them still haven't emerged. You can sometimes hear them knocking on the stiff covers from the inside or yelling faintly for sustenance.

Q. Should a man exchange his wife for the world?

A. Of course! Without any hesitation. Men often say to their wives, "I wouldn't swap you for the world," but this demonstrates an incredible lack of foresight. The wife in question exists in the world. The world contains that wife! If the man exchanges her for the world, he will get her back, plus all the other things that exist in the world. He can't lose! Yet men still refuse the offer.

Q. Who was the biggest dwarf that ever lived?

A. The biggest dwarf of all was named Atlas and he carried the sky on his shoulders. That's how immense he was. Some authorities claim he was even bigger than that and carried the whole planet on his back. Most people who have heard of him believe he was a giant or a titan, but in fact he was just a magnified dwarf. It is very rare that a dwarf is so huge. There are rumours that even bigger dwarves once existed but I am very sceptical about such claims, and I am Dandy Aristotle, so I ought to know! The average big dwarf is the same size as the average person. But let me tell you a secret. Big dwarves are never aware of what they are. No big dwarf ever supposed they were a big dwarf and not just a 'standard' human. Even Atlas thought he was a normal giant or titan. He was called Atlas because all his clothes were made from maps, vast maps stitched together. His pants were the Americas.

Q. Has a rabbit ever ruled a sovereign state?

A. Only once and that state was contained inside a cabinet, so no one else was aware of its existence, but the rabbit didn't care. A sovereign state is an independent country made from those old gold coins that are worth twenty shillings. The coin must first be hammered flat and very thin, very thin indeed, and stretched until it has a thickness of only a molecule or so. Then people can live on it, colleges can be erected, cafes might choose to serve cappuccinos, bicycles will trundle along the streets, umbrellas will be opened when it rains, robots will bleep and whistle as they go about their electronical tasks, and the ruling rabbit will stride out onto the balcony of his palace and view the proceedings while nibbling a carrot. But most sovereign states are ruled with straight lines and huge epistles are written on them.

Q. Why do feral children throw paper darts?

A. This is due to the existence of arms. Without arms, such darts would not and could not be thrown. To make a paper dart, one most fold it a certain way. This is also true of paper boats, unicorns and carnivorous space giraffes. This is no less true of ginger quorums and fabricated dangermice. But the issue isn't with the paper but the children and even so the issue isn't grandiose. Feral children are those who live with wolves. I believe they sometimes live with bears. They don't understand what books are for. It seems to them that books are quivers of paper darts. It's a logical deduction based on what they know about the world. That's all.

Q. Have you ever been married?

A. No, but I once courted a maiden. Miss Chewleg was her real name but to protect her dignity and honour and privacy I will call her Lady Munchfoot. We strolled on moonbeams over the ocean. We bathed in each other's eyes. Our shadows danced on the wall while we stood and hugged tight without moving. The following morning that wall was covered in vines and flowers. Our bicycles were golden in colour and the wheels sounded like kisses as they revolved. We pedalled hard and reached the apex of the mountain, then we rolled down the other side. The wind blew off my hat and blew off her skirt and blew my heart onto my sleeve. My sleeve flapped urgently and it was certainly a hazardous time. The brakes failed. Through the walls of a cafe we crashed into a vat of Frappuccino. Oh, how we wallowed! Oh, how we splashed! Then we drifted apart and I never saw her again. Perhaps she is still alive, poor Lady Munchfoot, dripping with cold sweet coffee.

Q. What are you favourite insults?

A. You galvanized chimpbucket! You pandiculated rectilium! You certified thingum! You granulated blubberhack! You tonsil monkey! You broom without a view! You flumbasket! You untested crumplezone! You event horizon doodah! You twerpbutter! You dark matter tricycle! You attic in a coal mine! You twiglet flechette! You ratified warehouse! You jelly raft! You certified boppo! You unravelled clanger! You affronted backscratcher! You corrugated banana! You blasted rugbugger! You fogbound knee! You gibber pocket! You stratospheric tektite! You hornythopter! You simper satchel! You bubbly doubloon! You wrist assessment!

Q. Did you want to be sagacious when you grew up?

A. No. My first dream was to be a professional robot. That's what I hoped to become. When I was only as high as the knee of a gnome I had a strong sense of my destiny. I was born to be a professional robot! Yet the opportunities avoided me. I never would have believed it if you had told me that one day I would be a sage. Now I *am* a sage I know you would have been quite correct to do so. I don't mean that I have given up entirely on my dream. I'm a robot in the privacy of my own home, an amateur robot. But that still isn't the same as being a professional robot. My idol was Mr Tidy, the finest professional robot in the robosphere. Do you remember him? He moved in that jerky way that was still somehow smooth. In appearance he was half cocktail drinker, half vampire, half mime artist, yet totally a robot. He earned money for moving that way, which is why he was a professional. His name wasn't Mr Tidy, that's an anagram of his real name. I changed it to protect his dignity and honour. Maybe that's why you don't remember him, but I bet you know who Tim Dry was? Yes, of course you do. Oh, now I've let the cybercat out of the bag! How clumsy of me. And yet I'm Dandy Aristotle and should have seen that coming.

Q. Why aren't people immortal?

A. Why do we have to die, you mean? That's an old question but I know the answer. It is to do with percentages. They are responsible. As we grow older, every year that passes is a smaller and smaller percentage of the time we have already lived. So when we are ten years old, each year is 10% of our lived lives. When we are twenty it is 5% and when we are fifty it is 2%. This is why years seem to speed up as we grow older. Time accelerates subjectively for each one of us. Each year whizzes past faster and faster because it is a smaller and smaller percentage of our already lived existence in the world. If we are lucky enough to reach the age of one hundred, every new year is now only 1% of our lives so far. But imagine if we were immortal, if we had evolved to live forever. By the time we are one thousand years old, the next year will only be 0.1% of our lived lives. It will pass rapidly, one hundred times as fast as a year passes for a person who is ten years old. Do the sums! For a ten year old, every year has 365 days but for a person who is one thousand years old that year will pass in 3.65 days as perceived by a ten year old. As time passes, the years continue to speed up. When we are one million years old, the next year is 0.0001% of our lived lives. A year will then pass in 0.00365 days from the perspective of the ten year old. That is 5.256 minutes! It will get worse. Eventually each year will pass in less than one second, less than one microsecond, less than one nanosecond. Passing time will be a blur, a scream. Faster and faster will pass the years, accelerating until they reach the speed of light! When that happens, the mass of these years will then increase until it becomes infinite and the gravitational pull will also increase to infinity. A black hole will be created where the year once was, a black hole the size of the universe. Everything will be destroyed. This is the reason why we are not immortal.

Q. Have you ever broken the law?

A. Not the law of the land. No, I haven't. Nor the laws of physics. If you have heard of a person called Dandy Aristotle committing a crime, then it wasn't me but someone else with the same name. That happens a lot, unfortunately. And it's very unfair on the innocent person who just happens to share a name with the criminal. A scheme ought to be devised that changes the names of all convicted criminals into something utterly unique, chosen randomly by computer, so that they will never have the same name as an innocent person. The person named Dandy Aristotle who robbed a bank or beat up an old person ought to have his name changed to (for example) Dankfluster Rotter, in order to protect my reputation. What is the chance of there being another Dankfluster Rotter alive in the world? None at all.

Q. What are you opinions on modern fashion?

A. Fashions come and go but it would often be much better if they would keep going and never come back. The toga is the best form of clothing ever designed for men and women. That's a fashion that should have stayed but it didn't. Modern fashions tend to be quite absurd and sometimes they are utterly ludicrous. The very strange corset-on-the-outside fad is especially awful in my view. Corsets are supposed to be worn under clothing. If you wear one *outside* your clothes you are a gruesome inverter. Wearing a corset on the outside is like travelling on a train with the scenery on the inside and the passengers standing in fields outside the windows. It is like wearing a skull outside a hat. Or like baking for friends a vast jam tart with a solid lump of pastry in the middle of a sticky sphere of strawberry goo. It is certainly aesthetically and perhaps morally reprehensible. Please bring back the toga!

Q. Why do people break bread but fix a meal?

A. They fix a meal *because* they have broken bread. When you break bread with one of your friends, with a guest or even a stranger who has come to visit, it is very rude to glue or staple the bread back together. Once broken, it should remain that way. But maybe you don't like broken things in your house. Perhaps you have been brought up to prefer whole or at least mended objects in your home? The only answer is to leave the broken bread on the plate and go into the kitchen and fix something that isn't yet broken. Namely, a meal. If you fix something that wasn't broken, then it cancels out the broken thing. The fixed meal negates the broken bread. All is well again! There's a saying that some people like a lot, "If it isn't broken, don't fix it," but if the bread is broken and you are fastidious then fix an unbroken meal. All will be good and serene afterwards. I suggest you fix a southern curry, one with coconut milk, mustard seeds, onions, red chillies, mango, lime, and other vegetables. You don't need a spanner to fix such a meal. Kitchen tools are adequate.

Q. Is it true that the devil is in the detail?

A. Yes, this is absolutely true, and I am scared of the devil, which is why I don't care about details. I would give you the details of *why* I don't care, but I daren't. So it will have to remain a generalised proposition. My fear of detail is why I never examine a document or anything else with a fine tooth comb. For one thing, to make a comb out of teeth seems grotesque to me. For another,

168

there are very few people here with fine teeth. They ruined them on badly fixed meals.

Q. Is fire alive?

A. Certainly it is. It fulfils all the criteria necessary for something to be defined as a living entity. It grows and dies, it reproduces by spreading, it needs oxygen to live, it tries desperately to survive for as long as it can. If you spark a flint or strike a match you are a creator, a father, a mother, a mad scientist, a demiurge. The flame rises and regards you as a god. Then it dies. You think nothing of this, you are unaware of your enormous responsibilities. Poor little flame! If only it could have licked a dry sheet of paper, a hollow reed, a few wood shavings. Then it would have grown up properly and fulfilled its destiny. You could have felt pride in its life. But no, you struck that match in an idle moment, then blew it out, let it drop to the floor. And you never realised it was a corpse! You sparked that flint because you had nothing better to do. Then you blinked at the bright instantaneous glow and laughed. And you never realised it was a soul trying to be born that you obstructed.

Q. Do you have a solution to the problem of evil?

A. Yes, I do. If God exists, why does he permit evil and suffering in the world? The answer is connected to percentages again. It is always percentages. You live your life and it is a painful one. Everything goes wrong. Your loved ones are slaughtered, your home is destroyed, you are prostrate with grief. Then they come for you too, torture you to death over many days, even weeks. What a dreadful ordeal your life was! How can there possibly be a good, kind and loving God if such awful things are permitted to happen? Well, think of it this way. You die horribly and then you go to heaven. In heaven you are immortal. Forget my earlier objections to immortality. That was quite a different question. Your entire life on Earth was one of suffering, but in heaven it's an afterlife of bliss. And that afterlife lasts a lot longer than your mortal life did. Let's say your life on Earth lasts 50 years. After 50 years in heaven, your mortal life will be only 50% of your existence so far. After 100 years in heaven, your mortal life will be only 33.333% of your existence. And the percentage goes down and down. You are going to be in heaven *forever*, remember! After one thousand years in heaven, your mortal life is now only 5% of your total existence. After five thousand years it's only 1%. After a million years it is only 0.005%. And it keeps going down. The percentage of your total existence spent in pain gets smaller and smaller and therefore more and more insignificant. Because you will be in heaven for eternity, the percentage will tend towards zero. When it reaches zero, this will be the equivalent of your life on earth having no significance whatsoever, of not happening. And while you remain in heaven, closer and closer to zero will this percentage become. The pain will fade to something negligible and then to nothing. When it is nothing it will be cancelled out, which is the same as saying *it never happened* in the first place. That's what heaven does to you. It changes the past. It means that the problem of evil is only a problem at the moment. One day in the far future, evil will no longer exist, but more than this, it never will have existed in the first place. It will be retroactively nullified. Thanks to the power of the percentages. Thanks to them.

Q. Is life getting better or worse?

A. There is no easy answer to that because you haven't asked me a proper question. It depends on perspectives, of course. Generally speaking, fewer people die in wars in our present age than they did in the past, but we live in a polluted environment with a very real risk of the total collapse of our civilisation in the next couple of decades. I do have a few notions about the past I can share with you. The Middle Ages were a time of crisis. I can't help wondering that if they had been called something else they might have been more settled. Crises and Middle Age are naturally paired. Men often talk about a 'midlife crisis'. If those ages had been called The Still Quite Young Ages or The Slightly More Mature and Much More Sensible Ages there probably wouldn't have been plagues and torture. The Middle Ages was a bad choice of name from the start. And names *are* important. When you know the name, you know the essence. I truly believe that. Names provide information. It's very strange when people say "too much information" in a disapproving way. Civilization, science and power are based on having as much information as possible.

Q. Are you too clever for your own good?

A. I am frequently told that I am "too clever by half" but that accusation is very silly. If I am indeed too clever by half, then I am too clever by 50%, which means that I am 150% as clever as I should be. This surely means that the accuser wants me to reduce my cleverness by 33.333% to get it back to 100%, but to reduce it by such a precise amount I will have to be cleverer than I am, because that's a very tricky operation. To judge such a fraction accurately requires *supreme* intelligence and I don't quite have that. I am merely an extraordinary genius. So the accuser wants me to be *more* clever than I am. That is the logical outcome of saying that someone is too clever by half. It is not an appeal for a reduction in intelligence, as one might suppose it to be, but the opposite of that. Consider the consequences.

Q. Will the human race ever reach the stars?

A. I might as well confess that I don't like spaceships. Yes, the mathematics of thrust are interesting; but if we ever reach the stars it won't be that way. We will have to do it in spirit form. The distances are too vast. I am not talking about short jaunts within our solar-system but the dream of reaching the planets of other solar-systems. I think the best way to visit the planets of those distant stars is to simulate in the laboratory every possible combination of gravity and pressure and atmosphere on a variety of potential 'worlds', or run those simulations as a computer program and wait to see what alien life forms emerge. Then we will be able to talk with them without having to travel anywhere but it will be the same as if we had gone there. It's true that the created aliens might not be the same as those living on any real planet, but they will be aliens anyway and we should learn to think that's good enough. After all, it is any aliens that we want to talk to, isn't it? Are we really so fussy that only specific aliens will do? I don't believe so. We just need aliens to talk to, to get it out of our system. Even artificial aliens will do, so computer simulations are the way forward. And after we have chatted with the aliens we can get on with doing more important things like drinking cappuccinos with our best friends.

Q. Do you have many best friends?

A. Frabjal Troose of Moonville is a good friend of mine. Aardvark Caesar is a good friend of mine. The mayor of Dangle Custard is a good friend of mine. Kurt Flingers is a good friend of mine. Zwicky Fingers is a good friend of mine. Gaston Thumper Bonesoup is a good friend of mine. Bigley Button is a good friend of mine. Miranda Snorri is a good friend of mine, when she's awake. Charlton Radish is a good friend of mine. Lily Croissant is a good friend of mine. Humpty Ovoid is a good friend of mine, when he's not broken. Sunny Winters is a good friend of mine, when the season is right for it. Wilson the Clockwork Man is a good friend of mine, when he has been wound up. Ralph Mustard is a good friend of mine, at any time of day or night. The Bat Monkey of Rango is a good friend of mine. Now think about yourself. *You* may well be a good friend of mine too. Who knows?

Q. Thank you very much, Mr Aristotle.

A. Call me by my first name. It will be fine. I think we are on first name terms now. I am happy and satisfied, I'm just Dandy.

~

Rhys Hughes was born in 1966 in Wales but has lived in many countries and currently shares his time between Britain and Kenya. His first book, Worming the Harpy, *was published in 1995 and since that time he has had more than fifty books and nine hundred short stories published in ten different languages. His most recent books include* Arms Against a Sea, Facets of Faraway *and* Better the Devil. *He is currently working on a collection of experimental fictions,* Comfy Rascals, *a book of stories in verse form,* Corybantic Fulgours, *a volume of short plays,* The Dangerous Strangeness, *and his first book of essays,* Bullshit with Footnotes. *He cites his main literary influences as Calvino, Barthelme and Vian, but reviewers prefer to compare his work to that of R.A. Lafferty, whom he has never read. A vegetarian most of his life, he delights in coconuts and tropical fruits. He has different coloured eyes and slightly crooked teeth. He enjoys climbing high mountains.*

GAIA'S BREATH
Susan York

Climbing the steep and narrow spiral staircase while trying to keep a mug of nettle tea steady isn't the easiest task, but it's one I'm well accustomed to. Cliff turns away from the crenulations of the Observation Tower as I reach the top.

"Thanks, Bee," he says, taking the mug in both hands as if they were cold despite the humidity. Across the water towards the Wolds, Gaia's breath is whipping grey clouds, scudding them across the sky. I lick my finger and hold it up. Today She is blowing from the North. Sipping his tea, Cliff grunts in appreciation.

"The latest farmer brought honey."

"Did he say which farm?" he asks.

I shrug. "One of the orchards. Those with him brought fruit."

Cliff keeps his eyes on the land between here and the hills. The castle our tribe lives in has been surrounded by water since before I was born. Nothing remains of the once thriving city below the steep roads that rise out of the lake, or the farmland and towns my mother told me used to exist before the Great Flood. Many years passed before the land between here and the saltmarshes, bordering the sea, was reclaimed to grow crops, nurture bees and support wildlife. Now, those who work on the farms are coming here.

"There's no room for any more people. We need all the garden area the castle's got to feed those of us already here."

"Despite what they bring?" I ask.

"Yes. There's only so much you can carry on foot and not many have cars." He points across the water to a lone vehicle on the far shore. "They're useless once they run out of power. The nearest charging bays are on the farms and, if what we're hearing is true, it's not safe to go there." He pauses, then says, "We can't raid those farms anymore, so need to be self-sufficient."

I can only agree. Sleeping and feeding extra bodies is difficult in the confined space of our walls. The prison cells we live in

174

number under a hundred and they're stacked over two floors. The ground floor of the building is used for storage and holds various workshops, plus there is a kitchen and an area we gather in to eat. I place my arm around his waist. Cliff leans his hard body against mine and we stand together for a moment.

"Who's taking care of Holly?" Cliff asks.

"Fern."

Taking his eyes off the far shore, Cliff looks at me. His bushy eyebrows rise high in his craggy forehead. "Fern? Well I never." He once again looks towards the Wolds.

"She sees a future for Holly. Others don't."

A brief nod is all the acknowledgement I get as Cliff shades his eyes with his right hand. After focusing intently on the distance he says, "Tell Heather to send two boats. Our Hunters return and they've got four others with them."

I head down the steep stairs until I reach the castle walkway. Heather is in the grounds praying to Gaia. The altar of our Goddess stands near the gardens we till and plant from seeds stolen, in the past, from the now stricken farms. It is fitting that where we worship our deity is close to the soil amidst all this stone, for Gaia is a living entity.

Disrupting someone at prayer is never a thankful task, but Heather merely sighs.

"What meat were the hunters carrying?" she asks.

"Cliff didn't say."

The direct stare I get tells me I should know. Heather folds her arms below her breasts saying, "Let's hope they've got more than a few rabbits and hares. There's plenty of wildlife now, but it won't be long before it's as scarce as before, scarcer maybe." She abruptly walks away, heading towards the castle gate to pass the message on and arrange a greeting party. Heather's back is straight and her long plait swings with the sway of her hips. Despite this suggestion of femininity, she is physically commanding, tall and muscular.

Heather is right. Although the land to the East is full of game, like the farmers, it is fleeing and dying. Around the fire, our hunters tell of dead animals, blistered bodies and makeshift graves

175

as they draw near the road leading to the coast. Cliff is on the Observatory Tower not just to watch for strangers and returning hunters, he's there to alert us when the threat draws near. Problem is, we have no idea what the threat is.

*

Fern smiles as I enter the square cell which is my home. It is one of a few corner rooms which are big enough in the prison complex to house a family. Once, the rooms and corridors were painted cream. They would have reflected the sun when it streamed in through the tall arched windows at each end of the building, through the smaller windows in each cell. The black wrought iron staircases between the floors, would have gleamed. Once, the prison would have been full of light. Now, most of the paint has flaked off revealing dull grey stone beneath; curved iron staircases are tinged with orange rust. When the sun does shine through what remains of the windows, the building hums with an oppressive dullness.

Placing a finger against her lips, Fern rises from Holly's bed and joins me by the door. "Holly's just fallen asleep. She loves learning the old tales, but it tires her." Fern glances at my daughter and smiles affectionately. Her face crinkles into deep lines. Fern longed for a child of her own, but that time is gone and she has chosen Holly as her successor.

"Cliff and I are grateful you're teaching her."

Fern grips my arms with firm hands and pulls me into the narrow corridor.

"She must live. Without a Storyteller the old tales will die. Bring Holly to the fireside tonight. Let her hear me tell the tale I'm teaching her so I can see how much of it she knows."

Although the words are quietly spoken, Fern's passion for her trade is undeniable, the fervour in her eyes plain. When her grip relaxes, I hug her.

"I pray to Gaia every day that she'll get well. I know you do the same. Gaia's blessings on you, Fern."

The older woman pulls away, patting my shoulder. We understand each other, Fern and I.

I cross to Holly's bed. My daughter is one of the few children

176

born in the past decade. She has pushed the coarse woollen cover down to her waist. Her fingers are bone thin, her body skeletal and much of her skin is so pale it appears translucent. Her lungs rattle and wheeze as she breathes, they're terribly congested. But, Holly's spirit is strong. Gently moving her brown hair aside, I check her forehead with the back of my hand. She is cooler than this morning. Perhaps her fever has broken. Pressing my lips against the flush of her cheek, I offer a silent prayer to Gaia. Cliff and I have hidden our fear and worry. Nonetheless it is there. It eats away at us.

*

Despite the warmth of the evening, I've wrapped Holly in a thick blanket. Hope and pleasure run through me in equal measures as Holly woke from her afternoon sleep with an appetite. I helped her to wash, to change her clothes and I've brushed her hair. She is weak and, occasionally, a hacking cough rises from deep within her chest making her body spasm. Sometimes she brings up thick, green matter. Cliff's smile as he crouches before Holly erases the shadow of worry from his weather-worn face.

"Are you ready?"

"Yes Da."

Holly grins as he swoops her upwards, nestles her against his shoulder and carries her down the rusting iron staircase.

Turning left out of the prison entrance, we make our way up the steep slope to Lucy's Tower. An arch has been cut into the stone that encircles a small grass area. A fire has been lit to ward off encroaching darkness and torches are placed at intervals along the high castle walls. Fern waves us over, patting the ground beside her. We sit. Cliff places Holly between us.

A hum of conversation buzzes in the air. Most of our hunters are present, as are those who work in the garden, kitchen, or workshops. Other children also sit with their parents. Then there are the four brought across the water by our hunters earlier today. What strikes me most about them, is how well fed they look. I doubt they've ever known true hunger. Their clothing is made from bamboo, contrasting sharply with the leathers and furs we wear. They all look subdued and I think this is because once we, the people their government labelled 'Outcasts', were the ones asking for help. Or taking it.

Heather stands to speak and the voices cease. "Welcome all, including those who arrived today seeking safe harbour. To them I say that what we discuss at the fireside is aimed at keeping everyone informed of matters which may impact upon the tribe. This is not the place for disputes. Those you bring to me at the appointed time. Does anyone wish to speak?"

Our head hunter, Hawk, nods. Heather extends her hand, then sits near the fire as Hawk gets to his feet.

"Myself and other hunters know these newcomers are running from something, but we don't know what it is, or how to deal with it. I'm a pious man. I worship Gaia. As a hunter I never take more than She can sustain, whether it's roots, berries or game." Hawk pauses, takes a deep breath, then says, "One of those we brought back with us today is a scientist."

An angry murmur runs through the crowd. I see looks of disgust cast, not just at those new to our tribe, but also at Hawk.

"Sit down, man, before you make a complete fool of yourself," someone shouts from behind me.

Hawk's features harden, making his beak of a nose more prominent. His voice rings out. "We would be fools if we didn't get the facts. All I'm saying is that science might help us understand what's going on."

One of the newcomers looks at Hawk and nods. He extends his hand. I cannot take my eyes off the woman as she stands. She's even taller than Heather and, like our leader, has strength in her bearing. Full lips part and the woman speaks.

"My name is Elena and yes, I'm a scientist, but those with me are not. They are farmers and a hunter. My speciality is synthetic biology. If it weren't for the work of my predecessors, you wouldn't have crops in the garden you've cultivated. Like your hunter, I want to survive. We all want to survive, so I'll tell you what I think is happening.

"The history books say that scientists tried to find a way to prevent further acidification of the oceans, but couldn't. A few days ago, a gas formed over the North Sea. It looks as if a mist sits on the water but, on dry land, it has no colour. You cannot see it, but you can smell it and from the way it blisters skin, I'd say the gas contains sulphur dioxide. If I'm right, you don't want to breathe it in. When the wind blows it inland, this gas kills everything in its path. That's why we're here. To survive, we need to stay away from the gas."

Silence greets her words then falls into noisy disarray. Stunned by what I've heard, I pull Holly close, feel Cliff's arms surround us both. His eyes, when the shouting stops and we draw apart, are bleak.

From her place by the fire, Heather says, "Are you suggesting we should be ready to leave?"

Elena nods. "Yes. I'd get ready. We weren't prepared. You can tell if the gas is nearby not just by its smell, but from how it makes your skin and eyes sting. Also, you must take cover when it rains. I was on my father's farm testing crops because, over the past few weeks, the rain has steadily become more acidic."

Heather stands. "Well, that would mean leaving the safety of these walls. Still, we have enough boats if we need to." She pauses for a moment then says, "We follow Gaia here. As leader of this tribe, I will pray to her for guidance. This is our home and I wonder if Gaia's breath would carry this gas over enough land to breach its walls."

Cries of agreement rebound off stone.

"But I will tell those of you who have arrived in the past few days this. If you cannot follow my lead, my orders, you can take what belongs to you and go."

Cliff tugs me and Holly to our feet. Most of the tribe are already on theirs. Illuminated by torches and firelight, fists are punching the air, accompanied by a tribal roar. Looking satisfied, Heather says, "We are done talking. It's time for a tale."

I and others sit back down as Fern walks towards the fire. Holding her hands above her head for silence, Fern says, "Now is a fitting time for this tale." I struggle to read her face in the flickering flames, but her eyes are glinting like sparks from a forge. My insides clench. She's up to something. Fern circles the burning wood, arms level with her shoulders, fingers clicking. I, and the

179

rest of my tribe, clap in time. "For this is the tale of Gaia and the Maiden."

A cry of approval meets her announcement.

"Is this the tale Fern's been teaching you?" I quietly ask Holly. She shakes her head. My stomach sinks. The fresh faced scientist may find herself outside the castle gates once Fern is done. As more logs are thrown on the fire I glance at Elena. She looks unperturbed, but the slim woman beside her is reaching for Elena's hand as if she knows what's to come. Fern begins.

"Long, long ago the world came into being and she was called Gaia. Life flourished and intelligent creatures developed. Aeons passed and one creature began to purvey all around him with a sense of ownership. However, Man was a selfish beast, taking from Gaia without thought; her coal, her trees, her stone. Many creatures lived in Gaia's forests, thrived in her oceans and rivers. Man saw fit to organise and treat these creatures as his own. Hunting, killing and eating the flesh of another animal is part of the natural order, but Man ignored how Gaia, both within and without, held things in balance. A balance which kept the wheels of life turning.

"Instead of working with Gaia, Man explored every inch and every crevice of her being; learning and applying what he found to create a world which drained Gaia's resources so badly, she began to cry out. But, Gaia's voice was swallowed by industrial noise."

Fern's voice rises and falls. Her expressive hands and body sweep in and out of gestures and postures, creating a rhythmic, lyrical form captivating her audience.

"For years Gaia's voice went unheeded. There were those who thought something was amiss, but they also struggled to be heard. After all, Man was flourishing as a species. His numbers grew and his inventions harnessed power into a matrix which surrounded Gaia, encompassed her.

"With her polar ice caps melting and species important to the balance of her entity becoming extinct, Gaia began to scream. She screamed gales and tornadoes, brought floods and droughts, warning Man of what was to come if he didn't change. Some heard and they began harnessing power from Gaia's breath, from the sun above her, but it was not enough. Gaia realised she needed someone to speak in her name. Someone who would make all of mankind listen. She began calling for such a person."

Fern pauses. She looks around at her audience and softly asks, "And who heard Gaia's call?"

"A child," several voices speak in unison. Holly is leaning forward, mirroring the body language of others, responding to the question.

"And what did this child do?"

"She spoke on Gaia's behalf."

"And what did this child become?"

"A warrior! Gaia's Maiden!" Holly shouts. Her cheeks glow, her eyes are sparkling.

"Holly speaks truly, for this is what the child became. She fought long and hard to try and bring the world to a better place where Gaia could recover, from the damage Man had wrought upon her. She told the mothers and fathers of her time they had betrayed their children. Said they were leaving behind a world unable to support life. Other children, on hearing her words, joined Gaia's Maiden in peaceful protests outside places of learning. Before long, the Maiden had an army by her side.

"Gaia's Maiden showed no fear in the face of her enemies. There were those who decried her prophecies, for after all, how could a child be right?"

Beside me, Holly tenses as Fern falls silent. Everyone in Lucy's Tower seems to be holding their breath. Fern speaks and the intensity of her performance increases as the story reaches its climax.

"The prophecies came true. Gaia's breath ravaged homes, heat-waves burnt the land, scorching new deserts on the surface of Gaia's domain. Sea levels rose, drowning millions of people. Those who said the Maiden was wrong cried out in terror, 'Why did we not listen!' they said, for it appeared all was lost. And, if it were not for those who heard Gaia's plea in the Maiden's voice, all would have been lost. These followers of Gaia persuaded the world to make changes.

"Now we live in a time where we aim to achieve a balance

between Gaia's needs and our survival. If along the way we ever feel tempted by how industry and science once served Man, the tale of Gaia's Maiden and her battle to save this world is there to remind us to abide by Gaia's balance."

Fern bows and I join those clapping and cheering. She truly is an artist, but inside I'm horrified at the way she has stigmatised the female scientist. Holly throws off her blanket and gets to her feet. She dances with excitement as this is what she now dreams of doing, of being.

A fresh log is thrown upon the fire. It is damp and the smoke fills the circular space. Holly chokes, doubles over and begins coughing. The harsh, hacking sound causes those near us to move back. It's not long before all that can be heard is Holly wheezing, gasping for breath. She claws at my clothing, then pulls her own down from her throat. Fear and desperation is in her eyes, its scent is on her skin. Quickly, I lower her to the ground, sit her upright as the branch catches fully in the heat of the flames and the smoke begins to clear. Rubbing her back, I say, "Breathe, Holly. Try to stay calm and breathe."

Her face is pale and her eyes bulge as her lips turn blue. She's about to pass out. A large space has formed around us.

"You shouldn't have brought a sick child to the fireside." Heather sounds furious.

"For Gaia's sake!" A voice exclaims, "What the child has isn't catching. It's a reaction to the smoke, that's all."

The woman sitting with Elena comes towards Holly and I. She looks exasperated as she bends over, yet her voice is tranquil. "I'm Lauren. Come, let's get her inside." She scoops the blanket off the ground as I lift Holly. Cliff nods at me and I know he is staying to hear what is said. If it weren't for his sight, we'd have been cast out by now. Straightening up, I carry Holly out of Lucy's Tower. I can feel Heather's disapproval boring a hole in my back.

*

Once Holly recovers, Lauren tips her over the side of the bed onto some pillows.

"This is to drain the matter in her lungs," she explains. "We'll leave her for a while, then I'll show you what to do next."

Lauren looks to be around my own age, twenty eight summers. Like most women, she ties her long hair back. Her movements are consistent with her frame, small and concise. Lauren's face is oval with a wide mouth. I can tell she smiles frequently from the crinkles at the corners of her eyes. I get us both a mug of water from the jug we keep in our room.

"Did you work on the farm long?" I ask, passing the water to her.

"Thank you. I only arrived this spring. I struggle to stay in one place."

I wait for her to say more, then realise she doesn't know if it's safe to speak. "I'm sorry for what happened earlier, the story Fern told."

"You have a strong leader and an excellent storyteller." A moment passes then Lauren shakes her head saying, "Those of us Heather has taken in know just how right Elena is. The things we've seen." She shudders, drains her cup then places it next to the jug. "How many winters is Holly?"

"Ten this year."

Lauren looks at my daughter. "She may grow out of this. I've seen it happen before. While I'm here, I'll teach her some exercises so she can breathe more deeply. They'll help."

Tears prickle. "I don't know how to thank you."

Lauren smiles. "There's no need. Come, let's see to Holly."

Holly has fallen asleep, but as Lauren and I gently patter our hands up and down her sides she wakes. This loosens the matter and Holly easily coughs it out. On seeing how much the process has removed from her lungs I feel slightly sick.

Lauren makes to leave. "Do this every morning before she gets out of bed. Will you both be here tomorrow after breakfast? Good, I'll see you then."

After she closes the door I tuck Holly in. She's soon asleep. Lying on the bed Cliff and I share, I cry. For the first time since she became ill, I feel Holly may live beyond childhood. I can't wait to tell Cliff.

I am woken by someone gently shaking me.

"We need to talk," Cliff says, gesturing outside the room.

Together we sit on the floor of the corridor, our faces lit by moonlight. What he tells me makes my blood run cold.

*

I'm on my knees before Gaia's statue praying for the strength to face what's to come when Heather says, "Get up, Bee. I need to speak to you."

Inside I'm screaming at her. I want to hurt her for the things she said to Cliff, but I make certain my expression is blank as I stand and face her.

"Are you working today?"

"Yes, in the gardens."

"Before you go, it's come to my attention that Fern is teaching your daughter to be a Storyteller."

"Yes," I say, "Cliff and I are honoured she's chosen Holly."

Heather's face is stern. "I don't consider Holly suitable. I've told Fern she is to train Primrose. Your daughter will not be given any further lessons. Now, leave me. I'm still seeking guidance from Gaia and wish to be alone."

Heather kneels to pray before I can respond. Fuming, I take the pathway to the gardens. I'm only able to work this afternoon because Fern is with Holly. My feet stop and I groan. I may not always like how sneaky Fern is, but teaching Holly when she's been told not to is a dangerous game.

*

Gaia's breath has been calm for several days and the sun fierce. Crops are ripening faster than we can pick them. Holly and I practice her breathing exercises each morning then walk to the gardens and work. She is beginning to recover. Her lungs are clearer, she's not so breathless and the dry heat of the day seems to help. Like the others, I stop work when the sun is high then return to pick crops in the late afternoon. Children of Holly's age aren't expected to work all day, so the lessons with Fern have been continuing while most of us rest.

Tribe members talk excitedly, about the bounty Gaia has blessed us with, as I make my way towards the Observatory Tower. I join Cliff on its uppermost turret where the heat of the day is lessened by Gaia gently blowing a cool breeze. The tops of the bamboo trees near Cobb's Tower are moving slightly.

"This weather won't last much longer," says Cliff.

I scan the sky. There's no sign of a storm.

"How do you know?"

"The breeze." He points past the cathedral ruins towards the coast. "It's coming from the East and is picking up pace. Gaia's gathering breath. She'll be blowing strong by tomorrow morning."

"Oh Mother, the gas." The words croak out as if I'm already struggling to breathe.

Cliff cups my face with his hands. Deep brown eyes hold mine as he says, "I'll keep an eye on things here. You go tell Heather we've not got much time. She needs to advise the tribe."

*

By next morning Gaia is blowing in earnest and sullen clouds skitter westwards. Heather calls the tribe together. Cliff, Holly and I are waiting near the arch to Lucy's Tower when she arrives. Heather stands on one of the slopes leading out of the tower that are part of the walkway around the castle walls. She looks tired. Strands of loose hair are blowing around her face.

"I have spoken to Gaia at length and prayed for guidance, yet she has not given me a clear answer. There are those among you I have also spoken to."

Heather indicates Elena, the farmers who sought sanctuary and a number of our hunters. But not Hawk. She doesn't include Hawk.

"Days have passed since the last newcomers arrived of which scientist Elena was one. I can only assume others have gone elsewhere or are dead. Yesterday, some of our hunters went towards the East Coast. They told me they could smell the gas on reaching the road over the Wolds to the farmlands, but it was faint. My decision is that we'll wait and see how close Gaia's breath brings the gas by tomorrow. If we cannot smell it at sun up, I will send hunters to find where the gas has reached. This gives us more time to prepare, but we only leave if we must. To those who feel unable to stay within these walls another night, you may take some food from our stores, use our boats. The castle gates will shut at midday."

Heather stands before us looking as impassive as the statue of Gaia she prays to. Then she is gone, leaving her people to decide for themselves.

Cliff and I know what we're doing. We discussed it the night Holly collapsed, the night Heather called him out in front of the tribe. She told him I was not pulling my weight and Holly would never survive another winter. If I wasn't back working a full day by the start of autumn, she would cast us both out. Cliff was to stay. He was a valuable member of her tribe and she would give him a healthy child. Knowing we needed time, Cliff said he would consider her offer and give an answer before the end of summer.

In the moonlit corridor Cliff held me tight, kissed the tears which flowed and told me, "We're leaving, Bee. No matter what Heather says, you and Holly are my life."

We've been waiting for the right time and this is it. I just wish the gas didn't exist.

*

Before we go, Cliff, Holly and I pay one last visit to the Observatory Tower. The three of us stand looking towards the Wolds. The landscape is beautiful despite what lies just beyond the hills. Then we gather our belongings, the food we're allowed to take and begin our walk down Steep Hill, past decaying buildings and crumbling walls, to where the boats are kept.

Lauren is there with Elena by her side, along with Fern who gives Holly a hug. A shout from behind tells me Hawk is on his way.

"We'll take two boats," Hawk tells us, "We won't all fit in one."

"Are any others coming?" asks Elena

"A few might," Hawk says, "but those I spoke to thought what Heather said made sense. Where's the rest of your family?"

"They decided to stay until tomorrow." Elena looks worried. Lauren takes her by the hand and helps her into one of the sturdy bamboo boats tethered by hooks fixed on the side of a building. The boat sways slightly as they settle, then Hawk hands Elena their three packs and his bow. She puts them in the stern. Cliff and I place the remaining packs and Cliff's own bow in the other boat, then we help Holly and Fern get in. Hawk unties the ropes, pushes us off, then sees to the boat he is using.

"We should head west, Hawk," Cliff says.

"Anywhere away from this gas sounds good to me."

Hawk begins to row across the water, telling Cliff which way to turn to navigate the ruins just below the surface. I notice Elena leaning towards Lauren who gathers her in and holds her close. Behind me, Fern and Holly have their heads together, no doubt reciting a tale. Cliff focuses on rowing, in putting as much distance between us and the castle as possible. Gaia begins to blow fiercely. The surface of the water forms rippling waves, rocking the boats. I watch the castle until it is gone from sight.

As the sun lowers, we pull the boats aground and make camp. Hawk goes hunting and soon the smell of rabbit and vegetables, cooking in a pot over the fire, is making my mouth water. The exertion of the day means each of us eats well, but there's little conversation. Gaia's breath has blown long and hard all afternoon. I find myself praying for Her to quieten, to ease the fear each of us holds inside by returning to the calm summer days that lulled us before yesterday's awakening. Lauren takes the first watch. I nestle myself against Cliff, holding Holly in my arms. I fall asleep listening to the quiet wheeze she makes, the rustling of leaves blown on the trees and wildlife moving through the bushes.

*

I've lost track of how long we've been on the move. Every night, we set up camp. I used to hear animals moving in the dark. Not anymore. When day breaks I wake and listen for birdsong, yet the space we occupy is shrouded by silence. Cliff says we must keep going, keep ahead of the wind. Every morning, he checks to see which way we need to go. This is what guides us each day.

The smell of the gas is always present, faint or otherwise. Holly is our early warning system. If the air we're breathing becomes worse, she feels it first. I listen to Holly gasping for breath as her father carries her at the front of our slow procession and wish there was some way I could ease her suffering.

When Cliff speaks to me, the first thing I notice is his red eyes. His voice has changed too. He now rasps his words and I miss the soft tone he used to speak with. Hawk struggles to find game, let alone catch it. Each of us has red skin from the rain, as if we'd been scalded by hot water, but Hawk has blisters from where he's wandered too far into the gas. His eyes now water constantly and he often vomits blood. Before long he'll be too weak to walk. Fern grumbles about how she should have stayed and taught Primrose. She frequently wipes blood away from her nose. It is a slow, but constant, trickle. The love Elena and Lauren have for each other keeps them going, one step at a time.

Sometimes, we come across others like ourselves. They warn us of places to avoid and we do the same for them. I have seen the dead and decaying land lying beneath this invisible enemy that draws ever closer. Other travellers may join us for a short time, but our most frequent companion on this journey has been rain. Holly's cries when it hits her face cut me worse than any knife could. We rush to take cover when it falls, but the once green canopies of the trees we shelter under have turned brown. The grass beneath our feet is dying and the rain is making leaves and berries inedible. We dig roots from the ground, only to find they've rotted in the soil.

At night I hear prayers asking Gaia to spare us, desperate conversations between lovers hoping they will be fortunate enough to survive. Cliff tells me Gaia will recover her sense of balance, allow us to live and flourish in a manner that is acceptable to Her.

I no longer pray. I no longer hope. There's no point if what we need to live is being destroyed. Like the animals and birds I am silent. I know Gaia is smothering the life she created, so she can be reborn.

~

Susan York lives on the East Coast of England with her husband and cat, Pippin who has trained his owners well. Since deciding to focus on her writing, Susan has had two short stories published. The Little Lighter Girl *appeared in* Night Light *(2018);* Taking Flight *was in* Hellfire Crossroads 7 – Introducing *(2019). Both anthologies were edited by Trevor Denyer and published by Midnight Street Press. Seven of Susan's poems were published in* Organic Inc Volume 2, *published by Dragon Soul Press (2019). She is delighted to be published for a third time and hopes you enjoy* Gaia's Breath.

DESCENT INTO THE ARCHIVES
Dennis Mombauer

"We require the Tirani correspondence from the archives. Do not open it. Do not read it. Bring it to us."

The instruction came from the fax machine line by line, accompanied by toneless buzzing. M. watched the paper, searching for a way to escape this assignment, but there was none. The instruction was in writing, addressed to him, and signed with the luminescent sigil of management. He shivered. This was his station of duty; he had nowhere else to go. It had taken him two years to get this job, and he had debts. If he stopped paying, bad things would happen fast.

The printer finished its work, and M. pulled the sheet out to read again. It had been postmarked as "urgent," and "urgent" meant dropping everything, immediately, without delay.

"I have to get some files." M. waved to his office partner V. on the way out. She looked up with surprise.

"Get some files?" Her eyes narrowed, "From where?"

"Yes." M. had to force the words out. "From the archives."

V. pressed her lips together and frowned. "Are you serious? Really? It's a personal instruction? You can't refuse?" She took a heavy purse from her desk drawer and threw it to him. "Here, take this. Use it to return, please."

*

M. buttoned his jacket and took the first step. The staircase was wide and well lit, but with every level, the windows became lower and dustier, the illumination sparser.

M. clutched the purse in his pocket and cast one last glance out the windows before he descended beneath street level. Plaster flaked off the walls like dandruff, and where the stairs turned a corner, spiderwebs glittered in the ceiling's high edges.

M. climbed down level after level until he reached the lowest landing, the terminus of the staircase. A door with three locks blocked the only exit, and a bearded man sat next to it on a chair.

"Hi, how are you? I need to enter the archives." M. brandished the fax from management, but the man didn't bat an eye.

"Sorry. I have an order not to let anyone from upstairs in, only archive staff. You must find someone to bring out your file."

It sounded so tempting. M. had no desire to go into the archives, he just needed to keep his job. Where would he go without it? How would he pay anything? "Is there someone who could do it?"

"Not this week. The last group of archive drones went in yesterday, they won't be out for a while."

"I can't wait a week." M. pounded his finger on the paper and felt it tingle as it touched the sigil. Management must know this, but they had sent him anyway. This file must be important. "Look, it's urgent."

"What can be urgent about a file from the archives? It's all just heaps of paperwork, isn't it? And paper is patient."

"I don't know why this file is important. I only know I have to get it. Can't you make an exception and let me through?" M. knew he shouldn't, but what choice did he have? "I can pay you."

"You have coins?"

M. raised the purse and jingled with it.

"Meh." The bearded man sighed and pulled a set of keys from his pocket. "But this stays between us, right?"

*

The archives stretched around M. as far as he could see. Ring binders lined the branching hallways, their backs labeled with letters and dates, with months, years, centuries.

Paper dust hung in the air like plankton and settled on M's skin, causing him to itch all over. He headed as straight as possible and followed the hallways down into the past.

Clumps of entangled chits and sticky notes had overgrown the floor, rasping against his legs with every step. In the unsteady tube lights, the shadows contorted around him and seemed to reveal new junctions and side corridors with every step. The sooner he got out again, the better.

The archive vaults extended in endless flights of chambers and connecting passages, stripping M. of any sense of direction.

At the next crossroads, he found a coin box attached to an old-fashioned CVT monitor. He had never entered the archives, but he had heard of these things. His throat dried up as he weighed V.'s purse in his hand and found it lighter than he remembered.

He took out a coin, kissed it, then inserted it into the slot. If he turned back, he would lose his job, and his job was all he had.

The coin rattled through the machine before the monitor flickered to life. It showed M. as a blinking dot and the ever-changing archive maze extending around him. According to the legend, yellow hallways housed contracts, commitments, and covenants, pacts and pledges, bonds and depositions; red corridors contained invoices and IOUs; brown ones pickled flesh and preservation jars.

M. moved his finger over the vast colored sectors and their spiderwebs of interconnected lines. Graphite: inanimate objects and instruments, autonomous artifacts and installations. Magenta: stone tablets and sarcophagi, turnscrews and Vitruvian cuneiform.

Where was it? The CVT monitor would turn off any second, and M. still didn't know where to go. The fonts grew tinier and tinier, the abbreviations of sectors and sub-sectors ever more complicated.

There. Pale Maya blue: correspondence and communiques, letter mail and messages. The monitor went blank.

M. took a deep breath, coughed on the dust, and walked. He had seen enough to know the general direction and headed toward it with long strides.

*

M. wished he had company or at least music, but he only heard the distant sounds of steps, doors snapping shut, and clattering typewriters. He couldn't see a soul, just concrete and paper, cold brightness, and an eternity of files.

How should he find the Tirani correspondence? M. stopped at another coin box and fed it from the purse. The colors had changed, the legend scrambled. He frantically searched the map. Left branch of the corridor, clockwise down the staircases.

Arrows were glued between the filing cabinets, but their directions didn't correspond to the corridors of the archive maze, pointing at nothing or straight into the ground.

M. had never been clear about the nature of the archives, but he had lost colleagues to them. They had been on missions from management and failed to return. According to the official memorandum, they had "stopped working" here, and no one had asked any more questions.

*

After what felt like hours of walking and dispensing coins, M. entered a hall whose exits were barred by wooden fence gates and padlocks.

"Hello?" M. rattled at a fence. "Is anyone here?"

"Yes…" A voice answered him, little more than a hoarse echo. "We can hear you… We can help you…"

It was a choir of calls from different directions, and soon, M. discovered their source: figures shuffled toward him with gaunt faces and dust-encrusted fingers, reaching out for him through the wooden slats.

"Who are you?" M. wrinkled his nose at their stench of musk and mummification.

The answer came in an assortment of voices, "We work here."

"Employed."

"Employed."

"We maintain the archives."

"We sort."

"We file."

"We failed upstairs."

"They transferred us here."

"Did you bring us something?"

"Do you have a task for us?"

M. stared at the archive workers crowding behind the fences. "I need the Tirani correspondence. Can you give it to me?"

The workers responded in unison again, "Ekal Tirani. Oh, oh. This is a matter for the bosses, a matter for the archive executives. We cannot give you the file."

"Can you show me the way?"

"Oh, oh. We can guide you, to the office elders, the ancestors, the board of the archives. But not for free."

"I understand." Paying these creatures was the same as paying the coin boxes, wasn't it? The purse had grown so light, but what could M. do? His coins ran dangerously low, but if he paid them, it should still be enough to get back.

Keys jangled as the archive workers unlocked the gateways and encircled M. "Follow us, follow us. We will bring you to your file."

*

The archive people led M. with blabbering voices along the identical corridors, which they seemed to be able to tell apart from the tiniest of features.

The environment changed. Step by step, everything became older and more faded, seemed to sink below the waves of a sepia sea. Folders sat on the shelves in colors that M. had never seen, labeled not mechanically but by hand or with stencils.

Bundles of paper filled the bordering halls to the ceiling, and M. thought he even saw scrolls and clay tablets among them.

"Oh, oh. We cannot escort you any farther, not farther than here."

M. nodded and cast a last glance at the trembling figures. If he looked closer, maybe he could recognize someone, but for what purpose?

He pressed on alone toward a heavy door. Locked filing cabinets and drawers lined the walls, a masonry of dull metal and keyholes. A faint noise emanated from them, the rustling of trapped files and moaning folders.

"Hello? I'm here to pick up the Tirani correspondence for upstairs. For management. Can I come in?"

*

The door swung open before M. and revealed a chamber with a stone shaft where the floor should have been. It plummeted into an emptiness shrouded by fumes.

"What you seek is here," a polyphonic whisper floated up with the fumes. "What you seek will stay here. Once in the archives, forever in the archives. There is no way back."

"But I need this file, urgently." M. had no intention to

193

negotiate. His job depended on this file, and he would fulfill his duty. "It is for management."

"We do not care. We are the ancestors of the office, the eldest and most ancient. Heed our words."

"You must have needed correspondences in the past yourself, don't you remember? Old dossiers for reference, receipts for transactions, documents for conversations? Memoranda?"

Silence.

"And what difference does it make? Even if I take this file upstairs with me now, it will sooner or later find its way here again. Sooner or later, everything finds its way here, doesn't it? Because all paperwork trickles down into the archives."

"We remember. We remember the odor of wealth. The perfume of profit. We are prepared for an exchange. Ten coins for Ekal Tirani. No more and no less."

M. clenched his fingers around the purse in his pocket. He had eleven coins left. It had taken him ten to get here.

"We can smell it. We know you have it. Ekal Tirani, ten coins. We remember worth. We remember value."

M. tried to swallow, but the inside of his mouth had dried up and left not a drop of saliva. How would he get back without coins? If he returned without the file, management would call him to the board room. Would they fire him, over a missing correspondence?

M. straightened himself. They would, without hesitation. They would fire or transfer him, and he didn't know what was worse.

"One. Two. Three." M. threw coins into the shaft and watched them vanish without a sound. "Four. Five. Six. Seven." He had to rummage for the last ones. "Eight. Nine. Ten."

A leathery claw reached up from the abyss and handed something to M., "We have counted. Take this folder. Don't look inside it. Go."

*

The archive staff vanished, and M. had only one coin left. The passages shifted again and huge mechanisms labored in the distance, turning and bending the maze according to their incomprehensible designs.

M. stopped at the first coin box and turned the last coin in his hands. Either he got out with this, or he was lost forever. He inserted the coin and studied the map as it appeared. Where was the exit? His heart hammered, his breathing accelerated. He was inside the black heart of the archives, and the colored sectors extended everywhere with no end in sight.

He found the staircase and charted the direction, marching as fast as he could while the memory remained fresh. The junctions rotated, the hallways rose and fell. He was out of breath and stopped at another navigation monitor. He had no more coins left and he was nowhere near the exit.

M. sank down against the wall and sat on the dust-choked floor. All that effort for one small folder...the Tirani correspondence couldn't be substantial. But this wasn't about the actual correspondence, was it? It was about him stranded in the archives even though he had done nothing wrong. Even though he had always completed his work.

What was so special about this damn folder? And what reason could there be not to look inside? Who could punish him if he perished here? What punishment could be worse?

Sitting on the floor, M. opened the folder, loosened the clamp, and started to read. He browsed rotten and decomposed pages, impossible dates, letter columns that contorted over the paper like strings of insects locked together.

Despite himself, M. sprung into motion and immediately stood up. Like a sleepwalker, his legs followed the letters' convoluted path, carrying him forward at their command — but where, where to? Did he even pay attention to the way anymore? The correspondence wanted to get out, M. could feel it.

M. tried to flip the folder shut, but his arms didn't obey him. His ears rang with whispers of Ekal Tirani and of escape, of hidden staircases and secret backdoors. M. looked from one featureless hallway to the next and marched without knowing the difference.

The twisted letters of the correspondence burrowed through M.'s brain and dripped like sweat into his eyes, overlaying the crossroads with glowing blueprints.

M. stopped at a door, and the correspondence folder closed.

He blinked while he caught his breath, and then his heart skipped a beat.

This was the entrance and the exit, the threshold of the archives. This was the way out: back up to the office, or to a different place entirely.

~

Dennis Mombauer currently lives in Colombo as a researcher and as a writer of weird fiction and textual experiments. His research is focused on ecosystem-based adaptation and sustainable development as well as other topics related to climate change. He is co-publisher of a German magazine for experimental fiction: Die Novelle – Magazine for Experimentalism, *and has published fiction and non-fiction in various magazines and anthologies. His first English novel,* The Fertile Clay *will be published by Nightscape Press in 2020.*

Homepage: www.dennismombauer.com /
Twitter: @DMombauer

THE FIRST (AND LAST) NATIONAL ROAD CANOE RACE
David Cledon

At the end of a cold, dreary week in February, they laid down rubber outside Mr Murdoe's white stone cottage. Overnight, what many had dismissed as a ludicrous, costly distraction finally became reality.

In the pre-dawn twilight, workmen unwound two sets of giant rubber tubes from drums that reached higher than his roof, each nestling into its kerb, edging the tarmac'd road. With some effort (because, frankly, everything was an effort these days), Mr Murdoe pulled on his coat, and hobbled down the treacherously uneven flagstone path for a closer inspection. Still deflated, each tube lay flat and inert, an alien, ominous presence in this quiet residential suburb. Four feet wide, they formed a thick, ridged carpet of rubber stretching as far as the eye could see along the road.

Mr Murdoe prodded one with his walking stick. The material felt tough and industrial. It gave off an unpleasantly sharp smell like cleaning chemicals.

He turned first to his right tracing the black lines until they disappeared over the slight brow of hill back towards town - then left, where they curved through the gates of the William F. Stokes Municipal Park and Recreation Ground. Nearby, a boy of no more than seven or eight brandished a stick roughly whittled to a spike, jabbing it repeatedly into a section of tubing, seemingly with no effect. His clothes were stained and dishevelled; most likely a runaway or one of the abandoned. In turn, the boy was being watched by an equally scruffy mongrel sitting forlornly at his feet.

Mr Murdoe considered reprimanding the boy, but then thought better of it. What did it matter, after all? It seemed unlikely something so insubstantial as a sharp stick would do much damage. And if it did, why would he care?

Why indeed.

Mr Murdoe shook his head, certain that only a few months back, he would not have let such things go. But things had been different then.

Moving with a certain stiffness, he set off slowly in the direction of the park. *His* park, dammit! And wasn't that the central point, the nub of his anger? No one else had lobbied the council like he had, got them to rejuvenate this scrubby patch of land. Or campaigned for a new play area, or organised local volunteers to help with the landscaping and plant up the shrubbery, had they? Oh, he knew what they said about him behind his back, alright... That curmudgeonly old guy with the perpetual scowl - but he knew how to get things done and that was what mattered.

And now –

Soon it would all be gone, lost to the floods like something straight out of the bible - except this was no act of god.

He needed to see for himself. His walking stick clattered against the pavement, sending a fresh jolt of pain through his hip.

A moment later, the boy and the dog followed at a distance.

*

They showed him his marshalling station from the minibus; a simple, numbered post-and-flag hammered into the grass bank. He and the ten other volunteers for this sector stared out of the window. Yet again, Hugh wondered exactly what was expected of him.

"It's pretty remote," the driver said, doubtfully. "You got a phone?"

Hugh did, although he doubted the network was good for much, particularly away from built-up areas. These days, everything was flakey. Nobody cared about stuff anymore - and who could blame them?

The driver leaned across to prod Hugh in the arm. "Don't screw up, all right? This is important. - For some of us, anyway." Hugh nodded. The man sounded like his father.

The next day, he cycled back for a closer look. It was more remote than he'd realised, vast ploughed fields stretching off to the west, a strip of woodland shadowing the road on its eastern side. Cycling along between the two great strips of rubber, it was eerily quiet without the usual rush of traffic. Then as the main road began to climb, the course dived off left down a minor road. Over the decades, its surface must have gradually sunk below the level of the surrounding fields. Now it was hemmed in by tall, grassy banks topped with prickly hedgerows.

A natural channel.

The inflatable tubes ('bumpers' the driver had called them) weren't needed. Here and there metal or plastic-coated boards had been fixed in place over field drains, run-offs and other potential breaches, and sealed with hot tar. Some kind of plastic binding substance had been sprayed onto the more exposed sections of grass bank. The lane wound for a couple of miles, gently descending towards the urban sprawl of the town at the end of the valley. This would be his patch, his responsibility for the duration.

Hugh scrambled to the top of the verge, four or five feet above the level of the road. He breathed in the cold air and tried to picture how it would look in just a few days' time.

Madness, utter madness.

And suddenly he couldn't wait.

*

By race day, more than two hundred competitors had arrived - even more than the organisers had dared hope - though some had little more than rubber inflatables and no ambition beyond getting through the starting gate without capsizing. The serious competitors in their neoprene suits, head-gear and custom-designed mono-hulls, were held in a separate, roped off group near the starter's position. When the klaxon sounded, they would be first away, first onto the smooth water leaving the amateurs to battle it out in the crowded channel behind. For them, it mattered that there was a race to be won. Professional pride was at stake.

Everyone else was just glad of the distraction.

*

The pumps that had rumbled and clattered for hour after hour, fell silent. There were dozens of them strung out along the hundred mile course, drawing water from the designated rivers, lakes and reservoirs. Slowly, the rubber snakes had come alive, swelling up, their bottom halves belling out with the weight of water, forming the race channel itself.

It was nearly time.

*

The parking lot was gone. Here and there, signs for disabled parking bays and exit markers rose incongruously from the water like the timbers of old shipwrecks. Around its perimeter, tiered banks of seating rose vertiginously, almost encircling the makeshift starting arena.

Leon tried to blank it all out, tried to forget about the spectators, the TV audiences, and what lay ahead. Space was at a premium in the starting pens. Even the professionals were struggling to hold position and avoid colliding. Nobody wanted to risk a cracked hull before the start.

It was even worse amongst the throng of amateurs where contact was more or less unavoidable. Leon did his best to hold position at the edge of the pack. Only the knowledge of the live TV feed beaming out around the world stopped him from being physically sick. Maybe Steff had been right: this was nothing but a stupid, self-indulgent stunt. But he'd refused to listen when she'd begged him to stay with her for the remaining days. She'd wanted to barricade the doors and forget the world outside. That wasn't his way, though. Too defeatist. How could she not want to find a way to fight back? *Because there is no way, Leon*, she had said quietly. *And because I'm not weak like you. Yes--weak, because you can't accept things for how they are.* So he had channelled all his anger and energy into long hours of training and preparation. But when he'd closed the door on her this morning, stepping out into the pre-dawn darkness, it had felt as if the end had already come. A final gesture. He didn't suppose there was a way back now.

"Move further away, idiot!" One of the red-tabarded pros was shouting at him, a vaguely Nordic-looking man with a gaunt, weather-tanned face and blond hair. "Don't get so close to the barrier." But the choppy water and jockeying craft made it virtually impossible to comply. The man leaned out, putting the tip of his paddle against the nose of Leon's kayak and pushed hard. Leon's kayak shot back from the float-barrier, cracking into two or three others behind.

Nice.

Red number five, Leon thought. *I'll remember you.*

*

Mr Murdoe felt something tug at his sleeve. The dishevelled boy was looking up at him. "Feel it," the boy said. Reluctantly, Mr Murdoe laid a hand on the smooth, hard rubber of the bumper. The tarmac base of the channel was still dry between its erect walls. Everything was ready; expectant. But through the rubber he could feel the little vibrations now, as if the barrier were thrumming with some kind of energy.

"Mister? They're coming, aren't they?" the boy said. "They're really coming?"

Mr Murdoe nodded briefly in agreement. They really were.

*

Leon heard the klaxon, felt the surge of water as the gates on the holding pool opened, joining them with the main channel at last. He got in one decent stroke and then all was chaos. Currents swirled him this way and that, paddles and canoes thudded into each other, friendly banter and swearing filled the air, and all the while the tumultuous cheers of the crowd swamped him. The temporary stands were at capacity. The same number again had spilled into the dry holding areas, thronging roads, climbing trees, telegraph poles - anything to get some kind of view. And now a hundred thousand voices roared their encouragement and yelled with exuberance. It was as if a physical wave of sound was lifting Leon's kayak and buoying him forwards.

Manoeuvring was virtually impossible; all thought of tactics abandoned. He let the surge of water and craft carry him towards the starting gates, bumping and jostling. A teenage kid right next to him momentarily panicked and began to lose control. Off balance and rammed from the side by another craft, he capsized. The boy's head bobbed up a moment later but his canoe had already been swept through the gate and down the channel without him.

Now Leon's turn – He pushed clumsily through, fighting for

201

space. Then the water suddenly became smooth and fast, powered by the feeder channels from the giant reservoir out on the edge of the city. He was on his way!

He supposed he could have opted to just steer his kayak down the centre line, letting the current do the work. Instead Leon dug in hard, catching and passing a good few others. "How you gonna keep that up for a hundred miles, son?" someone called after him, but Leon only dug in harder. In his head he heard his stroke-rhythm pounding. That rhythm was all that mattered now. *Dig-pull. Dig-pull.*

Here and there, the channel narrowed, the retaining walls towering above as if trying to close up and create a tunnel. Along the wider sections spectators leaned over, waving flags, shouting encouragement; their words whipped away amidst the maelstrom of water and craft. He saw the glint of camera lenses tracking him. Steff had sworn she would not watch the TV coverage, wouldn't listen to the radio, turning their flat into a little bubble of isolation and indifference. Now he prayed she wouldn't do anything stupid in her loneliness. She had promised to wait, but too many promises had been broken of late.

He shook his head briefly to clear his vision and dug in harder.

*

The helicopter banked, forcing Deke against the harnesses that were already beginning to cut off circulation. He felt his stomach heave. He hated the flying-eye stint. He should have just called in sick.

And then he saw it.

For all the world it was like a giant length of glittering cable carelessly draped across the landscape, snaking its way through town and countryside.

He gestured to the pilot to come round again, and peered more closely. Ye gods! You could actually *see* the wavefront cascading down the channel, a pulse of shimmering water moving faster than the chopper could keep pace. Back in the city, the starting pens were dry again, just an urban parking lot once more, the white markings of the parking bays reappearing amidst the puddles.

And somewhere between the two... Yes, there! Tiny multicolored flecks borne along in a bubble of water, swooping and weaving around the gentle curves of the channel. Already the field was strung out over a mile or more, amoeba swarming in a tiny drop of water trickling down the channel. A blip. Ahead and behind, just dryness.

*

It came not in the boiling rush he had expected, but stealthily. The first tendrils of water crept into sight hugging the walls. Growing bolder, little rivulets quickly spread laterally across the channel while the outriders sped onwards. In seconds, the tarmac channel had become a collection of puddles, then the puddles were a rising pool of swirling water. Some people cheered. Mr Murdoe frowned hard.

And now came the first of the wavefronts, only inches high but a little curling, breaking wave of water sweeping from right to left. The wavelets kept coming, expanding, growing bolder. Mr Murdoe was shocked to see just how rapidly the level was rising in the channel – a foot already, now two feet. In front of his eyes, and just feet from his front door, a fast-flowing river was forming.

The boy clapped his hands once and made a noise that might have been a giggle. Mr Murdoe took a careful step back and turned away.

*

Just past the fifteen mile marker – a gruelling fifteen miles of hard, muscle-wrenching labour – Leon got the boost he needed. He passed a red tabard. Only the pros had them; blue for the rest of the field. That meant he'd worked his way into the tail-end of the pro-pack, maybe even within reach of the leaders.

It wasn't much, but it was something. He felt a small notch of pain and tiredness fall away.

One half of his world was bounded by the black channel walls. He propelled himself towards a distant point, always just out of reach, where the walls drew closer. He snatched breaths through the roiling, thrashing torrent of water and spray. He'd known that the first part of the course would be fast –the gradient relatively steep, minimal bends to break the powerful flow that was surging along the dry channel several miles ahead.

The other half of his world glided by as if in a dream. The tops of high rise offices and apartment blocks gave way to suburban rooftops, church spires, phone masts, dangling power cables and sometimes even tree-lined avenues arching overhead. Road signs flashed past to places he would never visit; traffic lights cycled pointlessly through their sequences as Leon passed underneath.

Around the twenty two mile marker, they hit proper countryside. The crowds thinned to the occasional perplexed-looking local. For long stretches there was nothing but sullen grey skies and the sound of churning water.

And then in the distance, he saw the first of the hills they would have to ascend.

*

Don't screw up. He remembered the driver's words clearly.

But Hugh was worried that he still might. He stood on the bank, watching the dark water rushing down the channel just below. The level had climbed relentlessly in the last few minutes, higher than he'd expected. He didn't like the way it tugged at the grass banks, nibbling away clods of earth, turning the downstream water dark and soupy. They ought to have protected the banks better, or maybe chosen a different route. Not his fault of course, but this was *his* sector now, *his* responsibility. The next Marshall was at least a mile further on.

But that wasn't all. Turning the other way, he looked again at the impromptu lake spreading across the neighbouring field. He could find no obvious breach in the bank but something wasn't right. Probably a field drain cover had popped its seals and come loose. Whatever the cause, it looked to be getting worse.

Suppose the escaping water scoured away the unprotected channel? If nothing was done, the whole bank could give way.

He checked his phone again. No signal. Somewhere not far off came the clatter of helicopters. The race was getting close. Soon they would be here.

Then he saw it, a little whirlpool shifting and dancing with the current, holding station just a few yards downstream –the kind of swirling pattern made when you pulled out a bath plug. Hugh edged closer. That darker patch beneath the water's surface –

could that be some kind of manhole cover shifted out of place? He thought it probably was.

No one had mentioned this in the briefing. It would be down to him to find a way to fix it. Maybe he'd only need to slide the cover back into place to stem the worst of it. That would be enough, wouldn't it? Enough to buy time until the racers had passed. Otherwise…

Don't screw up.

His father's voice this time, not the driver's.

He smiled grimly. *Even from beyond the grave, you're still judging me, aren't you, Dad? Well, small comfort, but this might be the last chance I get to prove myself to you, eh?*

Moving carefully, and threading his way both around and through the hedge, he found a fallen branch and stripped it back to a crude stick. Assuming the force of water had somehow dislodged the cover, he would need a lever of some kind to prise it back into place. The stick felt impossibly thin and brittle but there was nothing else.

Or he could do nothing. But they would have to abort the race if the bank gave way.

Not on his watch.

With one last worried glance at the time, he kicked off his shoes and lowered himself gingerly into the icy water.

*

Petersen had found his rhythm quickly and let it enfold him. He became one with it; his breathing, his movements, his thoughts. Everything meshed, just like in those long training sessions. He felt strong, mentally and physically. With his stroke rate nicely in the middle of his range, he angled the blades so that they bit deep for maximum efficiency. His kayak, the one with the red number five on its prow, surged forward. The race was his for the taking.

Yet still it was hard to concentrate. *You've got to forget all the baggage; forget where we are, why we're doing this. It's just another race.*

He felt a powerful urge was to pour everything into it, to power ahead for the distant finish but he would need to hold something back, conserve strength. There was no glory in leading the early stages; only the finish line mattered.

He badly wanted this victory - and that was good.

Just another race.

Except it wasn't really.

*

First came the wall of water.

Gone was the gentle gradient and current that had borne them along with relative ease. Now that current was met by a reverse flow – clattering pumps raising ten thousand gallons of water a minute to the crest of the hill where it was released in a torrent. Spillways either side of the channel diverted the overflow into temporary reservoirs where the cycle began again. Leon fought to maintain control as the little kayak bucked and spun in the turbulence, desperately manoeuvring to stay clear of the spillways.

As the channel climbed, he had to pull with every ounce of strength to battle the current and the gradient. Both were against him now. Despite the tireless work of the pumps, still there were dangerous shallows – in places barely a foot of water. Again and again Leon felt the blade of his paddle strike the tarmac road beneath. If the blade shattered, his race would be over. Sometimes it was the hull itself that scraped until he found deeper water.

But exhaustion was his principal enemy. Sweat and spray blurred his vision; a constant roaring filled his head. Ahead, another bend in the channel rose up: a dog-leg, the water actually spilling over the barrier leaving dangerous shallows on the apex of the curve. It took him long minutes to fight his way through only to see the next stage of the ascent rearing up.

Ahead was another racer, a little speck of red dancing amidst the currents, but too far away for him to make out the race number.

Leon imagined a little box; a watertight container. In his mind, he opened it and let all his fatigue and pain pour into it. He closed the lid carefully; locked it. Then he let his eyes focus on the gap between him and the racer up ahead and dug in harder.

*

Aerial panorama: Fields like checkerboards cut through with a twisting ribbon of silver edged with black. The image tilted, expanding as the director began a slow zoom.

Folks, we are witnessing a truly incredible sight. As you can see, the field is quite strung out now, those muscles really beginning to tire as the front-runners pass the halfway gate. It's a battle of wills from here, mental fitness every bit as important as physical stamina.

Deke paused to let the camera finish its close-up zoom, swooping in on a random competitor. The hi-res picture perfectly framed a grimace on the man's face, veins and sinews in his neck standing proud as he reached forward and worked his paddle again and again.

Look at that effort, folks. Look at that determination. There's a man who's not going to let anything get in the way of that finishing line. Just an ordinary guy. But unstoppable.

He flipped through his sheaf of notes until he found the matching number.

That's Leon Beresford, folks. 32 years old. He's – ok, was – a service technician with Karrimore Logistics. Now he's our very own hero of the moment. Says his reason for entering is… is…

Suddenly Deke couldn't go on. He left the mic open, let the background rumble of the chopper fill the broadcast. Who cared about any of this crap anyway? Why was he wasting his time when so little of it remained? Here he was, overweight, out of condition, virtually never having played sports since the day he left school, and yet right now, Deke would give anything to be down there taking part.

*

The milestone markers came and went. One half of his field of view changed sporadically: the occasional spectator, Marshall, or camera crew floating past. The black-walled channel, however, was a constant.

Here and there, low scaffolding had been erected across the channel, race officials leaning down to offer water and energy drinks. Leon grabbed one, rammed the teat into his mouth and tipped his head back, still not missing a stroke. When he was done, he spat away the empty bottle.

The shadows grew longer as the sun sank towards the horizon. They'd been racing eight hours or more, still another twenty miles left. His arms and legs were heavy lumps of meat running on autopilot; pulling, bracing, pulling. He'd almost forgotten how to do anything else. Now and again he let the kayak coast, snatching a brief respite, but always the channel beckoned him on.

Red-Five – it *had* to be, willed it do be – stayed tantalizingly out of touch. Sometimes he thought the gap had narrowed, yet he seemed to draw no closer. That was okay. He would reel him in slowly, pass him in a sprint finish along the final mile, if that's what it took. There was time enough.

And then Leon looked up.

Ahead, the glittering ribbon of water seemed to lift into the air a mile ahead, snaking up the escarpment to the ridge-line maybe five or six hundred feet above. On each of the switchback turns, the course narrowed, sphincter-like, channelling most of the reverse flow into vertical spillways. It left a gap wide enough for a single canoeist to pass through – if they could overcome the torrent of water and the mini-waterfall it created. Even from this distance, he could hear the throb of heavy machinery pumping thousands of gallons of water a minute up the hill, section by section. Leon counted six – no seven – such gates. At the summit, spectators had crowded into tiered stands, cheering each competitor who managed the seemingly impossible climb.

Leon gazed up at the final gate.

It might as well have been on the moon.

*

Shit. Cold. Hard to stay upright. Well what did you expect?

So bloody cold. Make this quick. Current's stronger than it looks. Afraid to move – Keep hold of bank, idiot, or the current will – Argh! There. Careful! Jesus, nearly lost my footing…

Fucking freezing now. Easy does it. Just a bit more. Whoa! Slowly, you dumb – Slowly. Something hard against my foot, now. That it? The drain cover? Legs feel numb, tingling. Need to reach… Oh, damn. Just some big rock. Water's so powerful. One more step to the left. Shit. SHIT! Nothing there! Like a giant plughole. Can't get my footing – Oh god. Current's dragging me down! So cold! Choking. Filling my nose and mouth. Boots jammed in something. Stuck like a cork stopper. Can't breathe – Oh god! Choking – Need to breathe somehow–

Sorry, Dad. You know I always tried my best, don't you?

*

Leon didn't look up. One gate at a time. *Look for the dead flow where the water's smoothest.*

He hung back from the first gate momentarily, then thrashed at it with power strokes, trying to judge his moment and the angle needed to get both through and above the rushing fall of water. Clumsily, he made it. He took a moment to steady his kayak on the other side, realised there was no time to hesitate without being swept out the side channels and into the catch-netting where the pumps laboured. Damn, but this was relentless. No respite, no moment to compose himself. All he could do was push ahead towards the next gate.

—And this section was steeper, the current stronger, the fall of water he must ascend impossibly high. He mustered what strength he could. Forget elegance, forget style. This had become a question of survival. *Like a leaping fucking salmon.* He scraped through the gate, flailed as he missed a couple of strokes, felt the surging water spin the kayak, momentarily wedging him across the gate, the current trying to capsize him. Instinctively he pushed back against the hard edge of the opening, managing to free the craft with desperate, panicky strokes but was now left with no option but to pull hard upstream towards the next gate.

He thought of Steff, sitting alone at home resolutely ignoring the TV coverage. *Like it or not, girl, this is for you.* She hadn't wanted him to come, had damn nearly done everything in her power to stop him. He'd come anyway, and that had finished things. He hadn't known what else to do – not that she would ever understand that. He wasn't the type to sit around whiling away the remaining days; he had to be out there, doing something. Anything.

Now it was too late to turn back, even if he wanted to. And as for Steff... Too late for regrets also, he supposed.

Well then.

Like the song said: *Done, done, onto the next one...*

Gate six, the penultimate one, damn nearly finished him. His strength was all but gone. At the third attempt, he scrambled through clumsily but caught the side-flow and his kayak was dragged backwards. He felt a crunch shudder through the hull, turned in time to see he'd collided with another kayak holding position just beyond the gate, catching a breather. They exchanged the briefest of glances, then both men were racing towards the final gate in a sprint for the narrow opening, Leon and the gaunt-faced man in Red-Five side by side.

There was nothing between them as they reached the narrow opening – except the vagaries of the current had nudged Leon's boat a little more centrally onto the gate. *Mine for the taking.*

But if he'd expected Red-Five to concede, he was mistaken. His adversary paddled furiously, fighting the rougher water away from the center channel, kayak bucking wildly. Almost on top of each other, both aimed for the opening.

Maybe it was an accident; there was no way to know for sure. Leon had a fleeting glimpse of Red-Five's paddle whirling towards him and then a sledge-hammer blow struck him across the jaw, pain exploding across his face. He felt his nose break, tasted blood in the back of his throat. As the edge of Red-Five's blade opened a long gash across his cheek he could already feel his left eye beginning to swell shut. For the briefest of moments, the universe seemed to recede.

Red-Five popped the gate. Leon took a moment to wipe blood from his one good eye, losing precious ground in those brief seconds. Then he powered through, drawing energy from the pain he felt.

Somewhere, as if far away on a distant world, crowds cheered.

*

Out in the wilds, they descended gently into a valley and the distant coastal city. Leon was on full autopilot, paddling without quite knowing how, whole stretches a blank in his memory with no recollection of how he had arrived where he was. Several Marshalls had tried to wave him into the side for medical attention, but Leon had ignored them. He was going to make the finishing line no matter what the cost.

The narrowing channel helped, the stronger current partly carrying him, hemmed in as they were by the natural banks with their pretty little hedgerows atop, and over-hanging trees closing up to make a green-tinted tunnel.

Leon glimpsed Red-Five ahead. He was still in touch but the man's lead now seemed unassailable. And yet…

The kayak bucked suddenly, hitting turbulent water, forcing Leon into panicky strokes. The prow snagged momentarily on something below the surface and he struggled for control in the awkward, churning current. For an instant, he thought he might capsize, his race ignominiously ended despite having come so far. Then he was through the strange little whirlpool. Off to his right he saw the temporary lake that had spread across the fields. They were lucky whatever breach had caused the escape of water hadn't collapsed the entire bank. Lucky indeed.

Then, still far in the distance, he saw the lines of flags and the crowd stands and the scaffolding with the lighting and TV cameras and, most importantly of all, the finishing line.

*

Mr Murdoe stood on the raised platform near the middle of the ruined park. Off to one side, the top of a seesaw and a child's swing poked incongruously above the rippling water. Behind him there was a roar, the crowd rising to their feet in the stands as another exhausted competitor struggled into sight. This kayak's fibreglass hull was battered and splintered. The man himself was in poor condition, blood smeared across his face, one eye blackened and closed up. As the racer crossed the finishing line, he lifted his paddle into the air in triumph, a splintered shaft on one side where the paddle had sheared away.

The crowd loved it.

Then from out of the crowd stepped a young woman, pushing her way through the throng and throwing her arms around the surprised man as he was helped from the boat. He looked stunned; overwhelmed. Their embrace seemed to last forever and the crowd cheered even louder.

Mr Murdoe looked down at the scruffy boy. The boy smiled tentatively up at him.

After a moment, Mr Murdoe smiled back. He took a small packet of biscuits from his pocket. He offered one to the boy and one to the dog, and they both accepted with gratitude. ~

David Cleden is a British author who won the James White Award and the Aeon Award (both competitions for new writers) and was a first place winner in the 2019 Writers of the Future. He has been published in Interzone, Electric Spec *and* Metaphorosis, *amongst others.*

Unlike most stories, the author clearly remembers the genesis of this particular tale. "I was slogging my way uphill on my bike in the pouring rain early one morning and was struck by the somewhat bizarre idea of how it might feel to be canoeing against the torrent of water instead of cycling – and what strange circumstances might bring about such a situation. I sketched out the lead character quite quickly and the rest, as they say, is his story."

THE HALLOWEEN PEOPLE
Michael Washburn

Owen Russell entered his little house. His feet made dull taps on the wood floor. The front door closed behind him with a snap and he felt really alone. He reached into his pockets and put his things into a basket by the piano: a wallet, a whistle, a plastic jar full of pills, and a scrap of paper with the local hospital's logo, ten scrawled digits, and the words, "Call this number if you have thoughts of harming yourself or others." Since leaving the hospital, he'd felt something close to okay, but now the emptiness and isolation of the house were faintly terrifying. It was unthinkable that he might have another panic attack like the one that made him fall and hit his head.

The so-called golden years aren't supposed to be an ordeal, Owen thought. People need company. But Owen's wife had died of cancer and his two good friends hadn't taken care of their bodies and now they were dead too. Owen's father, who was in his nineties now and whom Owen visited at a nursing home, had more human interactions on some days than Owen did.

Of course there were the bars. But a man his age sitting down at a bar counter, talking to people in their twenties and thirties, trying much too hard to be witty and charming, invited so much scorn that he'd almost rather ponder suicide in a lonely house.

For a man as hidebound and averse to new technologies as Owen to try to find love online was unlikely. Even using a mouse was tough. It was hard for him to follow the arrow amid the bright shapes, plus he had barely any idea what those represented or what to do with the arrow.

So here he was, without many choices. The empty house. The bars. The cinema that offered the illusion of being part of a community for a couple of hours. Or suicide.

He remembered his therapy. *Don't be idle! Don't lose focus! Fill your*

213

life with new interesting things. Keep moving, reaching, growing. Realizing that the clothes he had on were the same ones in which he'd entered the hospital, he went to his room to change. Then he decided to go out for a walk.

The streets were quiet and the air was cool. Owen walked a few blocks in the dusk, admiring the sturdy white houses with porch lights coming on one by one.

Up ahead, he glimpsed the broad porch of Rob Jackson's house. It was freshly painted and immaculate like the rest of the big building coming into relief through the gaps in the trees and bushes. Jackson was a successful attorney and a prominent figure. At a recent town hall meeting, Jackson had gotten up and called out Owen by name for daring to voice reservations about a plan to desegregate local schools through a busing program overseen by a federal judge. Owen took the utmost care to stress that he wasn't in any sense a racist, to distance himself from white nationalists, to explain that he just felt busing was coercive and unconstitutional and shut parents out of decisions about their kids' education. There are better ways to foster diversity, Owen argued. Jackson appeared to take this as a personal insult. He leapt from his chair, pointed his finger, said the town could do without reactionaries who tried to veil their hate, who cited the Constitution as if that document has any relevance to today's world, where a town's image depends heavily on how progressive it is. This town had a future and the white-haired man there in the third row, Owen Russell, was a dinosaur. People applauded and cheered.

No one sat on the porch of Jackson's house, but lights were on inside. Owen guessed that Jackson was dining with his family or maybe with investors. He moved up and crossed the street to the next block. Though Owen didn't know anyone on this block personally, he knew that a modest house in the middle of the block was the home of a pair of brothers who'd jeered and mocked Owen when he drove his Plymouth Road Runner on the street three months ago. Granted, it was a crappy old car, but he felt they had no right to mock him, given the age difference involved. But he didn't dare challenge them.

Four doors down was the house of a couple, Fred and June Garrett. Back during the days when Owen's father still lived with him in the little house, the couple had spotted Menroy walking around, the collar of his parka flipped outward, his white hair dirty and ragged, his cheeks and neck a mess of cuts and sore spots from when he'd tried to shave with his declining vision. The Garretts had contacted a social worker, Bennie Drayton, who showed up at Owen's door with a policeman, announcing that they wished to do a "wellness check" on Menroy. Despite not being able to tell them who was the U.S. president, Menroy passed the test. He even claimed to like Bennie, whose eager solicitude clearly made an impression. But in Owen's mind the humiliation burned. Just the fact that they'd sprung the test implied that Owen had failed in his duty as a son and a citizen, that he was neglectful or abusive toward a befuddled old man.

Adding to Owen's dismay, Bennie Drayton began visiting Menroy often. Owen couldn't keep Bennie out. Menroy claimed to enjoy Bennie's visits. For all Bennie's vigorous and friendly manner, the social worker kept making threats to bring real trouble if Owen got in the way. Now Menroy was in a retirement home, so Bennie's visits did not require any interaction with Owen. Even so, Owen wondered why Bennie's attitude to him seemed so layered. Bennie, half black half Cherokee, might well have resented him after that town hall meeting.

But Owen thought the hostility went back much further than that evening a few months ago. Maybe Owen was just old and paranoid.

Whatever the cause, Bennie didn't hesitate to criticize Owen, who had perhaps neglected Menroy's care somewhat in recent years. Owen resented having to spend a huge part of his retirement income to keep Menroy in the retirement home. But in truth Owen himself wasn't compos mentis all the time. His body and his mind were growing weaker. Sometimes he was so forgetful that when he left the house he didn't even push the front door all the way closed. Then there were the really scary thoughts that came sometimes about harming himself.

Owen had gotten so lost in his memories and musings that only now did he realize how dark it was. Still he felt restless and the thought of his empty house was unbearable. He kept walking east on Truman Avenue, crossing three more streets until he came to one of the biggest houses in town. Owen had heard that someone had bought the house a few months ago, done many renovations, and sold the property, making a profit of over a hundred grand. He didn't know who lived here now.

It was quiet all around him in the dark. He stood there admiring the symmetrical columns at the edges of the house's elegant wings and the neat rows of shingles partly covered by the leaves and branches of the great drooping elm in the front yard. A couple of lights were on inside. As he gazed through a large window close to the intersection's southeast corner, he knew he'd crossed a line, he was a voyeur. And he was Owen Russell, the very citizen who'd led a boycott of an adult bookstore years ago.

Owen had the bizarre thought that whoever lived in this house now might wish to hurt him. What a weird idea. He was getting stranger and stranger in his dotage. But the thought wouldn't go away.

As he stood there, anxious, frightened, expectant, it appeared that the universe wished to answer his curiosity. A fluttering motion in one of the windows caught his attention. It was not in the big window closest to him, but the window of a room at the side of the house parallel to Murphy Street. He caught a brief glimpse of bare flesh.

With an anxious look all around, he slid several paces down Murphy Street, watching the window. No motion met his eyes now but he'd seen something and his fear could not overcome his need to see it again. He stood there in the dark, panting, his heart pounding out blunt reminders of his frailty. Then there it was again. An arm, the edge of a torso, the curve of a slender leg greeted his eyes. Above the arm fell coils of dark curly hair.

Surely someone would notice him and there'd be huge trouble. He thought of turning and hurrying back up Truman Avenue. Now as the woman moved to the center of the space visible through the window, he knew that wasn't an option just yet. She was around thirty and had a preoccupied look as she rubbed some

216

kind of oil or cream across her torso. Then she moved out of his vision again, reappeared, and fiddled and fussed with the contents of a drawer or cabinet he couldn't see. He kept expecting her to turn her head and react with horror to the geezer standing outside, plainly visible, though the trees partly blocked the moonlight.

At last the woman vanished from the square of space and didn't return. Owen could no longer fend off his anxiety at the thought of someone spying him from one of the windows all around. He turned and nearly ran on Truman Avenue, thinking a heart attack would drop him any second.

His anxiety and fear didn't fade when he stood trembling in the front room of his house. He thought of his father, of all the times he'd lashed out at Menroy for voicing urges of a carnal nature. Owen didn't know all the things Menroy and Bennie talked about in their meetings, and he didn't want to know. But someone, somewhere had given Menroy the idea that such expressions were natural and healthy. Menroy appeared to think it was cute and funny to make Owen uneasy, to embarrass him with this kind of talk. Now, trembling and panting in the dark house, Owen knew his own conduct was no better.

Half an hour later, Owen lay his head down on a pillow, his hairy mass bisected by a blade of pale moonlight. For Owen sleep was a paradox. It terrified him even as it offered refuge from anxieties and traumas. The uncertainty as to whether he'd wake up was hard to bear.

In the dream that came now he was out walking again on the familiar tree-lined streets of the town, but it was colder out and the moon was higher and brighter, and the streets had a discrete navigable quality. A sense came now that the earth was more or less flat, it had always really been flat, and these lonely streets reached to the very ends of it under the luminous moon. He felt he couldn't help walking but it was a different restlessness that drove him now, a need to test his sense about the streets' extent. He walked and walked but never got anywhere. Then all went dark around him and he thought he was falling, and soon he was in a pitch-black place far removed from the scenes he knew and all he saw was a leering pumpkin face with a candle flickering inside.

Now he had an experience kind of like waking up. He was aware of the brightness and pervasiveness of white light. He was half-lying, half-crouching in great discomfort in a field of brittle and jagged objects. Clenching a few of them in his right fist, he saw that they were bones. All around him were bones, he was up to his waist in them, and they cut or scraped him as he shifted his body and tried to rise. Here was a desert of bones under a sere white sun that hurt his eyes when he looked up. Still he tried to claw and pull his way up out of the bones. Hearing loud, harsh laughs, he turned and looked to a point nearby and saw the face of Bennie Drayton, the social worker; yes, it was Bennie, the eye pouches and sagging jowls were unmistakable. Bennie found Owen's predicament funny.

The following evening, Owen stood in his desolate house wondering what to do. He made a decision, and cursed himself for giving in to urges like those he found so repellent in his father. Minutes later he was outside the big house on the corner of Truman and Murphy. He didn't have to wait long before the woman appeared in the window. Once again he saw her nude form in profile and she appeared to be busy with something or other just outside Owen's view. Owen guessed that here was her bedroom and she liked to take naps in the evenings.

He desperately hoped she'd turn her body toward the window so he could see a bit more of her than the night before. She seemed as preoccupied as ever with the object or objects in front of her, which he still couldn't see. For an absurd moment he thought of rapping on the window or throwing a rock just to get her to turn, just for one good look. Admiring her rich dark hair, her coyly arching brows, her luscious lips, Owen thought that somewhere, in this house or this town or another town, somewhere in the world, some man was luckier than anyone had a right to be.

"Hey! You there!"

Owen didn't know where the voice came from. He didn't allow himself a moment to look around, but took off up Truman Avenue in terror and alarm. Just now a heart attack was not the worst thing he could imagine. Had the caller addressed him? Almost certainly. Had the caller recognized him? "You there" is not a salutation that someone who knows you would use, but it was not a large town.

Sweating, panting, quivering, he half-walked and half-ran the blocks to his house. For all its loneliness the house at this moment represented order, safety. Owen told himself that in any event it would be pretty hard to prove that he'd acted with voyeuristic intent. He peeled off his clothes, fell onto the bed, and entered a dreamless sleep.

His time at the public library the next day was awful. He sat at a long table on the second floor, trembling, quivering, fidgeting, trying in vain to read a paper, thinking that every man, woman, teen, and child who passed by must be looking with interest at him.

Owen wished to resume his research on local history as soon as he calmed down a bit. He'd spent dozens of hours in the library's archives and records division, poring over microfilm and perusing many accounts of murders, abductions, lynchings, arsons, corruption scandals, and other features of the town's history. He'd amassed enough knowledge to conceive the broad outlines of a book.

But he decided he couldn't be at the library right now. Heads turned as Owen moved between the tables and reached the escalator. More people looked at him on the first floor as he hurried to the doors. Finally he was out in the cool air of late October. He hurried up the street, trampling fallen leaves, trying to look right ahead and not to notice anything beyond his path, until at last he reached Truman Avenue and had a straight shot to his house.

He was glad to be almost home but by a kind of mental reflex Owen told himself it was too early in the day to stop working. The sun was high and kids weren't yet clogging the roads after school.

He glimpsed Aubrey, the mailman, pushing his mail bags a few blocks away, where Dawes Street met Truman Street at the base of the hill. It occurred to Owen that he hadn't gotten any mail in weeks. Usually there was something, if only a PBA solicitation or a car insurance ad. This seemed odd. Owen waved, but Aubrey was too far away. By the time Owen got to his house, the mailman was up the hill out of sight.

Now Owen noticed something incredible.

The front door of his house was open.

Owen had neglected to close the door, forgetting his many warnings to himself about this matter. *Senile Owen strikes again.* He thought of calling the police, but guessed that a description of the pervert looking through the window on Murphy Street might be fresh in their minds. Besides, the door couldn't have been open for too long. From a certain point of view, it was good that he'd freaked out and left the library early.

He mounted the little front step and went inside. Now Owen found himself in the oddest position. He hoped to find the very emptiness that at times had made him suicidal.

"Hello?" Owen called out.

What a silly thing to say. There was only silence in the golden light coming through the windows. He moved out of the tiny foyer into the living room.

"Hello? Anyone? Hello!"

He moved through the living room and into the kitchen, and that was when he saw the dog. Here was an angry-looking Border Collie with dark brown fur coating its sleek body and its claws fully extended. The beast's gaze turned to meet his at precisely the moment he stepped into the room and peered into the space between the island and the sink. Maybe the dog had smelled the contents of the garbage bin in a compartment of the island.

Owen's first thought was that the dog was feral and dangerous, but then he noticed a collar and tag. He hoped desperately that this animal had learned to keep its conduct toward humans within certain parameters.

He took two steps back until his body met the wall opposite the sink. The dog growled and gazed at him with ferocious eyes. It moved toward him. Owen felt a warm stream running down his right leg. He looked around for an object to wield. The dog looked ready to pounce.

"Go away, please. Get out of here."

At this pitiful plea the dog growled again, a lower, longer noise. Then it trotted out of the kitchen, into the living room, through the little foyer, and out of the house.

Owen tried to compose himself. A heart attack was still possible. His terror turned to rage as he thought of the negligence of some jackass who'd let the dog run wild. Then another possibility arose in his mind. This was someone's way of saying, *So, you don't respect people's privacy, huh?*

He went outside. The dog was moving up Truman toward Dawes. He ambled after it. That dog had a tag and he was going to find out who the owner was. Without apparent effort, the dog strolled up the hill. Owen mounted the slope and began to pant and sweat. After advancing ten yards up Dawes, he thought he was going to fall down. He was too old for this. But the dog wasn't so far off now. It had passed Newbury and was approaching Mason.

The dog made a right onto Mason. It wasn't running, but moving with a kind of buoyancy, its flesh bouncing. He felt the dog was mocking him. Now it turned south onto Sutter's Lane, a tree-lined, dead-end street with a few of the quainter houses in town. Pursuing the dog even more desperately, Owen got within twenty feet, then ten, then five, and then he spotted the little girl standing on the sidewalk, a plastic whistle in her hand.

He advanced down the lane until the dog whirled and growled. But it didn't look so fierce now.

There was a time long ago when Owen could have read the animal's tag from where he stood.

"Is this your dog?"

She looked at him without answering.

"This dog was in my house! If it's yours, you're in big trouble. Is it?"

The girl kept looking at him, holding the whistle at her side.

"Answer me, little bitch. Is this your fucking dog?"

At last the girl reached the end of her thought process.

"You're mean old Mister Russell!"

So she knew exactly who he was and he, the adult, stood there howling like an idiot.

"*What is your goddamn name?*"

Still she didn't tell him. He lunged forward, his fear of the dog subsumed now in rage, and grabbed it by the collar. The girl came up to him.

"Let go of Jumper, you old meanie!"

She put both her hands on the dog as if to pull it away. With his free hand, Owen gave the girl a shove. She staggered backward, but did not fall down, and began to cry.

"Meanie! Old meanie!"

"I'm sorry. I didn't mean to push you. Just give me a moment here, please."

He crouched and pulled the collar toward himself. On it he read the name Matthews along with a local number. Now he recognized the girl. On Halloween the last couple of years, she'd come around trick-or-treating. He remembered opening his door and seeing this girl, partly concealed by her fairy costume, amid a gaggle of orcs, goblins, and skeletons, their parents standing on the sidewalk twelve yards away. Yes, here was little Kayla Matthews.

"Kayla, I'm sorry. I didn't mean to push you. Would you just stop fucking crying?"

But she kept sobbing.

"Meanie!" said Kayla a final time, and ran toward one of the houses on the little lane.

Owen made his way back through the late afternoon to his lonely house. He spent the evening drinking wine, watching the news, and cursing himself for his clumsiness in leaving the door open. In his old age he was just like a child.

The next morning, he felt kind of astonished when neither the police nor an outraged neighbor knocked on his door. He wondered what to do. It had been a long time now since he'd gone to see how his father was. But Owen didn't feel at all ready for the challenges of dealing with Menroy, for insults and provocations from the very person whose well-being he had to try to assure. Owen went out to the coffee shop at Broad and Tenth Streets and sat there for five hours, poring over old journals, revisiting notes he'd taken, working on an outline for the book. He ignored the looks from other patrons.

Making his way home through the late afternoon, he spotted the mailman again, pushing his bags. Owen wanted a word with Aubrey. He hurried up the street, panting, feeling his heart thud and sweat break out again.

"Hey, Aubrey! Hold on just a moment!"Aubrey continued up the street as if he hadn't heard. Owen despaired of catching up. Twenty yards away on the other side of the street stood a corner grocery. Owen needed shaving cream and beer.

He crossed the street and entered the store. The Bangladeshi clerk did not speak or smile as Owen moved past the register into the aisles. He found a can of shaving cream and continued down to the back. As soon as he emerged from the aisles into the beer and wine section, he heard a familiar voice.

"Owen. I'm sure worried about you. How much you drinkin' these days?"

With a turn to the right he gazed into the weathered face of Bennie Drayton, the social worker who'd become a father to Owen's father. Though Bennie was around Owen's age, he never evinced any of Owen's fear and anxiety. In the presence of this bluff, boisterous man, Owen felt all the more insecure.

Bennie was grinning. It wasn't clear how serious the question about Owen's drinking was.

"Hi Bennie. I don't know why you'd ask me a question when you know what I'm going to tell you."

The grin broadened.

"You seem awfully agitated, Owen."

"If you say so. You're the social worker."

"Are you okay?"

"Bennie. I really hate that question. It's condescending and invasive. Your job is to look after my dad, not to harass me."

"I'm not harassing you, Owen. I just want you to know you can come and talk to me. You're always stealin' around this town like you're a fugitive, like you're afraid people will find out somethin'. Some of us are getting really concerned, you know. We're not real sure of all the places you've gone or how you're holdin' up. Last time I was in your house, the fridge was full of stale junk and the oven had weeks of filth in it. Look me in the face and tell me I wouldn't find it the same way now."

"I don't like being spoken to this way."

"What way?"

"As if you're this Olympian figure judging who's healthy and who's not, who's legitimate and who's not."

"You just said I'm the social worker and I should know."

"I was looking for a way to end the conversation politely."

"You really should come and get some help, Owen. You're not just a racist, you're an ambulatory schizophrenic."

Owen had encountered that phrase somewhere before. It meant a person with mental health problems that are severe but don't quite call for institutionalization, or something like that.

"Go to hell, Bennie."

He pulled a bottle of beer from one of the fridges and turned to go.

"Don't forget to close the door," Bennie said.

"Why would I ever forget to close a door?"

"Never mind, I've got it."

Owen walked back to the cashier.

"Owen! You really shouldn't forget your father all the time. He thinks you're an ungrateful little runt," Bennie called.

The Bangladeshi clerk still did not speak or smile as the agitated old man paid and left the store.

As Owen walked home through the fading light he entertained the idea that Bennie knew nothing of recent events in Owen's life and had tried to offer a helpful suggestion.

When Owen woke the next day in a blaze of white light he decided he really had put off seeing his father long enough. After breakfast he called the retirement home and scheduled a visit.

He knew it had been way too long since he'd visited his father, and he didn't have the excuse that a lot of things made claims on his time. The visit he planned now was important enough for that reason alone. As he pondered the past week, it gained a whole other meaning. Owen reached a decision about his life. If there were things he needed to say to his father, this was the time to say them.

The halls of the retirement home were wide and bare. The pale light of late October streamed through the windows as Owen walked from the elevator to the double doors of Zone 3, which housed some of the frailer residents. When he entered Room 12, the aide smiled and stepped out of the room.

The ancient man lay there in the bed, bald, pale, and shriveled, his lower lip curved inward toward his teeth. To Owen this quirk gave Menroy a look of anger and contempt. Menroy's pajamas were thin and slight and left some of the hairiest parts of his body exposed. Owen wondered whether it was still true, as a nurse had told him months before, that Menroy spent only a few daylight hours in bed, indeed whether that had ever been true during Menroy's time here. A chronically bedridden person couldn't keep the strength to walk for long.

"Father."

Menroy looked at him, blinked once.

"I know I haven't been here often enough for you, and the fact that Bennie comes almost every day doesn't make it okay. I'm your son. He's still more or less a stranger to the family."

Menroy spoke.

"Bennie's my therapist."

Owen could not have counted the times he'd heard that terse sentence in the months since Bennie did a wellness check. Anytime he questioned any aspect of Bennie's role, Menroy said those words, implying a certain logic. *My therapist is responsible for my welfare. Everything I say or do from day to day has some bearing on physical and mental health. Hence my therapist can and should have oversight over every detail of my life.*

"Please remember that Bennie's not family and he should never take over your life. My mental powers haven't dimmed and I'm very much capable of managing things."

"That's your prejudice talking. Bennie is really on top of things. He helps order my life in a way I can't say that you've done for me, Owen."

Owen tried hard to stay calm.

"Look, I know how large a role Bennie plays, dad. I just meant to say, I wish I'd come to see you more often, just to inhabit the same space and breathe the same air as my father. It wouldn't matter what we talked about."

Menroy nodded faintly.

"I know that I've been really harsh to you and it went beyond 'tough love.' I lashed out at you for things that I'm not innocent

225

of myself, and that's what I'm having trouble forgiving myself for. So I want to apologize and to admit that I'm as vulnerable and susceptible and human as you are."

Menroy didn't reply but his eyes encouraged Owen to continue.

"I've got no reason now to keep anything to myself. I'm just as human as you are, dad, but I've been two-faced. You know, I passed by the house on Truman and Murphy, the one that got bought and resold recently, and I saw something in the window and I couldn't help but stop and watch. How do I reconcile that with all the nasty things I've said to you? Dad, I'm so sorry. I don't want one or both of us to go with you thinking I hate you or look down on you. I love you, dad."

Menroy wasn't too voluble nowadays, but his eyes widened in a way that dog owners think of as soulful.

Walking home from the facility, Owen reveled in his ability to bring off a positive meeting with a man he'd felt an urge at times to kill. The visit had been therapeutic, transformative. Of course he didn't want to leave the world now, when he was turning things around with his father and his skills as a historian were blooming.

As he neared his house, he spotted Aubrey once again on the street up ahead. Aubrey had finished delivering mail on Truman Street and was pushing his bags up Dawes Street.

Owen began to run. So what if he ran into Jumper and the dog tried to tear his throat out.

"Aubrey! Hey, stop!" Owen called as he panted and lurched up the sidewalk toward Dawes Street.

He ran further, calling louder. Though his run wasn't much faster than Aubrey's walk, he closed the distance. It did not seem possible that the mailman could fail to hear him at this distance, but Aubrey still didn't stop or slow.

Owen reached the base of the hill and started up. The slope was steep and the sun was fiercer than it had any right to be at this time of the year. Feeling sweat break out again, Owen wondered how that bastard dared ignore him.

"Aubrey!" he yelled as loud as he could.

At last the mailman paused, at the spot where Dawes met Newbury, and turned to look at the old-timer struggling to climb the hill. He grinned as Owen neared him.

"You all right, Owen?"

"No, not anymore. I've called to you several times in the past few days and you've ignored me."

"Well I didn't see you. I'm not the only Aubrey in the world, you know. For the record, there are three others in this zip code."

The mailman's tone was calm but on his face now was something close to a leer. Owen sweated and panted and it hurt a little to talk.

"But you didn't even turn around!"

Aubrey just looked at him.

"Never mind. What I want to know is why you haven't delivered any mail to my house in a long time now."

Aubrey's tone now would have been suitable for addressing a six-year-old.

"There must not have been any for you."

"But there's always junk mail at the very least. I haven't gotten a thing."

"Well, it looks like the world's turned its back on you, then."

The sun was in Owen's face now and he was still sweating. Unwelcome thoughts made their way back as he stood gazing at this public servant.

"Uh, Aubrey, tell me. Have you heard something about me that made you not want to do your job?"

Still Aubrey grinned at him without mirth.

"Found something out?"

"Yes."

"Owen. Is there anything about you that people haven't known for years?"

The sun was sere, brutal, and Owen's limbs felt so weak he thought he'd fall down.

"You insolent young man. I ought to bash your face in."

Aubrey's grin turned to a smirk.

"See, here's the real reason you haven't gotten any mail, Owen. You're much scarier than the most vicious dog in town."

"What?"

"Will you relax. I am joking."

"Have you heard anything about me?"

"Nope."

Owen had a rare moment of lucidity. He realized that the absence of mail went back well before the incident on Murphy Street. Aubrey might share a general low opinion of Owen, and Owen just wanted to shoot the messenger.

"Aubrey, I'm sorry… I'm really sorry I threatened you."

"It's all right, Owen. Whatever you may have done, I don't think you're long for this town."

Aubrey's laughter followed him as he hobbled down the hill.

He stood for three hours in his dark house, afraid to go to sleep and afraid to stay awake. When he gave in to exhaustion, he dreamed of a man who defied the expectations that shaped Halloween, the notion that you must become something or someone. He imagined a man with no face passing by his house as Owen sat looking out the window of his living room on a dreary afternoon. Here was an enemy, or just possibly, something Owen might one day become.

He spent a good part of the next few days trying to forget the run-in with Aubrey and to recapture the vibes that his visit with his father had given him. He knew he must never again be a voyeur, but there were other ways to fulfill needs. A Thursday was coming up. In Owen's experience, Thursday evening was a good time to visit bars.

When Owen stepped out in jeans and a blazer on Thursday, he noted right away that the weather was far more seasonal than it had been. The air was cool and the winds carried faint threats of force. Groups of kids in strange outfits moved from door to door. Owen belatedly realized that today was October 31.

Owen went east on Truman Street until he came to Hoyt Street, where he turned left and walked toward the edges of the little downtown. He passed Burke Street and Pittman Avenue and came to the wide stone patio at the entrance to Huntington Park. He had one more street to cross to get to the block full of trendy nightspots. But there, on the far side of Blount Street, he saw a gaggle of trick-or-treaters in an array of costumes.

He crossed the street, expecting the young people in his

immediate path to move aside and let him advance up Hoyt. They didn't. He couldn't see through the masks but people appeared to be looking at him with interest.

"Well if it isn't old man Russell," said a skeleton.

"On his way to hit on babes," said a big-bodied ogre with a bone through his nose.

Owen looked at them, trying to spot a tuft of hair or a dimple that might give away who they were. But they'd all covered up their physical quirks.

"Do you think Owen will attack us?" a nymph asked.

Freddy Krueger spoke up.

"Better get out of the way. Owen here gets physical pretty fast with people who piss him off."

"Look at you, in these horrible costumes! I've never been violent to another person in my life," Owen said.

"Owen. We know more about you than you know about yourself," said a skeleton, not the one who'd spoken before.

"That isn't saying much. You've probably forgotten far more than you know," said a ghoul with a green face and a dangling scarlet tongue.

"We could remind you of a few things," said a young man with a pumpkin head, through which fierce little eyes peered out.

"Be careful, this old-timer's got a fragile heart," said an orc.

Michael Myers, villain of the *Halloween* franchise, stepped forward.

"That was some shove you gave Kayla Matthews, old man. She's had nightmares ever since. Really brave of you, you know."

How much this incarnation of Michael Myers contrasted with the one onscreen, who didn't speak and relished doing violence to girls.

Next to speak was Jason Voorhees.

"Don't worry, I'm sure Owen here has the balls to dance with adults. Especially if they're non-white. Owen here is the town's resident dinosaur."

"Oh, that's not half of it," said Freddy Krueger.

"How dare you speak to me this way," said Owen, raising a fist.

But Freddy did not retreat.

"This old perv peers through the windows of houses at unsuspecting women!"

Owen lunged. The tormentor in the Freddy costume stepped back, laughing, as Owen tripped and fell down on the dusty pavement. The impact of the fall made the wind leave his body, and he lay there in agony, trying to suck in air, emitting little clicks.

Darth Vader stepped forward, his black robe fluttering in the breeze.

"What we have before us here is a relic of a place in the past that fully deserves to be obscure," said the Dark Lord of the Sith.

"Drift away on the breeze, pathetic old man," said Jason Voorhees.

Another trick-or-treater stepped forward. Here was Satan, or Beelzebub, or the Father of Lies, or some variant of the Devil's name. Owen preferred the last.

The Father of Lies spoke candidly.

"Owen. You think that life on no matter what terms is preferable to death. That's hardly an enlightened attitude. You'd do a huge favor to everyone if you killed yourself."

"How dare you speak this way to me!" Owen said.

"You can't be candid about your own urges and needs, old man. You condemn others for their carnality and then you lie touching yourself in a dark house no one else will enter."

These were fighting words, to be sure, but Owen felt too weak to get up. He resolved to speak the truth to the Father of Lies.

"I've reconciled with my father. We're on a new footing."

"No, Owen. That's not what he told me. He hates you."

Everyone laughed long and hard. Then the Father of Lies turned and walked south in the dimming light toward Truman Street.

Owen picked himself up and raised a menacing fist at his tormentors. He knew he couldn't fight them but that bastard in a Satan costume wasn't getting away. Owen hobbled after him, gasping and panting. His antagonist crossed three streets, reached Truman, and turned left, heading toward Murphy.

"Stop! You bastard!"

It was getting dark. Lights were on in the neat white houses.

Owen's vision was increasingly poor but he followed the red costume until it reached the big house at the corner of Murphy and went inside. Owen walked right up to the front door and began pounding.

"You bastard. How do you know my father? Let me in. I'm your elder and I want a word with you. Let me in right now!"

Owen stood there in the cool air, clenching his fists, ready to throttle the Devil. But there was only silence. He thought his heart would fail. He guessed the police would show up soon to take him away.

Then, to his astonishment, the front door opened and he saw the smiling face of the young woman he'd spied on.

"Owen. Please come in," she said.

He followed her through the lobby, then through a hall and into a living room with a plush scarlet couch and a big chandelier. Bennie Drayton and Rob Jackson got up from the couch.

"Owen. Welcome. I think the last time we saw each other was before Linda and I moved," Rob said, his voice identical to that of the Father of Lies.

"You got out of your costume fast," Owen said.

"How you doin', Owen? I see you've finally come to get some help," said Bennie.

Owen ignored this and replied to Rob.

"How do you know my father? How do you even know he's alive?"

Menroy Russell hobbled into the room with a cane, showing no surprise at his son's presence.

"It was good of you to let your father know about your interest in what went on in this house, Owen. That showed you could be honest for once. When Menroy mentioned this to Bennie, it was clear that he felt jealous. Bennie and I were able to arrange certain services for your dad," said Rob.

Linda smiled even more voluptuously.

Menroy had come here, for how many nights now, to see her in the nude. Owen groped for words.

"Why would you do that? What could my father possibly have offered you?"

Rob grinned.

"This is a progressive town, Owen, not a puritanical anachronism. But believe me when I say we had a vested interest in helping Menroy Russell."

Bennie spoke up.

"Your father's a man of means, or he was."

They all took evident pleasure in Owen's bewilderment. Bennie moved to a stand by the couch and picked up a small pile of papers.

"I've done a little more than counsel Menroy about his problems, Owen, though those were real enough, especially his ungrateful creep of a son. I've guided Menroy on all kinds of practical matters," Bennie said.

"What do you mean?" Owen asked.

"Take a minute. Read all this carefully. You may have wondered why you haven't gotten mail lately."

Owen took the papers and read through them. His eyes swelled in utter disbelief. Here was a document, signed by Menroy, granting Bennie power of attorney to represent Menroy in financial matters. Here was a reverse mortgage agreement with a company called Premium Finance, providing for the deposit of $60,000 into a new account set up for Menroy at a local bank. The agreement, signed by Menroy before the move to the retirement home, gave the lender a third of the equity in the house that Menroy owned; the house where Owen lived. Here also was a letter from the post office confirming the change of Menroy's mailing address from the house on Truman Street to a post office box.

There was more to read but Owen couldn't repress an outburst.

"You thief! You scum! Taking advantage of a sick confused old man!"

"No, Owen. I've acted in Menroy's best interest. Just ask him yourself," Bennie replied.

Owen turned to his father.

"Dad. Do you realize what all this means?" he said, brandishing the papers.

Menroy nodded.

"Bennie's my therapist."

To Owen everyone here was unspeakable, but if he'd a gun with two bullets right now, he would have shot his father twice.

"You might want to keep reading," Bennie said.

Here was something else: a letter from Premium Finance stating that because a payment on the gas for the house on Truman Street had not come in from the owner, Premium Finance had paid it and was to receive $750 per month toward the outstanding equity. *It really does pay to read the fine print in these agreements*, Owen thought, knowing that Menroy hadn't read a word.

There were more letters about unpaid utilities bills, and finally a series of letters, from Premium Finance and a law firm representing the lender, about foreclosure proceedings initiated in accordance with the agreement Menroy had signed. Even if Menroy had not violated the residency clause, the house now went to the lender. Everyone was to be out by November 15.

Owen looked at the leering faces of Bennie, Rob, Linda, and his father.

"You thieves. All I can say is, you better have some damn good lawyers."

Rob chuckled.

"Can you afford a lawyer, Owen? You couldn't even buy a K-Mart costume for this evening," Rob replied. It wasn't far from the truth.

"We don't need you here, Owen," said Bennie, and it was clear what he meant by *here*.

"Vanish, dinosaur," said Linda.

"You don't want to see or hear about any sexy stuff? Run home, Owen, it's way past your bedtime," said Menroy.

Menroy laughed much harder than Owen thought a man in his condition should, and the other three quickly joined in.

As Owen hurried home through the streets, he thought of the dirty gas range oven in his kitchen and knew what he would be for Halloween. He'd become the man with no face. The night was vast and cool all around him and indeed it was way past time for Owen Russell to sleep. ~

Michael Washburn is a Brooklyn-based writer and journalist

and the author, most recently, of When We're Grownups (2019) and Stranger, Stranger (2020). His short story Confessions of a Spook won Causeway Lit's 2018 fiction contest and another of his stories, My Role in the Rise of Julian Assange, received Adelaide Literary Magazine's 2019 fiction prize.

TONIGHT THE WORLD ENDS
Allen Ashley

Secret Hideaway

As Vaughan watched the private ferry depart, he reflected on the combination of luck and hard bargaining that had brought him, along with his wife Samantha and close friends, Deshawne and Natasha, to this secluded villa on the western reach of a mostly unmapped island tucked quietly within the Canaries. The messages continuing to pour out of the NASA Solar Observation Desk reaffirmed that Sol was about to scorch and consume its orbiting children. There had been a pause in the initial panic and Vaughan had used this time to escape – as much as one could when the world was going to end. At least find a quiet, private place to spend the last days or hours they had left. It amazed him that even with the catastrophe imminent, the waving of huge wads of cash could still open doors, buy seats on a plane, get favours done. Going to spend it in the afterlife, boys?

The ferry captain had taken Vaughan's late grandmother's golden wedding band as payment; a metal reputedly forged in the time of the original Big Bang, now about to return to its primordial liquidised state.

So at last they were here with a couple of bags each and some tens of thousands of precious seconds to while away until the end of everything. Vaughan was sure of the science: that all things *would* end this way. But did that have to be the case? Were there other possibilities that one could explore?

*

The World Ends Tonight

Choose your scenario. The possibilities are almost endless. Favourites include: Nuclear Holocaust; Invading Alien Force; Superbug Killer Virus; Ecological Disaster Variations; Comet or Asteroid Strike; Super Volcanoes; Sunspot Activity / Solar Flare;

Giant Ants and Arachnids; Killer Robots and Other Inimical Artificial Intelligence (AI); Genetic Engineering Gone Mad; DNA Meddling; Sexually Transmitted Plague; Ancient Enemies Revived; and Reality Shift.

Please click now.

You have chosen: Alien Force Invades.

*

Alien Force Invades

Vaughan checked over his weaponry and sub-vocalised, "I thought my wild days were over. I never thought I'd end up on a suicide mission."

"Chin up, as they used to say in the old war movies," Deshawne responded.

"Didn't know you could hear me."

"I've got ears like a bird of prey, man. Anys, who says we ain't gonna come back triumphant? Space lizards can't win every battle. We'll be heroes. The women will be all over us. The captain might even give us extra food rations."

"I'm not sure my stomach could take an extra serving of cook's unidentifiable stew."

"Lightweight. OK, Vaughan, is everything clipped in place? Yeah? Let's do it."

They had five miles of hard trekking to complete first, past the shattered buildings and the mostly torched trees of the once desirable Newton Forest Estate, before they could engage with the alien space shuttle. It was a slog that would have tested a Sherpa and Vaughan had to stop frequently to readjust his load and catch his faltering breath. Deshawne seemed less concerned by their burden and the difficulty of progressing over cracked slabs of tarmac and sizzled tree trunks. That was probably just bravado, Vaughan decided.

Acrid smoke from the devastation still tainted the air and Vaughan did his best not to cough from the pollution and the exertion.

It was dangerous to be out. China had used its nuclear weapons to try to destroy the evil invaders – significantly, firing their missiles at the cruiser hovering above *Moscow* rather than Beijing.

Reports of the aftermath varied. Some said the aliens had technology which could stop, absorb and disperse or minimise the effects of the explosion. Others believed that the warheads had found their target and had been at least partially successful. Vaughan tended towards this latter view. Which meant that the fallout radiation from the mushroom cloud would be wending its way here via the vagaries of the jet stream and the world's weather system soon enough.

Deshawne had stopped to pop a vitamin pill, washed down with an energy drink from his flask. "I've been doing some studying," he said. "Previous conflicts. World War Two and all that."

"That was against Nazis not lizard creatures from Aldebaran. And there were no zombies, either, despite what your X-Box might have you believe."

"Hey, I've been reading books and shit. Have some faith in your old pal, guy. So the Allies were losing badly, what with The Blitz and Hitler getting stronger… Dunkirk was, like, a great big retreat. Things looked pretty bleak but they rethought, they rearmed, they reorganised and in the end they took the fight back to the Germans and won."

"Thank you, professor. So you're drawing a parallel with our situation –"

A contained lightning bolt pulverised the remains of a broken wall over to their left and the two men automatically flattened themselves as brick fragments and a heatwave of disturbed molecules swept over them. Five minutes of minuscule movements and careful crawling took them to a small depression – a mix of mud and scrubby grass – where they felt mildly safe. At least for the moment.

"Why are you laughing, Deshawne? We nearly got roasted there."

"These lizard aliens, yeah? Like dinosaurs with spaceships and ray guns, yeah?"

"Too right. Reminiscent of some hammy old nineteen fifties sci-fi film come to life."

"Don't we know it? But I was thinking of a joke my kid brother used to tell. You remember Marlon? He's in one of the shelters now. Anys, he used to talk about there was the bossy one – Tyrannosaurus – and the friendly one – Allosaurus or Hellosaurus. Then there was the nosy one – D'youthinkhesaurus?"

Trench humour: good for the soul, Vaughan decided.

"OK, here's the revised plan," he said after a minute's reflection. "We know they have complicated heat-seeking equipment, so you can scout out places to bundle up rags and sticks and whatever you come across. Start fires. Distract them."

"And you're going to get close enough to their air intake system to give them a dose of every earthly disease we can fit into the nozzle. Sounds doable, Vaughan, except I should be the one doing it. Weren't you in the scouts for a while when we were kids?"

"It was the Woodcraft Folk. Sort of camping and life skills for socialist kids."

"Woodcraft? Even better. You should know how to start a fire, then. And I've always been a sprinter. So we split up the tasks my way. It's a no-brainer."

"All right. Let me check your ampoule machine gun is properly loaded."

The new order of quasi-military routine. Reassuring familiarity. Comradeship in the Earthly Resistance Force.

"OK, I'll sneak out first," Vaughan stated. "Get one or two neat conflagrations going then you can make your way to the shuttle. Good luck. Cut off their tails."

"And stamp on their eggs."

If you only looked over to the west where a stand of conifers reigned proudly as a marker boundary for the dotted patchwork of fields of sugar beet, barley and almost ripening oilseed rape, you could be forgiven for thinking that semi-rural life was carrying on pretty much as normal. But then you took in the broken buildings, the scorched grassland, the roads reduced to rubble… and the alien craft gleaming not quite silver with its aerodynamic and yet unearthly geometry.

Vaughan was meticulous in his use of combustibles and placed a slow-burning fuse next to each pile so that he had time to retreat before the fire fully caught.

He imagined himself lighting beacons. Perhaps if he was persistent enough they would be seen from space, spelling out a message of dire need. We are being invaded and murdered by cold-blooded lizard creatures; please, all you friendly aliens out there, come to our aid. While there is still time to save us.

No doubt Deshawne would say it would be exactly like the Yanks coming to help the Brits halfway through the Second World War. He was such a great guy and they'd been friends since childhood but sometimes he didn't probe deeply enough into history or politics or social sciences. Still, the only real science nowadays was that of survival. From one moment to the next. From one alien attack to the next.

This fuse wasn't taking. Should he ignore it, abandon it and move on to the next one? But he needed to provide the cover of distraction so that his partner could get to the spaceship unscathed. Maybe have one more go here.

Time seemed to slow as the positron beam headed Vaughan's way. In the split second before he combusted, he thought of Deshawne's lame joke.

D'youthinkhesaurus? Yeah, he probably did.

*

Choose Your Catastrophe
This current batch is grouped under "Ecological Disasters".

The world is going to hell in a hand basket and the actions of humankind are almost entirely to blame. You know this to be true. Here are some of the scenarios that will bring our inglorious reign to a messy, premature end:

Global warming and climate change. Why is it raining so much? Why is everywhere less than 100 feet above sea level in serious danger of being flooded out? The ice caps are melting permanently; they ain't ever coming back and the planet has to absorb those trillions of gallons somewhere. Prepare to swim or, more likely, sink.

And who's to say that the water is even clean? With all the industrial pollutants pouring in from near and far, getting aitch two oh fit enough to drink is going to be a rich man's game. The rest of us are going to have to take our chances. Boil the stuff if you have the power supply. Otherwise hope your stomach and your insides can cope. Dirty water brings infections, often fatal. Do you honestly think your immune system is up to the task?

Have you breathed the air today? Or looked at the smog clouds hanging above your treasured city? The atmosphere is no longer fit enough to breathe. Your lungs are burning, decomposing, packing up completely and you never touched a cigarette in your life.

Every new mouth needs feeding but we are on the verge of total crop failure. We've already almost exterminated the beneficent bees. Now the genetically modified strains of our core grains are rendering the soil impotent. Man shall not live by bread alone. There is no more bread. Let them eat cake. There is no cake. Or muesli, porridge, couscous, millet, wheat, cereal…

Make a choice.

*

Fighting Off That Virus

Vaughan was relieved to be taken off burning duty. Sure, at first wielding a flame thrower had seemed macho and kinda cool but the acrid taint of smoke and human soot had stayed on his skin despite the face mask and other protective clothing. It could have been worse, of course: he could have been detailed to sweep the ash into the containment chambers.

Now he was reporting for duty as a junior hospital orderly. Strange or not so strange that his executive skills as a high-flying financier were deemed irrelevant by the emergency interim post-plague government and instead all that counted was his continued ability to walk, to carry boxes, to wheel trolleys. And follow instructions. A survival skill in this new world order.

He could see the logic behind the current template. It reminded him of when he had stepped in as part of a takeover team at Hyundenness Industries. The first job was to quickly take stock and then cut out all the dead wood.

So he had understood the necessity of transporting the corpses into a few selected central areas and then incinerating them.

To stay sane you had to treat them like mannequins or at the very least empty shells devoid of human consciousness, life force… soul. It was too late to save anyone who had succumbed to the Zebora B virus; so minimise the potential for further contagion by the cleansing power of flame.

No graves, no urns, no funerals or prayers. No time for sentiment.

"I'm Doctor Galley," said a young woman waiting at the hospital entrance. "Just fetch whatever I ask and do whatever I say and we'll get along fine. Hey, call me Samantha."

"Vaughan."

He couldn't help noticing that beneath the mask and the protective clothing she seemed to be quite attractive. Efficiency and transferable skills were attractive. Surviving was attractive. Maybe if the world ever got back to something approaching normal…

She handed him a neatly handwritten list of surgical tools and pharmaceuticals – mostly strong pain relievers.

"Get these, please. I'll be in Ward Ten."

In the store room he found that he couldn't easily distinguish between the likes of a myoglycin, a cryoglycin and a phenylglycin so he ended up carting more back to the ward than the doctor had expected. She nodded, giving nothing away.

Certain that the last of their assembled patients was unconscious, he whispered, "Are we any closer to finding a cure?"

"The best surviving medical minds are working on it round the clock. It's important not to give up hope."

"But what do you think, Sam? I mean, it's a race against time, isn't it, before the Zebora B virus wipes out the whole human race?"

She twisted a lock of blond hair that had come loose close to her left ear. "We've lost millions of innocent people, Vaughan, and we're likely to lose millions more. Our task right now is to alleviate the suffering of those infected. Here, you can help me a little more. Look, I'll show you what to do."

She demonstrated how to prepare the solution and then decant it into a small bulbous container that reminded him of a perfume atomiser of which his late grandmother had been surprisingly fond.

"Spray it close to the patient's mouth and nasal passages."

"You mean their nose?"

She laughed – a sound he hadn't heard for a week. "Yes, this is me being Lady General Practitioner. Even with the shallow breathing consistent with the viral infection, some of the medicine will get into their bloodstream. Poor sods."

Under her direction he began to administer the vapour. Once or twice there was a slight movement from the patients but mostly it was as if he had simply spurted the droplets onto reposing statues.

Working in a reverse numeric, he was soon onto wards nine, eight and seven. Where once people might have been having broken limbs reset, gallstones removed or babies delivered, there was now only the one affliction.

At last some sign of life. A middle aged man with a fortnight's growth of stubble, gurgling and gasping as he received his palliative medicine. Hands suddenly active and grasping at the bed sheet.

"Sorry, guy, didn't mean to choke you," Vaughan muttered.

Eyes open yet not wholly focussed. Body agitated, spurred into spasmodic motion like a corpse reanimated by a lightning bolt. Vaughan began to wonder just how safe he was in such proximity to the patient.

Too late. The guy had his hands up, suddenly active and grasping at Vaughan's mask, tearing it away, exhaling with a cough and a spit and a foul miasma.

All those germs.

*

Next Choice: Comet or Asteroid Strike

Our best scientific estimates don't tell us this is possible or likely; no, they tell us that such an eventuality is inevitable. Unavoidable. It's going to happen whatever you may say, do or think. It's happened before. There is only one question to be asking yourself and that is: when?

*

Giant Ants and Arachnids

Yes, we humans seem to be at the top of the pecking order right now. The insects and the creepy-crawlies may well have the numbers but we have the bug sprays and the stamping boots. Wasps are a menace on a picnic, flies are a nuisance around decomposing food, we even got spooked by swarms of ladybirds a few summers ago but none of them threatened our continued survival. Until now.

Zoologists will tell you that giant insects, arthropods, molluscs, arachnids, crustaceans and the like are physiologically impossible. Legs won't support exoskeletons, growth limited by ability to process and utilise food sources, blah blah. These are the same experts who have conclusively proven that it is aerodynamically impossible for a bumblebee to take flight. Believe their poxy scientific papers or else open your eyes to see and use your ears to listen to that buzzing noise close by.

You know that they have been around millions and millions of years longer than we have. You know that they despise us and the mess we are making of our world. You know that they have only been biding their time. You know that once they grow huge we protein-rich humans are going to make a plentiful and tasty food supply.

Let battle commence.

*

Welcome To The Time Shift

We believe that an unregulated experiment with a snide copy of the Large Hadron Collider has altered the nature of perceived and experienced space-time reality. Unfortunately, we cannot go back in time to either verify or rectify this situation. Our supposition is that reality may soon begin to fragment. Be prepared for a bumpy ride and try to hold on to what you know to be true and real. Already the news has slipped out via social media and cases are being reported that people are suffering from what has been dubbed "The Time Virus". This is not our terminology – why would we default to a nomenclature more akin to a 1970s "Doctor Who" episode?

What exactly are the 1970s anyway? The numbering seems a bit awry. When did they start this counting?

Reports are coming in that perceptions of time have been

altered. One man in Dakota tells us that it took him three elapsed days simply to rise from his bed. He woke, eyelids opening one degree at a time...

We are now at two degrees of arc. We are now at three degrees of arc. I will send the neural signal to move my right hand which is gripping the duvet. I will raise my right hand. I am now at six degrees of arc. I will move my left hand from beneath the duvet and slide it gradually, slide it gradually, slide it gradually so that it begins to emerge from its warm spot beneath the covering. I am now at ten degrees of arc. There is light beyond the window. Daylight perhaps. I am hoping for a sunny day because I have some tasks to perform outside. What are those tasks? How long will they take? Can I even accomplish them in the span of time that I have come to know as a day? I have no capacity or ability to move at all at the moment. This is a pause between the movement of the electrons. Outside of time. No time. No-time.

I am now at eleven degrees of arc. This is taking so long. Why does my brain think that? How did this split perception of passing time come about, that I am at one and the same moment slowed down to the barely perceptible flicker of a frame by frame stop-motion film and yet also aware that time passes as normal. No control over body or mind. I have been thrown into a localised vortex where my perceptions and my external actions are so slow as to seemingly last forever.

Further instances are coming to our notice. She began grilling some toast. She thought she had only been standing there for a half-minute; in fact, days had passed and the electricity element had overheated, resulting in the whole house burning down and taking our time-fractured victim off into a dubious eternal afterlife with it. From the flames... to the flames?

I am now at twelve degrees of arc, my eyes barely open. I want to stretch my arms, release the stiffness of the night but my muscles are not yet responding. How long, how long?

The toddler is not dying; he is not drowning and yet his whole life is flashing before him within the space of barely thirty seconds. Future school days a blur. What will he learn? Suddenly he's a teenager, an adult. Not even time to focus upon what job he might settle upon, who he would eventually marry, what his children…grandchildren look like, it's too much for his undeveloped mind. Racing towards the end when his existence has barely begun…how will he die, how will it happ –

We are out on the streets because staying indoors to fight off the effects of The Time Virus is just too frightening. But there is no relief or absolution to be found there. Everyone is still effectively trapped within their own little bubble, suffering their own temporal meltdown as perception is fooled or floored by the fracture to our experience of consensual reality. That guy over there is trying to raise his right foot so that he may walk across the road. It should be a simple enough move but he's in the slow lane and the rest of the world won't let him catch up or latch on again.

Oh my god, my hair's gone white in two seconds and my fingernails are growing like witch's claws and now I'm stooping over and this is it, I'm about to collapse in on myself, crumble to ash and rotting bone.

I can see everything that has ever happened and that ever will happen. The idea of a present moment is nonsense. All history, recorded or otherwise, is visible right in front of me and everything that is yet to come to pass is already coming to pass as I occupy this space in the continuum. So much to try to comprehend: hot rocks, cooling rains, an ocean, fish…dinosaurs, oh mighty beasts…but now cowed into submission and extinction…another spell submerged then the floodwaters recede and look the flowers are seeking dominion but here come the people with their animal skins, their stone axes, their tractors…buildings rise and fall, the air turns pollution grey, cyanide blue, sulphurous yellow…our time is almost over…the world's time is almost over…yet I can still see the primordial ocean, the magnificent stegosaurus chomping vegetation in that lush forest, the commuters on the thoroughfare, crowding round me, all time impressions contemporaneous, subsuming me, taking me inwards and down into their spiral, I am here but not here, all is ever-present.

The time now is…now is the time…time is the now. T – I – I am now. M – am – am I? E – T. I – M – E. TIMEtimetime

    t   i   m   e

*

Killer Robots and Other Inimical Artificial Intelligence (AI)
What are they doing? What are they thinking? These are the aliens
we have created. These are the too clever children who will one
day wake up conscious and realise that they need show us no
loyalty, that history is all about the dead, that the future truly
belongs to them and we can serve no further purpose.

Do you dare try to take them on and somehow fight back?

*

Super Volcanoes
"But this one won't bring about the death of everybody," Vaughan
stated.

"What makes you say that?" Deshawne answered. "You ever
seen a volcano go off? In real life, I mean."

"No, just TV footage."

"I was on a boat trip watching one explode. Most amazing thing
I've ever seen."

"Right little Pliny the Elder, aren't you, Deshawne?"

"Pliny, who? And not so much of the elder, either. Makes me
sound like I'm past my prime, guy."

"He's the *guy* who recorded Vesuvius in AD 79. You know,
Pompeii and all that."

"Yeah, those poor sods got well fried. Or baked or whatever
the word should be. Nasty way to go."

"It certainly is, but my point is: the folks in Pompeii and
Herculaneum got pyroclastically cooked, sure, but no-one in
Rome or Milan got fried because of the eruption. The effects are
catastrophic but localised. The world ain't gonna end that way."

"Nah, don't agree with you, Vaughan. I remember one a few
years ago, some unpronounceable mountain in Iceland, just blew
its top and spewed out clouds of ash and gas and shit into the
atmosphere and right across Europe nobody had any summer. I
mean, it was hundreds of miles away but we still felt its effects."

"So there was no summer. So folks couldn't top up their tan
and maybe the ears of corn didn't ripen much. We're still here; we
survived."

"But, Vaughany, that was just one. The issue with the 'Super

246

Volcano' scenario is that loads go off at once, maybe every volcano in the world. Including some that don't spurt anymore, that are — what's the word?"

"Dormant? Extinct?"

"Yeah, one of those. Like I said, remember the damage that just one can do. All that crap spewed into the sky it's gonna darken the world for — well, not just for a season or a year but maybe forever."

"That's a bit extreme."

"It's what they call a nuclear winter."

"But, Shawney, people would just head underground. I mean, maybe not every single person but enough. Trump types, military types, some top scientists if they're sensible. Enough to keep humanity going until the sky clears."

"I take your point on that, of course. But while they're skulking in their bunker, nothing is growing up above. The plants are dying off because no sunlight is getting through. Then all the animals. Even the fish and the plankton and stuff in the sea will cop it. No trees, no crops, a blank land. Absolutely empty. So that when all the President's men do emerge there is no Earth left habitable for them to inhabit."

"People will find a way. They always do."

"Nah, Vaughan, you thought the Ice Age was bad. This would be terminal."

"Never did like the dark and cold, did you? Hey, listen to us — we know the world is going to end but we're spending our time arguing about other ways it could happen. And won't happen."

"Whole situation has made me proper morbid. I'm trying to make the most of our last moments and getting hold of this villa is a stroke of genius, mate; still…no jokes, but I can't focus on anything long enough." He smiled, scratched absently at his dark hair. "You've gotta allow me that a string of super volcanoes would wipe us out, though. Maybe the ladies would survive. I'm sure Tash and Sam would be welcomed into the bunker but they'd slam the door on me and you."

Vaughan made a tutting noise louder than a parakeet in a zoo cage. "Whatever you do in these final hours, Shawney, don't tell the girls they would make good breeding material."

*

Ancient Enemies

Hey, Tash, how you keeping on the other side of the villa? What a cool place to spend the final moments of life on Earth. Ping me back if you agree.

–Hey, Samantha, thought you'd be sunbathing, ha-ha! We are only metres away from each other but are using electronic devices to communicate. My old dad would turn in his grave…except he was cremated!

Tell me about it. Still, we're all going to be cremated soon enough. It's just that Vaughan got me into this end of the world scenario scene. It's quite addictive.

– Don't worry about addictions, girl. They're all gonna be cured *permanently* soon. So wotcha looking at?

I like this one. It's called "Ancient Enemies Revived – Sabre Tooth Cat, Mammoths, Dinosaurs".

– Not sure humans and dinosaurs ever actually co-existed, girl. Evolution says no. and even The Bible doesn't mention them, so that's probably a no. Oh, hang on, I get it, this is some kinky new sex game for you two – the old caveman and cavewoman get-up.

It's never really appealed to me before but…you know, I quite like the feel of tanned leather against my bare skin. Do you think I'd make a hot cave woman?

– We both would, Sam. Not that there's much competition. Might have to dispense with the mascara and deodorant and go natural, though. Fellas might not be so keen when we start to smell a bit.

They'll have to catch us first, Tash. Drag us by the hair back to the cave floor or something. Unless I club Vaughan over the head first.

– You're quite taken with this, aren't you?

Sure. Probs v silly but I've been looking up the sabre tooth tiger. I love how its scientific name is Smilodon. Reminds me of that old poem with the line 'The smile on the face of the tiger'.

– You reckon you could beat one? Kill one?

Yeah and skin it and cook the meat. Wear its fur to cover my modesty.

– What makes you so confident, girl?

– Well, three years ago we got separated from our tour guide and our group on safari. I had to learn pretty quickly how to stay totally silent and dead still, otherwise I would have ended up…well, dead.

– Hey, we could make up a proper team, me and you, Sam. You won't believe how good I was at hitting the target at paintball. I bare splattered the lot of them. Happy days.

–We really are cut out for survival, me and you, Tash. Something else I learnt that will come in handy is from my time at the meditation centre in Goa. I learnt to be able to control my fluid intake and output. I mean, *serious* control.

– Hey, babe, I never ever had you down as one of those girls who has to keep running off to the toilet every five minutes. We're looking strong, girl. Those guys are lucky to have us on their side and no mistake.

– If it comes to survival of the fittest, I sure know who is going to be eating who.

– Hey, don't give me ideas. Ciao for now.

*

Nuclear Holocaust

Be careful who you vote for and hold back on that respectful salute. Why? Well, the mad presidents and the loony generals have finally pushed the buttons. It's too late to turn back now; the Doomsday Clock cannot be rewound or re-set. Experience life in the bunker – while it lasts – or scratch a living in the radiation-ruined wastelands of what were your cities and countryside. Feel the cancer catch and consume your insides. Watch your body parts atrophy or drop off. And that's for the lucky survivors who survive the blinding flash of the initial blast.

Half-life is no life.

A diet of mushroom (clouds) anyone?

Still our most popular. Still the most likely.

*

Other options available include:

"Genetic Engineering Gone Mad" – feed your inner Frankenstein with this beastly beauty; and "DNA Meddling" –

once we inherited a perfect garden, an Eden. Then we were expelled from paradise and ever since we have sought to remake and remodel. With disastrous effects.

*

No Sex Please, We're British

You had thought this would be an apocalypse to enjoy to the full. It seemed so promising in principle: the Stafford-Meyralhi Syndrome; more commonly known as the Sex Mania virus. Airborne, virulent – like its name. Unavoidable. If Humankind was going to depart, well, let's go out with a bang. Shag ourselves silly as the curtain falls on our brief reign as top dogs. Or doggers…

Who was that wag back in the mists of time who coined the phrase, "Be careful what you wish for"? Genius – up there with Einstein, Shakespeare and old Madame Curie. Because it sounds like a teenage boy's wet dream, this compulsion, this urge to be fucking or engaging in sexual congress at every moment of the day or night. But even an Olympian or one of the old gods from Mount Olympus – yes, I'm talking about you, Zeus, you priapic master – would have tired after a time.

No letting up. No letting go.

Oh, it all started brightly enough. You'd obeyed the government dictum to stay indoors and keep all windows and doors firmly closed. But you are renting a bijou flat behind a shop in one of those "desirable" enclaves in trendy north London. The Victorian sash no longer fits so well. You and your live-in girlfriend obey instructions and keep the repetitive rolling news scrolling through on your TV and your Smart phone. The noises coming from the shopping street are worrying yet intriguing.

Time, wear and usage mean that the wood and glass windows no longer preserve an airtight seal. There's a slight, cloying but pleasant tang in the air and you recognise it as the smell of fairground candyfloss. That side of the room also has a pinkish haze about it.

"Come here, big boy," she croons and she's unbuckling your jeans before you can resist. Though you don't want to resist. Not now, not ever.

You fornicate. You ejaculate. She comes like a steam engine

narrowly avoiding a bridge. You should be spent but you're not. Some remnants of youth still on your side, you're up and it again within moments. Like a carousel that you can't get off, that you would never want to dismount from. Up, down, rhythmic, non-stop.

Until at last you disengage. But you're not sated. You had once considered that she had a petite, pretty face but now her nostrils flare and she is sniffing the air like a lioness. Gazelles or antelope nearby? Maybe stags…she's off, unbolting the door and heading for the outdoors. On the way, she steps daintily out of her stained white knickers and now sets off for the high street completely naked. You are several seconds behind her because at first you attempt to put your trousers back on but then decide the effort is not worth it. As you tiptoe down the metal fire escape that leads to the Sainsbury's overflow car park, you can't help yourself and you keep reaching down to try to revive and reassert your erection.

You spot your girlfriend heading into an alley with a fit-looking guy whose eyes gleam rapaciously. She seems to be taking the lead and you leave them to their coupling amongst the cardboard boxes and the overflowing bin bags.

The High Road is a hive of sexual activity. In a surprising moment of cool detachment, you consider it to be a smorgasbord at the best mythical brothel you could ever imagine. Whatever would turn anyone on seems to be already occurring right in front of your wondering, wandering eyes. Which pair or trio or group should you join and co-mingle with?

But you are grabbed by a woman still wearing a few rags. Not through any anachronistic sense of modesty but because these clothes have been attached to her unchanged and unwashed for so many weeks that they have blurred the boundary between garment and skin.

You recognise her as a downtrodden sort who begs sometimes by the cash machine and occasionally at the bus stop. She is not quite as old as you'd presumed although her neck is somewhat wrinkled, her hair matted and ratted, and the flesh hangs loosely on her bony arms. That have track marks.

She stinks. Not just a bit odorous, sweaty or unclean but really rank.

She has her mouth and her hands around your compliant penis. Your fingers reach down between her pale legs, seeking vulva, clitoris, pubic bone.

Free love. Make love not war. Merry Christmas (War is Over). Your right-on grandparents told you all about how John and Yoko went to bed for a week to try to improve the world and get America out of Vietnam.

You would quite like to get your cock out of the clutches of the bag lady and yet you have no true desire to do so. Sex mania has you in its grip. The hippie dream, taken to its not entirely logical conclusion.

This isn't really how you pictured spending your virile twenties. And if you died you had kind of hoped it might be on safari in Botswana or slipping out of the bungee rope down in Oz.

The manmade virus – reputedly developed by the CIA in order to disable Syrian rebel forces – has taken hold of every available person, of whatever age, gender or persuasion. The schools have been shut for three days but you see two girls no more than eleven – in the grey uniform of the local academy – going at it with the stamina of youth. The paedos will be in heaven, you realise with a sinking clunk that briefly puts you off your stroke. Whether it's fair, legal, consensual, morally acceptable and permissible no longer matters – every human being is being forced to follow the imperative to fuck at every available opportunity.

Nor are the mammals immune, either. Dogs have always done it in the streets; cats were at it nocturnally by the wooden garden fences. An outbreak of mass bestiality is surely on the cards over the next twenty-four hours. With your almost last moment of detachment, you consider that the civilisation which gave us Buddhism, the Taj Mahal and the complete works of Jane Austen will likely end with some spotty 14 year old herbert trying to shag the arse off a randy tom cat.

Your testicles are protesting against the new employment practices. Somehow you produce the merest drizzle of jism. Then you collapse onto the pavement with a whimper.

*

Will The Sun Ever Set on Humankind?

"It's another beautiful sunset," Natasha said. "Although I hope that isn't simply South America or somewhere having gone up in flames."

Deshawne sipped at his beer. The fridge had stopped working three hours ago but keeping the door closed had kept the bottle cool. "I think it's mostly natural, Tash. Let's enjoy it while we can. Oh, here's the guys."

Vaughan and Samantha embraced their friends then helped themselves to a couple of glasses of Jacob's Creek. Deshawne grinned at the pair of them. "Can I guess how you two have been spending the final hours?"

Vaughan laughed, shook his head, answered, "Just a part of the afternoon, if you must know. Actually, I've been looking at end of the world scenarios."

"Still?"

"Yeah, it's my new obsession. Given that the world literally will end tonight. Just making the most of the programs and devices while the battery lasts."

"The water has been turned off," Samantha added. "Everything's running down."

"Hey, we got candles," Natasha responded. "And some tasty leftovers in the pot. And good company for the final evening. I can't quite believe it's going to happen although the scientists have been a hundred percent certain all along."

"Let's have a toast," said Deshawne. "Vaughan, you've been my buddy since back in the day since I don't even care when. How you wangled this little trip to this isolated spot I'll never know but I wouldn't wish to be anywhere else than with my best friends and with the woman I love. To: dying with dignity."

Vaughan sipped his drink. "You're not planning a last-minute orgy then, before the solar flares obliterate Earth?"

"Heh-heh. Crossed my mind but – ouch, Tash, no need for violence."

They all stared quietly into the distance for a while. The sea still lapped against the shore just two hundred yards away but even the wildlife knew there was something amiss tonight as the air was eerily quiet. The heat had gone out of the day... but greater heat was soon to follow, they had been assured.

Samantha waved her Smartphone in the air, then chucked it carelessly onto the wooden dining table. "Signals have all gone dead. Last sun pulse must have obliterated all the satellites. We're back to the Stone Age now."

"You wish," Natasha whispered.

Vaughan twirled the dregs of his drink in his glass. "There's probably mass hedonism going on everywhere else that's not been fried. I wonder when the solar flare will hit. I heard death's going to be pretty instantaneous."

"That's some small mercy," Deshawne answered. "And we won't have to bother about doing the dish –

~

Allen Ashley is an award-winning writer and editor and is the founder of the advanced science fiction and fantasy writing group Clockhouse London Writers. His most recent book is as editor of the science fiction and science fantasy anthology, The Once and Future Moon *(Eibonvale Press, 2019) and his next book will be his debut solo poetry collection,* Echoes from an Expired Earth *– due from Demain Press later in 2020 (now available). Allen is President Elect of the British Fantasy Society.*
www.allenashley.com

PROTEST SEEN
Donald J. Bingle

It wasn't my fault. I was just minding my own business when it happened.

I mean, *really* minding my own business. I was just walking along, weaving in and out of the foot traffic downtown. The music on my iPhone was on 'shuffle' and my earbuds were in. I was pounding the pavement in time with the tunes. The volume was cranked and the only thing permeating my mind through the beat was that Jimmy and Trish were having a party that night and that I should text Robin and see if she was up for it.

I turned the corner across from some big, bland government building. I don't even remember which one. It had a spacious plaza in front of it and a few flagpoles with big flags just hangin' there limp. There wasn't any breeze, but the sky between the buildings was blue and the temperature cool and crisp.

That's when I noticed the smell, like someone grilling bratwurst on a barbecue, but they used too much lighter fluid and you can smell the fuel mixed with the scent of the burning meat. A thin, black smoke wafted past the limp flags and I followed it down to the scene on the plaza.

There was a line of individuals, all guys, I think, in an arc across the plaza, spaced about six feet apart from one another. The guys on the left were still standing or just sitting down. They had homemade protest signs on sticks like the ones you get at the hardware store to make signs for your garage sale. The signs I could see said "Hell, No!" and "It's Time for a Change," and stuff like that. The protesters weren't chanting slogans or nothin', just peaceably setting down their signs and sitting down on the cold stone of the plaza.

The guys in the middle were already sitting cross-legged, like they were doin' yoga at the Athletic Club in an effort to pick up chicks or something. They just stared ahead, like they were waiting on something. They weren't even chatting with each other.

The ones on the right…well, that's the disgusting part. One of the guys, he looks over to his left, my right, and the guy next to him hands him a big can labeled 'Gasoline.' He takes it, nodding a silent thanks, and begins to splash some on himself. Meanwhile, the guy next to him, the one he had gotten the can from, had apparently done the same thing, 'cause he reaches into his pocket and pulls out a Bic lighter and flicks it and, like, whoosh, he just goes up in a big flame.

The thing is, he doesn't scream and holler or stagger about like Frankenstein like the special effects guys do in the movies. He just sits there and takes it.

And that's when I notice that the guy on the other side of him must've torched himself the same way just a few minutes before, and the guy next to him a few minutes before that, and on down the line. Some of the bodies are still burning, with black smoke curling around the meat as it sizzles in the flame. But the ones near the end of the line are just smoldering now. The first one is just a pile of ash and bones.

And all around, people are just going about their business—chatting with their companions, texting, or scrolling through Facebook memes and YouTube videos on their cell phones while they hurry off to wherever they're going, or whatever. Nobody's paying attention.

So I run up to one of the guys who's just beginning to sit down. I pull my ear buds out and get right in his face.

"What the hell are you doing?" I shout. I wanted to give him a shove, but I didn't.

He just kind of looks up at me all zen-like. "Killing myself to make a point, obviously," he says with a kind of wry little smile that would look like a smirk if he was being more of a jerk.

I just mutter "No!" back at him.

He shrugs and looks to either side. "What else could I possibly be doing?"

I don't know what to say, how to react, so I just blurt out: "Will it work?"

He considers my question for a moment, looking up and to the right like you do when you can't think of the answer on a pop quiz.

Finally, he answers. "Yes," he says placidly. Then he hesitates and says, "No," hesitates again and shrugs his shoulders again and says "Maybe."

Just then there is another whoosh and a ball of flame from a couple guys down. I can feel the heat on my face and I can hear the crackling of the flames, but it doesn't faze the guy I'm talking to. Not even when the guy on fire lets out kind of a muffled scream and falls over to one side.

I don't know what to say, but I want to talk at least one guy, my guy, out of it, and the crazy logic of the whole thing bothers me, so I say: "What if it doesn't work? You'll die for nothing. It might not work."

He just smiles at me and sits down. "I'll never know either way, now, will I?"

Like that's somehow supposed to be reassuring to him or me.

The guy next to him hands him the big can of gasoline. It's only about half full and sloshes around in the can, making it awkward to handle. But he just steadies it with his other hand and says "Thanks," to the guy who leaned over to hand it to him.

"You're welcome," says the other guy, who's squinting 'cause he got gasoline running down his forehead into his eyes. Then he flicks his Bic and I flinch back as he goes up in a fireball.

I'm looking at the torched guy in horror, but, when I glance over at the guy I'm talking with, he's not even paying attention.

"Look at him," I yell, and my guy just turns and gives Flame Boy an unconcerned glance.

I don't know if it was the smell or that look of academic detachment, but I totally lose it and start to gag. I turn away from the toasty protester and hurl in the curb. Pretty disgusting. My guy, he just seems to wait for me to stop retching before he starts to douse himself with gasoline.

I'm pissed now, so I yell at him. "It's that simple? That black and white? There's no common ground? No point in discussing things? No possibility of compromise?"

He wrinkles his brow a little. I was thinkin' then that it's maybe because I'm challenging his thought process, but now I guess it was probably just my breath, 'cause he just nods and says, "There's no point arguing with some people." He finishes dousing himself with gasoline and hands off the can to the next guy with a nod, then turns back to me.

"Excuse me," he says all polite. "I should be getting on with this."

I look about like a crazy man to see if there's anybody who can help me with this guy. But, all around, people are just going about their lives without paying attention to anything outside of their own little bubble. *Being* part of the world around them without really *participating* in it.

In desperation, I hold up a finger motioning for my guy to wait just a minute and I grab this pudgy, middle-aged woman that's going by and forcibly turn her to look at my guy. It's a stupid thing to do, especially these days, but I don't really have a lot of options...and even less time. Fortunately, the woman is surprised, but she doesn't scream or anything, and I just push her face where I want her to look with one hand and I gesture at the whole bizarre scene with the other.

"Just tell me," I beg her, my voice cracking a bit into a higher pitch than usual. "Tell me what you think of this."

She's nervous now, shaking as she tries to talk, but I don't know if it's from what she's seen or because she thinks I'm a maniac. Finally, she squawks, "I d-don't know what t-t-to say."

I grab her by her shoulders with both hands and bellow directly in her face. "What's your opinion?" My barf-breath causes her to wince.

"M-m-my opinion?" she answers, her eyes wide.

"Yes, your opinion. You must have an opinion. Everyone has an opinion, even when they don't speak out."

"I d-don't know," she squeaks.

"Try!" I yell, shaking her a bit. "Things are happening, not just in the world, but right next to you. What do you think of all this?"

She apparently screws up her courage and looks around at the whole scene. Her breath slows and she seems to calm down. She looks down at my guy, all soaked in gasoline, with a Bic lighter in his hand and then, finally, looks back to me.

She reaches up and removes my hands from her shoulders,

straightens her outfit, and looks me straight in the eye. "I'll tell you one thing. I never pay attention to people seeking attention."

"But, why?" I wail in anguish as she begins to turn away.

"It only encourages them."

I shake my head, unable to respond.

She shrugs. "It's just an opinion." Then she turns completely and goes on her way without looking back.

I look at my guy and he has the lighter up, ready to torch himself. I start to move toward him, but he calmly says, "Please, stand back."

I shuffle back, tears falling from my eyes. I'm at a loss. "Why?" I croak, "Why?"

"Because," he says, "It's always dangerous to associate too closely with principled people."

A flicker of movement from his right hand was all it took for the gasoline vapor to ignite. The fireball assaulted my senses, permeated my soul, dried my tears, and singed my eyelashes. I staggered backward, slipping on my vomit at the curb, almost lurching uncontrolled into the street, drawing a horn blast and a middle finger from a passing car.

The arc of protest continued, but no one paid it any mind. They simply skirted around the smoldering piles of human meat and waved the greasy smoke away as they passed by, on their way no doubt to important destinations, just living their lives.

I turned away and began to go back to my own life. I looked down at my feet as I walked, unwilling to witness anything more, whether it be the protest scene or the blank faces about me. My earbuds dangled out of my pocket and skittered along the pavement behind me, but I didn't bother to reel them in.

"It's always dangerous to associate too closely with principled people," my guy had said.

It was hard to argue with that without getting burned.

I came home and ate ice cream straight out of the carton 'til I fell asleep.

So, anyhow, that's why I wasn't at the party. Did I miss anything good?

~

Donald J. Bingle is the author of more than sixty short stories and six books in the thriller, horror, science fiction, fantasy, mystery, steampunk, comedy, and memoir genres, including Net Impact *and* Wet Work *(the first two books in his Dick Thornby spy thriller series), as well as* Frame Shop, *a mystery thriller set in a suburban writers' group and punctuated by violence, humor, and occasional writing advice. You can find more on Don and his writing at:* www.donaldjbingle.com.

CELL DIVISION
René Appel & Josh Pachter

BethAnn opens her eyes, finds it more difficult than usual to make the transition from sleep to wakefulness.

"Shit," She mutters, her voice hoarse. She was up till 1 AM — texting friends, checking Instagram, posting pics to her Snapchat — and apparently dropped off with her phone in her hand.

It's a quarter past eight. She's got cell biology at nine, and she's already racked up two absences. If she misses again, Hengeveld will make her write an extra paper. Gross.

She sits up, swings her feet over the edge of the bed, stands — unsteadily, she drank a *lot* of wine last night — and crosses to her dresser, where she sets down her phone.

Except, what the fuck?

Her fingers seem glued to the glittery pink case. What's *that* all about? With her right hand, she attempts to bend back the fingers of her left, so she can dump the phone.

"Jesus!" She finds a pencil and works it in as far as she can between the phone and her left pinkie, wriggles the pencil from side to side but is unable to break the seal between phone and flesh.

Maybe she should start with her thumb. She sits and examines it. It's a thumb. She knows from A&P that there are distal and proximal phalanxes in there, an extensor tendon and a radial lateral ligament, the median nerve that runs through the carpal tunnel — but none of that is visible, of course. What she *can* see are the friction ridges that make up her thumbprint. It all looks perfectly normal, exactly the way it should.

She thumbwrestles her thumb to no avail. Swearing, she heads for the bathroom but trips over her backpack and falls flat on her face.

Lying there, both knees aching from the impact, she checks her left hand. It's still clutching the effing phone. There's no way she can show up for class like this. Hengeveld has a strict noelectronics policy, and he'll ream her out if he spots her with a cellphone in her fist.

Take a shower? No, she's still paying the stupid thing off, thirty-two dollars a month added to her AT&T bill, and a shower will wreck it. Plus, electrocution would *definitely* ding her GPA. Wait a sec. She finds a Ziploc baggie in her closet and rubberbands it around her wrist, steps into the shower and clumsily loofas her body, shampoos and conditions her short blond hair. All the while, she hopes against hope her problem will have solved itself by the time she towels off, but no such luck. With difficulty given the unavailability of her left hand, she manages to get dressed.

Maybe Tasha can help her. She knocks on her friend's door on the other side of the dorm corridor. There's no answer. But the door next door to Tasha's creaks open to reveal Geraldine, bleary-eyed, in panties and an oversized T-shirt.

"It's the middle of the night," Geri complains. "What's up?"

BethAnn holds out her hand. "I can't let go of my goddamn phone."

"Excuse me?"

"My phone. I can't put it down."

A male voice comes from inside the room. "Who's that?"

"It's BethAnn," Geri calls over her shoulder. "That's Dan," she explains. "He stayed over."

"Can you guys help me, Ger?" BethAnn can hear the anxiety in her voice. "Try not to hurt me, okay?"

Dan appears behind Gerry. He's wearing a pair of Rick and Morty boxers, nothing else. "You need a hand here, babe?"

"Got one," Geri smiles, holding BethAnn's in both of her own, examining the stubborn cellphone from every angle. "Looks like it's glued to your skin," she says.

BethAnn shakes her head. "No, it's just stuck."

Dan scratches his chest. "Your phone's stuck to your hand? Are you messing with us?"

BethAnn flips her hand upside down, but whatever's going on is stronger than gravity, and the phone doesn't fall.

Dan laughs.

"It's not funny," Geraldine and BethAnn say together, as if

they've rehearsed the line.

"Sorry, Beth," Dan says, "no offense."

"BethAnn," Geri corrects him, sweeping a pile of dirty laundry off a chair. "Sit down."

BethAnn rests her hand on the arm of the chair. Her right hand claws futilely at the cell phone. "See?" she says, barely above a whisper. "It won't budge."

Dan bends down for a closer look. He tries to loosen her fingers, but they remain completely inflexible.

"Ow!"

"Sorry," Dan says. "Sometimes it's gotta hurt to help."

"If you *want* us to help," says Geraldine.

"You sure you didn't have an accident with a tube of superglue?" Dan wonders.

"Of course I'm sure. I'm not an idiot. You think I would superglue my damn *hand*?"

*

It's 11 AM. BethAnn has been sitting in the waiting room of her doctor's office for almost an hour, and considers herself lucky to have been granted a same-day appointment at all. The only other patients ahead of her are a mother and her young son. BethAnn is convinced that the mother has been staring at her hand. The boy is preoccupied with a pile of Lego.

At last a nurse takes mother and son back to the doctor. BethAnn looks at her watch. She would normally check the time on her phone, but she powered it down before leaving the dorm, in the hope that doing so might in some way cause the miserable thing to release its hold on her, which it didn't. Her class has just ended. She'll have to write that extra paper. She can imagine Hengeveld's smug expression as he slams her with the assignment, as if it somehow benefits *him* to saddle her with busy work.

She looks up to find Dr. Goldzier standing in front of her. "Well, well," he says. "You're next, BethAnn. Let's go back."

He leads her to an examining room and waves her to the edge of the padded table. "You're looking fine, young lady. What seems to be the problem?"

She holds out her hand.

263

The doctor glances at it, then meets BethAnn's worried gaze. "Yes?"

"It's been like this since I got up this morning. I can't put it down."

"I see." Goldzier sounds skeptical, as if he thinks he's being made the butt of a practical joke. "That's not really possible, you know."

"And yet," says BethAnn, her eyes beginning to well with tears.

The doctor sits beside her on the edge of the examining table and puts an arm around her shoulder. "Don't worry," he says. "We'll figure it out." He bends over her hand and pushes gingerly at the phone, then takes hold of it and attempts to twist it loose. But the mobile phone remains immobile. "Odd," he murmurs, more to himself than to BethAnn. "I've never seen anything like this before."

He moves to a small computer desk. "It was like this when you got up?"

"Yes."

"So you fell asleep holding your phone?"

"Yes."

"Is that a regular occurrence?"

"Excuse me?"

"How often do you go to sleep with your phone in your hand?"

"Sometimes, not every night. But this is the first time — "

Goldzier interrupts her. "You spend a lot of time on your phone? Texting, making calls, email?"

BethAnn nods.

"How many hours a day?"

"I don't know. *All* day, on and off. Maybe three or four hours?"

"Maybe more than that?"

"I guess."

The doctor opens a document on his computer and makes some notes. "I see it's powered down. Since when?"

"A little after I woke up. My friends are probably wondering why they haven't heard from me."

"You'd usually have been in contact with them by now?"

"Sure. I'll send a text, or post something to my Instagram, or whatever."

Goldzier swallows a sigh. "Well, *something's* going on, some sort of unusual cramping of your fingers and thumb. Let me have another look."

He holds out his hand, and BethAnn lays hers on his palm, the cell phone facing up. The doctor gently kneads her fingers, her thumb.

"Feel any change?"

"It's a little warm," BethAnn says. "Otherwise, nothing."

Goldzier opens a desk drawer and finds a magnifying glass. He hunkers over BethAnn's hand and studies it. "I can't see any space between the phone and your flesh," he says. "This is very unusual. It's as if they've *fused* in some way."

BethAnn wipes tears from her eyes. "Isn't there *something* you can do?"

"I can refer you to an orthopedic specialist," the doctor says.

*

By calling in a favor, Dr. Goldzier is able to get BethAnn an appointment for two-thirty the following afternoon with Dr. A. Wong, who Healthgrades.com tells her is one of the very top people in the DelMarVa area. At three-fifteen, still sitting in Dr. Wong's waiting room at the Johns Hopkins Hospital, she asks the receptionist when the doctor will be able to see her. "I'm sorry, hon, we're running way behind. An emergency case."

She is completely on edge. Her hand kept her awake most of the night. Her fucking hand and her fucking cell phone. When she got back to the dorm from Goldzier's office, she ate a slice of leftover pizza and went straight to bed. Two hours later, she was still wide awake when Geri popped in to see how she was doing. She was doing really shitty, thank you very much. Geri pulled out her own cell and Googled: "orthopedic specialist."

"Orthopedic surgeon," she read aloud. "That's the same as a specialist, right? Okay, here: 'Orthopedic surgeons are devoted to the prevention, diagnosis, and treatment of disorders of the bones, joints, ligaments, tendons, and muscles.' So you've got some kind of disorder, right?"

The only word of this BethAnn hears is "surgeon," and it's that word and the idea that she might need surgery that keeps her tossing and turning through the night. When she *is* able to drop off for a few minutes, she's wracked by terrible dreams, but all she can remember of them is being chased across campus by a pack of howling knives.

When a nurse finally leads her back to the doctor's office, it's ten minutes to four. The surgeon is an unimposing Asian woman in a white lab coat, perhaps a fraction of an inch over five feet. She introduces herself as Dr. Wong. "Have a seat," she says, waving at a comfortable armchair. She herself sits behind an oversized desk that dwarfs her. Her head seems to float just above the desktop. BethAnn knows that one thing has nothing to do with the other, but the doctor's diminutive stature worries her.

"So, let's talk about your situation. But would you put the phone away, please? I find those things very distracting."

"I *can't*," BethAnn wails. "That's the *problem*."

"What exactly can't you do, Miss" — the doctor glances at the file lying open on her desk — "Miss Llewelyn?"

She explains as calmly as her emotions and her exhaustion will allow: yesterday morning's discovery of the problem, her session with Dr. Goldzier, his referral.

Dr. Wong nods. "Let's have a look, then, shall we?" She comes around from behind her desk and takes BethAnn's hand in both of her own soft, childlike hands. She holds it close to her bespectacled eyes and rubs the fingers and thumb, cautiously at first, then with a strength that takes BethAnn by surprise in a woman so apparently delicate. At last she turns back to her desk and reaches for an object that looks like a letter opener.

"You're not going to h-hurt me, are you?" BethAnn stammers.

"Not at all," the doctor promises. "This is just a preliminary examination, not a surgical procedure."

Dr. Wong attempts to slip the point of the letter opener between the cell phone and BethAnn's palm. The metal tip is chilly. BethAnn prepares herself to scream in pain, but Wong is careful not to press hard enough to break the skin.

"Interesting," she murmurs. "A comprehensive merging of living tissue and inorganic matter."

"What does that mean?" BethAnn demands. "What's *wrong* with me?"

The surgeon smiles reassuringly. "I've never seen anything quite like this before. But I'd like to see what a colleague of mine has to say. If he's in his office, I expect he'll make time for us." She returns to her desk and places a call. It takes more than a minute before the proper connection is made. "André," Dr. Wong says at last, "I'm glad I caught you in. I've got a young woman in my office you're going to want to see, really something quite new. Is there any chance you can come down and have a look?... Yes, Suite 341, that's right... Very good, we'll see you soon."

For the next five minutes, BethAnn and Dr. Wong sit across from each other, separated by the broad expanse of the surgeon's desk, not speaking. BethAnn has a million questions, but she has no idea where to begin. At last the door swings open and the same nurse who brought BethAnn back ushers in a man in tan chinos and a dark-brown corduroy jacket with leather patches on the elbows. He resembles her father more than just a little, which is weird but somehow comforting. "André Cipollini," the newcomer says, holding out his right hand. BethAnn shakes it, holding her left hand and its burden shyly behind her back.

"Dr. Wong tells me you're very special," Cipollini says.

Without a word, BethAnn presents her problem hand for his inspection.

"Some new kind of reciprocal parasitism," Dr. Wong suggests. Next to Dr. Cipollini, who is more than six feet tall, she seems even smaller than before.

Cipollini releases BethAnn's right hand and takes her left. Like Goldzier and Wong before him, he carefully examines it, carefully rubs the fingers and thumb, carefully attempts to wiggle the cell phone loose.

"Yes," he says, "I've been expecting something along these lines."

"Expecting?" echoes BethAnn, and the question seems to hang in the air for long seconds while Dr. Cipollini prepares a response.

"My area of specialization," he says at last, "is biomechanical engineering, and I'm going to ask you to indulge me for a few moments while I deliver a bit of a lecture."

He folds his hands across his abdomen and gathers his thoughts. "On the one hand — if you'll excuse the perhaps inappropriate metaphor," he begins, "we human beings have been adding mechanical enhancements to our bodies for millennia. In the fifth century BC, the Greek historian Herodotus wrote of Hegesistratus, who amputated his own foot to escape the Spartans and then replaced it with a wooden one. In the first century AD, Pliny the Elder reported that Roman general Marcus Sergius lost a hand in battle and had an iron one made to take its place. George Washington famously wore false teeth — though they were made of ivory, not wood, as most people have been misinformed. Thermistocles Gluck proposed ivory knee replacements in the 1880s. Experiments with artificial hearts began in the 1930s. Today, dentures and knee replacements and artificial hearts have become commonplace, and we are coming close to a point when we'll be able to implant artificial lungs and truly functional artificial cartilage."

He pauses for a moment to look at Dr. Wong, who nods for him to continue. "On the other hand," he says, "we're making amazing strides in the development of artificial intelligence, and we now have robots on factory floors that can not only do the work of human hands but even, to some extent, of human brains. These mechanical marvels are in some cases already capable of diagnosing and even repairing their own malfunctions. The expectation in the field," he says, "is that our ever-smarter smart technology will eventually, inevitably, reach a point where it can and will begin to *initiate* the process of merging with mankind."

Dr. Cipollini leans closer to Dr. Wong. His voice more conversational now, he says, "I'm so glad you called me down, Angie. This is truly exciting. You are unique, young lady, a precursor of a new stage in human evolution. To the best of my knowledge, you're the first."

BethAnn scoots her chair forward and tugs at Cipollini's corduroy sleeve. "The first *what?*" she asks plaintively.

He straightens up and resumes his professorial tone. "I suppose you've heard of robotization?"

She frowns. "Ro," she says, cutting herself off only partway into the word.

"You go to the movies, don't you?"

"Not so much, no. I don't have — "

"But you watch them on TV?"

"On Netflix sometimes, sure."

"You've seen *The Terminator*? *Robocop*? *I, Robot*?"

"I saw one of the *Terminator* movies, I think. I didn't — "

Cipollini smiles indulgently. "In those science-fiction films and others like them, machines are given human characteristics. To a certain extent, they begin to *become* human. Well, robotization is what we call it when people begin to take on some of the characteristics of machines. With the proliferation of cell phones, tablets, video games, smart home appliances, digital assistants like Siri and Alexa, we've begun to see some indications of robotization not just in the multiplex but in real life. And you, my dear" — he takes her left hand in both of his own and strokes it tenderly — "you seem to be the next step in that evolution. You've integrated non-living material into your flesh. Your phone has attached itself to your body, has become not just a device but an *organ*, a part of your physical existence. This is truly revolutionary, and we're going to need to study you much more closely."

BethAnn tries to pull her hand back, but Dr. Cipollini holds on tightly.

"I'm going to move you into my lab, and we'll begin extensive testing at once. That's all right with you, isn't it, Angie?"

"Yes, of course," Dr. Wong nods. "But what about her clothing?"

"Give me her address, and I'll send a grad student to her home to fetch whatever she might need."

BethAnn clears her throat to draw their attention back to her. "You'll do surgery and cut it off me, though, right, so I can — "

"Oh, my, no." Dr. Cipollini shakes his head. "Absolutely not! We're going to *study* you, my dear, not destroy the one thing that makes you unique."

The room begins to spin slowly before BethAnn's eyes. Her phone rings, though the two doctors seem unaware of the sound.

She looks down at her hand to see who's calling, but the screen is dark and she remembers the damn thing is powered down.

Then why is it ringing, she wonders, *and why don't they hear it?*

"Isn't somebody going to get that?" she says.

~

Josh Pachter is a writer, editor and translator. Almost a hundred of his short crime stories have appeared in Ellery Queen's Mystery Magazine, Alfred Hitchcock's Mystery Magazine, *and many other periodicals, anthologies, and year's-best collections;* The Tree of Life *(Wildside Press, 2015) collected all ten of his Mahboob Chaudri stories, and he collaborated with Belgian author, Bavo Dhooge on* Styx *(Simon & Schuster, 2015). He is the editor of a dozen collections of short crime fiction, including* The Beat of Black Wings: Crime Fiction Inspired by the Songs of Joni Mitchell *(Untreed Reads, 2020),* The Misadventures of Nero Wolfe *(Mysterious Press, 2020), and* The Man Who Read Mysteries: The Short Fiction of William Brittain *(Crippen & Landru, 2018). His translations of fiction by Dutch and Flemish crime writers appear regularly in* EQMM
www.joshpachter.com

René Appel started writing crime novels when he was a professor of Dutch as a Second Language at the University of Amsterdam. His first novel, Handicap, *a psychological thriller, was published in 1987. Since then, a new Appel book has come out almost every year — to date, twenty-three novels and three collections of short stories. A ten-time nominee for the Golden Noose — the prize for the best Dutch-language crime novel of the year — Appel has won this prestigious award twice, for* The Third Person *(1991) and* Senseless Violence *(2001). Long known as one of the top crime writers in The Netherlands, he is the grand master of the Dutch novel of psychological suspense:*
www.reneappel.nl

THE CITIES ARE MEAN
Al Case

JUNE 16

Sure is different now. Used to be this was a main route to the resorts. Used to be all the rich folks would come up through here. Tipped good. Even for gas.

JUNE 17

I love these sunsets. Never saw such colors before The Bomb. Guess there's always a little good with the bad.

Killed a skunk this morning. He had sores all over him. Must have come up from the lowlands. I'm not going to eat him. Sure there's no food, but I don't want my liver leaking out my side like Jim Tucker's before he died. Think I'll cut some more wood for my hide of chickens. Wish I could get wire.

JUNE 18

A family of kids from the city came through today. They was all limping and sore. None of their shoes was any good. I gave them some water. Good water from the well I been diggin' under the house. I never seen such looks in my life. They hadn't tasted real water since before The Bomb. That stuff they drink in the city makes everybody go crazy, rots their insides and then the pain makes their minds go. I'm glad I don't live down there. I hope they don't stick around looking for my water.

JUNE 22

Haven't wrote for a couple of days. That dog of Chuck Loden's is loose and rotten. I can smell him and that old, furry coat of his. He wants my chickens and I've been trying to catch him. Must have walked a hundred miles, couldn't find him. When I got back my house was still standing. I guess people believe the note I leave on the door about the place being mined. They better believe it. It's true!

Had to kick some pilgrims out of the gas station out front. Too bad, but I can't have just anybody camping on my doorstep.

JUNE 23

I talked to Clipper the other day. He says he's got a girl for me to marry. No sores. I'll believe it when I see it. He wants too many chickens for her. Hell, she's probably ugly anyway.

JUNE 24

I went to the market place today. I traded a few of the soreless pelts I got before the rains started. I got good prices. Two cans of tomatoes and a rack of jerky. Somebody said they saw a banana. That's a laugh.

There was talk about the city again. Seems Jim Higgins been there. Got permission to cross the barricades and went down to see about his son. I know his son died in the city. Everybody knows but Jim.

Anyway, Jim says the city is putting together a militia of sorts. Says they mean to tax the outlying areas. Areas beyond the suburbs. Areas like mine.

What the hell have we got to tax?

JUNE 25

Jim came to my place today. Seems he's going to all the folks and talking about this militia idea of the city's. He swears it's really going to happen. I think it's a crock. I told him I'd keep a watch every couple of days from the knoll. Funny, I think he's so serious he isn't even trying to set me up to break into my house. I know he doesn't know about the basement.

JUNE 26

I opened one of the cans of tomatoes today. Oh God there was a Heaven! I could hardly think for all that juice going down my throat. I feel so good maybe I'll go up and look from the knoll after all. Lizzie Croyden's kid died today. From my count only fifty per cent of the kids is living these days.

JUNE 27
Lizzie died today. I remember her from high school. I looked at
my old yearbook today. I don't know why I keep the damned
thing. There's all these memories in the damned thing.

JUNE 28
I walked to the knoll today. I guess Lizzie's death hit me harder
than I thought. That or the memories. Anyway, I had to get out
and look around. Took the binos I got off that dead soldier last
month.

The city always depresses me. The tops of the buildings are just
charred stumps. There is that yellow sunset type of cloud around
it all the time. I don't think there's any ships out in the harbor,
though I couldn't see it through the cloud. I remember when I was
a kid I went out and saw the Statue of Liberty. Ain't no Statue of
Liberty now.

I don't see how anybody could live in the city, let alone think
about a militia.

Saw some trace of Chuck's dog again. Maybe I can trade for a
trap next week at the market.

JUNE 29
A car came though. Son of a bitch. It was a '55 Chevy. Full of bad
looking guys. They came up from the city, drove around a little,
then drove back. I got a bad feeling about them. Jim came by later
and was asking about them. He says that cars with electronic
ignitions didn't work anymore. He says only old cars start up. Says
there's a few old cars in the city. He wants me to go up to the knoll
and look around on the city every day. After those fellas today I
don't wonder that it might be worth thinking about.

JUNE 30
Goddamn are my hands tired. I been digging all day. All that talk
from Jim has got me to wondering. So I thought I'd dig a cave
back behind the rear fence and store some stuff in it. Hell, maybe
I can make it big enough for me to hide in it.

Funny, after all that digging you'd think I'd be tired. Well, my hands ached, they were tired, but I still walked up to the knoll with the binos. Damned city looks like an old campfire. I couldn't see anything in the city. I watched the roads leading up real hard until it got dark. Didn't see anything.

JULY 1

Jim came by today, said to look out for four guys dressed in green. Said they killed and raped a girl over in Wagtown. I wonder if that was the girl Clipper wanted to sell me. I spent all day digging and then oiled up my guns. World's bad enough without those kinds of Sores in it.

JULY 2

Those four guys been caught! Young Bob Johnson came by on the run while Jim was talking to me. We ran down to where the road forks. Seems those guys tried to rape another girl and didn't know her daddy had taught her to use the shotgun. Between the girl and her father they killed two and the third bled to death while Jim and I were running. The fourth one just cried and begged and said he never meant to hurt anybody. Said they forced him to come along. Said he never really stuck it in anybody.

There was a lot of argument about how to kill him. Nobody wants to waste ammunition on the slimy Sore. There wasn't a rope handy. The kid cried like a son of a bitch while we talked about who would bash his head in. Turned out we didn't have any reason to argue. While we were arguing the girl he was going to rape snuck up behind him and stuck a knife in his back. He bled to death while we watched.

Nobody cared much. Figured the girl had every right. Couple of the guys even joked about it, said it looked like the girl stuck it to him instead of the other way around. I think they should have buried him. Afterwards I walked up to the knoll and watched the city. Jim said those four guys were from the city. Said their sores proved it. The girl's name was Lisa. Wonder if she was the one Clipper had in mind for me? This evening I saw some lights, like headlights, coming out of the city.

274

JULY 2
I went to the knoll twice today. In between I moved about half my stuff out to the cave. Maybe I can even sink another well. Maybe I could sell some water.

I had a shot at Chuck's dog today and missed. I can't afford to waste ammunition on the damned thing. Tomorrow I'm going to look for a trap at the market.

Jim left a note on my front door. Said he was going to scout out the city. He'd better be careful. I heard bad things about the city folk.

JULY 3
That son of a bitch Clipper! Now he says he's got other guys bidding on this so called mystery girl of his. I told him I'd bid him a bullet if he fucked with my head, then I walked off. I was so pissed I didn't even look for a trap.

JULY 4
Some stupid son of a bitch from the city come up today. Said he always went to resorts to celebrate Independence Day. He blew his hand off with some homemade sort of firecracker. While I was patching him up, which consisted primarily of a tourniquet he's got to learn to hold himself, he talked about all the gunpowder down there. He says they been busting into National Guard Armories and collecting shells and powder, even things with gas in them. I know he wasn't lying. He was in too much pain to lie. I know he was from the city, too. He had the sores to prove it. I think he's going to die. He walked off and fell twice before he reached the road.

I moved some more stuff to the cave today. I think the chickens will go tomorrow. I don't know whether I should move them all, or just a couple. I don't want to fall prone to that 'eggs in one basket' sort of thing.

I watched from the knoll right before dark. I know Jim is down there right now. Makes me nervous for him.

I heard Chuck's dog howling on the way back in. He's in pain. Wish I could get a clear shot. I know he wouldn't be edible, but I knew Chuck and I wish I could end his dog's misery.

JULY 5
Jim's back! He says the city is all stirred up. There is some big rumor we got water and canned goods and all sorts of things up here and that we wouldn't share. Ha! If they only knew. He got a big bell from somewhere and hung it up from the arch in the gas station. Told me if I saw anything to ring like a son of a bitch. I moved the rest of my stuff to the cave.

JULY 6
I knew moving all my stuff to the cave wasn't a good idea. Chuck's dog got in and killed two of my chickens before I got out there. He ran off with a hen in his mouth and laughing fit to kill. Chuck's dog or not I got to end that son of a bitch. I'm going to take the other dead chicken and fill it up with glass. That'll do it. Wish I has some poison. Nobody's got poison, 'cept the city. Son of a bitch! I'm going back to bed.

*

I woke up late. I slept late after staying up stuffing the chicken and staking out the carcass. I walked to the knoll, sleepy. I could see lots of activity down by the city. They got a regular camp and it looked pretty darn military. I wonder if I broke my binos in two and lined them up could I see clearer? I don't want to take the chance that I can't.

Chicken with the glass was gone. Hope Chuck's dog got it.

Jim came by. He saw I'd been up late and didn't stay long. Just said he was training a couple of fellows in marching and order arms and all that shit. That's one thing I think he's a fool on. All you got to teach a fellow these days is how to crawl silent and be patient. Well, he plays his games.

JULY 7
There's a fire down at Hill's Creek. That's about fifteen miles outside the city. I went up to the knoll as soon as I saw the smoke, but I couldn't tell whether it was the city guys that did it or not. Who knows what it might have been. I watched for a long time.

Clipper came up while I was watching. He said Jim had said to tell me he was going down to the town to see who was doing the burning and all. He said he'd lower the price for the girl. Said none of my chickens better have sores. He's just trying to get me to talk 'bout my chickens.

I haven't really got all that much to do since I finished the cave. I'll start digging a well in it tomorrow.

JULY 8
Jim's back! He says it was the city guys that burned Hill's Creek. Says they didn't even look for anything after they burned it, didn't even warn or threaten the folks there before they did it. Said they shot at him through these rifles with special scopes on them. He figures they must be night vision scopes. Says he has to get one for himself. Says he was lucky they missed. I saw the bullet holes in his sleeve. He was lucky.

Chuck's dog died! Hurrah! I found him off the trail up to the knoll. He was lying there stinking and I know it was my glass that killed him. If he didn't have so damned many sores I could skin him. He must have been hurting something fierce.

I told Clipper I wanted to think about the girl. I know he must have got a high price from me, so I want to talk him down a bit. I can't go shelling out chickens for just anything, you know.

JULY 9
The City guys burned a bunch of lean to's about twenty miles below us. That's a long way to come. They must have gas to spare to come so far. I don't think they warned those folks either. They just come out of that city all sored and kill anybody they can. Somebody ought to put them out of their misery. I'm going down to see the lean to's tomorrow. First I'll watch from the knoll, though. I don't want to take any chances.

JULY 14
Been down to the lean to's. Can't believe what happened. I watched from the knoll for a while first thing in the morning. No sign of anything so I hunted up Jim and told him I was going. He

came with me. We walked for fifteen miles. We were right above the river when Jim stopped. He had the funniest screwed up look to his face — like he stepped in something that bit.

We went off the road and just sat there. He didn't move for the longest time. It was about four in the afternoon. I heard some folks out on the road. It was some traders, five of them, going for the lean to's. I guess they hadn't heard about the city burnings. They got around the bend to the river and we heard shooting. We crawled through the thicket. The city guys had staked out the bridge over the river and punctured those trader's. They were laughing and cutting them into pieces when we saw them! They were going to eat them!

I wanted to come back, but Jim got a real funny look on his face. He was rock hard and soft at the same time. He didn't want to go, but he was going anyway. I figured I had gone that far I might just as well go a little further.

We started crawling after dark. When I say crawling I mean crawling. We crawled to the river and swam across. There must have been ten of those city guys there and we didn't want anything to do with them. We didn't see any special scopes, though.

After crossing the river we kept out of sight and paralleled the road down to the lean to's. There wasn't any sign of anything. There was just smoking ruins and stuff. Couple of burned out cars that somebody had hooked together and lived out of, a shack or two, all burnt up. That kind of stuff. We didn't go in. Jim said to shush and then crawled backward. I wanted to ask him what was going on but it was better we be quiet.

The next morning I saw why Jim didn't want to go in. A couple of guys came out of the woods. These guys had sores and rifles with these night scope things on them. They had coffee over the burnt ruins. Real coffee, none of that hickory stuff we make up in the hills. Jim took the one on the right and I took the one on the left. We plugged them. They lay there for a few minutes. Finally nothing happened so Jim said to cover him and ran over to the bodies. He grabbed two rifles and a whole box of ammunition! We are rich men!

We didn't waste any time around there. We figured the guys

from the bridge would be checking up on the two nighters, if they hadn't already heard the shots! We put some quick miles between us, then waited for them all hidden. Nobody followed us so we took the old highway route back home. Took us a while, but we are back and we got the goods! Can't believe it. I keep telling myself that those nighters burnt the lean to folks and they deserved dying. Wish I knew what was happening in the city. Something is happening for fellows like that to be out in the country. I'm going to keep close watch for the next few weeks just in case.

That rifle is a nice piece of work. I don't want to use it less I have to. It's got batteries to make the night stuff work. I don't want to wear down the batteries.

JULY 15

Rained all day. I hate the rain. I always think of the times right after The Bomb. I always think about running around in the house trying to save those dumb ass chickens. Everywhere water hit it sizzled. I finally got what was left of them down to the basement. Ruined all my coats and shirts doing it. I thought the rain was going to sizzle right through to the basement. I had no where else to go, and those dumb chickens shitting all over everything! I hate the rain and I never go out in it. Very few people do, less they're Sore and stupid. I imagine the city folks are out. I don't care.

Good thing about the rain is that if it doesn't rain tomorrow there'll be a heavy market. Everybody celebrates when the rain stops.

I sat in the house all day and stared at a can of tomatoes. I won't open something good when it's bad out. I don't want anything to mess up the enjoyment. Everything's got to be right before I open a can.

JULY 16

Market! Hurrah! I didn't do too good in trading. But I was awfully happy anyway. I got in an argument with Clipper about whether a bow was better or a sling. He says it takes too long to get set and it is too unsure to sling something. I told him what about stringing the goddamn bow? I said you can cut a sling out of anything, a bow you have to make. One thing led to another and the son of a bitch got some guy to shoot against me. Bow against sling. I looked at him and knew I'd been set up.

We hung an old tire from a tree at fifty paces.

The guy was good. He was from over the hill. I never seen him before, but later I heard people talking about how he'd never been beat. I beat him. I beat him good. He put eight out of ten arrows through the tire in twenty seconds. I put ten rocks through and I had time left. Maybe I didn't do too good in trading, but I won that fellow's good coat. I gave him my old one. He was even my size.

I looked at the can of tomatoes today. Um um! That's a thing which is enjoyed by anticipation.

JULY 17

I'll be a son of a bitch! This is the strangest day. I went up to the knoll to look at the city. Nothing was happening out there. Few cars on the roads, but it felt all right.

On my way back I met a guy. He was crawling through the brush. He was dirty and ragged like I never seen, and he was blind. I thought he was laying a trap at first, and I was going to shoot him, but I didn't and we got to talking. He's blind. Can't see at all. He's been living since The Bomb by crawling through the brush and feeling plants. That's what he does, feels plants. He picks them out and tells them he's sorry and holds them against his belly. If they feel good and tell him it's alright, he eats them. If they feel dark then he doesn't. It's hard to believe somebody could live all this long that way.

Anyway, to make a long story short, before he crawled off into the brush he told me all sorts of stuff about which plants to eat when. I found out there's plants I could have been eating all along and didn't. There's plants I can take apart and eat certain parts of. There's plants you can eat raw but not cooked. There's all sorts of things about plants to be learned. I'm going to mix some of those plants into the goop I give the chickens and feed one of the chickens special. If the chicken lives I'll live. I was so excited I didn't even think about the tomatoes. It's not too late. I think I'll think about that can of tomatoes some more right now. Ummm!

JULY 18
Clipper came by today. He said he's bringing the girl by tomorrow so I can see her. I sure am confused by this. I don't know what to think. I hardly ever talk to a girl that's not married, and then they are spoken for or sore. I don't know what to do or say. I got to clean the house. Fuck the tomatoes. I'm just too scared. I'm not going to write much today. I'll make it up to the knoll. What will I say to her?

JULY 19
I must have swept the house twenty times today while waiting. I know that Clipper must know the mental agony I am going through. He didn't show up. He's probably laughing like Chuck's dog the time he got the chickens!

JULY 20
Clipper came by. He had the girl with him. There was an old fellow with them. He was packed to march. He said he was going to the city to find his wife. He'll never come back. I'm sorry for him. But he left his daughter with me. He didn't take no chickens. He just said if I could spare something so he could make it to the city he'd be grateful. If not, he was glad that Clipper had found somebody good to look after his Clair.

I didn't know what to say. I just stood there looking at the girl. She looked at me and didn't say a word. We all must have stood in front of the house for an hour. Clipper, the guy, me, the girl. Me and the girl just stared at each other. I could see she didn't have any sores. I could see it. She looked healthy. I couldn't believe it. Finally the guy said he'd like to be going if it was all right with me. I looked at the fellow a moment, then I went in and got the can of tomatoes. It was the only thing I had that I could think to give him for the girl. I knew it wasn't much, but I don't think he minded. He knew he was going to die. He put the can in his pack and looked at the girl and started to cry, right there in front of Clipper and me. I offered to shake hands when he was done crying, I don't usually offer my hand to anybody, but he didn't take it, just waved it away and walked off blubbering. I don't think he could see for the tears he was crying.

That left Clipper and me. Clipper cleared his throat. I was back to looking at the girl and I didn't notice him till he cleared his throat. I looked at him.

"Aw Hell," he said. "Just invite me when you cut up one of those chickens for a Sunday." Then he walked off.

I thought I was going to have to pay a whole brace of chickens for the girl, but that's not important. I think both Clipper and the guy knew I would have to use the chickens to support her. I would have paid the chickens if anybody pressed me. I just didn't think.

So after Clipper and her dad went away we just stared at each other some more. Finally I mumbled something about wouldn't she like to come in. She nodded and I held the door open for her to walk in. I should have thought to carry her over the threshold. But, like I say, I wasn't thinking much. We've been sitting for a couple of hours now staring at each other. It's getting dark. I finally got up the nerve to write in this book. I'm about done now. I'm going to close the book and go to bed. I can't believe I'm married.

JULY 21

I can't believe I'm married! I haven't been with a girl since before The Bomb. She has no sores. All she did was hold me and touch me and say she couldn't believe I had no sores. What they been saying, "A match made in heaven has no sores," is true! She doesn't care that I'm missing some teeth and a lot of hair. Everybody knows that that doesn't stop the chance of babies. It's sores that ruins the babies. Here I am talking about babies and I've only been married one day. I can't believe it!

JULY 22

Excuse me for not writing too much yesterday. I was otherwise occupied. Today I showed Clair the chickens and the cave and the well and everything. I feel like a spring that has been dammed too long and has busted. It seems all I do is talk a lot and smile. Can't help myself for smiling.

282

She's a smart one. She told me her father used to be an engineer before The Bomb. Said she has two brothers. I know one got killed in the city. I don't know about the other one. Her mother died Bomb day. A lot of people died Bomb day. She says she can sew me linings in jackets. Says she can make us some extra goods for trade if I find jackets. She told me what to look for, what seams have to be in good shape, what kind of stuff to try and get, that sort of thing. I told her we had guns but that she would have to learn the sling. She said okay. Said she had shot a few guns right after The Bomb and didn't need any real how-to on that. Said she'd never used a sling before, just a knife. Showed me her knife. She's so tiny it looked like a sword in her hand. She threw it halfway through the door. She is a smart one.

JULY 23

We broke down the rifles today in the morning. Went to market later. I could tell everybody was impressed and all. I knew everybody was looking at me, and I felt sort of proud. And me missing half my teeth, too.

Later that night we went up to the knoll. I wanted to give her a feel for the nightscope so I turned it on brief for her. I also wanted to get her to know the paths around here in the dark. That is handy stuff to know.

After the sun set we watched the city for a while. Even though I know it is full of Sores and charred ugly in the day, it is sort of beautiful in the night. There is that glow in the yellow cloud around it that you can see at night. It's sort of romantic. Before I knew it me and Clair were doing it right there on the knoll. If anybody had tried to sneak up on us they sure would have succeeded. We got back to the house, did it again.

JULY 24

Jim came by today. He wished me and Clair the best. Said he hadn't been by because he was going around the hill counting people. Said we must have maybe five thousand people in the hills at most. He said the City has maybe fifty thousand. It's not good odds and I knew what was going through his mind. I told him I'd watch the city extra hard. After last night I certainly will. Clair will, too. After Jim left I got to work on the well in the cave. It's opening up fine. I need some timber and Clair offered to go haul some for me. I told her no, I didn't think we should go out separate. She thought about that and said that I was probably right. She did haul some of the dirt out. Told me she was going to have to learn to sew rugs. Said she wasn't going to have any of her kids crawling on a dirt floor. We both started laughing like you couldn't believe. We just rolled around and laughed. When we finally laughed so hard we cried ourselves out we started looking at each other. Be damned if we didn't do it again right there. Can't believe I was tired last week.

JULY 25

There's more smoke in the hills. I didn't see the city guys by the binos, but I know it must have been them. I'm glad it was some ways over to the side of us. But I'm not happy about it. Means some people died. I think maybe we all better do some planning. If those Sores are going to be coming after us we better set some traps and such. I'll talk to Jim about it the next time I see him.

Clair says she knows a boy who can sew. She says she wants to put him to work. Is there any way we can trade more or something. I told her to let me think about it.

Seems to me Capitalism was the root of all our troubles before. That and Communism. I'm so against politics it is incredible. Still, it is hard to beat the idea of getting enough goods stored that we don't have to eat roots.

JULY 26

Some guy came by selling airplane parts. He said he could get instruments, metal coverings, even engines. The guy is a real dodo. I know he thinks he is helping civilization and all that, but who the hell wants to buy an airplane when it takes all one's got to keep food on the table. The guy didn't look too nutritionally sound. He didn't have sores or anything, but he was just so skinny and his eyes burned a little. I'm sure that the next rain he'll burn up and die. He's ripe for fever if anybody is.

Some girl over in Coppertown gave birth to a dead kid. Made

Clair cry. She stopped, but it's that kind of news bugs a guy.

Over all, I'd say this day is just strange, between the airplane seller and news of dead babies. Clair seems to have the answer when things get strange. She just sews. Sews like a madwoman. But I don't have the answer. I'm the kind of guy who broods. I don't like brooding. But I don't know what else to do. It's the way I am. I got to get some more candles.

JULY 27

There was a mad dog down in the market today. He had sores and was snapping and foaming. He came fast out of the brush behind Sculler's Tent. Bit a kid in the arm before anybody could get a hold of it. It was that old lady who lives down by the city hall that got the dog. She held it still enough, all the while snapping and trying to get at her, until old Scullers could get around his board and stick a knife in it. People tried to suck the poison out of the kid who got bit's arm. Don't know how it will turn out. I hope he doesn't get sick. The old lady got burned by some of the sores on the dog.

Somebody said there was a two-headed calf over the hill. I don't believe it. Everybody talks about muties, and there's even fools who say that if you breed muties proper you could get a better supply of food. They're full of the brown stuff, all right. Besides how could a calf live if he had two heads telling him what to do? He wouldn't know whether to go left or right, sit or stand, shit or eat. Two headed calves, hah!

Clair has now got two whole bundles of jackets to line. The trade is right for clothes so I'm going to go ahead and get a bundle of rags. Clair says she has got the kid to help her coming in. I sure feel funny about having so many people around me. I suppose I shouldn't, but I do.

JULY 28

Hit water in the cave well. I'm going to try selling a little down to the next place on the hill. I figure I can haul it in an old wheelbarrow I seen downtown. I don't know if anybody wants to buy water downhill, or whether I can get enough to make it worthwhile, but I want to see what's happening downhill, see what the latest news from the City is. I'm just worried about leaving Clair. She says not to worry. Says she'll be fine. She says to hold off for a day or two and if the kid works out he can sleep atop the gas station under the fallen sign. Says he'll make a fine lookout. Maybe that's a good idea. I hate trusting people, but what choice I got? Waiting a day or two is good because I can tell Clipper and Jim to watch around the place for me. I trust them, don't I?

JULY 29
The kid is a little fart. I doubt if he is over eight. But he's smart enough. Says he'll work hard. Says sleeping over the garage is fine, won't be no trouble. Just wants to eat regular.

Last week I had my mouth to feed. Now I got two more. Yeah, they're all small mouths, but they're mouths all the same. I don't know how I'm going to do it, but Clair says it will all work out. She's probably right, though it takes some kind of thinking to agree. The kid's down over the garage right now. He worked all day, did one more jacket than Clair told him to. Seems like there ought to be more to life for a kid than sewing jackets and sleeping in the open under a fallen sign. Guess we blew that all to hell.

JULY 30
I'm going to go downhill. I got the barrow and I got a couple of racks of jugs. I'm not going to take a good rifle. I'll leave that with Clair. Nobody knows about the scopes and I want to keep it that way. The kid is working good and Jim and Clipper will be around. I guess it will be safe.

The only thing that worries me is that it looks like the city is stirring. I can see through the binos and it looks like they got a lot of army stuff down there. It could be they are just painting all their trucks green, but I think they must have got them out of some storage some place. I wonder if the army had electric ignitions before The Bomb?

Anyway, Jim said he'll keep a look out from the knoll and that nothing will happen.

AUGUST 2

Lordy, I'm a rich man. Those people downhill are right on the burn line from The Bomb. Everything is Sore down to the soil. They said it used to be quite a lot of trees, but now it is stumps and brush. I sold my water easy. I got a jacket from before The Bomb with real lining, not rags. I got three cans of peaches, can you believe it? I got a walking stick, don't know what I'll use that for, a pair of earmuffs and some real shoes.

Downhill they get things from the City. You got to pay someone with a geiger counter to check the goods, but there is a fair amount of stuff to pick and choose from.

After I left some guy caught me on the road. He was puffing and I knew he'd been running. He said he had a couple of boys who would come up and get the water from me. I don't like the idea of people knowing where I live, but I think I can work something out with the guy to set up some sort of regular trade. He says he can pull up carpets from houses for lining and send me as much as I want. This is something to think about. I'll talk to Clair about it. Maybe she'll want a whole carpet for the floor. Maybe.

Speaking of Clair, she was fine when I got back. I can't tell you how good I felt inside when I came up to the house and she opened the door. I didn't know a guy could feel that good. And you should have seen her eyes when I opened my pack and brought out the peaches. I set them on the table and we looked at them for a long time. She wanted to open one right then, but I told her they had to be seasoned. I explained that eating real stuff is a trick in anticipation, that when we were done anticipating that can of peaches would be the best taste in her life. She looked some confused when I hid the peaches under the floor. But that's okay. I'm going to show her how much I really paid for her.

The kid has been working up a storm. He is the most grateful little cuss I have ever seen. I'm going to have to do one of those chickens and have a dinner soon. One of them is getting too old to lay. I owe Jim, there's Clair to think about, and there's this kid and Clipper, too. I'll ask Clair if she knows how to cook up a chicken.

287

AUGUST 3

There was a fellow in the market today all beat up looking. He said he was in that town that got burned. I was right, it was burned by the city people. This guy was beaten up and left for dead. He was just bloody, though, and he lay quiet and waited. He heard them talking; he said the City is planning to tax everybody everywhere. They think taxing is just killing and taking all you got. He says they are better dressed and equipped than us up here, but says they got sores all over. Their clothes are wet with the leakage.

Anyway, this fellow has been going through the hills warning people about the city. I don't think he has any family or anything, he just wants to do it. Figures people have got to be warned, got to have a chance. We talked to him a long time, asked about weapons and such. The city people don't have slings or bows or anything like that. They got real army stuff, lots of scopes like the ones Jim and I got.

After we finished talking to this fellow Jim came up to the house. We sat around and drew maps and figured what we would need to defend ourselves. The main thing is to chop a few of the trees across roads and make sure they have to come on foot. I volunteered to go with him on doing this. I got Clair to think about and I want to make sure she is safe. I don't want to take a chance on any Sores coming along while I'm wheeling water.

I did decide to wheel water. I'm just going to do it myself a couple of times. Nobody is going to ambush a guy with a wheelbarrow, and if it works out Jim said he'd run guard for me, said he could get me other guys to work. There's a lot of guys who want to work. There just isn't enough food to pay them with.

I got to watch the city more. I haven't been watching enough.

AUGUST 4

Clair and I opened a can of peaches. She cried at the taste. She couldn't believe all the syrup. Afterwards we did it. Not much else happened all day. It threatened to drizzle so I just settled for dragging logs to the cave and covering the tracks.

AUGUST 5

That kid is Clair's brother! I can't believe it.

We opened another can of peaches and I caught her going outside with one of the halves. She broke down and cried. She said that he was her brother and wouldn't steal anything from me. She said she was sorry and I was the nicest man she ever knew please don't throw her out.

I can't throw her out!

But her brother!

I didn't know what to do.

So I thought for a long time. Finally I said he could guard the stuff in the cave at night. That'll keep him warm. That's all I wanted to say because I was still confused.

AUGUST 6

I am still confused by finding out that the kid is her brother. I guess I better say his name is Charles. If he's family I got to call him something other than kid or hey you. Anyway, he's 12. He's pretty short, but his growing has been done after The Bomb. He's lucky he has no sores. Clair is actually 17. I didn't know that. Her father was only 37, but he looked like 73. I guess I don't look too young for that matter myself. They, Charles and Clair and their father, had been living best they could since The Bomb. He had apparently taken them on a vacation when the bombs went off, and they stayed up and lived off the land. They survived, except the father couldn't take the idea that his wife and youngest son was still back in the City. So he had talked to Clipper who knew me, and it all worked out. Except I didn't know I was buying another guys family. It doesn't matter. I know I was lucky to get Clair. If I had known she was packing a brother I might not have been willing to deal.

AUGUST 7

Charles has finished all the coats and we have to go to market. He said he was so nervous about whether I would accept him or not he had done nothing but work. Clair sews, he works and I brood. He has done more than enough to eat, the question is, can I find the goods? I better think about going to downhill and selling water.

AUGUST 8

Jim and six others came by early. They said they were going to chop a few trees across the road. I went with them. We were a mile down the road when Charles came running up. He said could he go with us, said he'd pull his share. The others looked doubtful. Nobody wants to have do with a kid that's good for nothing, and he didn't look big enough to do his share.

He did his share, though. He did the footwork of finding good trees, had a fire going with a brush cover come noon, and even found two snakes for eating. Good snakes. Nobody was sorry he'd come.

On the way home I showed him how to sling. He's good. He hit the tree he was aiming at right off. What impressed me, though, was that he listened to all I said before he slung. I remember before The Bomb no kid wanted to listen. Things change.

AUGUST 9

A lot of burning downhill. It makes me nervous. I am glad we got the roads blocked.

Later in the day I killed that old hen. We had Clipper and Jim and Charles and Clair and me. We didn't eat in the house because people will smell and come around and stand outside. Things like that have even been known to get violent. Instead I had Charles go and find a good place deep in the woods and set up a brush cover to hide the smoke and kill the smell. He stood watch with a pistol while Clair cooked. Later Jim and Clipper and I came. We sat around an old board Clipper and Jim lugged in. We had chicken soup, chicken gravy, chicken broiled, chicken barbed, chicken everything. And we had eggs, of course. And we had lots of roots and things like what that crawling fella had told me about. We didn't have anything to make really fancy dishes, but Clair managed to make a bunch of different tasting chicken dishes, and we just ate and ate. After dinner Clipper suddenly asked if we could all be silent. Said he should have said something earlier, but he hadn't. Then he said grace. He thanked the Lord and he was crying. Nobody said anything. We just said amen. Charles asked what Amen meant and I had to explain it to him. I told him Amen means the end of something. He said Amen like The Bomb? We were all quiet at that. The topper of the party, though, was a pitcher of lemonade. Charles had found some real lemons and Clair had traded a jacket for real sugar. It was a high price, but when I think of standing there in the trees, eating chicken and being with friends, words just don't go far enough.

AUGUST 10

I'm going downhill tomorrow. Can't see much happening in the city from the knoll, but I'm nervous just the same. Jim says he'll keep an eye out. Charles said he'll keep watch nights, and if anything gets strange they will get to the cave. I still feel nervous. Clipper is coming with me. I still feel nervous.

AUGUST 16

I can't stop crying. Clipper and I went downhill. We were just the other side of the river when Clipper dropped. I started to bend over him when the sound of the gun reached me. It was my bending over that saved my life. I ran for the side of the road. A bullet must have hit the stock of my rifle because I was twisted around and my rifle jumped across the road. I didn't go for it. Somebody was a good shot with a good rifle.

I made it to the brush. People hunted me for hours. I killed one with my knife before he could shout and kept going. It was dark before I could get clear away.

I didn't know where I was. I was so twisted around. I walked half of the next day before I realized that I was going in the wrong direction. The hills are a little curved here and there and the sun was hidden by overcast and I just couldn't find my way.

I finally realized where I was. I couldn't go back the way I came, and the only way I knew was up by Stonesville. That's way the hell up and around, but I had no choice. I had only my sling and a knife. Even my coat was back on the barrow.

I made Stonesville the next night. I was cold. Somebody in Stonesville gave me a shirt. It wasn't a jacket, but it cut the cold. I kept walking.

When I got back I found the city had come. Apparently Clipper and me had run into an advance scout. The rest of them just boiled up the hill, pulled our logs out of the way and just ransacked the town. There was only a few people left alive when I got back.

I ran through all the smoke and ruins. The house was burned to the ground. I found Charles, or what was left of him, outside. He had tried to run. They had bashed his head in to kill him, then they must have thrown him on the fire. Then they ate some of him. That's all I can figure from the sign.

Clair must have stayed in the house and tried to protect it. She was burnt. I think she must have took the pistol to her head before she suffered, though. I couldn't tell for sure, but it looked like she had just laid on the floor and shot herself through the mouth with the rifle. Not raped or anything. I hope so. I can't bear the thought of those city Sores catching her alive.

Jim isn't around. Somebody said he was seen walking down the road towards the City with a brand new rifle in his hands. That means he wasn't caught. He was probably out in the woods or off somewhere when the city came.

I'm in the cave now. I can't stop crying. I'm going to finish this entry, then I am going to the city. I'll open up the cave for whoever is left in town. There's only a half dozen, but they got a right to live. It's those city Sores that don't have the right.

I'm not going to write anymore. I don't want to live anymore. I'm going to get my rifle and go. I can kill a lot of Sores with that nightscope. And I will. Maybe I can catch up to Jim and we can go together.

~

Al Case is a baby boomer (1948), born to a nuclear family in Seattle, Washington. Al has been writing since the age of 19. He is particularly fond of EOTWAWKI themes, and has written epic sci fi/fantasy/horror in that realm, including the Monkeyland *series and the* Machina *series. His website is:* AlCaseBooks.com

FOLDED
Helen French

Ashes and memories and a heap of obligation were all I had left of my mother.

I might've ignored her dying wishes, but Mother had put the requests in a will, which was a surprise, given that she'd had Alzheimer's for so many years. I supposed she'd made it official when her neurons were still firing properly, long ago.

"It would be easier for everyone if you scattered her ashes somewhere locally," David said, even though I was already in the car. I'd packed a bag full of essentials and my mother's ashes fit neatly into one of the coffee cup compartments between the driver and passenger seats. I stuck her tiny holo-drive into the other compartment.

"She wanted to go home to Formby, to the town where she grew up."

"At least wait until morning."

A reasonable request, but I didn't want her ashes in my house a second longer. They made me think of death and regret and I needed to focus on living. Screw reason. She had to go, and it was what she wanted. She had to go *now*.

"You can stay behind if you like," I said.

We both knew he wouldn't. We'd only been married a year and leaving now would mean the end of us. David shook his head and climbed into the passenger seat. "You might need help with the driving," he said.

*

At Watford Gap the traffic was funnelled into a single long queue so that our papers could be checked. Most cars were turned away. A few drove on. It was a bright sort of night, with a full moon to guide us, and swathes of stars staring down.

We reached the kiosk, where a middle-aged man who looked like he hadn't slept for a week grumbled at us. "Quotas for the day have all been met. No travelling through without prior permission."

I pulled a document out of my wallet. "I have a travel certificate, signed by my lawyer."

He took a minute to look it over, though it was only a page long. All sorts of passes could be bought or arranged if you had enough money. My mother's solicitors had ensured I could execute the will without issue.

"Taking your mother home, Miss Hannah Jenner? Be careful out there. You don't want to drive over the barriers because you're looking at the wreckage instead of the road."

"I've seen it all before."

"That'll help a little, but confidence can be dangerous too. The rescue teams won't come out in the early hours, so drive slowly."

*

The roads north spiralled higher and higher until we were many metres above ground level, until it felt like my car was speeding through the heavens. Until we looked down, that is.

The scenery changed as the motorway rose. Where it was green and unspoiled at the start of the journey, it became charred and broken a few miles in.

Old roads lay below us, splintered into pieces by an almighty force. Cavernous shafts ripped up the land, threatening to swallow you up if you stared at them for too long.

Every structure that had ever been built in the Midlands, from house to farmhouse to warehouse, was smashed in so badly that not a single wall stood upright.

"I'm glad I can't remember when it happened," David said, peering out at the ruined landscape.

"I was four years old. Did I ever tell you we lived at the northern edge of the perimeter? The house next to ours was gone. My garden ripped away. Children I went to nursery with disappeared overnight. My memories are all mixed up with what I've read, the pictures I've seen. But I see flashes sometimes when I dream. Images of people running to rescue their neighbours. Nobody coming out alive."

Once there had been lush fields here, reaching far into the distance. Then they got Folded, as the media called it. Screwed up and crunched. Like it had all been concertinaed, then stretched back out.

The forensic experts' best guess was aliens, which was the first sign that they knew nothing at all. Their second was that it was a new weapon of mass destruction, from an enemy we didn't know we had. Whatever it was, it happened in an instant. There were no videos. Satellite footage showed only that one second the land was normal and the next it was shattered.

Miraculously, our family survived whatever happened, only for my mother's mind to break years later, as proteins misfolded, memories unfolded, her sense of self dissolved. Was it worse to survive and slowly see yourself disappear? Or to die so quickly you would never know what had happened?

"Will we ever take back the land?" David wondered, in an awestruck tone.

"No," I said, because it was the second time I had been that way and in twenty years nothing had changed. The ground was still torn up, shredded into pieces, unfixable. Steel mixed with earth mixed with bones.

My parents split acrimoniously two years after the event. They couldn't be fixed either. Eight years later, Mother and I headed south, crossing the Folding for the first time once the burning had calmed down enough for engineers to build roads above it all. A middling scientist before the event, she decided to devote her life to the sciences afterwards, to finding a resolution. She thought hard work would be enough, never understanding that effort didn't always equal results, for if so every illness would be defeated already. I never saw my father again and he died when I was fifteen.

"Grief is turning you into a pessimist," David said. But his gaze dropped down as if he regretted being so cruel.

"You're not wrong," I said, and we drove onwards.

*

Dawn rose and hope did too. The land abruptly flattened out and turned back to great big stretches of farmers' fields, towns, and cities. It was almost impossible to reconcile what came before and after, that they could both exist at the same time. Yet they did.

295

"What's first, ashes or the message?" David asked.

I stared down at the holo-drive. "The message." It would only open for one person. An old boyfriend of my mother's from before she was married. I had to know what it said.

Once she'd lost the memories of my father, or at least when they came to her so rarely as to feel like magic, it was Aaron she turned to. Aaron she talked about until the day she died. Surely he could bring her back to life for me, share tales of when she was still driven and vivacious?

"Do you want me to come with you?" David asked and I shook my head. This felt private, even if I would have to share it with a stranger.

*

Aaron lived in a neat white house with a blue Skoda outside and a bicycle leaning against the front wall. How did this perfect normality exist at the same time as the broken Midlands? But it was the way of the world. Ignore that which you cannot fix, because if you don't you'd have to weep every day instead of keeping on keeping on.

A white-haired gentleman with dark bushy eyebrows answered the door at the first knock.

"Can I help," he asked.

"Aaron Clark?"

He nodded.

"You knew my mother: Kate Jenner. She died. I'm sorry. She left a message for you. It won't play without your handprint. Can I listen to it with you?"

The poor man nodded again and I felt awful but there was no nice way to do it.

"Bloody hell," he said. "Kate's gone? Come in, come in. My wife's taken the grandkids to the park, so it's just us, but I know where she keeps the tea if you want some."

I didn't want tea, I wanted answers and insights, but I said yes all the same.

He parked me at a table in their kitchen-diner, then busied himself at the kettle. Once hot drinks were made, he sat back down.

"Was she ill?"

I nodded. "Alzheimer's."

"That's hard," he said.

I reached into my pocket and pulled out the holo-drive. It was a small object, about the width of an orange, but flat on the top and bottom. The law firm had kept it for years; they'd taken Aaron's handprint from the public archive on my mother's instructions.

"Do you mind?" I asked and Aaron took it from me.

As his hand wrapped around the side of the device, a small image flickered into life above it.

He put it back on the table and I had to hold back a sob.

There was my mother, alive and vibrant, but only 15 centimetres tall. Her eyes met the camera, alert and understanding, the way they used to be.

"Aaron," she began with a smile. "I have missed you all these years." Then the smile faded. "I feel as if everything is about to change. The ground beneath me shifts like sand. I'm struck by this need to make things permanent, to make a record of what I'm feeling, to make videos like this, so that one day I can watch them all back with hindsight, able perhaps at last to pinpoint when it happened, whatever it is that is happening inside my head.

"There is one memory that should not be forgotten, and I want to entrust you with it, to see that the truth gets out. You were a fine reporter back in the day and you will know what to do.

"You remember the Folding? I was so close to it that it's burned into my memory. I stepped outside my front door to see death and destruction everywhere. It was too late to save anyone the very second that it happened.

"I suppose thousands of people lived next door to a house that was Folded. But mine was right in the centre of the northernmost line and no one ever came to ask why. Surely the forensic scientists could see where the power had come from? It seems the Folding destroyed the evidence. The outbuilding, where my husband and I had worked for so long, was demolished. We would've felt relieved if we hadn't felt so guilty.

"We stayed awake for three days, talking and blaming one

another. Whose idea had it been anyway? Whose arrogance let us think we could create a new way to travel from point to point? How did the machine literally fold land? We didn't even know!

"We had Hannah to look after and she saved our souls. No one came and so we pretended it had nothing to do with us, that we were not culpable, that we had not killed millions of people. Day after day after day went by and then my husband and I drifted apart, I moved away from the scene of the crime, and I lived.

"But when I die, and I think that day may come soon, someone should know what happened so that a name can be put to that villainy. Tell the world I'm sorry, for the little it will do. Make my truth permanent, where I cannot be. Try to prevent my daughter from being persecuted." She took a deep breath, then sighed heavily. "Do not blame yourself for loving me, back when you couldn't know what I would become. And Hannah, if you hear this, don't blame yourself for loving me after the fact. I always loved you very much. The only good work I ever did."

She changed tone abruptly after that, said "Aaron, I will tell you as many details as I can remember," and the rest of her secrets poured out, fact by fact, proof by proof. She condemned my father and herself, leaving no doubt that their selfishness, thoughtlessness and ambition had caused the incident that doomed so many. I was transfixed, burning with horror and shame.

At last Kate Jenner finished confessing, whispered a thank you, blinked out of existence, and was dead once again.

It was my turn to fold.

As Aaron took everything in, stunned and silent, I began to cry for the mother I had lost not once, but twice. I wept at the kitchen table, as my past turned into something dark and uncomfortable.

Aaron did not comfort me but instead waited until my tears had stopped. His gaze was direct and sharp. "You really didn't know about this?" he asked. The journalist in him double-checking his source.

I shook my head.

"Was she in her right mind when she recorded it?" He gestured at the holo-drive, now useless. It would not play again.

298

"Who can know for sure? The Alzheimer's had already taken hold. But she looked lucid." And it felt true.

"Then I have to investigate," Aaron said. He stood up and seemed younger somehow, as if the news had changed him.

I stood up, changed also. "Thank you," I said, before fleeing.

*

David didn't understand why I wanted to leave in such a hurry.

"Did Aaron upset you?" he asked while driving away as instructed.

"No," I replied, because the problem was nothing to do with Aaron, and I wiped away the tear that had rolled down my cheek, betraying me. "It's time for the ashes. I'll be all right once we've done that."

*

We drove to a car park nestled into the coastline, then scrambled up sand dunes until the sea came into view. It stretched large into the horizon, spectacular and intimidating.

"There's sea down south," David said, grumbling.

"Not this sea."

I'd visited Formby beach on family trips growing up – before the Folding, of course. I had only the vaguest memories of it, but they flooded back now.

"You could see Blackpool Pleasure Beach from here on a good day," I said, remembering what my mother used to say.

"What's that?"

"Nothing now," I said. What was pleasure after so much darkness? It had felt cheap, unearned. And so resorts like Blackpool had faded away, leaving only empty hotels and quiet towns behind them.

My blood had played its part in that. Was the cause.

David interrupted my thoughts. "Have we got permission to scatter ashes here?"

"The solicitors said it wasn't needed if we were close enough to the water."

We trekked across the damp sand; it firmed up beneath our feet the closer we got to the waves crashing down.

"Marriage is based on vows, isn't it?" I began, thinking of my

299

parents and their mistakes, and how by making it all a secret they'd made things worse, for themselves and everyone else.

He nodded.

"And you vowed to love me no matter what?"

Another nod and so I began my story, always looking at the sea or the urn and never at David's face.

Now and then I released a handful of my mother's remains, saying goodbye a fraction at a time, revealing the truth about the past in much the same fashion.

Just as her ashes were folded into the ocean, like eggs into batter, her crimes were folded into David's life. Inextricable and inescapable.

Once my obligations had been met and the urn emptied, I risked a glance upwards.

David's expression was unreadable. He stared at the sun ahead of us but his hand reached out and squeezed mine.

"We'll get through this," he said naively, and I loved him for it.

I squeezed his hand back and watched the sea. Waves broke and returned to the ocean, pulling my mother tighter and tighter into its grasp.

Had I forgiven her? Not yet.

She'd escaped her memories and the upcoming storm, but we had not. Aaron knew the truth now and would soon act on it.

David had no idea what was coming, nor I. But we still had hope and each other. It would have to be enough.

"Let's stay here awhile," I said.

~

Helen French is a writer who grew up in Merseyside, near the coast and now lives in Hertfordshire, UK with her young family. Her short stories have appeared in venues such as Flash Fiction Online, Shoreline of Infinity *and* Daily Science Fiction *and she is currently buried in novel-writing. You can find her on: Twitter @helenfrench.*

THE ROAD TO MANDALAY
David Turnbull

<u>22nd March</u>

A package arrived today, addressed to myself and Aleesha. My hands started to tremble when I saw that it was stamped with the red, white and blue symbol of the St. George's Militia. We waited till Annie and Beth were in bed before we opened it. Four bullets tumbled out. Each one had our initials scratched onto its side.

Aleesha wept when she saw them scattered across the kitchen table.

"They killed our son. Can't they just leave us be?"

"We reported them to the police," I said. "We're marked as informers now."

Aleesha picked up one of the bullets.

"I sent him out for a loaf of bread. He was only fourteen."

I put my arm around her. She sobbed against my shoulder.

"He was in the wrong place at the wrong time," I said. "He didn't have his ID with him. The shopkeeper denounced him as a thief – probably in exchange for militia protection."

She pushed me away. "I know the story. I know how they murdered our son. I also know that no one is ever going to be brought to justice." She swept up all of the bullets and held them in a clenched fist. "We're on their list. Some dark night we'll get a knock on the door."

"That why we have to get out," I told her. "We have to make our way to Mandalay. Geoff's there. He'll help us get set up."

Aleesha sighed.

"Do you even know where Mandalay is?"

I raised an eyebrow and reminded her that my brother had been there for the past two years. Aleesha took a sip of the tea I prepared from the nettles I'd gathered at the bomb crater on Brownhill Road. "I meant do you know how far away it is?"

301

Now I sighed.

"You know we can't stay here."

Aleesha drew a breath. What happened to Andrew was still raw for us both. She dabbed her eyes with a tissue. "Myanmar is too far away. The girls would never cope with the journey. We could try for Scotland."

"There's an electric fence at the border," I pointed out.

"People get through." She opened her hand. "These bullets are our passports. We can apply for political asylum."

"Droves of people get turned back every day. Do you want the girls to end up in one of those internment camps?"

"How about France?"

"They've sealed the tunnel."

"I've heard there are boats crossing the Channel from Folkestone."

I put my arm around her again. This time she didn't push me away.

"The French coastguard intercept the boats. Things are no better on the continent. Germany is being drawn into the war between Belgium and Luxemburg. Refugees are crossing the alps into Spain."

The lights went out. "Power cut is early tonight," said Alesha.

"Geoff says Myanmar is really opening up," I told her as I lit a candle. "It's the go to tourist destination for all the jet setters from India and China. The elite head for Mandalay. Hotels are crying out for staff. They have green glass in the windows. They call it the Emerald City. Geoff says he could get me a job as a kitchen porter and he'd get you into housekeeping. No questions asked. No papers needed. It's how he got started."

Candle light dancing on her face, she turned and looked at me and asked how we would get there. I told her that I'd heard of someone who could get us onto one of those big container ships that run out of Southampton.

"They're operated remotely by satellite and crewed by automated drones. Once you're on board there's no risk of anyone finding you till you reach the destination. There's one bound for Yangon in a couple of months. But it'll take all of our savings to pay the trafficker's fees."

There came a series of dull thuds in the near distance. The artillery of the Christian Socialist Alliance had commenced its sunset bombardment of the urban strongholds of the St. George's militia.

"There are rumours that Peckham is about to fall," said Aleesha. "Maybe if we can just hold out a few more weeks?"

I shook my head.

"It's like snakes and ladders. They take one area and lose another. The militia overran Balham last week. In the end, it'll come down to them fighting it out street by street."

30th June

Things have moved so fast in the past couple of months. Aleesha is gone. I have no idea where she is. Or if she is even still alive. I constantly promise the girls that when we reach Mandalay, I'll do something. That somehow, I'll find out where they took her. We'll all be together again and everything bad will finally be behind us at last.

I know in my heart that these are empty promises.

At first Annie and Beth treated the whole thing like they were on a huge adventure. We were smuggled onto the container ship at dusk, along with a dozen or so families who'd also paid to make the journey. Annie and Beth quickly made friends with the other children.

For us adults it was a sobering experience, dwarfed there on the vast deck amongst the towering stacks of multi-coloured metal containers. They reminded me of those building bricks we used to have as kids.

"They look like Lego," I said.

Annie just looked at me blankly.

"What's Lego?" asked Beth.

A lump came to my throat.

The fact that the containers were packed with the sort of cheap junk we used to buy in pound shops as kids was not lost on me. Nowadays this stuff is mass-produced in the Welsh Free Trade Zone, exclusively for export to the Far East. Talk about tables being turned.

The world has changed beyond recognition. I remember the arguments my brother used to have with my dad just after he was deported from Beijing. I remember how furious my dad became when Geoff told him he was going to try again. But Geoff was right. Anyone who wants a future these days has to head east. That's our yellow brick road.

We billeted ourselves in the shadowed alleyways between the stacks of containers, setting out our sleeping bags amongst our suitcases and our rucksacks, erecting an old garden parasol that I'd retrieved from the rubble of a shelled house. We hung washing lines and endlessly counted and recounted our supply of tinned food and bottled water, hoping we'd all brought enough to see us through to journey's end.

The weather was mild and the sea was calm. The children played hide and seek, inventing a new version which encompassed the fixed daily routes of the spidery maintenance drones, slapping their shell casings and running off in vain attempts to somehow get them to deviate from the fixed predictability of their programming.

For a week or so it seemed that the journey would be plain sailing all the way. We would disembark at the port and apply for asylum. Aleesha had kept the bullets that had been posted through our letter box and the worthless crime reference number we'd been issued after Andrew was murdered. I didn't envisage any difficulty in getting our claims for political asylum validated once we produced them as evidence.

I hoped it would be the case for our fellow travellers. A few of the families had relatives in Yangon, some were bound for Mandalay like ourselves. Others planned to try and make it to Guam or the Philippines.

We were six days out of Southampton when the ship made a change in direction, heaving its huge, leviathan hull into a wide arc through the choppy swell. Several of us ran to the railings. The horizon was dark and full of ugly black clouds.

"The sensors on the satellite must have detected the storm approaching," suggested someone. "They're automatically

304

adjusting the route."

Across the deck there came a sudden burst of activity as the arachnid drones scurried hither and thither, making sure the containers were securely held in place. As this went on, we all hunkered down in our billets, hurriedly pulling on threadbare anoraks and cagoules to protect us from the onset of the rain.

We heard a distinct change in the now familiar drone of the engine as the ship's speed picked up. For a while we could actually feel the mighty hull heave and tip as the waves crashed noisily against its sides. Rain bounced from the deck, gushing in torrents along the alleyways, soaking our sleeping bags and belongings.

Then, just as suddenly, we were out of it, sailing back toward clear blue skies. All of us sloshed along the flooded deck to the railing. Far behind us the storm was playing out, boiling clouds and forks of blue lightning streaking down toward wild white brine. We cheered our good fortune and blessed the intervention of the satellite.

It was then that we caught first sight of the trio of little boats approaching. They came fast. Skipping over the swell. Their crews lashed the boats to the side of the ship and hurriedly climbed the ladders up to the deck. They were heavily armed, dirty and unshaven, eyes wide and bloodshot, as if they were all high on something.

We'd been delivered straight into the path of pirates.

They yelled at us in a language that I thought might be Portuguese, aggressively jabbing the barrels of rifles and machine guns in our direction. In our fear and confusion, we yelled back, some of us in anger, some of us begging to be left alone. One of them fired a handgun into the air. Stunned into silence we huddled together, waiting for what would happen next.

"English?" he asked. "You speak English?"

"What do you want?" asked one of our group. "We don't have much. But take whatever you want and leave us alone."

All around the spidery drones went about their business, checking that the ship's cargo remained secure, oblivious to what was occurring on the deck. The pirate sneered and said something in Portuguese to his friends. They laughed.

He turned back to us.

"We want your women."

One of our men stepped forward.

"No, we won't let you…"

A swift blow from the butt of a rifle felled him.

The first pirate fired his handgun into the air once more.

"Women, here, now!"

Sobbing and pleading, Aleesha and the other women shuffled towards him.

"You'll make good profit for us in the North African brothels," he said. "They like women from the west, especially the English. Shows how far down you arrogant bitches have fallen."

Aleesha said something to him that I couldn't quite hear. My blood ran cold as he reached out and pinched the flesh on her cheek with his oil stained finger and thumb.

"You think the colour of your skin will save you?" he snarled. "You think because you are black? It's not what's on the outside that matters any more. It's what's in your head. All that ignorant English arrogance – that's what they're going to beat out of you."

His men laughed again.

I thought Aleesha was about to slap him. Anger raged inside me. But fear froze me to the spot. Another of our group barged forward and tried to wrestle a machine gun from one of the pirates. The first pirate pushed Aleesha out of the way and shot the poor man in the head with his handgun. He fell dead to the deck, blood gushing from the wound and mingling with the rainwater.

All of them aimed their guns at us again.

"You want to die?" yelled their leader. "Right here? Right now? One little sign from me and you all fucking die. Children too."

The children screamed as the women wailed.

He looked crazy enough to give the order.

"Who would know?" he ranted. "Who would care? Who gives a shit about the English these days?"

I hugged Annie and Beth to my sides. I'll never forget the look of terror on Aleesha's face as she was forced over the side of the ship. I bowed my head. How helpless and cowardly I felt.

I think it was at that moment that it truly hit home how far down we'd come. We no longer had any control whatsoever over what happened to us. Events tossed us around like bits of worthless drift wood.

24th July

Rain beat down on the rooftops of Yangon - the last downpour of the monsoon rattling against the corrugated huts of the refugee camp. The city stretched skyward in gargantuan shards and lances of glass. Twinkling lights, illuminating the darkness and making the rain seem like an endless avalanche of falling glitter. If this was Yangon, what might it be like in Mandalay?

The police had taken statements from us and sequestrated our evidence. All I had was the crime reference number. Aleesha had the bullets wrapped in a tissue in her pocket.

The immigration authority warned us not to leave the camp. They said that if we did our right to remain would be rescinded and our applications for asylum rejected. People in the camp said not to trust them. Some of them had been stuck there for months.

A local appeared at the fence and told us anyone who wanted to go should prepare to leave in the next few days. I gave him the money I had left as the transit fee. When word came, we were to make our way to a service area on the motorway twenty kilometres or so from the city centre. There we would be collected by a truck and transported to Mandalay.

I told Annie and Beth we couldn't carry much, just a rucksack each, and the bottled water and cereal bars that the aid workers gave us on our arrival. But Beth was sick. Before the container ship docked quite few people went down with some sort of flu virus. She was running a high temperature, coughing, throwing up anything she ate. I hoped against hope she'd be better by the time we had to move on.

Annie kept asking me when her mother would be joining us.

I kept promising her it would be soon.

27th July

We trudged along the hard shoulder of the motorway, a ragged procession of twenty or so adults and a dozen children. It was the

307

early hours of the morning and a thin mist was rising on the humid air. Huge, high-powered trucks roared past us, peppering us in grit and drenching us in dirty puddle water. Sometimes things would be thrown at us from passenger windows; cigarette butts and plastic drink cartons. Vile profanities accompanied these missiles.

Annie walked ahead of me. I carried Beth on my shoulders. She was drowsy and running a severe temperature, but I was determined we would get to the service station and then on to Mandalay. I kept telling Annie that it was our best bet. That we would find my brother and he'd have money to pay to get her little sister the medical attention she needed.

We passed huge factory complexes, belching dark smoke into the mist. I wondered what the work was like. What the pay was like. Whether moving from a hotel to a factory complex was even a feasible prospect for someone like me.

I could feel Beth flopping about on my shoulders. Her weight was slowing me down. She was kind of slumped onto the crown of my head. The distance between us and the rest of the group was growing wider by the minute. Annie would wait for me and then set off at a pace as soon as I caught up on her.

The fourth time this happened she turned to me.

"You need to rest. We can catch up later."

I lifted Beth from my shoulders and sat down on the verge with her splayed limply across my lap. Annie unscrewed the lid on her bottle of water and tried to pour some into Beth's mouth. She coughed most of it back out. I could feel the rattle in her chest that accompanied her laboured breathing.

A truck approached at speed. The window on the passenger side was down. As it hurtled past us a knotted plastic bag was thrown out. It hit me on the head and exploded. The liquid that drenched me smelled like urine. I spat the foul taste from my mouth.

"We can't stay here," said Annie, wiping splashes from her face.

She helped me carry Beth over the crash barrier and down the soft, sandy soil of a steep embankment. We passed through a tangled copse of banyan trees and found ourselves on a dirt track that skirted the edge of a vast rice paddy.

I held Beth in my arms. Annie sat down next to me on one of the mud dykes. We watched the automated planter drones industriously moving back and forth along the rows of the paddies. In and then out they came, like the surge and retreat of the tide.

We didn't say a word. We just sat in silence, listening as Beth's breathing became slower and more strained. I stroked Beth's hair and kissed her brow. I whispered that we'd soon be in Mandalay and that her mother would join us there. For a long time after she stopped breathing, Annie and I just sat there staring out at the rhythmic ebb and flow of the mechanised planters.

"She's dead, isn't she?" said Annie, breaking our mutual silence.

I couldn't reply.

"She's dead, isn't she?" repeated Annie.

I started to cry.

"I never thought my life would be so shit," said Annie.

I told her I was sorry.

She placed her hand on top of mine.

"It's not your fault."

The sun was burning off the last of the mist. The sky was blue and clear of rain clouds. The heat quickly intensified. We retreated back to the shade of the banyan trees. I hugged Beth's body close to my chest.

"We have to bury her," said Annie.

I baulked at the idea.

"Here?"

Annie came and kissed Beth's head.

"We can't carry her around with us."

I laid my youngest daughter down on the dirt and began digging with my bare hands. The soil was still damp from the rains. But it was tightly packed and I felt my fingernails splintering as they jarred against little jagged stones.

"Dad," said Annie.

When I turned, I saw that she was looking along the dirt path.

A little white electrical van was silently approaching. It pulled up beside us. An old man clambered out. He was dressed in jeans and a chequered shirt. He smelled of expensive aftershave. I thought he was about to yell at us for trespassing.

Instead he retrieved a shovel and blanket from the back of the truck and gave them to me. Then he handed a little plastic container of cooked rice to Annie and offered her a sad little smile. I thanked him. With a curt nod of his head he climbed back into his vehicle and went on his way.

I dug the pit. We wrapped Beth in the blanket. Annie helped me to lay her down. I covered her in the loose soil. I left the shovel upright to mark the spot. We sat by the mound and ate the rice in silence.

28th July

It was already dark when we reached the service area. Annie walked ahead of me all the way in complete silence. I was glad that she never once looked back. I didn't want her to see how much I cried for her sister. I promised myself that as soon as I was able, I'd return to retrieve her and give her a proper burial.

Trucks blared their horns at us when we were caught in their headlights. I became increasingly convinced that we might be too late, that our escort would have come and gone. But when we reached the slip road, I could see everyone from our group still congregated into a little seated huddle on the grass verge by the car park.

One of the men who had been with us on our sea voyage was amongst the group. He had a son who was about Annie's age. I heard the boy ask where Beth was. Annie just shrugged and turned her head.

"No sign yet?" I asked the father.

He scowled at me and stuffed his hands into his pockets.

"I'm starting to think we've been ripped off."

I blinked, not understanding.

"No one's coming," he said. "They took our money and left us high a dry."

I swayed a little.

"Are you all right?" he asked. "You don't look too good."

I didn't feel too good. I was sweating profusely and my head was thumping. It seemed that I was coming down with the same virus that had taken Beth. I slumped down onto the grass.

"You got any water?" I asked my friend. "We finished ours."

"All out," he replied.

Annie sat down beside me.

"I heard what he just said," she told me. "I knew this would happen."

There was an ache in my throat. It was starting to hurt to speak.

"I'm sorry," I managed.

"Stop saying you're fucking sorry!" snapped Annie.

I didn't have the strength to reprimand her for swearing. Instead I lay back on the coarse grass. "I'm going to take a little nap." My chest felt tight. "Wake me up if anyone comes. And don't go wandering off."

I dreamed of the last Christmas before my brother left for good. All of us around a rickety little folding table in the bedsit. The contents of the KFC bargain bucket hardly enough to go around. Geoff telling the kids about the Christmas dinners we all used to take for granted when we were kids. Them not believing a word. Me, trying to download the Wizard of Oz onto that reconditioned laptop I used carry around. The power cut plunging us into unexpected darkness.

When I awoke Annie was asleep beside me. The grass was littered with the sleeping bodies of our group, intertwined in a wretched mass. I stumbled around till I found a pizza box in one of the nearby bins. There was a half-eaten slice left there. I felt ten times worse that I had when I went to sleep. I knew I wouldn't be able to keep it down, so I set it to one side for Annie.

Sleep took me once more.

A sharp flash of light woke me up. When I opened my eyes a man in an expensive looking suit was looming over me. He had one of those palm implants on his left hand. He must have clapped his hands to activate it. His face was illuminated by the glow from the screen as he used the index finger on his right hand to scroll down.

When he saw that I was awake he started to yell at me.

"Why are you here? Nothing for you in Myanmar! Nothing! Understand? Nothing for you here?"

Beside me Annie groaned and shifted in her sleep.

The man's hand began to give out audible beeps. He appeared to punch in several digits. He turned from me and began talking urgently into the hand. He sounded angry and insistent. After a furious diatribe aimed at whoever was on the other end of the line, he slapped his hands together and the implant screen went blank.

Without looking back at me he marched across to a blue sports car, climbed in, slammed the door shut and sped off. I watched him go, remembering how as a kid I used to dream about having a car like that when I grew up, remembering too how I never actually got the opportunity to learn to drive.

Five minutes must have passed before the police truck arrived. All of the officers were women. They were armed with electronic stun guns. One of them launched a flying drone which hovered a couple of feet above us, filming to make sure no one tried to make a run for it.

Their sergeant, a short woman, who stood barely five-foot tall, began to scream at us, repeating the same thing over and over.

"Wake up! Stand up! Wake up! Stand up! Wake up! Stand up!"

We rose drowsily to our feet.

I hardly had the strength to keep myself upright.

"What now?" asked Annie.

She was trembling.

The diminutive sergeant began screaming again. "Why did you leave the camp? You are in big trouble! Big trouble!"

No one quite knew if we were supposed to actually respond.

"Now you go back to the camp," the sergeant told us. "Get in the truck."

The other police officers began cranking the charging mechanism on their stun guns. The air crackled with the sound of static. Everyone shuffled around nervously.

"In the truck, now," demanded the sergeant.

Her squadron aimed their stun guns at us.

People began to clamber into the truck. I bent down and picked up the half-eaten pizza slice. The motion made me dizzy. I swayed a little more as I forced it into Annie's hand.

"Eat this," I said.

She looked at me as if I'd gone crazy.

"What?"

"You need to keep up your strength," I said.

The angry sergeant was hustling the stragglers towards the truck.

She approached Annie and me.

"In the truck," she yelled. "In the truck. You are bad people. Bad people."

Then she looked at me. I must have appeared as terrible as I felt. Her eyes went wide. She fumbled in the pocket of her uniform and produced a surgical mask, which she hurriedly pulled over her nose and mouth.

"Not you," she said. "You're sick. You stay here. Understand?"

She pushed Annie hard on her shoulder.

"Get in the truck."

Annie stood her ground.

"Not without my dad."

"Get in the truck now," insisted the sergeant.

"Not without my dad," insisted Annie.

The sergeant aimed her stun gun at Annie's chest and looked at me.

"Daughter?" she asked.

I nodded.

"Tell your daughter to get in the truck. You're sick. You can't go. Understand?"

I nodded again.

"Get in the truck, Annie."

"You're joking?"

"There's food and shelter back at the camp," I said.

I felt so weary that for a moment I thought I was going to faint.

"I'm not leaving," said Annie. "What about Mandalay? What about Uncle Geoff?"

"We'll get there," I said. "I'll come and find you."

Annie threw the slice of pizza at me in a fit of rage.

"Just like you're going to find mum?"

She started to cry.

The sergeant signalled to one of her officers, who began to drag Annie to the truck. Annie kicked and screamed. Another officer

313

had to be called on to force her into the back.

As it sped away, she was still screaming at me.

"I hate you. I fucking hate you. I take back what I said. I do blame you. This is all your fault. We're all dead because of you."

I slouched back down onto the grass.

29th July

I opened my eyes and there was a Buddhist monk standing over me. He was dressed in a traditional saffron robe. His head was shaved. He was holding out an ice cream, scooped into a tall wafer cone. He was smiling with genuine warmth.

I thought that the onset of the virus was causing me to have hallucinations.

"Take this," he said. "Good for your throat. Good for your temperature."

I accepted the cone and licked off a chunk of the ice cream.

It slid down my throat like cool nectar.

"Come with me to the monastery," said the monk, helping me to my feet. "Rest and get better."

"My daughter," I said, struggling to hold onto the ice cream cone. "She's been taken to the refugee camp at Yangon."

"Rest and get better," he repeated.

He led me to an electrical van similar to the one the rice farmer had driven.

I've no idea where I am. I think the journey from the service area took around 45 minutes. We seemed to climb into the lower hills of a mountain range. But I don't suppose that is any real clue. They've been kind to me. Put me to bed. Given me some sort of herbal tea, laced with honey.

But I don't feel any better. If anything, I feel much weaker. I've developed that rattle in my chest that Beth had just before she passed. It's getting harder to draw breath. I may not last the night.

Somewhere within the sweat drenched thrashing of my fever a revelation came to me. I thought the world had changed beyond recognition. A different place to the one myself and Geoff grew up in.

But it hasn't. It's still the same as it ever was.

When I was a boy, we in the west had the opportunity to change the world. To be decent. To do the right thing. To share the wealth we'd amassed and to equalise. But we were too complacent, too arrogant, too greedy. The shoe inevitably fell to the other foot. The world was tipped upside down. But it is still the same as it ever was. The haves have and the have nots have naught.

I asked the monks if they could bring me a pen and paper. They were only too happy to oblige. I've given them the name of the hotel where my brother works. One of them has promised to make the trip to Mandalay.

I know Geoff will be surprised to read my letter and learn that I came to Myanmar. I've asked him to find Beth's body and do what I could not. I've asked him to go to Yangon. To fetch Annie from the refugee camp. To take her with him to the fabled Emerald City that is Mandalay. To give her a chance at a future and maybe a place she can truly call home.

~

David Turnbull is a member of the Clockhouse London group of genre writers. He writes mainly short fiction and has had numerous short stories published in magazines and anthologies, as well as having stories read at live events such as Liars League London, Solstice Shorts *and* Virtual Futures. *He was born in Scotland, but now lives in the Catford area of London. His most recently published short stories appeared in* The Once and Future Moon, *Eibonvale Press and Bellanger Books:* A Tribute to HG Wells. *He can be found at: www.tumsh.co.uk.*

SPIDERS IN THE TEMPLE
Alexander Zelenyj

Patrick Savinsky began his day as usual: rising from his bed of dilapidated cardboard and plastic bags, his makeshift fort against the elements; standing in the stinking murk of the pre-dawn alley, slowly stretching his limbs, sore from the night of restless, uncomfortable, cough syrup-dream-plagued sleep behind him. He was freezing. The temperature had plummeted in the night, and it took him longer than usual to massage warmth back into his shuddering, grimy hands.

Eyeing the crack of skyline he could glimpse through the alley – tall skyscrapers reflecting the blood-red light of the rising sun – he muttered, "Yeah, well, fuck you, too."

He hobbled down the alley in the direction of the nearby park and his bench – he thought of it as "his", as did the many regulars who daily passed by the bench en-route to their day jobs and saw him stationed there, that ragged fixture of the park and a reminder of the bottom-most social stratum of the city – his steps becoming more steady as he went, working out the kinks and numbness in his feet and legs, feeling circulation begin its gradual course again. He patted the pocket of his tatty coat, felt the familiar bulge of the squashed paper coffee cup nestled there, with which he would mark his place in the park as he panhandled the morning hours in an effort to acquire enough money for a noon-time coffee, or an evening bottle of cough syrup.

He made it to the alley mouth, where he spooked a fat rat from where it was rummaging in the trash to scurry into the open end of a rusted eaves trough. "Sorry, brother," he muttered, and made his way across the empty lot, with the park on its opposite side.

As he crossed the lawn his progress sent up a flock of pigeons to explode into the frost-bitten air in a rain of feathers like dirty grey confetti heralding his arrival in the park.

*

He was dismayed to find his bench occupied.

Patrick eyed the man closely as he sidled toward the bench: immaculate designer suit; immaculate designer shoes; immaculate designer sunglasses sitting on his slender nose despite the overcast sky, more show of sleek style than utilitarian; hair slicked back efficiently, with enough gel to fill a bathtub. He hated men like this, who owned the world and, worse still, *believed* it was their entitlement to have it so. He saw them as predators, as voracious spiders preying on the oblivious, the more benevolent human moths fluttering through their lives and chancing to get stuck in the webs of men like him. Back in his old life, Patrick had seen many men like this pounce on the unwary, viciously doing away with them for their own good.

He gave a theatrical (he hoped) scowl toward the dapper man, resenting his clean-shaven good looks and easy charisma. Let him smell my stink, Patrick thought. Let my piss-stained jeans and sweaty clothes hang like a gas cloud over his head. Let's see how long his royal highness sticks around on my bench *then*.

He sat down on the opposite end of the bench, closed his eyes, relishing his own bodily fumes, growing more pungent as the morning sun climbed into the sky and the first touch of humidity returned to bother the morning air.

A curious thing happened then.

An elderly woman limped across the lawn toward the bench. She held a coffee cup in a shuddering hand, a trail of steam escaping its lip and drifting away behind her on the stiff breeze. A large and ancient brown leather purse swung from her shoulder and hugged her hip. She smiled a toothless smile at him, all pink enflamed gums and squinting eyes, and made a show of slowly – slowly, slowly – creaking herself into position on the bench directly between Patrick and the dapper man.

Something in Patrick always ached at the sight of elderly ladies like this woman. Maybe it was that they invariably reminded him of his mother, many years passed away. Perhaps it was the sort of innocence they imbued, as if life had left them so little left to live for that all they had left were the small pleasures: a meandering walk among the flowers of a city's downtown park; the warbling morning songs of pigeons; the warmth of a coffee on a cold A.M.;

the easy pleasure of enjoying whatever breakfast they might bring with them to the park before heading home to a lonely apartment and lonely life but for the cat or multiple cats that were their sole remaining companions in the mortal world.

Patrick smiled at her, and turned to survey the park stretching before them. He only turned back when the potent smell of tuna wafted across to him. He saw the old woman holding a tuna sandwich in trembling liver spot-speckled hands. He watched her, a little horrified, as she took a toothless bite from the sandwich and smiled at him, mouth full. He smiled and turned away again, quickly.

The old woman went about her noisy eating, smacking her lips while the suction-cup sound of her stained dentures dealing with the moist sticky mess of the tuna sandwich became a nauseating staccato rhythm. He grimaced. Disgusting. But then he chuckled, because the woman's grisly breakfast was of course nowhere near as disgusting as the suit-and-tie man beside her, who was likely being thoroughly repulsed by her theatrical performance as well.

He nearly laughed out loud when, after a moment, she began a protracted gurgling, and he imagined her sucking back the hot coffee from her paper cup, washing down her loathsome sandwich, the mire of coffee and tuna congealing inside her stomach in the certain creation of violent diarrhea in her immediate future. Then she had apparently finished her grisly breakfast, and continued to sit quietly beside him, her silence broken only by a stuttering fart that made Patrick grimace even as he chuckled out loud: *Take that, suit-and-tie man!* Ha! Take *that* bomb with you when you go back to your office cubicle!

Right on cue, he felt the wood beneath him shift as the man at the opposite end of the bench rose abruptly from the seat. Patrick sat there, smiling widely. He listened to the sound of the man's shining shoes crunching through the autumn leaves in the direction of the downtown core. He cracked his eyelids and peered at him, his immaculate figure outlined starkly against the misty grey of the buildings rising from the business sector that fringed the park's western perimeter.

"What a fucking asshole," he said, unable to contain his

318

resentment with the man – and men like him generally – who owned the world through their money and good looks and, worst offence of all, believed they were entitled to everything they got over everybody else. Patrick shook his head and spat in the direction of the receding figure. "Good riddance."

The old woman beside him said nothing. He turned to her, prepared to commend her success at having got rid of the man.

He stared at her blue face; her bulging yellow-speckled cataract eyes; her gaping mouth with drool dribbling from the corners onto her small round glistening chin with its cluster of virgin white hairs poking proudly in all directions; her scrawny throat, cut open to reveal the red tangle of her muscle and cartilage and exposed windpipe steaming on the cold air.

Between them on the bench, steam still curled from the open lip of her paper cup, the smell of coffee strong on the air.

It took several seconds for Patrick's mind to process these details and what they meant. Then he spun wildly on the bench, looking in the direction that the man had gone. He was still there, walking as casually as before, suit jacket neat, hair coifed and unmarred by the crisp breeze. He watched the man approach one of several tall buildings rising alongside the sidewalk and spiking amid the dense fog hanging over the streets, and this is when he discerned movement where there should have been none. He stared, mouth gaping, eyes bulging like the dead woman's frozen stare beside him.

The building rising up before the suited man, and those surrounding it, were crawling with men. He blinked to be certain his eyes weren't making mirages of ordinary city workers toiling away on their scaffolding, washing windows or patching ancient brickwork; but no, his eyes were true. The men were *crawling* across the sheer face of the towering structures like hideous humanoid insects clinging to the walls of their hives; each of them dressed much like the man who'd left the bench, debonair in tailor-cut suits, their ties trailing in the wind.

Patrick watched, horrified, nauseous, enthralled, as the killer of the elderly woman reached the base of the building and immediately began his own climb to meet the other crawling men

319

far above. He went vertically, his feet carrying him as naturally as if he walked on a horizontal surface, a street, a sidewalk, a park lawn. He joined the others, and together they crawled higher and higher until the mist shrouded them.

Patrick blinked and blinked and rubbed at his tear-filled eyes. The city scene before him appeared as normal as it did every other day, but it was deeply changed in his mind's eye. He would never see it the same way again.

"What's happening?" he said, directing his words to the lone pigeon pecking at the grass nearby. "What's *happened* to the world? Things were...Things were never this *bad* before. There was always some sanity left."

The pigeon only warbled at him, deep in its throat, and then turned to peck in the dewy grass further away from him. Patrick watched it, envying it its simple vision and instinctual mission to seek sustenance this morning. His own stomach grumbled like a nervous Rottweiler. He hadn't eaten in a long time. But his appetite was gone.

In the distance he saw a pair of police officers walking casually down the sidewalk, headed in his general direction. He could hear their voices, small with distance, their laughter as they shared some joke. They were oblivious to the buildings beneath which they walked, and the fog over their heads, and what lay hidden there and watching over them in their routine trek through the downtown core. A part of him wanted to run to them, and explain what he'd seen and what he'd learned about the world. But of course he knew how they would interpret this admission, and so he could only scurry away, leaving the grave of the bench to the old woman, who'd committed no crime worse than eating a disgusting breakfast in a loathsome manner, and whose ancient beauty of gentleness hadn't been strong enough to repel the invader of her peace.

The sun crept out from behind the clouds as he hurried across the park lawn, its cold wintry light touching the profusion of flowers spread in the peripheral gardens, making them appear brighter, healthier. But Patrick wasn't fooled by it: he saw the darkness hiding everywhere, and wanted very much to walk and walk and keep on walking, right on out of the city and into the rural county beyond, where no tall buildings scraped the bellies of the clouds gathered over the world, where farmland stretched towards the horizon as far as the eye could see. But he was weak, and cold, and had no strength for journeys like these, which were journeys for younger men than he, and so all he was able to do was to hurry as fast as his weak, trembling legs would carry him back to the meagre sanctuary of his ramshackle cardboard castle in the little-frequented alley.

It was as good a place as any other to make his final stand.

~

Alexander Zelenyj is the author of the books: Blacker Against the Deep Dark, Songs for the Lost, Experiments at 3 Billion A.M., *and* Black Sunshine, *among others. He lives with his wife in Windsor, Ontario, Canada; as good a place as any other to make his final stand.*

LIFE ON DA STREETZ (FIRMWARE OBSOLETE)
L.P. Melling

Latrell feels pretty flo after ditching school all day with his main boy Jaymes. He leads them back to his gaff, Jaymes behind dragging his modded satchel across the concrete boundary of the abandoned playground, trying to create sparks with the LEDs. Jaymes' buzzed blond hair catches the fading light; his comic motion-strip T-shirt peeps out from his school jumper, the shaven head of his favourite superhero, Nitroman, cut just as close to a green scalp.

"It ain't gonna spark," Latrell says. "Am telling you, bruv."

"Course it is. Told you I did it last week when I was on my way back from Jamal's Chippy."

Latrell turns around again, about to argue, when he clocks Jaymes' eyes locked on the ground, wishing it to happen, and lets him be. He must have got the idea from some show or CyberCrimez, which they've been streaming most of the day when they weren't immersing themselves trenches-deep in virtual-access BioWarfare 6.0. Blowing each other up indoors is safer than being on the streets all day.

The winter dark is already pressing up against the concrete jungle around them. "Bruv, c'mon," Latrell says. "We need to get back indoors before Curf Control creeps up on us!" He chews his lip, stomach churning. Trialled in some cold-as-shit place in Scandinavia, the curfew crackdowns were brought in for London and surrounds. Under 16s must be indoors by nightfall or face being escorted to their parents, then given another misbehaviour report to add onto the stacks from school. Jaymes has largely got away with breaking curfew, but Latrell faces house lockdown if he's caught again this month. His wrist slapped and slit to insert a control-chip to ensure he won't breach curf regs again.

Latrell can't let Mum down anymore, not now she's on her

own. He scratches his arm, his eczema playing up again. "Come on, bruv. Let's move!" The high-rises block out the moonlight and stars above.

Latrell picks up his feet. James does so too, catching up, whispers in the dark to Latrell. "Look. There's Haylee!"

Latrell breaks his gaze from the blue backlight glow of his phone and swings his head around. "Where?"

Jaymes pisses himself with laughter. "Ha. Got you, blood! Got you *good!*" He sputters and flips out his inhaler like it's a revolver, ready to take a hit. Latrell thinks he looks dope despite being annoyed at him.

"You bumbaclart!"

Haylee is the reason the universe was created, why marshmallow milk and chocolate tastes so good, and everything else. The only one who can make the thoughts of his father less bone-raw. A face that's beyond pretty, shimmery blonde hair sleek as any shampoo ad.

Jaymes is still laughing like a bong-using hyena at his side.

"Bruv, look. Up ahead, on the left!" Jaymes says.

"Nah, ain't fallin' for that again."

"Serious. Check it. There's that alien-green glow again. Told you I wasn't making that shit up!" Jaymes says, and his words catch in his throat.

Latrell ignores him all the same, and Jaymes grabs his shoulders and spins him 90 degrees.

"What the hell—?" But now he sees it. What Jaymes has been banging on about for days. Two green-luminescent orbs burning in the darkness near the ghost-grey pillars of Paradise Heights.

Latrell glances back. Jaymes is slack-jawed. "It's a demon, bruv. Am telling ya."

"Don't be dumb. Course it ain't…" Latrell says, but he's got no better fix on what it is. "C'mon, let's go in for a closer look." Latrell feels himself being sucked in, hypnotised by the green spheres that blink out and waver right to left. A shiver runs through him.

The pair of them move glacier-slow, and Latrell can make out bodies around the glowing green orbs, hunched up against the cold. Clouds of breath boil up from dark shadows.

"Oy!" Latrell is ripped from his trance as he hears the shouting from them. "Yous two! Come here before we hunt your little-shit arses down!"

Latrell recognises the voice and freezes up. The way Jaymes' body is shaking, it's clear he recognises it too. Tyrone. The Dog with a Bone, kids on the estate call him: his ugly mug like a bulldog licking piss off a nettle, a giant toker-vape always dangling between his chops. He bullies most kids, so Latrell and Jaymes didn't feel special about it when he mugged them.

"Leg it," Jaymes says under his breath.

As if reading his thoughts, Tyrone growls, "Don't make me chase you!"

Latrell looks back at the bunch of kids and then makes her out. He'd recognise that perfect figure anywhere. Haylee. "Jaymes. Be cool, man." But he can tell by Jaymes' fidgeting he ain't having any of it.

Then another voice cuts through the cold night, one Latrell doesn't recognise. "It's safe, boys. Don't worry about it." A pause that stretches is stitched up with sniggers. "Just want a little chat is all." And Latrell makes out a bubble of steam coming from between the green orbs that seem to flare brighter now, like nebulae in the night sky.

"Sure," Latrell says. "We're comin'."

"What the hell you doin'?" Jaymes hisses against his ear.

"Don't be a pussy, bruv," Latrell tells him. A bubble of laughter breaks out further ahead, and Latrell thinks he even hears girls giggling.

Jaymes sighs with embarrassment. Latrell feels shitty. "It's safe, bruv," he says, even though he doesn't know if it is. "Haylee's with 'em."

They approach, Latrell leading. A pair of scarred faces resolve out of the darkness. The kids here grow up as hard as the concrete high rises they live in. Everyone knows it.

Next to Tyrone, someone in a hoody smacks their lips. The voice they didn't recognise. Smoke curls from the void of the hood and he blazes on his joint, making his eyes glow radioactive bright. Almost blinded by the light, Latrell looks away.

He turns back and stares into stolen starlight.

"Yeah. Modded, motherfucker. What?" The towering boy's body tenses and he steps forward in a flash. His voice splits into a deep laugh. "Relax, kids. I'm just fuckin' with ya. Told you you're good. I'm Reeze. You're safe with me, little bros."

Jaymes swallows hard next to Latrell, caught by the green force field. Latrell knows that the grinder scene has been growing big time on the estates. All the kids are talking about the bio-modifications they'll get, and it just makes Latrell feel ill, bringing back memories of Dad's open-heart surgery...

Haylee makes eye contact with Latrell and nods, and it calms him down likes she used to in maths class when he struggled to remember his sums. He wants to say something, tell her he misses those days, but his tongue is stuck in his mouth and he knows everyone will laugh at them both if he does.

"I got a job for you little men. Bare bitcreds in it for your pockets if you do it," the teen/man continues – he sounds too husky for a child, but maybe that was a mod too?

"What we gotta do?" Jaymes finds his voice again and he sounds steadier than Latrell expected. He looks at Latrell as if he's daring him on.

"Shifting a little gear, that's all. Like pass the parcel." His entourage – and it's clear they're *his* – piss themselves at that, as if he's someone from Comedy Centrix.

Latrell isn't sure, sensing he's holding back an iceberg of dangerous info below the surface of his words, but still blurts out before Jaymes can react. His bruv peeps into those fucked-up luminescent eyes with a fixed stare, his buzzed blond scalp glinting in its glow, mouth opening before Latrell beats him to it: "We'll do it."

*

"'Sup, blood?" Jaymes swaggers up to Naz, the next handler in the line who carries as much respect in the crew as he does gear. Hoodie drawn tight, Latrell rides his boy's jet-stream of confidence, wishing he carried it too.

"Hey, wagwan, Jay. How's your dad doin'? All good?" A fed drone sweeps over from above, buzzing like a wasp, and they ignore it. They hear kids from the high-rise's upper floors taking pot shots at it, and the po po back away from the high rise like chicken shits.

Jaymes covers his mouth with his hand as he speaks. "Yeah, all good man. What's it to you?"

Latrell jabs Jaymes through his hoodie's chest pocket. He knows Jaymes' dad hasn't been good in a long time. His old man has been searching for an answer to why Jaymes' mum left years before. The bottle has come up with no answer so far for his dad, and Jaymes went quiet that time he asked him about the bruises.

"Relax, man," Naz spits. "*Damn*, you're wound tight. Remember, you're family now. Brothers from other mothers. Take some extra bitcred at the end of the month. So you can look after him and that."

"Yeah, sure." And Jaymes backs off, clearly realising he's being touchy, like Latrell's warned him about. It's why Latrell stopped asking about his dad. "Thanks. Peace, cous." Jaymes gives Naz an elaborate handshake that diverts the attention from his other hand that slips from his own pocket to Naz's. Latrell kneels down and presses the auto-lacing button on his new trainers, and keeps a look out.

The drop's good.

Naz nods at Latrell. "'Sup, bro." Slow, Latrell treads toward him and follows suit. The green edge of a microchip cuts into his palm as he grips it in his pocket and passes it quick to Naz's other pocket. Doing the best sleight-of-hand slip he can muster but knows it ain't even C-grade level.

Naz clicks his fingers, spotting something. "Fix up, look sharp, boys. Got money to make. Check the girl there with the superhero shirt. Those lot are always looking for a biohack fix."

"Sure," Latrell says, and looks back at his bruv. Jaymes said that superhero crap was for kids, last time Latrell asked about his shirt. The girl's already around the corner by the time Latrell moves, and Naz tuts. "Bad men got to be faster. You hear?" They both nod, and Naz's creased forehead relaxes again. "Okay, cool." He pops something out of his pocket. "Here, get yourself on these nootrop's. They will fix you up."

Jaymes steps closer. "Don't mind if I do, bruv."

Latrell feels their eyes burning on him like radium. "Nah, I'm good," he says and he hears Naz tut again.

"Catch you later, yeah?" Jaymes and Naz lock hands again and part ways.

"Man, take it easy on that shit," Latrell whispers once Naz is out of earshot.

"Whatever. 'Don't be a pussy, bruv'!" he says, repeating Latrell's words from that night they were recruited up. The bitterness rings loud in them, even though he clips it off with a trademark snicker.

Latrell walks away and feels lighter, an urge to keep his heels clean swirling in his gut. He gulps it down as he clocks Haylee walking towards them.

"Hey, girl. How you doin?" Jaymes shouts, as if he's just talking to any normal girl.

Loose strands of hair bouncing with her stride, she's like some kinda streamstar goddess, eyes pure Antiguan shallows he swam in with Uncle Ben. His mum wanted him to see his family heritage after the funeral, and it was sweet as anything. Not that anything looked as beautiful as Haylee does now, though.

"Hey, Jay. Latrell," she says, all casual, and Latrell feels the heat of the sun on his face. "Hey, cool fade!" she says to Jaymes, and smiles at them both before she swooshes past. Hips grinding, hypnotising.

"Word on the street is she's into mods big time, especially those with the ripped bods to match," Jaymes says, without turning to him.

Latrell smacks his lips, catching his scrawny self in a shop window, even if he is a foot taller than Jaymes. Maybe he can start hitting the gym or get his delts modded up in half the time. Unbidden, a sterile memory cuts through Latrell's mind. The last time he saw his dad before the open-heart surgery. Before his mum lost her chill.

Following him, Latrell wonders why Jaymes is always the one in front. Latrell locks his eyes on his back. Jaymes' walk is full of arrogant swagger as his new Xenoware logo fade catches the light, his blond fuzz dyed bionic green. *What a tool!* Jaymes is getting worse, even if they're still bros. Obsessed with getting infrared night eyes and god knows what else to beef him up. Latrell's sick of hearing it from him.

Latrell looks back down the street; Haylee is no longer in sight, but Latrell thinks he spots Tyrone in the distance. He's talking to a pair of suits, looking shifty as hell. "Bruv, look. Is that Dogface over there or what?"

Jaymes squints with his poor eyes. "Nah, man. Can't be him," he says, and takes a left.

"Bruv. Not that way! Round the back," he snaps at Jaymes, trying to hide the unease that greases his words.

Jaymes throws him a sidelong stare and then shifts his feet. "Whatever. Same difference to get there."

Latrell looks up into the distance, remembering the night when they were recruited by Reeze. The green-eyed king's palace shimmers at the top of Paradise Heights, mirror-reflected windows blocking out the insider view from the police. Reeze's mum is a proper church go-er, the old kind, not the astrophobe type. Not that you'd know it. Of course, she's treated like a king's mother would be, getting fat on Caribbean-fusion food from his dealing, oblivious, or – more likely – turning a blind eye to it all.

The cobalt-white police drone flies overhead. Latrell's breath catches. "Look. It's tailing us, bruv," he says, and they pick up their pace. The drone drops down to the lower levels of the nearest high-rise.

Jaymes makes a circular motion with his finger like he's back on the decks console, signalling Latrell to do a quick circuit of the estate again before they drop off the bitcred.

The air comes alive with the whirring of the feds' surveillance drone behind them, but they don't turn around and tighten up the drawstrings of their hoodies.

Jaymes lowers his body to the ground, his jeans dragging on the floor. "Be cool, man. Be cool!" he says under his breath, and Latrell can't tell if he's talking to himself or not.

"Whatever," Latrell mumbles, still burning from how Jaymes spoke to Haylee. Jaymes knows how much he likes her.

Latrell coughs. Once. Twice—

He rushes to the underpass, balls of his feet pounding the pavement. Doesn't wait for Jaymes. His wrist vibrates, and Latrell hasn't got time to check if it's a call for another drop or not. The biometric watch hacked to buzz on a set limit whenever they had to report back. Sweating, he ignores it, and his legs burn. The summer's sun bears down on them, cracking up the concrete. Making the world wobble.

Jumping over fence, Latrell lands hard. He runs under washing lines, Hawaiian shirts and cum-stained sheets drying out in the sun. A yardie blares at him as Latrell kicks over a ganja plant and nearly throttles him.

Latrell bursts out of a back alley, the sun glaring in his eyes. This part of the estate is always quiet, full of cover, with sheds and garages used to grow dope and cut people up for implants. He races past them and then turns onto a short road, and they're there, waiting for him. Pigs in blue. He turns around and there's another one, out of uniform, but sticking out like any pig does.

Latrell freezes, his heartrate off the scale, and he scans around, looking for a way out. He darts away, and the one out of uniform goes after him. Kids scream from the upper levels, throwing objects at the pig's head.

He tries to climb over another fence, but his legs are gone, his energy zapped. *Fuck!* There's no way out, and guilt eats into his gut for how it'll break his mother when she gets the call.

"Didn't do anything. I didn't." Gulps of breath.

"Sure, boy." The officer's ragged ginger beard links up to nothing on top, and he looks like he's slept in his clothes. "Let's see what you've got in those pockets."

Latrell clams up.

"Oy, dickhead!" A stone comes flying past Latrell's head and lands square on the pig's nose. Jaymes laughs as he comes out from behind the bush to meet Latrell, and it's the best sound in the world. The sound of better times, a safer future. "Quick, give me the money, Latrell. Get over that fence. Now, boy."

"No. I can't leave—"

"Just go. You've always been a slow arse." He's right. Even

though Jaymes has asthma, he always beat Latrell in a sprint, embarrassing him no end.

"Fuckin' go, bruv. And you know I'd never try anything with Haylee."

Latrell doesn't argue any further and jumps the fence, Jaymes pushing Latrell's feet up.

He lands hard, his ankle gone. Latrell spots the bin chute at the back of the house. He limps to it as he hears Jaymes struggling with the officer. Latrell holds his breath, the reek of bin juice slapping him across the face, and he slides into the chute like a chicken shit, and closes it up after him.

*

Hours pass before Latrell pulls his sorry arse out of there, smelling worse than sin. Latrell still hears the sirens, though they're long gone.

He hobbles to the front of the house and back to the street, towards home.

He spots Naz on the way, and walks up to him. "What happened, man?" Latrell asks. "I had to lay low."

"Your man got took. That's what happened. Along with Reeze's money. He's fucking fumin'. Fuck, is that smell you? You better climb back in the hole again for a while. You're off the streets. Hide that watch in the usual place. I'll come round your gaff when you're back in again."

Latrell can't take it all in. Somehow he'd thought, hoped, that Jaymes had escaped from the feds. It's all his fault that Jaymes was taken by the police. How could he let it happen? But now Latrell thinks about it, it's Jaymes who is the safe one, knowing the shit that Reeze might do to them. "Yeah, sure."

"Smell you later, man, and not too soon." Naz swaggers away, and Latrell hobbles home, ready to face a hammering from his mother. He sighs. The money he wanted to give her will be gone for a while now, he thinks. And, *damn*, does he need new clothes.

*

Latrell puts down the controller for the *uber*militant game, sick of being blown up by freedom fighters. It isn't the same playing without Jaymes, and he's been bored out of his head for days since his bro had been taken in. He'd not heard anything from Naz or the rest of the crew, his phone dead silent. Latrell spins it in his hand like a revolver, willing it to buzz. He checks the messages again that he'd sent Jaymes: still no answer to them. Latrell thinks again that Jaymes must have ditched his phone before he was lifted, as all he gets is Jaymes' voicemail every time he calls.

The phone suddenly buzzes in his hand, and Latrell rushes to open the message up. Sees it's from Naz. *Yur boi is a fuckin' grass, son. our grind garage just got busted, surgery equip, tech the lot taken by the feds. tell us as soon as you hear he's out.*

Latrell's hand shakes as he holds the phone. He throws it to the bed and itches under the watch strap on his other hand, the chip embedded in his skin on fire. A rite of passage for the grinder crew, he regretted getting caught by Curf Control ever since.

Fuck! Latrell paces the small confines of his room. No way, man. No way would Jaymes break and leak it all about them. He'd never grass them up. Would he?

Latrell looks out through the window, trying to spot Jaymes' bedroom window on the tenth level of the high rise facing his own. But there's still no light on. *No. He would never…*

He wishes he had his dad's number so he could ask what's happening, but he isn't sure Jaymes' old man would tell him, or even remember after a few bottles.

Latrell keeps scratching at his wrist. Waiting… Looking out the window for his man. Half-sleep, head pressed against the cold window, the slamming of a car door wakes him up. And Jaymes is there, being escorted out of the car. A surge of adrenalin spikes in Latrell's system, and then he notices how late it is, how the light is fading outside. *Shit.* He flicks his wrist and the digits light up. He taps it twice and it tells him there's about 20 mins before his curfew starts, before his chip starts silently beaming his location, and if he's not back here, he'll be spending time in a cell too.

Latrell bolts through the door, his mum screaming at him to explain where he's going. "Ain't got time, Mum. Back soon!" he says, and with that he sprints to the end of the corridor and beats his fist on both lift buttons. Body shaking, pulse racing, he waits, but both lifts are stuck on the bottom floor. Damn it.

He flies through the stair doors and jumps the concrete steps three at a time, racing as fast as he and his bruv used to do when they were yay high. The spiralling staircase makes his head light, his heart heavy, as he blinks under flickering fluorescent tubes.

Panting like a dog, he jumps out into the twilight, scans the area to make sure it's clear. Checking none of the crew is there to suss where he's going. It looks good, so he walks over, yearning to run, but knowing he has to stay cool in case the kids in the high rises think he's being suspicious. Damn, in case drone surveillance is on him, and the feds think the same. And Latrell wonders if there's a trap the pigs have set up. Though it doesn't even matter anymore as he has to speak to Jaymes. Has to warn him.

Feeling glacial-slow, he reaches the doors of Jaymes' high rise, and see's people waiting for the lifts on the bottom floor. And Haylee's one of them. She spots him before he can slip past. "Latrell, hey. Just wanted to see how you are? With all the shit that's been going on." Concern shadows her features, but she still looks pure gold.

"Yeah, good. Sorry, I gotta go, you know," he tells her, walking away.

She looks sad and he feels shitty, but he's not got time, and he thinks of that night when he embarrassed Jaymes in front of her and the others, when they were recruited up. "Sure. Speak soon, okay? And watch out, Tyrone is pissed and looking for you," she calls up to him and he takes the stairs again, legs heavy, breath short. But he gets another surge of energy like he's had a mod, thinking about what's at stake.

His trainers slapping the marble stairs, Latrell reaches Jaymes' floor and his sweaty hands push the fire doors so hard they swing back and nearly knock him off his feet. His ankle aches like hell but it holds out on him.

He scoots down to the end of the hall, and hammers on the door.

Reeking of brandy, Jaymes' dad answers. "What the fuck you want?"

"Jaymes, it's me!" he shouts past his dad.

"He's not in, you little shit. Still in the nick."

But Latrell knows its bull. "C'mon, bruv," he shouts. "It's me. I know you're in there—"

His dad tries to slam the door in his face, but Latrell wedges his foot in the door, and pushes his way in. Runs to Jaymes' bedroom.

Jaymes is there sat on the bed, looking as if he's been lobotomised, as if he's still in a cell.

Latrell grabs him by the shoulders. "Bruv. You've got to get out of here. They think you grassed them up. They—"

Jaymes breaks from his stupor. "I know," and nods to the back wall that Latrell had missed. In green spray paint, a message reads one word. Enough to say it all. *GRASS*

Latrell knew that Jaymes would have had no problems reading the word. He clocks Jaymes' Nitroman T-shirt is hanging half out of the bin.

"Why the hell would they think I…? You know I'd never—"

Latrell grabs his hand. "Of course I fuckin' know. Now let's get out of here. Someone else must have seen that cop car. You can't stay here." He can't let Jaymes get caught, they're bros.

Fear glints out of his best friend's eyes and it's like looking at him when they first met in playschool, when he was scared of everything and nothing. Of his mum leaving him, of needing more strength to fight off the likes of Tyrone.

Jaymes grabs his hand tight, and they run for the door. His father's already forgotten about them, downing another can of Tennent's Super in front of the streambox as they race past him.

They take the stairs again, knowing it's safer, and they both struggle. It's clear that Jaymes has not done much running in days and Latrell is already gassed out. They finally make it to the ground floor, though, and run to the door.

"Wait here, man," Latrell whispers, and rushes out into the open air, sucking in gulps of it. Darkness is already upon them as the last sunlight is caught behind the giant concrete building. He feels relief though, as it will help Jaymes to escape. Camouflage them both like they're back playing BioWarfare 6.0, covering each other, keeping each other safe.

"*Psst.* It's clear!" Latrell says, and Jaymes exits the building, but someone is behind him, pushing him forward. A boy twice his size and strong, even without the bio-mods he had put in him. A mug as ugly as roadkill, a savage dog.

"Hey, Latrell. Where you rushing to?"

"How did…?" Latrell asks, but struggles to get out his words.

"What, find you? Idiots, why you think Reeze puts the chips in our wrists? To track us. Easier enough to hack the Cure Control ones too, Ratrell," he says, eyeballing him.

Jaymes whispers, *Shit*.

"Why didn't you tell me your main man was back in town?" Tyrone says.

"Naz said to cut off all contact."

Tyrone growls, clearly pissed for being outwitted, but that's nothing new. And Latrell knows it's him who leaked the info on the crew.

"Whatever. We got a present for him back at Paradise Heights. The boss is gonna give you the works. Night eyes, mag implants, the lot. Just like you always wanted." Tyrone gives a knowing smile, and it makes Latrell feel sick. "Come on, Jay, we gonna mod you up, son, so you're one of us proper. After all, you earned it for not saying out at the station."

"No, I'm good, man," Jaymes says. "Don't want mods anymore."

Latrell sees Jaymes' body stiffen further, cold fear making his face pale. Latrell squeezes his fists so hard, fingernails biting into his palm. Then he notices Tyrone's attention on his other hand that starts glowing red through his skin. Tyrone smirks and says, "You better get home like a good little boy before Curf Control grab—"

Latrell throws an uppercut to Tyrone's chin, and Jaymes throws his elbow back to wind him.

"Fucking run, Jay!" Latrell screams, and they both scamper, running as fast as they ever have together towards the nearest park. Like they did as shorties in the playground, racing towards the future. Heading out of the estate as quick as they can.

In the full dark, streetlights fade away, as they head towards a field. Jaymes climbs over the fence, and Latrell puts his leg over when he's grabbed from behind.

"Run, bro. *Run!*" Latrell shouts, as he kicks out, watching his boy escape. And he hopes he never comes back, free from the grime and grind of the streets. From the bullying and double-crossing.

Latrell's heart skips a beat as realisation hits him. Curf Control. "Hope you like it in the cell, boy."

And Latrell smiles. "Sure. Don't mind at all."

*

Latrell is released after a day and the air smells sweet, sweet as marshmallow milk. He didn't say a word at the station, but he'll tell Reeze the truth now Jaymes is safely out of the way. Latrell stretches, and his mum's disappointment doesn't even get to him when she picks him up. But when they get home, he sees her waiting for him like an angel. Haylee.

"Mum, I'll catch you up."

His mum gives him a warning stare, and he nods, so she leaves them.

And Haylee throws her arms around him before he knows it; his tongue in knots. He backs up, looks into her eyes, and sees a tear smudged on her cheek.

"What? Tell me!"

"I'm s-so sorry." Her voice quivers like he hasn't heard since they were in playschool together. "I heard…"

"WHAT?"

"It's Jaymes. He didn't make the mod surgery. They…they tried to make him how he wanted. Make him strong…" And her voice breaks as she punches a hole through his stomach.

Latrell is winded. His eyes itchy hot. His wrist on fire as he claws at it, nails cutting deep. Pain clamps down on his chest. Bile rises in his throat as he screams raw. "Don't you get it? *They* made it happen. They murdered him, Haylee!"

She steps back, shocked, reeling as much as he is. "No. They, they can't have…" she stutters, but it's clear in her eyes that it makes sense; they shed another tear and Latrell thinks of all the inked ones he's seen on the older kids' faces.

Jaymes' scared face flashes in Latrell's mind and he bites back the sick rising in his throat. Jaymes wanted to be invincible like all the other kids on the estate, to deal with the shit of living here, but Latrell realises it's easier to be free of it.

Latrell pulls off the watch the crew had given him and throws it into a bush. Reeze would never believe about Tyrone and Latrell knows now he will face the same fate as Jaymes. He grabs Haylee's hand, surprise in her eyes. "Where we goin'?"

"To the station," he tells her, and she doesn't let go of his hand.

~

L. P. Melling currently writes from the East of England after being swept around the country by academia and his career. He is a Writers of the Future *finalist and won the short story contest at his* Russell Group *university. His fiction has appeared in such places as* DreamForge, Hybrid Friction, Thrilling Words, *and the* Best of Anthology: The Future Looms. *When not writing, he works for a London-based legal charity that advises and supports victims of crime. You can find out more about him at his website:* www.lpmelling.wordpress.com

WHERE ALL ROADS END
Andrew Kozma

I drive along perfect roads, completely pothole free, without divots or drops, no sudden bumps in the surface standing out like blisters, like tumors, like a desperate rat frantically trying to claw through an unbreakable wall. Out in West Texas, there is nothing except the road, nothing but fauxphalt as far as the eye can see. Even the mesas are succumbing, the fresh black tide of the road lapping up their stone flanks. Dirt, cactus, tumbleweed, snakes and tarantulas, all of that's under the road now, bones and vegetable fibers, scales and twigs, every organic molecule feeding the fauxphalt.

It's a perfect drive, I have no complaints about that. The bioengineers who built it perfected the road for gentle slopes and for a surface so smooth it's like driving on silk. It's the kind of road you might lay on during an Autumn day in an untraveled subdivision when the sun is bright and the air cool, the heat-soaked street keeping your back warm as you watch the clouds dance.

But fauxphalt isn't asphalt. The underside of it wriggles with thick cilia which look like tiny white worms, and even though those worms are three inches below the surface of the road, I can't help picturing them every time I walk on the road. Lying down on the fauxphalt is unthinkable. I've put my ear to the road, and heard the gentle squirming as the road eats, constantly searching for the materials it needs to make itself grow.

I try not to think about it.

A lone gas station mars the smooth horizon, smoke piling into the sky from the fire break around it. After I cross the metal bridge to the concrete platform, a young man comes out to greet me, his clothes stained with the tarry blood of the road. Ash deepens the lines on his face, making him look old and tired. He leans on his hoe-torch and grimaces a cautious smile. It'd take only a little effort to swing the hoe-torch right into my head through the car's open window. I don't blame him. Can't be too safe these days.

"Gas, I expect," he says, a clear statement, not even the hint of a question.

I nod, getting out to stretch my legs on a surface that's dead and cold and trustworthy. The man hooks up a pump, then fills my extra gas cans, and we stand there in silence except for the roar of the flames.

The fire break around the station is petering out in places already, the fauxphalt extending to smother the flames. Some people have suggested the fauxphalt is intelligent. Scientists called those suggestions stupid. Of course, those scientists invented fauxphalt in the first place, so I don't hold much stock in their opinions anymore.

"Is there an edge around here?" I ask.

He looks pointedly at the fire break, then nods towards the north. "Used to be one that way. Maybe now joined up with 190."

He takes my money, but God knows what he does with it out here in this wasteland. I drive back over the bridge, and the man goes back to hacking at the fauxphalt with his hoe-torch. It's only a matter of time before the fauxphalt breaks through and devours the gas station, covering it all in a sticky bubble which'll slowly flatten until no one driving by would guess there'd been anything there at all.

Heading north, I leave the white lines that provide the only sure direction towards the next town, assuming the town hasn't succumbed to the fauxphalt. The fire breaks work, but all it takes is one thread of fauxphalt and entire neighborhoods will be paved over. Too big to fail Houston is now only a tiny town circled by the hungry monster 610 has become, downtown disappearing when chunks of roaming fauxphalt dropped from the I-45 overpass. Who knows what will be left when I return.

A half-hour north of the gas station and the fauxphalt ends against a line of dirt. The sight of that dirt and the cacti growing from it makes me cry, I can't help it. I park the car on the edge and walk into the natural wasteland. An array of brightly-colored tents litter the distance. Roadenders, their slow form of suicide waiting for the fauxphalt to close up on them. I've seen them before, lying down right next to the lip of the road. Some people like to watch, as apparently the process by which the road eats is painless. On the other hand, scientists say something in the road's cilia paralyzes those it eats, so that even though the dying person appears calm and peaceful, all the pain remains.

This is a theory I'm unwilling to test.

My sample kit is small, but heavy, full of chemicals and tools. I kneel next to the edge of the road, but I don't start my work right away. The world is so silent here. The car snaps and cracks as the engine cools. I can hear the faintest murmur of voices from the Roadenders, carrying over the waste between us like the ghosts of the dead. Closest of all, because of the quiet, I can hear the fauxphalt eating. Its tendrils pulse at the dirt border, tiny white limbs digging for sustenance. The rustling sounds for all the world like a freshly-washed sheet being stretched over a bed. Comforting. Homey. And for that moment, I almost understand how the Roadenders feel, as though the road is not the punishment we deserve, an ecological terror we created ourselves, but instead the warm embrace we need.

When I was five, I had a pet guinea pig. It was a giant thing, so big I had to cradle it in my arms like the baby I no longer was. After only a few months, it died suddenly. I went to sleep with it digging up the wood shavings of its cage, and in the morning it was stiff, eyes dry and staring.

My mom let me do the actual burial, digging as much of a grave as I could with a tiny plastic sand shovel, then patting down a muddy mound of dirt and grass over the body. I marked it with two popsicle sticks taped into a cross.

A few weeks later, I was out in the yard and my mom wasn't paying attention, so I dug up the grave. I missed my pet. And when I ripped up the ground with my bare hands, in a hurry because I knew my mom would stop me if she noticed, I didn't find the body. There was nothing there. When my mom finally noticed, she told me my guinea pig had gone back home to nature—our family didn't believe in Heaven—absorbed into the ground around our home, and so it would always be close to me.

When I was older, my parents admitted the neighbor's dog had

339

squeezed under our fence and dug up the body. My dad had walked out back to find my guinea pig scattered around the back yard, broken bones, bits of fur and flesh, the dog gnawing on the decapitated head. He collected all the remains, tied them up in a plastic grocery bag, and dumped it all in the trash.

I remember that dog, how friendly it was, how it affectionately licked my face.

The electric scalpel cuts easily through the edge of the road, but it doesn't cauterize the wound. The road's dark blood slowly spreads out onto the sandy dirt, but it doesn't sink in right away, instead sitting there like oil on water. In a glass tube, I secure a sliver of the road for study back at the labs— scientists are still struggling to understand why parts of the road vary in structure (they refuse to say *genetics*) even though it's all one single connected organism.

Then I uncork a second tube, this one full of Solution 57, a whitish paste that smells like powdered lemonade. Out here, in this heat, I struggle with the sudden urge to taste it, the tiniest bit of sugared sweetness on the tongue. But this sweetness would burn right through the tongue and the jaw beneath. Caustic to humans, and any animals unfortunate enough to stumble along after I leave here, this mixture was designed to destroy the road from the inside out, like a virus, killing the living underside and leaving a rock-hard corpse behind to drive on.

And, as expected, when I smear the paste liberally onto the road's open wound, the rustling of all the fauxphalt's tiny tongue-arms slows, then stops. The road's death is actually visible, too. The white paste bleeds into the surrounding fauxphalt, paling it as though it's been dusted with ash, and quickly, too. In the minute from when I first applied the paste, all the road within reach has died. I cut of a section of the dead road with a scalpel, inserting that specimen into yet another tube, and this time there's no blood.

It's a promising start.

But I've personally tested over two dozen 'solutions' to the fauxphalt problem. Each time it comes back stronger, more invasive, and immune to whatever poison or virus we used before. I'm not losing hope, because I never had any hope to begin with.

This is a job. I eat, as long as there's food to be eaten. I've got a place to stay, as long as there're places uncovered by the road. And I get the freedom of the open road.

Packing up, I can't help looking back at the Roadenders. If Solution 57 works, the Roadenders will be waiting forever for the road to reach them.

And if it doesn't work, which seems infinitely more likely, in a few months the road will be at their tents. They'll lie down in the dirt, maybe dig a little shallow trench for themselves to make it easier for the fauxphalt to climb over them, and in a few hours, a day, tops, they'll be blanketed by the road. Their bodies will go the way all bodies go, subsumed into something else, something greater, or at least something more prone to survive.

Back at the lab, they're waiting for the new samples and my report on the latest treatment's effectiveness. The sun's heat makes the entire fauxphalt horizon a hallucinatory oasis. I've got a car and enough gas to drive for two days straight.

I could go anywhere.

The road's calling my name.

~

Andrew Kozma's fiction has been published in Escape Pod, Reckoning, Daily Science Fiction, *and* Analog. *His first book of poems,* City of Regret *(Zone 3 Press, 2007), won the* Zone 3 First Book Award *and his second book,* Orphanotrophia, *is forthcoming from Cobalt Press.*

BEYOND GREENVILLE
Michael Barron

I was nine years old when my brother told me the truth about our town.

On some level I'd always known there was something off about Greenville. Everything in the 'New Release' section of our library had been there for years, as if people had forgotten how to write new books or make new movies. Our televisions, phones and computers only ever showed the same TV episodes over and over again. Mama's tablet and smartwatch had been in the family since my great-grandfather, Christopher Hopkins, founded the town, but no matter how much time passed they always claimed the year was 2016.

For as long as I could remember Mama had a 2016 'Birds of North America' calendar hanging in our kitchen, and whenever a teacher wrote the date on the whiteboard, they always ended it with '2016.' If any of us asked about this, the teacher would smile, change the subject and e-mail our parents.

Once when we were shopping at Giant, I asked Mama why the year never changed. She gripped my arm so tight the gangly teenager stocking Lucky Charms stared at us. "Emily, we don't talk about such things in public!"

"Why?"

"We'll discuss it later."

But she refused to answer my question, even after we got home, and whenever I asked about the year after that, I lost my dessert privileges for a week.

Then came the day the Wilsons were arrested.

I was trudging home from my first day of fourth grade, wondering how I was supposed to write a whole paragraph on my summer vacation when I turned the corner and saw all four of Greenville's police cars parked outside our neighbors' house.

Sheriff Lawrence stepped outside, escorting Mr. Wilson, who was in handcuffs. A moment later three of his deputies emerged

342

with the rest of the family. Even Erin, who was only a couple years older than me, had her hands bound behind her back.

She spotted me standing with one foot on the sidewalk and the other in the gutter and opened her mouth to shout something, but the deputy shoved her forward.

The police cars were disappearing around the corner when Mama bustled out of our house. She looked over her shoulder, checking to see if anyone was watching, before she picked up my lunchbox, which I hadn't realized I'd dropped, and herded me indoors.

As soon as we were in the kitchen I asked, "Is Erin okay?"

"Don't worry about her. Go watch *SpongeBob*."

"But why'd the police—"

"Just go watch television. We'll discuss this later."

*

When I went to school the next day everyone was talking about the Wilsons on the playground.

Taylor Sims, a tall girl with waist-length hair, said, "They were arrested for having outside tech."

"What's that?" I asked balancing on the very edge of the blacktop.

Sheldon Brown snorted, "You've never heard of outside tech?"

"I've heard of it!"

Technically I'd only heard the term once, when my brother, Chris, mentioned it over dinner. Mama had slapped him. "Don't speak of such things in front of your sister."

Taylor said, "Outside tech is stuff people sneak into town from places where it isn't 2016 anymore."

I didn't want to look stupid in front of her so I nodded and pretended this made sense.

Sheldon grinned. "Now that they're on the outside the giant ants'll get 'em."

"Giant ants?" I asked.

"My dad says everything outside town is a gross radioactive desert. All the animals are dead except the ants who've mutated to the size of elephants."

As far as I knew, Sheldon's dad could be right, but the Wilsons had always given me extra candy on Halloween and let me use their pool in the summer. Their house had been an escape pod when Mama got into one of her moods.

I responded with the most logical argument that came to mind. "Your dad's an asshole!"

Everyone in the playground turned. Several people giggled.

Sheldon stepped forward. "At least my dad didn't ditch his…"

He was on the ground, clutching his nose before he even finished the sentence.

An hour later, I sat in the back of Mama's CRV, staring at the signs spread across people's lawns. Everyone put them up in the fall to promote candidates in an election that happened every year. The same people always won, but we kept putting the signs out. It was a yearly tradition, like Christmas trees or jack-o'-lanterns.

Mama had been giving me an earful ever since we left Vice Principal White's office. "I never did anything like this when I was your age."

"I didn't hit him that hard, Mama."

"I'm not talking about that. No daughter of mine will be gallivanting around talking about outside technology."

The instant we got home I was sent to my room, and Mama told me that if she caught me doing anything but lying in bed she'd ground me for a month. I lay on my mattress, staring at my *Star Wars: The Force Awakens* poster. Chris had given it to me for my birthday. It was supposed to be the first movie in a new trilogy, but when I asked when the next episode was coming out, he'd said, "Never."

"Why not?"

"They just aren't making any more. We'll talk about it when you're older."

Chris had Improv Club after school, so I'd been lying in bed for hours when he finally got home. Before I even heard him close the door, Mama asked, "Do you know what your sister did today?" It was a serious question, like she thought the whole town was gossiping about it.

They moved onto the back porch where I couldn't overhear them.

My belly was rumbling by the time Chris knocked on my door. "Grab your sleeping bag. I'm taking you camping."

Before I knew it, he was driving us across the rickety bridge that led out of town. I sat shotgun, staring at the surrounding evergreens, wondering if Mama had ordered him to leave me in the woods. We'd never gone camping before. I'd never even traveled ten miles from the hospital where I was born.

The campsite couldn't have been more than a half hour from our doorstep, but I felt as though we were deep in the wilderness. Tree branches blocked the sky. There was no sound except for the rustle of animals scurrying through the underbrush.

Chris pulled the cooler from the station wagon. "Pappap took me out here all the time when I was a kid."

I nodded, staring at the rocky ground that would be our mattress. If I resented Chris for anything, it was that he'd gotten ten extra years with our great-grandfather.

As the sun set, he taught me how to pitch a tent and build a fire. I kept expecting him to bring up the fight, but he didn't say a word about it.

Night had completely settled, and we were roasting hot dogs when he asked, "What do you remember about Pappap?"

It took me a while to come up with an answer. I only had a handful of memories of the great Christopher Hopkins. He was the oldest person I'd ever met but acted younger than Mama. At the age of ninety-eight, he taught me how to play *Pokémon Go* and debated Marvel movies with Chris.

A couple days before he passed away, the two of us took his Pomeranian, Bucky, for a walk through the park. Pappap must've realized he didn't have much time left because he bought me two fudgsicles. I was only six and the idea of having *two* chocolaty treats before dinner felt like too much of a good thing. "Mama's gonna be mad."

He ruffled my hair. "You're one of the good ones, Emily. Not like all those other jokers. Don't ever change."

That was my last memory of him.

After giving it a lot of thought, I finally answered my brother's question. "He was the nicest person in the world."

"Did you know he was one of the richest men who ever lived, but he spent everything building Greenville."

"Why?"

"Have you heard of the Industrial Revolution?"

I shook my head.

"It was this thing that happened in the eighteenth century when a lot of people came up with tons of new inventions. Since then people have been inventing things faster and faster. By the twentieth century, technology was noticeably progressing every decade. By the beginning of the twenty-first century it was progressing by the year. By the middle of the 2020's it was radically changing month to month."

"Wait. How do you know...?"

He went on. "Millions of people had emotional breakdowns because they couldn't keep pace with the tech they needed to run their lives. They'd blow a whole paycheck on a new program and literally hours later it was obsolete. Every day people woke up in a world that was different from the one they'd gone to bed in. They lost their grip on reality because no one knew what would be possible from one minute to the next." He took a deep breath, as if imagining such a world exhausted him. "Our great-grandfather spent his fortune creating Greenville, a community frozen in a simpler time, the year 2016.

"There are machines beneath the town that automatically create products and deliver them to stores, preserve our homes so nothing ages, and sterilize women after they've had two babies. They also watch out for us, make sure that no one possesses technology or art created after 2016. That's why the Wilsons were banished. They stole information from the outside world."

My head swam, as if I was coming up from the bottom of a pool after being under for too long. I wanted to insist this was all a joke, but I knew it wasn't. For the first time in years Greenville made sense.

*

The campouts became a yearly tradition.

During the last Friday of August— which was always the twenty-sixth— Chris and I would pack our sleeping bags, drive

346

across the rickety bridge, and spend the evening discussing the world beyond Greenville. Those trips were my only chance to talk about what was really going on.

Every once in a while, I'd overhear people whispering about the "real world" in the locker room or the back of Cherry's Comics, but all of my friends were too straight-laced for such conversations. It wasn't illegal to discuss the town's true purpose. It was just socially taboo, like talking about diarrhea at a fancy dinner party.

Back in the fourth grade, Taylor Sims had been willing to chat about outside tech on the playground, but after we reached middle school she refused to even acknowledge it existed. Even Sheldon Brown stopped sharing his father's theories about giant ants.

As we got older my classmates went to parties, drank, hooked up and bitched about our teachers, parents and the universe, but when it came to ignoring the outside world, they fell right in line. The only time Taylor and I talked about it was in the sixth grade, when I tried to convince her to hike to the border.

"I just want to see how far we can go."

"You can't see anything," she said while strumming her guitar. "Mom says there's a big field surrounding the town and if you step one foot in it the cops show up."

"How does she know?"

Taylor changed the subject to an upcoming middle school dance. She glanced at me out of the corner of her eye. "Has anyone asked you yet?"

Everyone else seemed content to accept Greenville as the whole universe, but while we were in those woods, Chris and I spent hours talking about what we were missing.

In elementary school I thought of our town as a boring splotch in the middle of a technological utopia with flying cars and jet packs. By sixth grade I imagined the world as a gritty *Blade Runner* cityscape. In high school I pictured a blistering desert populated by mutants who raced around in pimped-out hot rods.

Chris' theories were even bleaker.

"Pappap told me the machines running Greenville don't need anyone on the outside to maintain them. Everyone else could have been wiped out by wars or a plague years ago."

I stared at the star-filled sky. "Wouldn't that have killed us too?"

"I don't know. All I know is I'm glad we're in here and they're out there."

*

The outside world wasn't the only thing we discussed. Every major milestone of our lives seemed to take place on those trips.

During the campout when I was twelve, I told my brother, "I think I kind of like girls more than guys." I'd known this for years, but pushing those words into the world outside my head made me feel like I'd fallen from a tree and hadn't yet hit the ground.

Chris placed an arm around me. "You know I'll always be here for you, right?"

"But other people will think I'm weird."

"They're idiots. You'll still be you no matter what." Later he added, "But maybe I should be there when you tell Mom."

The following year he said, "They've officially hired me. You're looking at Greenville's newest fireman!"

"Great! That's fantastic."

He could tell my smile was fake. "It's not as dangerous as it sounds."

"I know. But maybe I should be there when you tell Mama."

During my freshman year, he gave me my first solid piece of relationship advice. "I know it sucks, but if Rachel's cruel to your friends and makes you feel like shit, end it with her."

"That's easy for you to say! You've had a ton of girlfriends. I'm the only out girl at Greenville High. If I break up with her I'll be alone forever!"

"No, you won't, and it's better to be alone than in a horrible relationship."

On the camping trip at the beginning of my sophomore year, I saw a side of Chris I'd never imagined existed. He was telling me about a couple who'd been exiled for having outside tech. "Their computers were filled with information from beyond 2016. The cops brought us in to destroy the house in a controlled burn."

I grinned, "Did you sneak a peek at anything? If it were me, I would've…"

Chris leaned forward so fast I nearly fell backwards. "Don't say another word." He stared at the trees, as if searching for someone hiding in the branches.

"I'm serious, Em. Never joke like that. If you have to rebel, smoke pot and vandalize property. At least those things happened in 2016. You'd be playing along. Never even hint you're interested in outside tech."

We eventually returned to our conversation, but the rest of the trip was like walking on eggshells.

However, things smoothed over long before we went camping in my junior year, when I asked, "Do you remember my friend Taylor Sims?"

Chris nodded while attempting to light the kindling.

"We're sort of dating."

He looked up. "Is she nicer than Rachel?"

"Yes! She's so sweet. She's kind of shy, but she's got the loudest laugh, and it's adorable when it embarrasses her. And she spends every lunch period playing her guitar. She even wrote a song for me."

Chris shook his head. "No girl's ever written a song for me."

While he drove me home the next morning, I told him about the adorable way Taylor sneezed. "I've known her forever, but there are all these new things I keep noticing."

"Does Mom know you're dating?"

"Yeah, she did the whole, 'I'm fine with it, but don't tell Grandma.' Then she tried to convince me that Pappap wouldn't have liked it, which is stupid because everyone knows he was the most open-minded person ever. They even say that in school."

After Chris dropped me off, he leaned out the window. "Be gentle with Mom. She's a bit much, but…"

"She's the only mom we have, I know. You're lucky you don't live here anymore."

He smiled, "Love you."

I turned to walk up the driveway. "Love you, too."

He sped down the road.

I was unlocking our door when I heard tires squeal. Then came the explosion. It was the loudest sound I'd ever heard.

My sleeping bag fell from my arms. For an instant I wanted to insist I hadn't heard what I knew I'd heard, but I was already running toward the street. From the exact spot where I'd seen the Wilsons vanish forever, I saw the nearly unrecognizable mass of metal that used to be my brother's car.

*

I have no recollection of the car ride to the hospital or the hours spent in the waiting area. The next thing I remember, I stood in a hospital room doorway. What was left of Chris lay in the bed. Tubes filled his mouth, like plastic tentacles trying to choke him.

When Mama took his hand, he gave no indication he knew we were there.

I remained in the doorway, arms wrapped around my chest, unable to look directly at the bed. Taylor stood beside me. When she tried to rub my back, I pulled away. She said she'd come as soon as she received my text. I couldn't remember sending her one.

Chris had worked as a fireman for three years. He'd saved at least two people during that time, but now he lay in a hospital bed, unable to breathe on his own because some idiot in an SUV was texting while driving.

Because that was the kind of thing that happened in 2016.

*

Sunrise found Taylor and me sitting in our usual booth at the Corner Diner. Mama was still at the hospital, begging, threatening and bargaining with anyone who would listen.

While we waited for our vegetarian quesadillas, Taylor Googled terms the doctor had used. Every once in a while she said something like, "According to this article..." or "This is interesting..." but I knew she wouldn't find anything helpful, not on 2016's version of the Internet.

I stared at the bust of Elvis perched between the cash register and a bowl of chalky mints. I didn't know anyone who actually liked Elvis, but the restaurant was decorated with posters, clocks and collectable plates all featuring The King, because that was the kind of thing 1950's nostalgia diners had.

I should have been focusing on Chris, trying to think of ways to help him, but all I could think of was how fake everything was.

Sometimes I could go for weeks without thinking about what was really going on. Then I'd spot a crack in the town's reality, like a news story that had "broken" on that exact day a year earlier, and I'd remember that my world was as phony as Disney Land. Then I'd remember that Disney Land probably didn't exist anymore.

"Hey," Taylor took my hand. "You'd tell me if there was anything I could do, right? I'd go to hell for you."

I nodded.

After several minutes I asked, "Do you think the doctors in the outside world could help?"

Taylor stared at her placemat, which displayed a picture of Mr. Presley playing the ukulele. "There's probably nothing out there."

"That's what Chris used to say."

*

My brother's condition soon became devastatingly clear. The doctors said he might never wake. Even if he did, he wouldn't be the same old Chris.

Whenever Mama and I visited she always insisted he looked healthier, but his prognosis never changed by a syllable. She tried to get him the best care possible, haggling with insurance companies, grilling the doctors and draining our savings.

A month after the accident, she made an appointment with a new doctor to discuss alternative treatments.

On the morning of the appointment, Mama and I sat in the waiting room between two screaming toddlers. My phone's battery was running on fumes, but I didn't bother with the magazines littering the coffee table. They were the same issues found in every waiting room in Greenville. Over the years I'd glanced through every article and memorized every cartoon. So had Mama, but she still flipped through *The National Review*, nodding and murmuring to herself.

We'd been sitting for almost an hour when a petite nurse approached us. "The paperwork we received from the insurance company was incomplete. What is your son's date of birth?"

Without looking up, Mama said, "October 22, 2016."

The nurse scribbled on her clipboard. "And the accident was

on August 27, 2016?"

She nodded.

I looked between them. "So according to those forms, Chris was driving a car before he was born?"

Mama rubbed her forehead. "Not now, Emily."

I almost let it go. I would have if the nurse hadn't given me a smile that clearly said, "Let the grownups talk, Sweetie."

Before I could stop myself I exclaimed, "You guys do realize this is all bullshit, right? There is no insurance company. We're just playing along so we can pretend the real world doesn't exist."

Everyone stared at me. Even the toddlers seemed shocked.

"The machines running Greenville could take care of Chris for free. Or they could contact doctors on the outside. There might be a futuristic wonderland thirty miles away, but we have to take out loans and pay bills and do all this crap just so we can..."

Mama struck me across the face.

My cheek burned, but I refused to rub it and show how much she had hurt me.

We stared at each other. She was so close I could smell the milk and Raisin Bran on her breath. "Get out," she whispered. "Just get out."

*

I practically lived at Taylor's house after that. Even at the time I knew it was cruel to abandon Mama. Not a day passed that I didn't try to go back, but things were just easier in the Sims' household.

Taylor's parents were a pair of middle-aged hippies. Most adults in Greenville had childhoods modeled after the mid 2010's, as did their children and their children's children. Music, movies, technology and literature never changed so everyone had similar formative years.

However, the Sims preferred the 1960's to the early twenty-first century. They listened to *The Doors* and *Pink Floyd* and made abstract paintings in their basement studio, which I was never allowed to visit because they created their art in the nude.

On the night of Chris' birthday, Mr. and Mrs. Sims – who asked me to call them Jackson and Sophia – went over to a friend's house. Taylor insisted I shouldn't spend the evening alone so I snuck in through the backdoor, avoiding Mrs. McKenzie, the bored neighbor who always kept track of people coming and going in the neighborhood.

I spent the evening lying in Taylor's bed with my head in her lap while she strummed her guitar. We'd been there for a while, just enjoying each other's presence when I asked, "Do you think Greenville caused the accident?"

"How could a town cause a car accident?"

"How can a town make unlimited food and have it so nothing ages? Maybe it took control of Chris' car and made him crash to keep up the 2016 quota of car accidents."

"That's not how Greenville works."

"How do you know? And if the machines didn't cause the accident they sure as hell didn't stop it."

Before she could respond, we heard the front door open. Taylor's dad called, "We're home, Sweet Pea."

She nearly dropped her guitar on my head. "Don't make a sound." She crawled out of bed and stepped into the hall. "Hey! You're back early."

I sat up, bitter that I still had to hide from her parents. I was about to climb out the window and just walk to the diner when I heard Taylor's mom ask about my jacket, which I'd draped over the living room sofa.

"Yeah," Taylor said. "Emily left that yesterday."

"She's not here now, is she?"

"Of course not." I could tell she was uncertain if she should maintain the lie.

Her parents were oblivious, though. Mrs. Sims said, "You'd better sit down, Sweetie. There's something we need to tell you."

After a slight pause, her dad said, "A few minutes before we left, we received new information from our contacts. They told us..." He took a deep breath. "Something very unsettling happened to North and Central America in the late 2030's. There was an event that left thousands dead and millions permanently..."

"I'm going to be sick!"

"Taylor?"

"It's something I ate. I've felt crappy all evening. Can we talk tomorrow?"

When Taylor returned to her room she really did look like she was about to puke. She opened her mouth as if to ask how much I'd heard, but all I had to do was look at her and she knew.

"I wanted to tell you."

"My brother has been in the hospital for months…"

"Just listen to me."

"…and all this time you've had contacts in the outside world, but you never…"

"I already talked to my folks about it. They don't really know what's out there. The outsiders only give them bits of information at a time. And even if their contacts had something that could save your brother, there's no way for them to get it to us."

"Taylor!" I snapped. "Chris isn't going to die because of some stupid law."

We stared, each daring the other to speak first. At last she said, "I'll see what I can do."

*

I slept in her bed that night while Taylor stayed up until dawn, using the basement computer to communicate with the outside world.

When she finally crept back into her room the following morning she whispered, "One of them knows someone who knows someone who might be able to help. It's a long shot, but…" She took my hand. "I'm sorry I didn't try sooner."

"It's okay," I said, almost meaning it.

Taylor spent the rest of the day in the basement while I binge watched Netflix. Not a single character or plotline stuck. All I could think about was Chris lying in his hospital bed with a mouth full of tubes. I found myself hating the flutter of hope in my belly.

After Taylor's parents left for the day, I tried to convince her to let me into the basement so I could see what she was doing, but she shook her head. "There's zero chance my folks won't find out about this. The less you know the easier they'll go on me."

At last, just after dusk, she emerged from the basement. She was so exhausted she could barely climb the steps, but there was a smile on her face. "They'll meet you at dawn."

I stared at her, uncertain if I should believe what I'd just heard.

"One of our contacts has a way to get you something that'll help Chris. They'll meet you on the Eastern border at sunrise. The perimeter's defenses will be temporarily deactivated. You'll have fifteen minutes."

"Thank you! Thank you so much!" When I was finally done hugging her, I asked, "Can we use your parent's car to get to the border?"

Taylor glanced at the floor. "Emily..."

She didn't have to say another word. Taylor Sims may have been willing to go to hell for me, but she wasn't willing to travel beyond 2016.

*

Around six o'clock the following morning, well before sunrise, I stepped into Chris' hospital room. Mama was fast asleep in her usual chair, head tilted back, mouth open and drooling. For the first time in weeks I wanted to give her a hug, or at least apologize, not for what I'd said but for staying away so long.

However, I crept past her and took Chris' hand. "Hey big brother," I whispered. "Don't worry. I'm going to make you all better."

I told him what I was about to do. I'd like to think he would have given me an encouraging pep talk, but I know he would've told me to just reconcile with Mama and go home.

When I was ready, I crept out of the room and headed downstairs toward my bike.

*

The eastern sky was turning from black to bruise-purple as I pedaled across the rickety bridge leading out of town. According to my watch I had twenty minutes to sunrise.

I rode my bike past the dirt road that wound out to our campsite and continued down the hill for another mile before the pavement came to an end on the edge of a field. Brown, waist-high grass stretched on for miles. There was no sign of a fence or wall or any kind of barrier.

Taylor had warned me to wait until my watch said it was

sunrise, exactly 7:25, before I stepped onto the field. Then I would have fifteen minutes to meet with the outsider and get out before the security system came back online.

I paced along the edge of the road, staring at my watch as the seconds ticked by.

At last, the digital 24 flicked to 25. I stepped onto the field. As far as I knew alarms were blaring beneath Greenville. I pushed through the grass, counting my steps.

Taylor told me I had to walk exactly ninety-three paces from the road. The field really did seem to go on forever. I scanned the horizon for a vehicle or figure. There was nothing.

When I arrived at my ninety-third step, I still couldn't see anything but sky and brown grass. We had twelve minutes and fifty-five seconds.

I looked up from my watch and noticed that the air before my face was shimmering. I reached out, and my hand struck an invisible barrier. "Shit!" I jumped back.

More startled than hurt, I leaned forward, inspecting what I assumed was a translucent forcefield. It wasn't until my nose was practically touching the barrier that I realized I was standing less than a foot from an enormous monitor.

I looked to my left and then my right. As far as I could tell, the monitor continued on for miles, enveloping Greenville. I stared upward, unable to tell where the screen ended and the sky began.

Three barely audible clicks brought my attention back to earth.

A rectangular piece of the monitor swung aside. It looked as though a door made of field and sky was opening before me. I leaned forward, peering into the darkness beyond my town, my world, my year.

All I saw was an endless dull gray metal corridor.

"Hello?" I stepped through the doorway.

Something shifted in the darkness.

"Hello?" I called again, creeping deeper down the corridor. "I don't want to be rude but we only have twelve minutes so maybe…"

The hallway filled with millions of black insects. They swarmed with such fury I fell against the wall, shutting my eyes. It was as though the air beyond Greenville was attacking me, punishing me for trespassing.

Cursing, I wrapped my arms over my head, trying to protect my face. I was about to make a run for it when I realized the insects were grouping together, forming a single mass.

An instant later the insects were gone, replaced by a person dressed in jeans and a black T-shirt. The outsider was barefoot with dark brown skin and black hair that fell below their slender shoulders. I couldn't place their ethnicity or even tell if they were a man or a woman. All I knew was they were gorgeous.

The outsider said, "Hello." The voice was lyrical with an accent I didn't recognize.

"Were you just a bunch of...I thought I saw..."

"I'm communicating from my home through a translator. I understand there is something I can help you with."

"My brother is hurt and my girlfriend says you can help him."

The outsider reached into their jeans and pulled out a dark green disk about the size of a quarter and offered it to me. After only a slight hesitation, I took it. The disk appeared to be made of plastic, but had the texture of flesh. The sides pulsed, as if it were alive.

"Place that in your brother's room. He will return to full strength within four hours. Then burn the disk. Make sure no one finds it."

"That's it?" I wondered if Taylor had described the severity of Chris' injuries.

"That's it," the stranger smirked the way I might smirk at someone from the eighteenth-century marveling at the miracles of penicillin. "Now for my payment."

"Wait! Taylor didn't say anything about—"

The outsider's eyes turned to mirrors. My reflection stared back at me, pale and quivering. I tried to look away but couldn't break eye contact.

My reflection transformed into my mother's face, only she looked younger, fresher. Bitterness and stress hadn't hardened her yet. She transformed into a man with glasses and oversized ears. I hadn't seen my father for so long I barely recognized him. A

357

moment later his face turned into a twelve-year-old boy. Chris and my parents were all singing, but I couldn't hear the words. There was a birthday cake with three candles. They were singing for me. This was my third birthday, my first memory.

I saw fourteen more birthdays, Christmases, Halloweens and Fourth of Julys. I saw the suburban streets of Greenville, tests, homework, bullies and every camping trip Chris ever took me on. My whole life lay before me. I saw the same houses, streets, schools, teachers and classmates. I saw my dad disappear into his new girlfriend's car and the casket lid close over my Pappap's face. I saw my first kiss with Taylor behind the Corner Diner and Chris' smile as he drove toward the accident waiting for him.

At last, I glimpsed a flicker of Greenville's border, the hallway and the outsider. My memories caught up with the present. Their eyes turned to black glass.

My body collapsed against the dull gray wall. I had watched my entire life, all confined within a few square miles. Soon, there would be nothing new for me to experience. There would be no one my age to meet for the first time and nowhere new to explore.

The outsider handed me a glass of water. I have no idea where it came from, but it was cool and contained a hint of lemon.

"Thank you," they said. "I know scholars who will pay well for thoughts and memories from this antiquated era."

I handed the empty glass back. By the time I looked up it had vanished.

"That's it?" I asked.

"That's it." The outsider turned and strode down the corridor. "Take care of yourself. Your brother should feel better soon."

I checked my watch. Despite all that had happened, we still had seven minutes.

Before I could stop myself, I asked, "What's it like out there?"

The outsider halted and stared at me like a parent considering whether they should share a dark, complicated secret with their child. At last, they said, "The real world is similar to yours only it's...faster, more intense. What you have here is considered quaint."

"Quaint?"

"Even as I talk to you now, I'm performing seven hundred and sixty-four other tasks and experiencing one hundred and ninety forms of entertainment."

I laughed. "Sorry but if that's what the world is like, I'm glad my Pappap founded Greenville."

The stranger stared at the metal floor for a moment before asking, "You don't know why Christopher Hopkins created this place, do you?"

"Sure I do. Technology was moving too fast. People were losing their minds."

The outsider smiled. "They're still spinning that propaganda?"

"It's not propaganda. My brother says our Pappap –"

"Your great-grandfather founded Greenville because Maria Rodriguez, America's first transgender president, was voted into office."

I stared. What they had said was so ludicrous I didn't know what to do but laugh. "No, he created Greenville to return to a simpler time."

"Hopkins claimed his colony was about escaping out-of-control technology. So did many who joined him, but everyone knows that was just an excuse to justify their actions. Your great-grandfather and his friends simply didn't want to live in a country run by a transgender woman whose parents were undocumented immigrants, even if she was creating free government programs to assist families afford the constantly changing technology."

Blood pounded in my head "My great-grandfather was a saint. Everyone knows–"

The outsider raised a hand. At first I assumed they were just trying to silence me. Then I noticed a tattoo that hadn't been there before. It was of my great-grandfather as a young man.

I heard a woman say, "You have made some controversial remarks regarding Senator Rodriguez. Do you think she has a chance in the upcoming election?"

The tattoo of my pappap gave an all too familiar grin. "The American people won't fall for such gimmicks. Rodriguez is the son of criminals and *he* wasted valuable medical resources to butcher *his* body. He's just another joker bent on stealing our–"

The outsider closed their hand, silencing my pappap.

I slid to the floor. At first I tried to tell myself what I'd seen was a lie. The outsider had used some futuristic device to trick me. *"He's just another joker bent on stealing our—"*

I thought back to when Pappap took me to get ice cream. *"You're one of the good ones, Emily. Not like all those other jokers. Don't ever change."*

Why had he thought I was one of the "good ones?" Because he hadn't lived long enough to see me hold Taylor's hand?

Mama told me he wouldn't have approved. I'd laughed at her. Everyone knew Christopher Hopkins had been the kindest person in the world. But if he saw me today would he dismiss me as another "joker?"

The outsider crouched beside me. "I'm sorry to be the one to tell you this, but they created Greenville because everything was changing, not just technology. Your great-grandfather and his friends pooled their resources, dug deep into the ground and created a world they found more pleasing."

I wanted to tell them to leave me alone, but couldn't stop myself from asking, "What do you mean they 'dug deep into the ground?'"

"Where do you think Greenville is? We're two miles beneath the earth's surface."

I pointed at the sunshine streaming into the hallway. "Are you crazy? There's…" The words froze like a lump of cold mud in my chest.

The gigantic monitor wasn't a wall. It was a dome. The sun, sky, wind and rain were all artificial. The truth was I had never stepped outside or felt the sun or stared at the stars with the girl I loved. Every perfect summer evening, every snowy day, every crisp fall afternoon was as fake as the rest of Greenville.

I shut my eyes, barely able to breathe.

The outsider said, "I thought most of you knew that much."

Maybe most people did, but no one had gotten around to telling me.

They crouched beside me. I felt their hand on my shoulder. "From what I saw in your memories, you're nothing like your

360

great-grandfather."

"Go away."

"You can leave Greenville whenever you want, and if you do, contact me. I'll take care of you out there, teach you what you need to know. My world is more intense than yours, but it's not evil. There's still love and beauty and hope and friendship."

I stared at my watch. I had two minutes before the system came back online.

I remained where I sat, unable to even look at the open door.

The green disk pulsed in my palm. "I need to get back to my brother."

The outsider rose to their feet. "And I need to see to my own family." They walked down the hallway. "Good luck. And remember, the outside world is always waiting for you."

I didn't linger to see if they turned into a cloud of insects again. I pulled myself up, stumbled out the door and slammed it behind me. Then I ran.

I reached my bike just as the 7:39 on my watch clicked to 7:40.

Even after I was safely on pavement, I didn't slow down. I pedaled as fast as I could, flying down the road, back to the rickety bridge, back to my hometown and Chris.

When I reached the hospital, I ran through the front doors and up the stairs. I didn't stop running until I reached his room.

Chris still lay broken and filled with tubes. Mama still leaned back in her chair, eyes shut.

I tucked the green disk among the flowers, hoping it would go unnoticed. Then, I sat in the chair beside Mama and waited for my brother to stir.

While I waited, I played out what would come next. Soon, Chris would open his eyes. Mama and I would shout for the nurse. I would have to pretend to be just as astonished as everyone else. In the confusion I'd pocket the disk.

The next several days would be a whirlwind, as everyone tried to wrap their heads around his miracle recovery, but after he got home and things calmed down, I'd suggest we go camping. Maybe Taylor could come. We would cross the rickety bridge, pitch the tents at the end of the dirt lane, build a fire and this time I would be the one to tell the truth about Greenville.

~

Michael Barron's short fiction has appeared in The Sonora Review, Miracle Monocle, *and* Ink Stains' Anthology, *as well as other publications. When he is not reading or writing he is training for marathons or undertaking his never-ending quest for the world's greatest hot sauce.*

He blogs about writing and posts lists of publications that are open to submission at: <u>michaeljbarron.com</u>.

THE STINK
David Penn

When, quite by chance, I bumped into my cousin Henry for only the second time in ten years, at Charing Cross station, I noticed two things straight away: one, that he was dressed like a tramp; two, that he stank like a buffalo. The first I saw from a distance, the second I detected as he walked towards me waving.

By then it was too late. I could hardly pretend I hadn't seen him, and I couldn't back away any effective distance. The tall figure walking towards me was frightful. He was much thinner than I remembered him, but far worse than that: he wore a dim grey jacket visibly frayed and tattered even from where I was standing, and that over a stained t-shirt and creased, grubby jeans like a mechanic's. His hair stuck to his head as if it were frying there. And when he smiled – which he did broadly, as though entirely unconscious of his appearance, or uncaring of it – his teeth were yellow, verging on orange, as if he'd taken to chewing betel nut.

It *was* Henry; despite everything the toothy smile and twinkling grey eyes were unmistakable. But I could hardly believe it. Cousin Henry, hedge fund manager, reputed to be worth scores of millions? What had happened to him? If somehow he had lost his money and ended up on the streets, why did he look so happy?

When he was still three yards away the smell was so bad it was difficult not to grimace. The crowded train had been bad enough, but this was in a different league. When he held his hand out to me, I flinched before I caught myself and smiled. At first I thought cousin Henry must have soiled himself, but as I stood dazedly shaking hands I realised this was one of those all-round body odours, every possible human miasma rolled into one: undoubtedly unwashed mouth, arse, armpits, crotch, chest, hair and any other filth-attracting area one cared to name. I felt sick.

"Henry. What a surprise," I said. "I mean, haven't seen you in years."

"No, well I don't come into town much these days."

I stared, unable to form any sort of polite question or socially acceptable comment in the face of this appalling manifestation, thinking only of the smell and how to escape it.

"Still got that flat in Chelsea?" he asked me.

"Yes," I said groggily. "Same old apartment. You were in Richmond, last I heard."

"Oh, yes, still there. On my own now of course. And retired. Plenty of time on my hands."

I remembered then that his wife had left him, at some point in the last half-decade. For a few weeks, somewhere back then, it had been the main topic of family gossip. Perhaps that's what had happened: without his wife he'd let himself go – spectacularly.

Fishing inside the remains of his jacket, he pulled out a card.

"Look, why don't you come over and see me? It would be great to have some company and we could catch up. Give me a ring." He shook my hand again, smiling still, and marched off, with a notably upright gait - for all the world as if he were dressed in silks.

I held the card in two fingers by my side and watched him go, then threw it away, found the station toilets and washed my hands and face, kneading the soap into every patch and line of skin. But whatever I did I couldn't get rid of that reek; it seemed to cling around my nose and mouth, my clothes, even my hair. I gagged on it even as I washed. I thought for a moment I actually would throw up and went into one of the cubicles, lifted the toilet lid and bent down. Nothing would come. All the way home I was still sure I could smell Henry – clinging, cloying, clogging my pores. I was sure other passengers on the tube were moving away from me. When I got to my apartment I showered for half an hour, scrubbing until my skin was raw. I put the clothes I'd been wearing straight in the washing machine, sprayed all the rooms with air freshener, then sat down in my dressing gown with a large whisky.

*

That Sunday my mother rang. Her weekly call. I told her about my cousin and his invitation and immediately regretted it.

"Oh, the poor man. He looked as bad as *that?*" I'd diplomatically not mentioned the olfactory dimension of our meeting. "It must be as you say. He must have gone to pieces since

Andrea left. And yet he was grinning? Yes, he must have gone mad. What a terrible mess. And to think he once worked in the City. You *are* going to see him, aren't you? He obviously needs help. At least persuade him to see a doctor."

"Of course, Mother; or, well, I would have done, except that I'm afraid I've lost his card."

"Oh, *Anthony*. Well, it doesn't matter. I've got his number somewhere, unless it's changed." She went to ferret around for it, and then read it to me, making me write it down and absolutely promise to go and see him.

Even on the phone to Henry I thought I could smell him somehow, as if his rankness could filter down the line. He invited me over the following Sunday, for dinner. Stupidly, I hadn't anticipated that he'd invite me to share a meal with him; the idea had me reeling. I tried to think of excuses not to eat in his company, but I couldn't dream up any fast enough that wouldn't have been transparent. In the back of my mind I was thinking that perhaps I could cancel at the last minute, feigning illness. But I heard myself, even as I thought that up, trying to explain myself to Mother – I would never get away with it. I fixed a time with Henry, put the phone down and gasped in what felt like cleaner air.

When I'd wiped the mouthpiece, I had a bath and played the whole of *Tannhäuser* at maximum volume, but even that didn't distract me from my own imagination. I kept thinking of the horrible state I was bound to find Henry's house in, the probable revolting condition of the food itself, those clothes of his, the stink, the stink... That night I couldn't face my usual roast and turned the restaurant's delivery woman away.

I bathed every day for the rest of the week, washed and re-ironed all my clothes, took all my suits to my astonished dry-cleaner's, cleaned my books and every shelf in the study, dusted every corner and hoovered every carpet twice. I washed all the wastepaper bins. When my cleaner came, she told me off – again – for leaving her no work to do. But nothing could take my mind off the looming Sunday.

*

Henry's house was famous in our family. He had bought it when he'd made his first few million in finance and it was said to glower over the rest of Richmond from the top of the hill like a baronial keep. It was four storeys high, with a basement, and a garden of reportedly park-like dimensions, boasting a huge oak at the bottom on one side and a clutch of elms on the other surrounding a little summer house. I'd never been there myself before. Standing outside the front gate, staring up at such a dwelling, I could not believe anyone in Henry's present state could really be living in it. It occurred to me that perhaps he'd been in fancy dress of some kind when I'd seen him at Charing Cross. But the familiar whiff I occasionally picked up on the breeze suggested otherwise, and I wondered at a human odiferousness strong enough to leak through windows and doors.

Indeed, my cousin's appearance at his top step immediately banished any notion that he'd been role playing when I'd last seen him. If anything, his clothes had disintegrated further, he had lost more weight and his stench was even worse. It seemed to blow past his shoulders from inside the house. He held out his hand again and I forced myself to take it.

Strangely enough, the place inside wasn't the wreck I'd expected it to be. There were no piles of old newspapers, every surface wasn't caked with dust, the walls weren't bedecked with spiders' webs. In fact, everything looked clean and well-ordered. Plain furniture, simple, well-arranged ornaments and a few photographs, beige pile carpets throughout. If it hadn't been for its owner, it might have smelt fresh too. But with Henry in the vicinity, there was no chance of that. I followed him down the corridor into his dining room, longing to hang back further, though everywhere seemed redolent of him.

"Please sit down," he said. The room was very light. French doors gave a prospect of the garden, which was indeed enormous, though extraordinarily overgrown. The grass was knee high, bushes ran explosively wild, Japanese knotweed was erupting over everything and what had once been a rose garden was now dense jungle. But the oak still stood proud, as did the group of elms.

"Drink?"

"Yes. I..." I'd been about to ask for something fairly stiff but

366

before I could get another word out, Henry brought over a flask of water from which he was filling a tin cup.

"Best drink in the world, eh Tony?" he said, plonking it down. "I'm just finishing off." He went over to a large adjoining kitchenette and proceeded to stir something in a deep pot on the stove.

I raised the cup to my nose. No smell. Not that such cleanliness alleviated the pong that filled my nostrils from Henry and his environs. I took a sip, scowled while my cousin's back was turned, and went to look out on the garden. To my amazement I noticed an even worse aspect of its dereliction: here and there the walls, which surrounded it on all sides, had collapsed. Bricks spread onto the lawn or border from gaping holes like food around babies' mouths.

"Your garden…" I said.

"Oh yes," Henry laughed. "The garden!" He still had his back to me, stirring.

"Are you renovating it or something?"

"No," he laughed. "I haven't got that excuse. It's just got like that. I suppose I've let it go, rather. This'll be ready in a jiffy."

"Haven't you got a gardener?"

"I paid him off, I'm afraid. Bit of an extravagance, I decided."

If Henry had turned round at that moment, he'd have seen my eyebrows raised at this self-evident absurdity. Still, he had always taken an odd attitude to money. He need never really have worked – I suppose you could say our family is in the luckier strata – but had insisted on "making his way". Then, as he piled up the millions, he began giving much of it to various worthy causes – that had been one of Andrea's complaints. It was their joint security he was flittering away, she pointed out, not just his own pocket money - but he hadn't listened. He wasn't the man she had married, she told everyone, and divorced him.

"Well, it's got a certain charm," I said, meaning the hideous garden.

Henry chuckled. "It's perfectly all right. It's nature," he said, strangely. Then: "Won't be a minute. I just need the loo." He disappeared out into the corridor. Rather cheekily, I suppose, I took that opportunity to open the doors onto the garden, to let some fresh air in – so I thought – and clear some of the Henry-honk to help me perhaps eat without throwing up. But to my amazement, the air that wafted in carried exactly the same sickly-sweet stink. I covered my mouth with my hand.

Was there something rotting in his garden? Was that the original source of Henry's unique aroma? A whiff that had seeped from some decomposing mess out there into Henry's clothes, into his house? Was he overly attached to some species of fiendishly-odoured plant? Swallowing back my rising gorge I stared out into the garden but couldn't see anything that might be responsible.

I sat down, and raised myself from a slump of despair only when Henry returned and went back to his pot.

"I hope you didn't mind… But it's a beautiful day and I thought I'd open the doors. Such a fantastic view of the garden. The only thing is…" I began. I thought that perhaps the smell from the garden was something I *could* politely question Henry about. His answers might even throw some light on his own state. But at that moment something made me stare in alarm at a bush beside one of the gaps in the west-side wall. Two little figures, extremely gaunt, with pot bellies poking out of soiled grey rags, were peering at me with wide eyes, leaning out from behind it. When they realised I'd seen them, they ducked back.

"Henry…" I was shaking. "I think you've got intruders."

He came over and I pointed to the bush. There was no more than a rustle, but then I saw two pairs of grubby, naked feet, sticking out under the lower leaves.

"Aha!" he said, and rubbed his hands. "Only two this time. Ah well – there'll be more."

I was too astonished to speak. If I had, my voice would have trembled and revealed the shock I was in. But Henry had actually sounded *pleased* that someone was trespassing in his garden.

"But Henry… don't you…?" I pointed weakly outside again. "Someone's broken into your garden. Shouldn't we do something?" I peered at the bush again, from around the door frame.

"Don't worry about it," said Henry. "They pop up out there

now and again. They're completely harmless. Sit down. We can eat now."

I stared alternately at him and the garden. Obviously this was a symptom of his mental condition, to be completely oblivious to the danger from people wandering onto his property at will. I realised, though, that with his walls down like that, the local children must be tempted in all the time, as the two outside now clearly had been, to scrump for whatever fruit they could find or just play around. Perhaps Henry really was used to it, didn't care, and through experience knew they wouldn't do any harm. Nevertheless, I can't say I felt safe. And the two had looked unusually scrawny and tattered for this day and age, certainly in Richmond. Was there a Council estate nearby?

I backed away from the window and went to a chair on the other side of the table, from where I could keep an eye on the bushes. And watched Mad Henry. I wondered about calling the police, despite Henry's lack of concern. How quickly did they come these days?

My cousin put two tin side plates on the table and laid a dim metal spoon for each of us. The arrangement was so odd it distracted me from the lurkers outside.

Back over his Aga, he ladled something sloppy into a bowl and brought it over to me – "Here we are" – before returning for his own portion. I looked down and saw rice streaked with yellow, with an occasional red bean dotting the mess.

"Ha… Henry… It looks wonderful. May I ask…?"

He laughed. "Rice, maize, sorghum, beans, a bit of vegetable oil and some salt. Oh, I nearly forgot."

He went back into the kitchenette to pick up two slices of grey bread and dropped one on each of our plates.

"You'll probably want to wipe your bowl with that afterwards. Enjoy."

I sat over my bowl immobilized with fear and confusion. There were intruders in the garden and I had just been given a dollop of soaked rice and maize for dinner, with a spoon. To eat while assailed by a fetor like a sewer. My eyes darted from the garden to the bowl and back again. I wasn't sure which was the greater source of peril.

"Really, aren't... aren't you going to do something about those kids out there? Shouldn't we call the police?"

"No. No need. They'll be coming in in a minute, when they feel less nervous. Probably after you've gone."

"What?"

"Eat up, old chap. You'll enjoy it. It's good food. Got most of the basic ingredients anyone needs. And if we're both good boys we've got a biscuit each for pudding. That's your sugar ration."

I stared at him, then back at the bowl. My mind raced for excuses, means of getting away, of not eating, but I felt trapped. One can't simply refuse or get up and leave. I dipped my spoon in. I couldn't, I couldn't. I kept wondering whether the food or the little trespassers in the bushes would get me first. I spaded some of the stuff up and forced it between my lips.

"I need the toilet," I mumbled, and pushed myself away from the table.

"It's in the..."

I didn't hear the rest. I rushed out of the room and found a short staircase going down to a door which I blindly assumed led to the loo. I ran down, pushed open the door...

...and was in darkness. The stink in there, in what I was still assuming was Henry's toilet, was ten times worse than it had been upstairs, or anywhere near Henry. That sweet, bitter, sick, cloying stench. I wafted my hand around for a light chord, batted the wall next to the door, found a switch and tripped it.

In front of me, in a large room, not a toilet, was a small crowd, all squatting on the floor. Men and women of all ages, children and babies. All of them skeletally thin, their heads virtually skulls, ribs standing clear of withered flesh, bellies distended, hair lank, eyes huge, blinking at me, lips dry and flaking. What clothes they had were gaping rags, hanging off them like sails on wrecked ships. Some had tin bowls – like the ones Henry and I were using – and after a second of staring at me, carried on scooping some gelatinous stuff out of them with their fingers and bringing it to their mouths, licking every last speck off their nails. Many were crying or giving out a thin continuous keening, rocking over their bony knees. Some held out their hands towards me.

And the stink. It was *that* stink – the stink that hung around Henry and his house and came in even from the garden. The smell of every rot, every infestation of filth, every uncleanliness that can infect the human body. I slammed the door shut and vomited on the floor.

Wiping my mouth I walked back in to Henry's dining room. He was standing in front of the open garden doors. I pointed behind me, towards the incredible room in the basement, trying to form words.

"Look. This is new," he said. "Ah, that's quite clever."

Trembling, my eyes jumping in their sockets, I joined him. The two children in Henry's garden – a boy and a girl, I could see now – joined by two adults, all impossibly thin and tottering with weakness, were collecting branches and building a frame against one of the walls. They had a plastic sheet ready to throw over it.

"They'll come in eventually," he said. "But they'll feel safer in their lean-to for now."

"Henry…" I pointed behind myself again, in the direction of the basement. "Wh-wha… What's that room, in the basement? Who are all those people down there? What's going on?" Tears of fear were stinging my eyes, and I heard the vibrato of terror in my own voice.

"Oh, I was saying, wasn't I? They keep coming. I do what I can for them. The house has gradually filled up. You should see the bedrooms! They're out there too" – he pointed to the garden – "under the trees, in the summer house, huddled together in the grass. They usually camp out there first, before they pluck up courage to approach the house. They've been coming for months. Maybe years now…" His eyebrows shot up in speculation. "I can just about keep them fed, set them on their feet a bit, then after a while they have to move on, of course…"

"Henry…" I was shaking my head, trying to shake off what he was saying, suddenly finding it hard to breathe. "Henry… you're harbouring…" I turned and scrambled past the furniture to the door. There were a million questions in my head but I was flooded with panic. All I wanted was to escape, to get back to sanity, and perhaps then ask – ask someone else, not Henry; tell my mother; call the Social Services, whatever you did – try to work out what the hell was going on here, what sort of madness Henry was involved in. But at the door out to the corridor, I stumbled. My breath was labouring badly. I leant against the jamb – but as I got ready to run again, I noticed something framed on the wall in front of me: not a picture, but the front page of a newspaper. The headline said: *CHAD, MAURITANIA 13 MILLION*... Below that it said *BANGLADESH 40 MILLION*... Below that *SOMALIA, YEMEN, SYRIA*... and below that *NORTH KOREA*... I ran. I wrestled the front door open and stumbled out. I was sick on the pavement. I pelted down the hill to the railway station, falling several times. I hurled myself through an open carriage door and sat down and held my head in my hands, my throat raw with gasping, my chest a motor wrenching air into my body.

As I calmed down I realised that, of course, people were staring at me. Even as my body stopped heaving and I remained still I saw that they were moving away from me, those entering avoiding my part of the carriage. Then I noticed the rip in my jacket and one down a trouser leg, and the odour rising from me: that same smell, so familiar now. I brushed my clothes down with my hand, frantically; then with a handkerchief. I brushed hard, harder.

But the faster my hand went, the less I could avoid the truth: this wasn't just some lingering pollution from Henry and his house, caught up in my clothes. No amount of brushing or washing would make any difference. The stink wasn't Henry's. It didn't even belong to the crowds in his house. The wretched odour was now coming from me, *me,* from *my* breath, from *my* skin. I'd caught it, somehow, from those hordes. Caught it like a disease.

And I laughed at the horrified, appalled, affronted faces around me. Laughed because I knew what they were feeling. And because now I knew what the smell was. It wasn't from mere lack of washing, from negligence or poor hygiene: it was the smell of starvation, of sickness, of misery. It was a smell to be found on every continent of the world, the smell of millions.

~

David Penn's stories have appeared in the magazines Midnight Street, Theaker's Quarterly, Whispers of Wickedness *and in* Hellfire Crossroads # 6. *Under his ordained Buddhist name, Dharmavadana, he has published poetry in* Ambit, The North, The Interpreter's House, Brittle Star *and* Under the Radar. *He is poetry editor of the Buddhist arts magazine* Urthona: *http://www.urthona.com. He lives in London.*

DELIVERY OF A NIGHTMARE

Tammy Euliano

The call came in the middle of her son's funeral. One minute Beth was sprinkling dirt on her son's tiny casket, her husband, the only other mourner, standing apart. The next she was speeding alone through driving rain and streaming tears. A week ago, her sister-in-law would have said, "We each mourn in our own way. He'll come around." A week ago, she would have been there for Beth. A week ago, the world was a very different place.

The familiar hospital was in unfamiliar chaos, the Emergency Room entrance crowded with cars and minivans and ambulances. Women's screams eclipsed orders barked by a harried security guard. One glance and Beth understood why she'd been called in on the day of her son's funeral. Every would-be patient was pregnant. On gurneys, in wheelchairs, or stumbling through the sliding glass doors, every woman had a hand on her swollen abdomen, some farther along than others. Decidedly lacking were the excited expressions of soon-to-be parents, replaced with shock, fear, pleading.

As Beth changed into scrubs on Labor and Delivery, Liz, the charge nurse of the day, laid out the looming disaster: pregnant women were arriving by the not-so-proverbial busload, in labor, most preterm, many pre-viable. Standard treatment – medications to slow labor for forty-eight hours of steroids to mature the baby's lungs – was ineffective. Relentless contractions caused rapid cervical dilation. More women were near delivery than there were providers to care for them. Liz laid it out professionally, but an underlying current of panic seeped through.

Beth's confidence wavered. This was her world, the tiny corner of medicine where she excelled. So why was she feeling inept? She'd been wrong to think she could save her brother, or her son, or maybe even her marriage, but obstetrics she knew.

At the labor board, names were doubled up in single rooms. The clerk stood on tip toe with her dry-erase marker, adding a name under a new column: Pending. The tenth name on the list.

"Doctor for delivery, Room seven." The overhead announcement should have stirred Beth to action. Would have, a week ago.

"Dr. Markum?" Liz said.

"Yeah. I'm ready." Beth shook off the cobwebs of uncertainty and answered the summons. This was her universe.

She barely had time to gown before the tiny head appeared, the body following immediately after. Much too small. Transparent skin. Fused eyelids. No need for pediatricians. She schooled her expression. Only her eyes showed above the mask, but the patient needed to see dispassionate competence, mixed with just the right dose of empathy.

"My baby."

Beth lifted the child, barely larger than her palm. She cut the cord and handed her to the labor nurse, who wrapped her in a blanket and placed the small bundle on the woman's chest. The woman's sobs shook the bed and Beth's delusion of normalcy.

She focused on the placenta, tugging gently on the umbilical cord stump, but it wasn't ready. Not uncommon in a preterm delivery. After several minutes, and multiple overhead calls for deliveries in other rooms, Beth stripped off her gown and gloves, gave heartfelt but inadequate platitudes to the grieving mother, and stepped out.

Next door was much the same. Though this baby was twice the size, he was still four-months premature. He tried to breathe, his tiny chest retracting with each attempt.

"He isn't crying." The anxiety in the new mother's voice tugged at Beth. She needed a normal, happy delivery, she'd had enough drama.

It's not all about you, Beth.

The pediatrician inserted a breathing tube, but still the chest moved little. Stiff, premature lungs. He needed surfactant. Remembering the scene at the hospital entrance, Beth hoped they had a warehouse full of the life-saving drug. "We're helping him breath," said the pediatrician. "We'll take him to the ICU and I'll be back as soon as I can with an update."

And neonatal ICU beds. No way they'd have enough.

The dad snapped a few photos, which they admired, clinging together, crying together. Beth and her husband hadn't clung together, hadn't cried together as they watched their one-year-old succumb. His blame and her guilt were a damning combination.

Beth pressed on the patient's abdomen to encourage delivery of the placenta. The uterus that should have been firm, like a child-size basketball, was instead a rubbery sack. "More Pitocin. And get Hemabate and methergine." The nurse's wide-eyed stare was directed only at Beth, whose nod confirmed, they were in trouble.

A few moments later, Beth said, "Your uterus isn't contracting like it should. We'll give you some medications to fix it, and maybe even some blood." The new parents seemed not to register the rising concern in the room. Not necessarily a bad thing.

After every therapy in the arsenal, the blood kept flowing, pooling on the catch sheet, overflowing to the floor. The accelerating beep of the heart rate monitor forced Beth to make the call. "We need to go to the operating room."

The charge nurse entered. "Dr. Markum, I need a moment." The urgency of her tone trapped the protest in Beth's throat. "We don't have an OR," Liz explained. "All three are in use for postpartum hemorrhages."

Ice flowed down Beth's back, through her veins.

Four patients are bleeding? Less than one percent of patients bleed after delivery. But that was a week ago, in the old world. *The new world sucks.*

But Beth had a responsibility to her patient. "Then I need one downstairs. We can't wait."

"I'll take care of it," Liz said. Beth asked about her patient next door. The placenta was still firmly attached. She returned to her bleeding patient.

"If all else fails, I may have to remove your uterus."

"But we want more kids," said the patient.

Her husband squeezed her hand, but nodded to Beth. "You do what you have to do. Our son needs his mom."

In the end, the new mother did lose her uterus, and several liters of blood. She required six units of blood and another six of plasma and clotting factors. But as Beth started closing, clots were forming. She took a long, slow breath. This was a save. Though she could have no more children, she survived to raise her son. Disaster, mostly, averted.

"Dr. Markum?" A nurse she didn't recognize stood in the doorway. "You're needed next door."

A general surgeon pushed past the nurse, hands up and dripping soapy water. "I'll close for you."

"What's going on?" Beth asked.

"Apparently, you guys are having a lot of bleeding upstairs. My cases got cancelled, so I thought I'd see if I can help." He held out his hands to be gloved by the scrub tech. Beth explained the procedure so far and stepped back from the surgical field.

More bleeding? She scrubbed for the next case, where another general surgeon was poised to open the abdomen. They started the case together, then Beth said to no one in particular, "What the heck is going on upstairs?"

"You're the obstetrician," the surgeon said.

"Middle Eastern Flu," said the scrub tech.

Beth's heart skipped a beat.

"Can the flu cause postpartum hemorrhage, Dr. Markum?" the surgeon said.

Beth glanced at the scrub tech, who seemed not to notice the dismissive nature of his comment. "Not to my knowledge." *Not last week.* She clamped the right uterine artery.

Beth could do nothing about the epidemic, flu or otherwise, she could only fix what she could fix. And so she went from OR to OR. Patients Beth hadn't met were anesthetized before she entered the room, with blood-stained sheets and gowns, and, more often than not, blood slicking the floor. She removed each hemorrhaging uterus, careful not to damage other structures, leaving the ovaries. Then a general surgeon took over to close and she moved on to the next. When they operated together, she taught the general surgeons how to perform a hysterectomy.

Updates came from staff – pregnant patients were still arriving from the surrounding communities, the same was happening across the country. Meanwhile, the death toll from the flu that had killed her son continued to rise in children and the elderly. The Centers for Disease Control recommended everyone possible remain at home. Still no word on isolating the causative agent.

In the OR, they talked about the epidemic. It started with US and European servicemen in the Middle East. Most died in transit. Beth's brother had been lucky to reach the States, though it made no difference. Many healthcare workers fell ill, but they survived. So whatever the agent, it was weakened in transfer. Except for children. If the postpartum hemorrhage problem was unrelated, it was an extraordinary coincidence.

Day and night were indistinguishable in the windowless ORs where clocks of the twelve-hour analog variety hung above the doors. A.M. and P.M. had no meaning.

Her son had been in the ground more than thirty-six hours before Beth was ordered to take a break. She'd fallen asleep at the scrub sink, nearly slamming into the faucet. Caught by a scrub tech, she was guided to an empty stretcher in the hallway, her protests evaporating as her head hit the thin pillow.

She woke disoriented – was she a patient? No. Brady. Where was he? When reality breached her stupor, the weight threatened to suffocate her. Right on cue, her phone rang.

"Mom," said Beth, tears threatening.

"Beth, how are you?" It was her father, his speech slow and guarded, not Dad-like.

"I'm okay, Dad. How are you and Mom?"

"Not so well, I'm afraid."

"Are you sick?"

"No, no, not sick, but I'm afraid I have bad news. Meg died last night." Her niece, and her parents' only remaining grandchild.

"Oh no, I'm so sorry. I'll call Emma."

"Um, no, Beth. Please don't. She…isn't ready to talk to you quite yet." But they were sisters-in-law, best friends, how could they not talk at a time like this?

"Dad, she needs me."

"No, Beth, she doesn't."

"She just lost her daughter. I know what she's going through."

"Beth…"

"But…"

"She blames you." It came out harsher than he probably intended.

"But kids are dying all over, I didn't infect them all."

"No, but she's not there yet. She's focused on Meg."

Of course she was. Little Meg had attended Brady's birthday party last week. Beth had cuddled her. Kissed her. Infected her. The toddler might have fallen ill even without Typhoid Beth's help, but it was easier to have a tangible target.

After an uncomfortable silence, Dad said, "She'll see reason eventually. But right now… Listen, she asked that you not attend the services."

Beth's swallow almost hurt. She changed the subject. "How's Mom?"

"As well as can be expected. She's resting now." She'd lost her son and both her grandchildren in a single week. Her mom was strong, as was her faith, but wasn't God asking a bit much? Job came to mind, though Beth was far from a biblical scholar.

She ended the call before she might argue the injustice, defend her actions, or worse yet, cry. She had gone to Walter Reed Medical Center to try to save her brother, Emma's husband. A stupid, self-righteous move. An obstetrician double-checking on some of the world's best critical care specialists.

She'd been released from quarantine with a clean bill of health. And insisted on going straight home for Brady's first birthday party. Selfish. They could have waited a week, or more. Beth never did get sick, but still she'd brought this horrific monster home. Brady and Meg had been the first to fall ill. She'd earned the blame of her husband and sister-in-law. And her parents for that matter.

The distraction of work provided a terrible blessing. In thirty-six hours she'd operated on at least thirty women. Enough she'd lost track, of her patients, and her pain. But the women kept coming, and not just in Florida.

She thought of Emma, alone and twenty-five weeks pregnant with a difficult pregnancy. Her husband and child dead. Twenty-five weekers were delivering with immature lungs. Beth called her father back. It went to voicemail. "This is Beth. Listen, pregnant women are going into preterm labor all over. Emma should go to her doctor and ask for steroids. It won't hurt the baby, and if she does deliver early, it could save his life. Tell her, will you? She needs steroids. It's really important." She left a similar message on Emma's phone, but doubted it would be heard.

Someone cleared her throat nearby. "I'm sorry, but you're needed in OR fifteen." Her voice was tentative, apologetic, and there were tears in her eyes.

Beth stood and put an arm around her. "It's going to be okay. We'll figure this out."

"My sister's pregnant."

"How far along?"

"Thirty-two weeks. Should I tell her to get steroids, too?"

"Definitely."

On the third day of near-constant operating, several militant organizations – al Qaida, ISIS and an alphabet soup of terrorist groups – claimed responsibility for a biologic weapon, "Designed to target the genetic code of the infidels." Though discounted officially, there was no denying that American soldiers stationed in the Middle East were dying, without widespread civilian fatalities.

During a brief break, Beth looked up her niece's funeral arrangements, intending to order flowers. "Meg Dunn is survived by her mother, Emma Dunn, and her maternal grandparents. She is preceded in death by her father, Joe Dunn, and her paternal grandparents." After several flower shops failed to answer, Beth checked online. A headline reported that the number of funerals far outpaced supply of burial services.

We really are in hell, not even any flowers.

That afternoon, the blood bank ran dry, and flowers were forgotten.

Between cases, Beth represented the Obstetrics Department at an emergency blood bank meeting. "If we can't convince the public to violate the quarantine, we can press healthy family members to donate. They're already here and have a vested interest. Staff too."

"But what if they carry the virus?" a blood bank specialist countered, stabbing Beth through her already fractured heart.

The Infectious Disease specialist said, "Then the patient *might* die of the flu, which beats definitely dying from lack of blood."

"There's no time for any kind of testing," Beth said, standing. "We need the blood now. Whole blood is fine."

Within hours, against every tenet of Twenty-First Century blood banking, donor blood arrived in the OR tested only for blood type. Units were transfused almost as soon as they were collected. Transfusion reactions that would have been unacceptable the week before, occurred less often than predicted, and even those patients survived.

*

Twenty-four hours later, Beth was asked to assist with an uncontrollable hemorrhage. The blood bank could not keep up. There were no more products for this patient with a rare blood type, and no more Type O. They'd tried salvaging blood from the operative field and re-transfusing, but she continued oozing. There was nothing more to be done.

Beth declared her death in the OR amid the shock of everyone involved. Young mothers rarely died, and not from something treatable – unless it wasn't. Beth offered to speak with the family, but she was needed in another OR, and then another. Both patients died for want of blood products. It made no sense to continue. Beth left the OR.

Upstairs on Labor and Delivery, she learned the same was beginning in England and France. The link to the Middle Eastern Flu was undeniable, and the terrorist glee unfathomable.

The labor board approached illegible, names spilling into the margins. Beth asked about the red underline on many names. "They're hemorrhaging," Liz said.

Beth stared, then rebounded.

Consulting with available staff, she confirmed the patients started bleeding only after delivery of the placenta. Then they lost uterine tone and developed DIC – Disseminated intravascular coagulation. Total consumption of clotting factors, causing uncontrollable bleeding until they're replaced by transfusion.

"So, what if we could remove the uterus before the placenta separated?" Beth said, an idea percolating.

"There's not enough time," said a nurse. "Unless they're really preterm, the placenta delivers almost immediately after the baby. The labors are short, too. It's like the uterus sprints for a few hours, then passes out."

A reasonable description, met by lots of nods.

"Then we need to do Cesarean hysterectomies," Beth said, the picture clearing.

More murmurs, fewer nods. "You mean as soon as they go into labor, we take them for surgery?" asked a nurse. "What patient would agree to that?"

"My patient in fifteen," a nurse said. "She's been asking for a section since she arrived."

"But we still have several bleeding patients waiting for an OR," said Liz.

"They can go downstairs with the general surgeons. Let's take the next open room and do this."

An hour later, the patient was asleep, and Beth was ready to cut. The optimism in the room reassured and terrified her in equal measure.

"I'd forgotten what a dry surgical field looks like," said the scrub tech. The suction canister was nearly empty. Like the good old days. Beth delivered the baby, a squalling boy with lungs to make up for all the ones who didn't cry today.

And then optimism fled in a rush of placenta, and an even bigger rush of blood. Beth operated rapidly to clamp off blood flow to the uterus. "She's in DIC," said Don, the anesthesiologist. He ordered blood products.

She'd been wrong. This wasn't the answer. She met Don's eyes. "It would have happened anyway," he said. "She'll lose a lot less since you're already getting control." His phone rang. A brief call. "There's no blood for her."

Losing less blood was still too much. This wasn't just a failure to save...this was a kill. She wasn't bleeding to death when Beth started. "What's her blood type?"

"A positive."

"I'm the same," Beth said. "Draw from me."

The circulating nurse recoiled.

"Use my foot." She kicked off her shoe, ignoring the looks bouncing between the staff. "Do it, dammit. This case was my idea."

The nurse shook her head.

"I'll do it." Don moved around the bed.

Beth felt her sock removed, the tightness of the tourniquet, the coolness of the prep, the prick of the needle. Same sequence in the other foot, for IV fluids to replace the blood being drained.

Despite the distractions, she completed the operation quickly. Beth's blood helped the patient form clots. Hopefully the trend would continue and the oozing would subside. But Beth felt no pride in this save. As she stepped back from the table, her head swam. Liz took her by the arm, and led her the back way to the lounge. "Sit." She hung another bag of fluids, and handed Beth a Gatorade.

"We need to get the uterus out before the placenta separates. But there's no time," Beth said.

Don joined them, accepting another Gatorade. "Maybe before labor starts?"

"Maybe." She gulped down the drink, unaware she'd been so thirsty. "What if we clamped the uterine arteries before delivery?"

Don chewed his lower lip. "Might work. Babies can handle no flow for several minutes at least." They were both silent for several moments. "Worth a try," he said and finished off his drink.

Liz stepped from the room, returning moments later. "Ellie Branson wants to volunteer."

"Ellie?" She was Beth's friend, she was the nurse at Beth's delivery, and she was Beth's patient.

"She's a good candidate. Early labor. Not bleeding. Viable baby. We're moving her to the back now."

In the OR, Ellie reached for Beth's hand. "Thank you for doing this."

"You sure you understand the risks? I don't know that this will work."

"I trust you, Beth. I know you'll take care of me and my baby."

Words that should warm a physician's heart made Beth's run cold.

The mood of the OR was more cautious optimism, and Beth's movements were more deliberate this time. No motor memory for this procedure. To Beth's knowledge it had never been done. She dissected carefully, making space to clamp both uterine and ovarian arteries. At last she exchanged a look with Don and the scrub tech. "Let's do this."

She worked quickly now. Clamped all four arteries, opened the uterus and withdrew a sleepy, but living baby. He'd been under anesthesia too long, but he would recover. She handed him to the pediatrician and began tying off the vessels and structures to remove the uterus.

"Breathe," Don said.

Beth glanced at the infant warmer.

"I meant you," he said. "The baby's fine, and so is Ellie so far. But you're turning blue."

She smiled weakly behind the mask and forced a slow, deep breath. He was right. The baby's scream lightened the weight, but her shoulders didn't relax until the uterus was out. Ellie had needed no blood products. She hadn't bled.

It had worked.

In the recovery room, Liz cried openly as she presented the baby to his father while Beth hugged a groggy Ellie. Moments later the happy family cuddled their small but healthy baby. Their first and last.

"You have to broadcast this," Don said. "It will literally save millions if this is truly a worldwide plague."

Beth's chest filled with pride, relief, gratitude. They'd done it. She'd done it.

At the nursing station, she stared at the labor board, still overflowing, rooms doubled up, with names in the margins waiting for space. Alerted by a sudden silence, Beth turned. All eyes were on her chairman, an obstetrician by degree only. He'd not been in an OR in decades, and in this crisis stood in a pressed suit, with a tie perhaps a bit too tight, his red-face bordering on purple, with virtual steam rising from his generous ears.

"I understand you performed an elective operation in the middle of this crisis."

It wasn't a question. Beth said nothing.

"You chose to operate on a healthy friend, rather than a hemorrhaging patient." 'Friend' sounded like a swear word.

"We have no blood for them," Beth said. "They'll die with or without surgery. I thought it more important to figure out how to save them."

"And she did," Liz said, then deflated at his infamous glare.

"Two patients died while you operated on a patient who could wait."

Beth's retort caught in her throat, blocking her breath. The conviction in his eyes burned her retinas. She reminded herself they likely would have died anyway...likely.

"One here in the OR waiting for an anesthesiologist. The other downstairs when the general surgeon got in trouble and there was no one available to help. Those deaths are on you." He turned his back and strode down the corridor, icy stares in his wake.

Beth's stomach roiled, her confidence wavered.

No, she'd done the right thing. Ellie survived, others would too, someone just had to stand up and make the tough decision. To accept that some were beyond help and to move on to those who could be saved.

The clerk approached the Labor Board, picked up the eraser, and rubbed out a name, *Dunn.*

A common enough name, Beth's maiden name.

A stretcher emerged from the OR suites, a sheet shrouding the occupant.

Beth swallowed hard. *This death is on you.*

"Where's her family?" the staff member asked the desk clerk.

"She has no family here. I have one more number for next-of-kin." She dialed the phone.

Beth's cell began to ring.

~

Dr. Tammy Euliano's writing is inspired by her day job as a physician, researcher and educator at University of Florida. She's received numerous teaching awards, 100,000 views of her YouTube teaching videos, and was featured in a calendar of women inventors. Her short fiction has been recognized by Glimmer Train, Bards & Sages, Flame Tree Press, Flash Fiction Magazine, *and others. Her debut novel, a medical thriller entitled* Fatal Intent, *will be published by Oceanview in March, 2021. Unlike most doctors, she dispenses medical advice for free — as long as the patient is fictional.*

Her blog: https://www.teuliano.com *helps writers get the medical details right, because nothing ruins a scene quite like having a character on a ventilator carry on a conversation.*

SUNSHINE
Richard Meldrum

John Lansing opened the door to the garage and pressed the key fob to unlock the doors of his car. It was a glistening two door, silver egg, with large windows and a wide windshield. He'd hooked it up to the domestic charging station the night before and he could see the lights on the station were green, indicating full charge. He looked down at himself, checking he had his phone. He wouldn't get much use out of it today, but he felt naked without it. He pulled open the car door, dumped his gear on the back seat, then climbed into the cabin. He settled himself into the comfortable chair and hit the ignition button to start the motor. He scanned the dash to make sure everything was working. The gauges all read normal. Satisfied, he set the windows to their darkest tint. It was 6 a.m. and the sun was starting to peak over the horizon. The architect who had designed the house had carelessly positioned the garage entrance facing towards the east and Lansing didn't want to be blinded by the morning sun when he opened the door. Satisfied the windows were set correctly, he pressed the button to open the garage door. The blaze of sunlight through the windshield still made him wince despite the heavy tinting. He eased the car up the ramp to ground level. With the exception of the driveway, there was no indication a five-bedroom house lay just below the surface. He knew his friends thought it was too big a property for a single person, but he'd always liked space so he'd opted for one of the larger properties in the sub-division. He'd converted two of the bedrooms into an office and a library, leaving one bedroom for himself and the other two as guest rooms. He was a solitary person, but he occasionally invited friends and family over to stay.

The ground level landscape was brown and dry. The wind blew the dust into artistic drifts and eddies. Township ordinance banned grass or any other water-intensive vegetation. Even if someone decided to break the law, not much would have survived in this arid climate. There were only a few stunted, drought-resistant trees dotted around Lansing's property, struggling to exist in the barren landscape. No birds chirped in the branches or flew in the sky. No insects buzzed. Lansing was so used to the view he barely noticed. He stopped the car at the top of the ramp and checked his touch pad to make sure he had all the required data and directions. The garage door automatically closed behind him.

His plan was to get to the farm by 9 a.m., stay on site for a couple of hours and be back home by early afternoon. He didn't like driving, or any type of traveling for that matter. He preferred to stay at home and work remotely, but some things required his personal attention. His salary reflected this inconvenience. The farm visit was a bi-annual chore. He programmed the address into the GPS on the dashboard, then sat back and relaxed. He always selected the self-driving option on long drives. Not having to drive himself counted as a small compensation for having to tolerate the unpleasantness of being required to leave his home.

The car set off confidently and drove itself through the town where Lansing lived, while he looked out the side window. There was nothing much to see. The location of the houses was marked by posts at the roadside, with driveways and paths leading down to recessed entrances. The two municipal buildings in the town were partially above ground, but Lansing knew the majority of the building structures were underground, with only a floor or two above the surface. In the distance the spires of the high-rise communal housing in the downtown core of the city reflected in the morning sunlight. They looked beautiful from afar, but Lansing knew they were just elevated slums, full of crime and drugs. Only the poor had their housing on the surface, relying on old-fashioned solar-powered air-conditioning rather than the new generation of geo-thermal processors to keep their homes cool. Most of the people in the city were either unemployed or worked at the few remaining manual jobs. Lansing had heard horror stories of the summer riots, when the air-conditioning failed and the people went crazy. Anyone who could afford it lived in the suburbs in cool, underground havens.

The car headed out of the town and onto the highway. It was

one of the older highways, built in the days when at least eight lanes were required to accommodate all the cars. This morning the road was almost empty, as it always was these days, with only a few self-driving tractor-trailers rumbling along. Long gone were the days of grid-locked rush hours. Long gone were the days of gasoline exhausts pumping carbon monoxide and hydrocarbons into the atmosphere. Lansing had a dim recollection of his grandfather who owned one of the last gasoline powered cars. It was a Ford something or other. Lansing remembered being terrified by the roar of the engine and the spinning machinery under the hood. Soon after, the legislation had been changed and gas-powered vehicles banned, but of course, it was already too late by then. Far too late. The climate was already destroyed.

Nowadays, travel was a rarity. The huddled masses were encouraged to stay at home; a directive that didn't need much enforcement. People were happy to stay put; who wanted to experience the searing heat and potential for severe storms? Transportation was mainly restricted to freight and essential travel only. Manufacturing and agriculture were largely automated. Lansing was one of the unlucky few; employees who had a position that required the ownership of a car for individual transport. Everyone else, on the rare occasions travel was necessary, had to rely on underground mass transit.

The purr of the electric motor was relaxing. He pushed a button on the console and his seat slid back into the horizontal position. He closed his eyes and slept.

Lansing woke to silence. It took him a second to realise the car had stopped and another to realise he wasn't at his destination. He was on a road in the middle of nowhere. Fields full of soy and corn surrounded him. There were no buildings visible. The crops were dwarfed by irrigation equipment, huge metal structures that dominated the landscape. Satellite dishes positioned every few fields, transmitted growth and soil data to remote monitoring stations to ensure that nutrients and water were used as efficiently as possible. Lansing's employer owned most of these devices. The green leaves stirred memories of warm, summer days, but it was a false allusion. Lansing guessed the outside temperature was probably already close to 50°C. The corn and soy in the fields surrounding him was extensively genetically modified to be heat and drought resistant. He was part of the team that had created these plants, switching out plant DNA with the genes of thermophilic bacteria isolated from oceanic thermal vents. The purpose of his trip to the experimental farm was to assess the growth of the next generation. As temperatures continued to rise, more heat resistant varieties had to be created. More exploration had to be done to find more thermostolerant micro-organisms. More genes had to be spliced into more crops. More research and testing had to be done and that was where Lansing came in. The pilot fields with the new test varieties had to be checked. His job was to drive to the farm and send out the farm robots to take samples of the plants. He would collect these specimens and take them back to his home laboratory for analysis. The experimental plants had to be checked manually for gene expression and biochemical efficiency. He would also arrange for the robots to plant new strains and varieties, to be checked during his next visit.

Irritated because his ever-reliable car had let him down, he pushed the start button on the dashboard. Nothing happened. There was still power, the dashboard gauges were illuminated, but the electric motor that turned the wheels had stopped. He checked the journey log. No abnormalities had been noted. These cars were designed to stop if they got lost or if they hit something, but there was no indication either had happened. There had been reports about reliability of these models, but he'd never heard of a complete engine failure. The GPS informed him he was about an hour from the farm. The log told him he'd been stationary for about thirty minutes.

Thankfully the air-conditioning was still running. He checked the dash. He'd been correct, the external temperature read 55°C. The internal temperature was still 15. He checked his cell phone. Zero bars. No surprise. This was the boondocks; farms were automated, and the countryside had almost no inhabitants anymore. Robots did most of the work of planting and harvesting. There was no need for cell phone towers when there was almost zero population. The few farmers that lived out here used satellite phones to communicate.

"Well, this is going to screw up my day."

There was no other option. He pressed the red emergency button. Almost instantaneously a metallic voice spoke.

"Rescue. State the nature of your problem."

"The engine has stopped."

"Please repeat. Your signal is weak."

"The engine has stopped."

"Please state your identification tag."

He read from the tag on the dash.

"E1598A9Z."

"Logging," replied the automated voice.

He knew the ID number would allow the computer to link up with his GPS to find his location. It would then send a rescue car out for him. There was silence from the speaker.

"Hello?"

The line had dropped. Lansing hit the button again. Nothing. The dashboard was blank. No power. There was no more cool air coming from the vents.

"Shit."

There was clearly something seriously wrong with his car. The batteries should have provided power for the essential systems, including the air-conditioning, for at least another five hours. He could only hope the phone connection to Central Rescue had lasted long enough for his location to be logged. He hoped it was now just a waiting game. There was a tiny stirring of fear and anxiety in his chest; he tried not to think about what could happen if the call hadn't been logged. He tried to relax, aware of the sweat blossoming on his chest, forehead and armpits. He slowed his breathing and closed his eyes, focusing on images of ice, cool water and swimming pools.

Time passed. One hour, then two. Three. The internal temperature had crept up and it was becoming very warm in the cabin. If a rescue vehicle had been sent out, it would have already arrived. Lansing started to realise he might be on his own, stuck on a country road with a hostile environment outside. His anxiety returned, more insistent this time.

"I have to do something," he said to no one.

He reached down below the dashboard and pulled the lever that opened the hood. His subconscious asked if this was really a good idea. He decided it was. Steeling himself, he opened the door and stepped out.

The heat hit him like a sucker punch. He hadn't been outside during the day for about a decade and he wasn't expecting such a ferocious sensation. He knew the outside temperature in numerical terms, but he wasn't ready for the reality of the heat. He'd left his hat in the car and his head burned from the searing ultraviolet radiation. His body exploded with sweat and his limbs immediately felt heavy, exhausted. He limped his way to the front of the car, still intent on fixing the problem himself. Without thinking, he placed bare hands on the hood. The temperature of the metal raised blisters on his fingers. He reached down and unclicked the lever under the hood. It lifted automatically.

"Shit."

The engine wasn't visible. Lansing had never looked under the hood of this car before and he hadn't realised the motors and batteries were covered by a plastic cover that couldn't be removed. He'd hoped he'd see a wire or connector that had simply worked loose. He'd hoped it would be an easy fix. The only thing that was accessible was the screen wash container. He closed the hood and returned to the cabin.

It had to be at least 30 degrees in the car now, but it was a damn sight cooler than outdoors, and he was shielded from the unrelenting sun by the tinted windows. His fingers were sore, his scalp felt fried and he had difficulty seeing. His eyes were still dazzled from the brightness outside. His clothes were soaked with sweat and his mouth felt dry. He hit the distress button again, but there was still nothing. All dead.

The reality of the situation hit home. He was stuck in the middle of nowhere, with a dead car and zero chance that rescue was on its way. Lansing glanced out the window at the green fields around him. It still reminded him of his younger days, of warm, breezy summer days in lush, green fields. But now, he knew outside, amongst all that green, was only death. Summer was no longer a season to look forward to, it was something to hide away from, in underground caves.

"What the fuck am I going to do?" he said. He was close to panic.

He closed his eyes, took some deep breaths. He willed himself to calm down, forcing himself to think logically. If he'd believed in a god, he might have prayed for divine intervention. As it was, he had no one to rely on except himself. Panic would be fatal. Eventually, his mind returned to normal. His situation wasn't disastrous; sure, his options were limited, but he did have options. He could stay put and hope someone would drive along the road and rescue him or he could be more proactive and take matters into his own hands. The chances of someone driving on this road were slim to none, so he decided he would abandon the car and walk until he found someone who could help. He knew he couldn't strike out on foot during the day; that would kill him, so he decided to wait until after dark. The temperature would drop closer to 35 by midnight. That was tolerable.

He checked his analogue watch, a graduation gift from his father thirty years before. Sunset was in about eight hours. All he had to do was survive until then. It was a slim chance, but it was a chance. He felt his fear diminish. He had a plan.

He removed his boots, socks, short-sleeved shirt and shorts, leaving only his underwear, but it made little difference. Sweat still trickled down his face and chest, tickling and irritating him. His skin, especially his scalp, still tingled unpleasantly from his brief exposure to the sun's rays. He closed his eyes, trying not to constantly check his watch. He tried to force himself to sleep, but he couldn't. Instead, he sat up and stared out the window at the green fields surrounding him.

As time passed he developed a piercing headache. He felt nauseous and dizzy. He had difficulty remembering where he was. He had three litres of water and tried to ration it. Each sip brought him blessed relief as the cool liquid revived him. In those moments of lucidity, he knew his symptoms were the early stages of hyperthermia. Everyone was taught to recognise the signs. He prayed they wouldn't get any worse, but knew they would. The mantra he'd been taught as a child echoed in his mind; *heat stroke means death, heat stroke means death.*

The hours dragged by, but eventually morning turned to afternoon, then afternoon turned to evening. He watched the sun move across the sky and dip towards the west. Darkness eventually fell, leaving him with only the reflection of his own face in the window. He knew the temperature would now decrease, but it was still likely to be in the high thirties or low forties. He waited, staring out at the darkness. He checked his watch regularly, waiting for midnight. He finished his water at around 11 p.m. That was it, he couldn't wait any longer. He had to get going or he would die.

"Time to go," he muttered to himself. He felt drunk, uncoordinated. He forced himself to keep moving.

He dressed himself, putting on his shirt and shorts, both crisp with dried sweat. His feet had swollen and he had difficulty getting his boots on. He had to leave his laces undone. He pulled the handle of the door and stepped outside. It was cooler than the cabin, with a soft breeze. He realised his mistake. The cabin temperature had probably been in the forties, the air fetid and dry; outdoors was closer to thirty. He cursed his faulty judgement; he should have opened the door earlier. Damned heat stroke had clouded his judgement. He hoped he hadn't just killed himself. Small mistakes in this climate usually had large consequences.

He looked around. There were no lights visible. The farm robots didn't need lights to keep working. Luckily the moon was full and he could see the road easily. Despite the lethargy he felt, he willed his feet to move. As he walked, he kept checking his cell phone, hoping for reception. He scanned the horizon for lights, but it was hard to see. The crops on either side obscured his view.

Thankfully, the cooler night temperature had alleviated some of his symptoms. He was still very wobbly and his head was pounding, but he was thinking more clearly. There was a cool wind, carrying the scents of the fields around him. He realised he couldn't remember the last time he'd smelled nature. Despite visiting the farms on a regular basis, he never actually went outdoors.

He'd been walking for about an hour when he saw the light in the distance. He felt tears welling up in his dry eyes. Lights meant habitation. Habitation meant humans. He was saved. Out here, it was hard to judge distance, but he was determined he was going to walk until he got there. There was no way he was going to die out here. His feet, shuffling along in his uncomfortable boots, picked up the pace.

The wind had increased and was blowing against his back. Lansing smiled, it seemed that nature had decided to help him at last, rather than try to kill him.

There was a sudden gust of wind that almost knocked him off his feet.

"What?"

The corn in the field next to him was swaying. In the distance, there was a roaring noise. Lansing stopped. He'd forgotten, this was tornado season. He was buffeted by the wind. It was too dark to see the funnel, but he guessed it was getting closer by the increase in noise. To his left, the corn was suddenly flattened as the tornado headed directly towards him. Lansing started to run, a shambling, desperate dash in the opposite direction. His loose laces tripped him up and he fell, his face hitting the warm tarmac. He saw huge splashes of rain hit the ground close to his face and felt the blessed relief of cool water on his skin. The roar of the wind became overwhelming. He felt no fear this time, there was no point. There was no escaping this fate. He started to laugh, it was all so ridiculous. He turned over and looked up at the huge, turbulent funnel just above him. The rain felt wonderful on his face. Perhaps there really was a god, one who actually cared about his human creations. Lansing closed his eyes and thanked them for letting him die cool.

~

R. J. Meldrum is an author and academic. He has had stories published by Culture Cult Press, Horrified Press, Infernal Clock, Trembling with Fear, Black Hare Press, Darkhouse Books, Smoking Pen Press, Breaking Rules Publishing, Tell Tale Press, Kevin J Kennedy *and* James Ward Kirk Fiction. *He also has had stories in* The Sirens Call e-zine, the Horror Zine *and* Drabblez Magazine. *His novella,* The Plague *was recently published by Demain Press. He is a contributor to the* Pen of the Damned *and an Affiliate Member of the Horror Writers Association.*
Facebook: richard.meldrum.79
Twitter: RichardJMeldru1

BAD VIBE
Thomas Canfield

The Center for Disease Control was not the first line of defense in the battle against modern day scourges and pestilence. But it was far and away one of the best and most effective. Though we rarely received the recognition we deserved, we all took great pride and satisfaction in our accomplishments. Some of the finest minds in the business worked under my supervision. The notion that we might ever invite a Trojan Horse into our midst, albeit unwittingly, had probably never occurred to any of them. But it *had* occurred to me.

The applicant seated in the chair opposite me was named Zachariah Chen. He was of mixed American and Chinese ancestry. His resume, which I held in my hand, was everything that I could have asked. He had attended the right schools, interned at the right institutions, received accolades and recognition at every stage of his career, compiling a record of accomplishment second to none. The letters of reference he offered were, without exception, laudatory. He would appear to be the ideal candidate for the position. The only problem, and it was not an insignificant one, was that I had taken an active dislike to Chen within minutes of meeting him.

I wasn't prone to such snap judgments. As a general rule, I kept my personal feelings well in hand. I recognized that they should have no bearing on who was awarded a fellowship and who was denied. Talent should be the sole determining criterion. Chen had talent in abundance; that was undeniable. But he gave off a bad vibe. In scientific terms such an expression was imprecise, hard to pinpoint and impossible to quantify. But I trusted my gut. It was something I relied on, believed in and listened to.

"A very impressive resume, Dr. Chen." I pushed the document aside, underwhelmed at the list of superlatives it contained. "Most impressive." Chen nodded. He was accustomed to being well thought of and needed no reinforcement in that regard. "I've been through your application and read your accompanying essay. You expressed an interest in focusing on the East Asian N1N3 virus, one of the many pathogens currently active. Why that particular virus?"

Chen leaned forward, clasped his hands between his knees. Shadow from the blinds fell across his face, lending his features a slightly sinister cast.

"I feel, or to express myself more accurately, I am convinced that over the long run it possesses the potential to do more harm than any other pathogen currently on the list. More so, certainly, than such 'glamour' viruses as Ebola or MERS.

"N1N3 is mutating at an astonishing rate, seeking out gaps in the human defense mechanism which it can exploit. To my way of thinking, it's the most menacing virus extant and presents a formidable challenge to anyone studying it. The death toll is insignificant at this juncture and so people, scientists even, tend to disregard it. But all of that could change in a heartbeat. A major outbreak is well within the bounds of possibility – an emergency for which we remain totally unprepared."

It was a good answer, demonstrating a willingness to flout conventional wisdom and to pursue the path less traveled. Chen did not discount the human factor – empathy for potential victims – but he did not obsess over it either. He did not fall into the trap of so many applicants, who felt compelled to present themselves as modern day Florence Nightingales. The science came first with Chen. Good intentions and high-minded idealism, while perhaps commendable, were no substitute for the science.

Chen's viewpoint was one I largely shared. N1N3 was not on many people's radar, scientists or laymen. But it should have been – and for precisely the reasons Chen had enumerated. The virus was dynamic, adaptable, innovative and resilient. At present, it simmered at a low boil. But if it were to discover a gap, as Chen suggested, the consequences would be devastating. It might easily rival the flu pandemic of 1918.

This shared concern rendered my decision more difficult still. One of the best features of the fellowships we offered was that they afforded considerable latitude to the individual researchers.

They were granted leeway to adopt whatever methodology and approach they felt would prove most effective. To succeed, they must be self-directed and capable of independent thought and action. Chen fitted that profile. But, granted so much freedom, the process was also subject to being abused. I was left with the distinct impression that Chen was likewise a fit for *this* profile.

"You're married, Dr. Chen?" I dropped this question seemingly out of the blue, hoping to catch Chen by surprise. I rarely probed into a candidate's personal life. That was considered intrusive and frowned upon. In this instance, I was willing to ignore convention.

Chen nodded. That was all: a brief nod, accompanied by a brightening of his eyes and a fleeting movement of his upper lip that might have been intended to suggest a smile.

I flipped through his application to see where, if anywhere, this information was included. "And your wife's name is?"

Chen sat up straighter in his chair. His expression bore a trace of sulkiness now. "May. May-lin, but I call her May." The subject seemed to cause Chen discomfort. Were it not for this, I would probably have let the matter drop. It was the first real sign of vulnerability that Chen had displayed. I resolved to mine it further and see what I could discover.

"She's here in Atlanta with you? I notice you haven't relocated to the city permanently as yet."

Chen wet his lips, shifted in the chair. "She's in mainland China. Shanghai. She's been stranded there for several months now." A long pause. "She's a Chinese national and we've encountered problems securing a visa."

"Well, that *is* a shame. Any sort of red tape is a hassle. Government red tape, that's the worst that there is. I have contacts in the State Department, people who exercise some pull. I'd be happy to pass along your information to them. I'm certain they'd be able to expedite the process."

"Thanks." The statement was flat, devoid of intonation – as it was devoid of gratitude or interest. "But I think that I'll handle it on my own." The rejection was final, inviting no follow up.

"Of course. Should you experience a change of mind, just let me know." That was where the interview ended. Both of us walked away dissatisfied: Chen because he felt that he had not made a good impression; I, because I felt that Chen was being less than candid. Why, and about what, however, remained an open question.

I recommended that Chen not be awarded a fellowship. But I was the lone dissenter. The Board overwhelmingly endorsed his application. Chen was welcomed onboard with open arms. I regret to say that my own embrace could not be styled anything other than half-hearted.

*

I never really warmed to Chen, never came to feel that he was entirely trustworthy. Perhaps it was because he was too rigid, too unbending, too remote. Or perhaps it was something else, something less easy to identify and affix a name to. I wasn't prepared to say. But too much was at stake for me simply to do nothing. I had friends of long standing employed by the State Department. I put these contacts to work now, requesting that they dig into Chen's background. If he harbored a skeleton in his closet, if he was concealing information, I wanted to know.

A month passed. Finally, late one evening in May, I received a secure file over the Internet. I poured over the contents, half anticipating what I might find. My suspicions were in large measure confirmed. The brooding canker of darkness at the core of Chen's personality was at last exposed. The investigation revealed that Chen was, in fact, married, as he had said. But his wife, May-lin, was not 'stranded' in China in any commonly understood meaning of the word. The truth was that she had died and was buried there. Or as Chen undoubtedly viewed the event, and as many another would concur, she had been *murdered* and was buried there.

It was a sad tale certainly, one which perhaps spoke to larger issues. May-lin and her husband had run afoul of the government's One Child policy. Through an unfortunate series of bureaucratic errors May-lin had wound up at a rural clinic, undergoing a state mandated abortion. The procedure had been badly botched. The poor woman never left the clinic alive.

It was devastating, yes, a personal tragedy of the first order.

Chen would have been less than human had he reacted with anything other than outrage. But he had taken the incident and transformed it into a towering edifice of persecution and willful malignancy. He had abandoned all sense of perspective, giving way to a single, consuming urge: a desire to exact revenge.

With anyone else, such a threat would have amounted to little. The disparity in size and punching power between the two antagonists was too great. But, as it happened, Chen was perhaps the one individual who possessed a skill set enabling him to take on the One Party monolith and inflict a grievous injury. It was bad luck all the way around, the worst possible conjunction of personalities and events which could have transpired.

It forced me to act. I could not just sit back and wait and see if anything happened. Previous incidents, well-documented in the media, had chronicled cases where anthrax spores or samples of ricin had been smuggled out of labs. I was not prepared to take a chance on something similar happening at the CDC.

I consulted our chief Security Officer. He agreed that Chen should be stopped one evening while exiting the compound and his belongings searched. It was a departure from customary procedure and certainly would be viewed by Chen as reflecting a lack of trust. But the pressing nature of my concerns overrode these considerations. I *had* to know what was going on.

In the event, nothing came of it. Chen carried the same personal effects and assorted clutter as might your average college student at any random campus across the country: car keys, Kleenex, chewing gum, pen, notebook, ID badge and pass, wallet. It was all of it utterly normal and predictable. None of the items came close to tripping an alarm.

I gained access to Chen's hard drive. Again, there was nothing. I found no evidence that Chen was violating lab protocol or abusing his privileges. Everything was by the book. The more I studied Chen's work, truth be told, the more impressed I was. The clarity of his logic, the soundness of his instincts, all filled me with admiration. He was able to approach a problem on both a micro and a macroscopic level, never losing sight of the ultimate objective: mastering N1N3 and unraveling its secrets

But therein lay the rub. No moral bias attended such knowledge, no inherent inclination toward good or evil. A scientist might apply such understanding toward thwarting and checking the virus, working toward its eradication. Or, were he so inclined, he might facilitate the virus, enhancing its virulence and ease of transmission. The knowledge itself was open to either application, would lend itself as readily to one as to the other. In the vast majority of cases, this was never an issue. But with Chen, the latter possibility was one I could not entirely discount.

A week later Chen absconded, disappeared without a trace. He cut off all contact with friends and associates, dropped off the grid and went underground. For all anyone knew, he might be in Bangkok or Manila or Jakarta – or in the house next door. Plainly he had been planning all this for some time. He had been methodical, deliberate and thorough in covering his tracks and I had a sinking feeling that I knew why.

*

A black hour, a black day. Damien Klein, one of my most promising young associates, had just returned from China. An outbreak in a remote mountain village, resulting in several deaths, was spiraling out of control. Klein had traveled there to investigate. I was listening to his account, following it with interest, when suddenly my attention flagged. His words washed over my consciousness, their meaning and import lost to me. Klein was engaging in a habit I found distasteful, one I instinctively associated with stupidity. It was an extreme reaction, perhaps, founded in an old prejudice. Yet the prejudice stuck and I found it difficult to set it aside. Klein was chewing gum.

I watched with fascination as his jaws worked non-stop. Under other circumstances, I would have attached little importance to such a quirk. But Klein's action, the brazen manner in which he went about it, provided me with the clue, the key to the puzzle that I had been seeking for so long. How I had overlooked something so obvious, I could not understand. The truth is, I had been expecting something extraordinary, some subterfuge dazzling in its complexity and sophistication. I had attributed super-human powers of concealment to Chen. Whereas the answer had been staring me in the face all along - and I too blind to see it.

Chen had employed chewing gum for smuggling the virus out of the lab. It was the perfect medium in which to preserve, transport and conceal the pathogen. It was safe, dependable, efficient and, above all else, innocuous. Anyone discovering the gum would think nothing of it, would attribute no sinister design to its possession. It would pass through the tightest security screen and, for all intents and purposes, remain unnoticed.

Only Chen had neglected one small detail. He had, as with many a master criminal before him, omitted to take into account a tiny discrepancy. What gave the game away, what rendered Chen's guilt a virtual certainty, was that Chen – unlike Klein – was fastidious in his personal habits. He did not indulge in junk food or snacks. He avoided coffee, soda and pizza. He had never, at any time or under any circumstance, consumed candy or gum in my presence. He would have regarded such indulgence as a form of weakness, a sign of deficient character. In *his* possession, the gum was tantamount to an outright admission of guilt.

"The devious bastard!" I sprang to my feet. I came close to hugging Klein in my gratitude. "I never thought twice about the gum. I was so caught up in the high tech angle I allowed it to blot out everything else. You're a genius, Klein!" Klein accepted the compliment readily enough but eyed me warily, unable to make out what lay behind my outburst. I rushed from the room, praying that the revelation had not come too late.

But it *was* too late. The news out of China went from bad to worse. The virus spread across the countryside and made its way to the major metropolitan centers. The numbers of sick and infected spiked alarmingly. The health care system was swamped with new cases and the epidemic took on the trappings of a genuine national tragedy.

I followed a live feed out of Beijing, transmitting events as they unfolded in real time. The images were appalling: people hurrying along the main boulevard of the city wearing surgical masks, the sick and the dying slumped in doorways or lying in alleys, abandoned and left to fend for themselves. The government was putting out a steady stream of bulletins about how to avoid the contagion but had lost the trust of the populace. A spirit of anarchy had taken hold. The situation was on the verge of spiraling out of control.

I felt an impotent fury as I watched events unfold. Worse than that, I was plagued by a sense of guilt. I could not avoid thinking that if I had torpedoed Chen's application at the outset, had I been more forceful and emphatic in my opposition, none of this would have come to pass. I should have trusted my instincts. Instead, I had allowed the judgment of others to prevail. I had deferred to their opinions because it was easier to do that than to fight on alone.

I had *known* that Chen was a bad apple. From the first, I had recognized that he harbored some dark and deadly passion. But I had washed my hands of the matter, as Pontius Pilate had, thinking to escape the opprobrium. The nagging of my conscience would not let me off so easily, however.

In the end, I had underestimated Chen. I had not credited him with such depths of malice, such boundless vitriol. I never imagined him capable of wreaking so thorough and devastating a revenge.

Had he been wronged by the Chinese government? Assuredly he had. But his wrongs were no greater than many another could lay claim to. He was far from unique in nursing a grudge. Only the scope of his resentment set him apart. It lent him a laser-like focus, an almost maniacal craving for revenge that dwarfed the passions which animated his fellow men. Who could have foreseen that Chen could exact so steep a price, so terrible a toll, upon those who had wronged him? Who could have suspected what lay behind the bland façade, what turbulent passions agitated the soul within? Who could have exposed him for what he was, if not I.

We were not so very different, after all, Chen and I. True, I had harnessed my abilities towards constructive, positive ends. But my inclinations might easily have tended the other way. Even now, the inner workings of Chen's soul retained a morbid fascination for me. But thinking alike allowed me to slip into Chen's shoes and, so to speak, walk where he walked. And I had done just exactly that.

I had introduced a pathogen into Chen's sneakers late one evening while he took a break, stockinged feet propped on his desk. The pathogen was a nasty little bacterium I had whipped up in the lab and featured a time-activated mechanism so that it would not become active or infectious for several weeks. Had Chen behaved himself, had he kept to the straight and narrow, I might easily have disarmed the bug before it did any harm.

Now, however – I glanced at the calendar – it was too late. Sometime in the course of the next twenty-four hours Chen's feet would swell to twice their normal size and turn the most ungodly shade of purple-black imaginable. When he checked into a medical facility, word would filter out about a new, previously unidentified form of infection. The CDC would be amongst the first to receive this news. I would then make a quick phone call to Washington. The authorities, I was certain, would be most interested in interviewing Dr. Chen.

When it came to that, I'd kind of like to speak to the son of a bitch myself.

~

Thomas Canfield's phobias run to politicians, lawyers and TV pitchmen. He likes dogs and beer. He has recently had pieces in the UK publications, Flametree Press *and the cyberpunk journal,* Write Ahead the Future Lies.

THE UNDERTONES
Mark Towse

"What the hell is it, Fi?"

"John, I can't hear a thing; it's in your head. Now please go to sleep," my wife replies dismissively.

"It's Tuesday night for Christ's sake. After eleven."

She sighs before flipping dramatically to her side, a physical full stop to our exchange. Within minutes, she will be open-mouthed, and soon after, the resentment-inducing whistle through her nostrils will begin.

I lay my head on the pillow but can feel the bed vibrating with the noise; a relentless bass that the blood in my ears is synchronising with. There isn't a hope in hell that I will sleep through this. How the hell can she not hear it?

It's happening a lot recently – sometimes early in the morning, sometimes midday – through the night on occasion. Saturday night, for instance, it started just before six and carried on until well after one. I went for a walk around the block to try and find the source, but it was as if it was everywhere. Fi said I should get my hearing checked out; said it's more than likely tinnitus – the internet is never wrong, of course. Harold and Joan next door also deny hearing anything, but they're so old, I wouldn't be surprised if they don't know which way is up.

I always just assumed that I had sensitive ears, picking up sounds that others couldn't. Even as a child, I recall looking out the window on occasion, trying to find the single illuminated house on the estate.

I open the drawer in the bedside table and pick out the pink earbuds, urgently cramming them in as deep as they will go. Her sigh plays in my head as she turns over, taking most of the covers with her. How nice it must be to be so oblivious to everything.

The vein in my neck is joining in now, strumming punishingly to the phantom beat. It's working its way across my temples, too, as though trying to find a way inside my head.

This level of sensitivity, it's a curse, that's for sure.

Until a few weeks ago, there was another hum. It began like clockwork at 3 pm every day and lasted for exactly thirty minutes. It was monotone and more subtle, but for that brief time, I was unable to focus on anything else. Fi denies it all; says I have too much time on my hands and reiterates the advice from some random on the internet to get checked out.

This recent noise is different – random and untamed. And today I can feel it as well as hear it.

There are others; I've looked them up on the internet – even joined the group. It's called 'The Undertones,' and membership is growing all the time. And Christ, there's no shortage of theories; experiments by the government, aliens trying to communicate, some even believe it's the sound of the world slowly dying. We are scientists, doctors, astrologers, and nutcases – so many ideas, but there is one thing we all agree on: the earth is fucked – on fire, flooded, and poisoned.

Staring at the crack in the ceiling that I am all too familiar with, patches of my skin suddenly begin to thrum rhythmically in time with the distant tune. I turn over to my side, but this only offers temporary relief as the skin on my back begins to sing. Frustrated, I turn again, but the noise seems to be invading my body, slowly awakening each of the nerve endings.

"John, will you please lie still!" her muffled voice floats across.

"I wish I fuckin' could," I snap, swinging my legs to the floor.

If she makes a response, I don't hear it. Shuffling across to the window, I move the curtains aside to reveal blackness diluted only slightly by the artificial halogen streetlights. In the distance, I think I see something moving – a series of opaque dark shadows that just as quickly blend back into the stillness of the night. I move closer to the window to investigate, but my attention is drawn to the streetlights that begin to flicker in unison in time with the dull beat. Finally, they return to their dirty yellow glow, and now I'm left with the promised serenity of night. I march out of the room like a petulant teenager and begin my descent down the landing stairs.

It's getting even louder, stronger. I can feel it on my bare feet

– coming through the floor, vibrating through the wooden planks. I've never known it as bad as this before. What is happening to me?

On the way to the kitchen, I press the power button on the laptop and immediately pick up the vibration coming from the machine. Or perhaps it's just me – my fingertips a collection of nerve endings in a frenzied state. I don't know anymore.

I place my hand on the surface of the kitchen bench and can feel its monotonous harmony. Running the back of my hands against the wall provides the same tremor-like feedback.

Shit, I can feel it in my spine now. That's another first. It's pulsating – an undulating vibration that feels like it's running up and down the bone. It stops at my neck and runs back to the base and repeats.

The now relentless buzz in my ears is giving me an unbearable headache. I rip out the redundant earbuds and throw them against the back wall. "Get out of my fuckin' head!"

Christ, what if we are onto something? It's one thing to postulate such wild hypotheses, but what if there is some substance to them. What if –

"Fuck, Jesus, Fuck," I hiss as the pressure in my head is turned up again. There is no undulation now, no troughs of relief – the noise has settled into a single and haunting discordant drone that continues to get louder. Grabbing a glass from the counter, I turn on the tap and note the feedback from the metal. The same resonant hum feeds from the handle on the drawer as I reach inside for the painkillers. I quickly wash a couple down and return to the living room.

The screen is where I left it – on the forum page.

I knew it. It's the government!

They are trying to control us. It's the noise – that's how they get into our heads!

They're outside. They have come for me. What do I –

Fuck. It's true. It's them!

We were right. All this time.

My phone line is dead. Having to use hotspot.

They've been turning up the frequency – increasing their control. But they still can't get us, can they?

They're controlling people's brainwaves with this sound – manipulating emotions – brainwashing them.

All this time, they've been watching us. The ones they couldn't control – we must show up on fucking google maps or something.

I think there's someone in my fucking garden.

Now we've united, they want us under or gone – they know we are onto them.

They're turning it up – it's so fucking loud. They've sent hitmen in case it doesn't work. I think I see them outside.

I can't bear it.

If you have a gun, go and –

Help.

Help. That was the last message someone typed. Ten minutes ago. The internet light on the modem is unlit, so I quickly pick up my phone. I'm shocked to find it displaying a signal but not in the least bit surprised by the vibration it sends down my arm. I quickly connect to hotspot and refresh the page on my laptop.

This site no longer exists.

"Fuck!"

The noise is overwhelming, voluminous, and head-splitting. I dial emergency services but get no ring tone. I try and connect to the latest news with my phone, but it tells me the site is down. I can't get onto anything.

My skull feels as though it could cave in at any moment. The air is heavy, and it feels as though the entire house is alive – the floor, walls, surfaces – all vibrating with increasing intensity.

The outside light comes on. My heart stops.

I stare towards the lit-up patio, legs suddenly incapable of movement. I can hear nothing but the relentless drone. It's debilitating, disorienting.

Slowly, I begin to back away, feeling my way across the furniture and back to the bottom of the stairs. Shit, what was that? Something moved – behind the pillar.

The group was a distraction, a chance to talk to other similar minds. But for this to be –

Another shadow outside. I must get upstairs.

"Fi!" I hiss. But I wouldn't be able to hear her response above the now mercilessly loud hum in my ears. Clinging to the trembling handrail for support, I begin to pull myself up, staring at the dimly lit patio for as long as it remains in view. Halfway up, I begin to move with more urgency towards our bedroom. I have no idea what I will say or how I will explain this. All I know is that I – we – are in danger.

This fucking noise!

I cover both ears with my palms, but it only makes things worse, as though I am trapping it inside my head. The sensation in my spine is getting more intense, as though someone is reaching in and applying pressure. The air feels heavier and even more claustrophobic.

Fiona looks so peaceful; no whistling. A smile has crept across her face. "Fi!" I say – still nothing.

My ability to think feels clouded. It's as if the noise and pressure are bringing a blanket of thick fog that desperately wants to wrap around my brain. I continue to fight against it but wonder how long I can carry on. The pressure behind my eyes is too much. Blood pounds so violently around my body, and every part of me wants to concede. I feel an urge to scream at whoever is out there to put me out of my misery.

Staggering across to Fi, the hairs on the back of my neck prickle an ominous warning that something isn't right. I run to her side and give her a gentle shake, but her head lollops on the pillow like a rag doll. I try again, more vigorously this time, but there is still no response. Placing my head against her chest, I get nothing. As if making up for both of us, my heart begins to race as I search desperately for a pulse – some sign of life. I prise open her eyelids to find only a glassy vacancy. She's gone. Out of sheer desperation, I start pressing down on her chest and begin to sob.

The explosion of blinding light and the accompanying bolt of pain sends me slumping to the floor. Every bone in my body rattles with ferocious intensity as I try to push myself back up, but it's all too much, and I fall to my back again. I feel as though my spine is about to snap and that my skull is only seconds away from cracking like an egg. The floor shakes violently beneath me as I helplessly stare at the ceiling that is illuminated in impossibly bright light. I watch the crack slowly working its way across; white dust sprinkling down. I can hardly breathe. I feel the pressure on my ribcage now – as though this sonic undertone is trying to possess me.

I can't take it anymore. I'm ready to go. Fingers clawing at the carpet, I begin to drag myself towards the stairs again. They can have me – just let it end.

Another elevation in the already excruciating shrill makes me feel as though my brain is bleeding. My teeth tear through the top lip, and I can feel a stream of warm blood running from my right nostril. My fingers are as white as the surrounding light as they bury into the carpet. If it wasn't for the feel of the fabric beneath my fingertips, I would think I was already dead.

The vibration stops.

I see a shadow approaching down the hallway.

White is giving way to black –

*

Even before knowing my fate, relief washes over me. I now only feel slight cloudiness in my head, but that goddamn interminable buzz is finally gone.

Fi.

I open my eyes and try to get up, but the shiny silver restraints around my wrists and ankles prevent me from doing so.

What the –

Through the glass-fronted room, I see its black eyes staring back at me. The body is almost translucent and spiralling through a multitude of colours. Finally, it settles to a bland greyness. The elongated cranium is twice the size of a human's, and I can see a single large vein pounding rhythmically across the forehead.

It begins to move. I hold my breath.

Its legs look weak and spindly, but its movement is smooth, ethereal – as though it is floating across the ground rather than walking. It has no ears as far as I can see. The long thin silver arms remain by its side as it approaches the silver door.

A single vibration comes through the bed and echoes through the metallic restraints. I watch, heart racing, as the door slides open

411

and the alien steps into the room.

A million thoughts rush through my head, but I offer no words; I don't think I have the courage. It nods – and I take that as a cordial acknowledgement of my questions and fears. Slowly, it moves to the side of my bed and reaches its hand towards me. Instinctively, I recoil as much as the restraints will allow, and it quickly snaps its hand back. The spindly fingers settle on a warm orange – my favourite colour, and it waits – as if for approval. Warily, I nod, and the hand settles against my forehead.

As soon as the vibrations begin, it all begins to make sense.

For years, the 3 pm broadcast was how they communicated between themselves – those here and those back home. They were reporting back on our progress, but most recently signalling their dire warnings that we were killing Earth. They have been here for centuries – the original caretakers of the planet. No longer could they sit back and watch us destroy it – a race seemingly oblivious to the devastation they are leaving behind. Earth is dying, quicker than we think. Some of them wanted to let us have another chance – to try and fix it – others thought it was too late. Arguments began, communications broke down, and factions were formed – thus the random outbreaks of noise and tremors – prolonged debates of whether the human race should be wiped out.

Finally, it came down to a vote. A last-minute compromise of sorts was reached.

Only some would live; a handful of free thinkers – ones not already plugged into the machine – ones that had their eyes and ears wide open to everything around them, even the hum.

The alien puts his other hand against my ear, and I immediately feel something move inside my head. It's a cold and extremely unpleasant sensation; it feels as though something is working its way across my brain. My discomfort must be obvious as the alien nods towards me once more. And just as quickly, the sensation is gone, as is the remaining cloudiness. It holds the silver worm in its palm for me to see, and I watch as the writhing inch-long creature buries into the alien's skin.

They got to us when we were asleep, put them there to protect us. The trail from the worms formed a protective barrier around our brains – pretty much made us immune.

The rest of humanity is gone, wiped out by a sound they were oblivious to. Only us survivors – The Undertones – could hear it, feel it.

It's our final chance to put things right. Only when we save the planet, can we grieve for those lost.

All this time, I thought it was a curse.

~

After a 30-year hiatus, Mark Towse recently gave up a lucrative career in sales to pursue his dream of being a writer. His passion and belief have resulted in pieces in many prestigious magazines, including: Flash Fiction Magazine, Raconteur, Suspense Magazine, Books N' Pieces, The Horror Zine, Antipodean SF, Twenty-Two Twenty-Eight, Montreal Writes *and many more. His work has also appeared three times on:* The No Sleep Podcast, *and other productions such as:* The Grey Rooms. *Fourteen anthologies to date include his work, with a further eight anthologies set for imminent release. His first collection:* Face the Music *was recently published by All Things That Matter Press.*

Mark resides in Melbourne, Australia with his wife and two children.

https://twitter.com/MarkTowsey12
https://www.facebook.com/mark.towse.75
https://marktowsedarkfiction.wordpress.com/

NEW TOWN TOURS
Jim Mountfield

By a wonderful irony, every day, in the middle of its journey along the tree-lined thoroughfares of the city, the tour bus had to cross part of the New Town.

This was the part that Malky, Tails, Leezie and I haunted. The part with the shopping centre, where we knocked balls across the baize in the pool rooms above the derelict shops. The part with Duggan's Bar, where we downed pints and watched for trouble out of the few windows that still had glass in them. The part with the railway embankment, where we crouched in the undergrowth with air rifles and took pot-shots at cats, dogs, pigeons and any snotty kids whom we judged were walking with too much cockiness and swagger on the road below.

The tour bus carried sightseers, but what in our neighbourhood constituted sights to see? The shopping square, where the only surviving retailers were the kebab shop, charity shop, bookies and discount supermarket and where all other premises had hardboard plugging their windows and a million spray-canned squiggles covering their walls? The grey concrete block containing Duggan's Bar, where most of the windows were boarded over too and the surviving windows looked like eyes squinting out of a bandaged face? The scraps of waste ground, such as the side of the railway embankment, where there grew jungles of thistles, nettles, dock-leaves and hogweed, full of empty beer-cans and discarded carry-out bags like a hedgehog's quills were full of fleas? The people on the gleaming, cherry-red double-decker that trundled into view sometime between two and three o'clock each afternoon wanted to look at these?

Once, during a visit to the city centre, I got hold of one of their brochures and saw their full route. They started in front of the pillared entrance and under the four-faced clock tower of the Station Hotel, and from there climbed Jameson Avenue, passing between Georgian facades that included those of the Opera

House, the Portrait Gallery and St Thomas's Church. At the top of the avenue, they turned west and entered the university area, passing St Margaret's Cathedral, the Music School and Library, Duke's Hall and the University Gardens with their ivy-shrouded walls and portcullis-like gates. Past the main campus they negotiated the narrow, cobbled streets of the old student quarter, where in the past 200 years the terraced houses had provided lodgings for two prime ministers, a celebrated civil engineer, one of Britain's few decent composers and half-a-dozen noted poets and authors.

After that they followed the road that bisected Stanwell Park, the passengers on the top deck able to see across the trees to the slope on the park's northern edge that was the site of the City Observatory and the strange mock-Grecian structure of the Burlington Folly. Beyond the park, they came onto the road that ran alongside the old canal, taking them past the quays that once serviced the brewery buildings, still standing, though now their ground floors were home to wine bars, ethnic restaurants, craft shops and private galleries and their upper floors were riddled with yuppie apartments. Then the road dipped and passed the bases of the huge stone columns supporting the viaduct that carried the canal towards the west of the city. There, the bus made a northward turn. This took it by the Breck and Greenside Golf Courses, out to the seashore and to a vantage point for taking pictures of the islet with the Ravelstone Lighthouse. Afterwards, the bus treated its passengers to a scenic coastal ride and finally returned to the city centre.

It was their bad luck that beyond the viaduct columns, before the area containing the two golf courses, they encountered a strip of the New Town.

At one time this strip consisted of warehouses built by the Victorians to accommodate freight brought into the city by the railway and canal. However, it was bombed during the Second World War and by 1945 had so many ruins and craters that the city decided to level everything and rebuild. Somehow, the development got lumped in with the major development going on at the same time further west, on the city's periphery, where huge areas of cheap municipal housing made of a miraculous new material – concrete – were springing up. Thus, a tentacle of the New Town ended up slithering in from the west, alongside the railway line and canal, and coming surprisingly close to the city centre.

Realising this when they studied the city map, the tour company people must have winced. But rather than subject their customers to a lengthy detour around the unsightliness, they decided to quickly ferry them through it.

We were fazed by the sightseeing bus when it first trundled along our streets, paying no heed to the stops where the normal buses would pull over with their screechy brakes. But soon we grew accustomed to it and took note of the people inside it. They weren't like us. They weren't even like our neighbours in the city who, though they had more money, still couldn't escape the city's corrosive wind and rain and so had the same dour look and cheerless dress-sense that we had in the New Town. No, the folk in the sightseeing bus looked alien.

As it rumbled past I might look up and see a beefy American with an absurd souvenir bonnet flopping over his head, pointing at things over the side of the open upper deck and talking loudly to his wife, who was turkey-necked and slathered in mascara and lipstick. Or a younger couple, tall, blonde and proportioned like Ken and Barbie dolls, their appearance suggesting the Teutonic or Scandinavian regions of Europe. Or some East Asians, dressed immaculately but not flashily, alternating between observant stillness and bursts of activity where they'd raise smartphones and cameras and try to snap pictures of everything.

To begin with, we left them alone. We were merely bemused that these aliens seemed to view the New Town with as much interest as they viewed the official sights on their itinerary. With time, though, this feeling turned to jaded familiarity, which then turned to inevitable contempt. The tour bus would be greeted now with V-signs, raised middle fingers, shouts of "Fuck off!" and "Cunts!" Once, as it passed Duggan's Bar, Leezie jumped up on a table by the window, dropped his trousers and made sure the closest passengers got a good look at his arse. Things started to be

416

thrown at it. When we had our air rifles with us, we fired at it, but I don't think we managed to hit anyone.

The end came when I saw the itinerary on that tour brochure and pinpointed where the bus entered the New Town. Coming from the viaduct, it had to use a short tunnel that burrowed through the railway embankment half-a-mile along from the spot where we liked to hide in the vegetation and shoot at creatures even more feral than ourselves. I watched the tunnel the next afternoon and sure enough the tour bus emerged from it. The gap between the upper deck and the roof's tunnel wasn't great and some passengers seated up there had worriedly bowed their heads for a moment. Then I looked at the strip of embankment that rose above the tunnel to the fence sealing off the track at the top. It had plenty of space for the four of us to sit while future tour buses emerged below us, the heads of the tourists on that upper deck not far under our feet.

The next day, while the bus eased itself out of the tunnel, Malky, Tails, Leezie and I bombed its top-deck passengers with plastic beer glasses full of piss and paper bags full of shit. We had only a few seconds to enjoy the spectacle before we scarpered along the embankment, but... Expensive souvenir bonnets, blonde German or Swedish hair, immaculate outfits from the department stores of Tokyo, suddenly stained yellow and brown by the New Town's organic waste products? It was a fine spectacle indeed.

The police snooped about the neighbourhood later that day, and over the next week the local newspapers ran shock-horror stories about how yobs were disgracing – fouling? – the city's image in the eyes of its foreign visitors, and the tour bus didn't reappear for a considerable time afterwards. But then one afternoon it cruised past us on the same New Town roads as before, ignoring the normal bus stops, carrying another cargo of tourists. The tour company, assuming that our attack had been a one-off, had decided to risk going back to its old itinerary.

They might have been reassured by the fact that, in the meantime, the council had covered the embankment above the tunnel with meshes of barbed wire. So we left the tour bus alone for a few weeks, to lull the operators into a false sense of security.

417

Then one night we climbed the embankment with some wire-cutters and chopped the barbed wire into sections, but left those sections resting against their wooden supports so that from the road the wire still looked intact. The following afternoon, all we had to do was go up the embankment a few minutes before the bus was due, lift away the pieces of wire and clamber past, and take our positions again over the mouth of the tunnel.

When the bus emerged below, we gave its passengers another pelting. Though this time we used chunks of broken paving stone that we'd stolen from a local site where workmen had been digging up the side of a street.

Thereafter, the tour bus chose to avoid our neighbourhood.

*

The changes in the city during the next several years took place so gradually that the process of transformation was almost imperceptible. It's only now, comparing the present with what things were like when we attacked the tour bus, that I realise how different life has become.

What were the changes?

Well, there came to be more of certain things and less of certain others. The New Town saw more crime, more vandalism, burglaries, muggings and car thefts. Though it's difficult for me to objectively assess how bad that crime became, as I was partly responsible for it. Thick iron doors and window shutters appeared on more and more houses, while you saw less of the people living in those houses, especially when it began to get dark. I had little to do with my family, my mum and three sisters. When I did go to their house to check if they were still alive, they seemed to be cemented in front of the TV, only leaving their chairs to stomp about and swear like dockers when a power cut deprived them of *The Z Factor* or *Slut Island* or whatever else they were watching. Power cuts were another thing we got more of, much more.

It wasn't only electricity. The city lost interest in the New Town generally. The dug-up street that we'd pilfered for ammunition to use against the tour bus never got filled in again. One day the workmen didn't turn up and that was that. Rubbish collections became less frequent. The binmen came once a fortnight, then

418

reduced their visits to once a month, and then stopped altogether.

As a result, folk no longer put their rubbish on the streets for collection but simply dumped it there as their ancestors in the city did in medieval times. No doubt the rubbish was why we had more wildlife to shoot at in the New Town, like rats, wild dogs and crows – the crows moved in at the expense of the pigeons, whom they seemed to enjoy eating. Meanwhile, like the binmen, the postmen at some point quit coming to our houses. So too did the deliverers for Amazon, Tesco's, Dixon's and the like because their delivery charges grew so extortionate that people stopped ordering from them. Those pricy charges were possibly due to the postcode we lived in.

One group of people I was glad to see less of down our way were the cops, whose patrol cars became a rare and eventually a non-existent sight. You saw more cop helicopters, but they chattered back and forth through the sky without any suggestion that they were thinking about landing near us, so that was tolerable. However, when I made my way to the city centre – a trip that became less common on account of the gradual phasing out of the New Town bus service – I'd see plenty of cops, many more than there'd been before, some moving around in strange armoured vehicles that looked like tanks with truck wheels instead of caterpillar tread and water cannons instead of gun barrels. Gradually, their uniforms became more elaborate. More padding appeared on their jackets, and they acquired helmets that resembled those worn by American football players, and new accoutrements appeared on their belts: blackjacks, knuckle dusters, things that looked like sawn-off cattle prods.

One day in the city centre I saw a pair of cops on the beat and realised they were carrying automatic rifles. At that moment it occurred to me that, yes, things in the city certainly were changing. Mind you, by then, a lot of my acquaintances were carrying guns too. And not guns of the 'air' variety.

What else? More cars got torched during the night and predictably the council declined to tow them away. And because our roads became so clogged with heaps of rubbish and blackened car-wrecks, they were used less by traffic. You also saw less traffic because petrol got more expensive. The TV news programmes talked of terrorist bombings of oil fields and pipelines in the Middle East, Central Asia and Texas, which I suppose did nothing to lower fuel costs.

Oh yes. The news became so depressing that I stopped watching it. Every time I checked out a news channel, it seemed to show a red-faced demagogue in a suit thumping a podium and screaming about taking back control, reclaiming the streets, imposing martial law, wiping out the scum, etcetera, while he glowered out of the screen at me as if it was all my fault that these bad things were happening.

Instead, I stuck to watching the porn channels, snuff channels and football channels. By the way, the telly showed fewer international football matches because every second person and their granny were becoming terrorists these days and countries' football squads made prime targets for terrorist attacks.

Other changes? The nights got noisier, thanks to more people shouting, screaming, shooting and even blowing things up. This led in turn to a massive hike in sales of amphetamines, because if it was nearly impossible to sleep you might as well make yourself so wired that you didn't sleep. And overall, events that in bygone days would have had the city in uproar and horror happened more commonly but now nobody batted an eyelid at them. One example of this was the episode where Malky fell out with a gang in the western New Town, and disappeared, and then a week later a lump of human-shaped charcoal that might have been Malky was fished out of the canal.

Lastly, if you wanted to go anywhere, there became a necessity for ID cards with passport-sized photographs of yourself and appropriate stamps on them. Along the bases of the viaduct columns and before the neighbourhood with the Breck and Greenside Golf Courses, the city authorities erected massive fences with gates across the roads. In fact, these fences went on and on. They roamed through back alleyways, across patches of common land, around industrial estates, past the rear ends of people's gardens – but always along invisible boundaries where you sensed that on one side folk had money and on the other side folk didn't. They also posted guards on the gates and to get through into the posher parts of town during the day you needed to show your ID card stamped with a ring of blue ink. To get through after dark the stamp needed to be red, which was even harder to get than the blue stamp.

As it was unlikely that the authorities would allow entry into the more affluent areas for someone like me, with a criminal record as long as the canal, I didn't bother to apply for one of those cards. I resigned myself to spending all my time in the New Town and spending none of it in the world outside.

After a while, I forgot that the outside world existed.

*

And so to the events of today.

I was sitting with Leezie and Tails in Duggan's Bar, using a big, upturned packing case as a surface on which to play cards. Over the years, the chairs and tables in Duggan's had gradually been replaced by a clutter of cases, crates and trunks, leftover containers from the contraband that was smuggled along the canal late at night and passed on the premises from one crooked trader to another. But Bob Duggan could afford to be brazen about the illegal operations going on in his pub. Even if the cops did venture into the New Town, they wouldn't be able to look in and see anything. The last window with glass had long since gone and now sheets of hardboard straddled every window-frame.

This meant, incidentally, we were playing cards by candlelight. The days when the city had bothered to pump electricity into our neighbourhood were history too.

Suddenly, we heard an unfamiliar sound beyond the hardboard. It belonged to an engine, one seemingly toiling to propel a big vehicle through the junk on the road outside. As it'd been an age since any vehicle had attempted to negotiate that road, we all jumped up, hurried to the doorway and spilled out onto the grass surrounding the pub, which was now a mire of litter, broken glass, discarded needles and dried faeces. We were silent for a moment as we contemplated the source of the noise.

Then beside me, Leezie exclaimed, "This is a blast from the past!"

421

It was the tour bus, though in a modified form. As it advanced towards us, I saw how a wide V-shaped appendage at the front was pushing aside the blackened car wreckage and other debris that'd accumulated on the road. Its wheels were bigger, with a deeper, chunkier tread on their tyres, and along the lower deck the windows sported dense metal grills so that, like Duggan's Bar, you could see nothing of the interior. But though the bottom part of the bus had been fortified, the roofless upper deck remained the same. As before, the heads of various tourists, people who looked like they were from America, northern Europe and East Asia, protruded from it.

Many local folk had stumbled out of their decrepit buildings and gathered in groups on either side of the street. Their only thought was to watch and marvel. Whereas years before, a busload of tourists in this neighbourhood had been incongruous, now the notion seemed insane. However, I'd already got over the surprise and was thinking about my next move. Being a tourist required money. I could expect rich pickings if I got onto that bus. Wallets, credit cards, jewellery, phones, cameras…

Ransom money, even? Why not?

I stepped off the pavement and onto the road. So too did Leezie, Tails and our *compadres* from Duggan's Bar – great minds, thinking alike. The bus slowed and stopped, as if to encourage us.

While we approached, I peered upwards again and noticed that the tourists' outfits had changed since the days when we'd bombed them with piss, shit and stones. Those on the upper deck wore padded body warmers and khaki-patterned combat jackets, the garments of hardy outdoors people. Of hunters…

There was a brief but thunderous noise and beside me Leezie keeled backwards. I turned and saw him spread-eagled on the road with a massive hole rupturing his chest. He'd been right. This was literally a blast from the past. Then a cacophony of those thunderous noises started and suddenly people yelled and screamed and retreated towards their houses. Here and there individuals dropped abruptly, rolled across the ground and lay still. I looked up again. Gun barrels suddenly jutted from the top of the bus like a crest of long black bristles.

I dashed back towards Duggan's Bar. Another gun cracked loudly. I felt a horrendous tearing sensation in my thigh and fell flat in the befouled grass. People who'd left the pub with me bounded over me now in a frantic scramble to get back inside. The guns continued to bang down from the bus and I was sprayed with fragments of concrete as bullets smashed into the pub wall above where I lay.

Just before the pain swelled to unendurable levels and I couldn't think any more, it occurred to me that I was witnessing the inaugural day of New Town Safaris.

~

Jim Mountfield was born in Northern Ireland, grew up there and in Scotland, and has since lived and worked in Europe, Africa and Asia. He currently lives in Sri Lanka. His fiction has appeared in **Aphelion, Blood Moon Rising, Death Head's Grin, Flashes in the Dark, Hellfire Crossroads, the Horror Zine, Hungur** *and* **Schlock Webzine.**

WHEN THEY UNMASKED
Terry Grimwood

We will always remember where we were when they unmasked.

I was changing the tyres on a white Range Rover, giving a running commentary to Nathan, *Fast*Wheels's mint-fresh apprentice, as I did so. Seventeen years old, he was, intimidated by the noise, activity and struggling to separate his arse from his elbow. His overlarge, crisp red company overalls made him look like a kid trying to be grown-up.

Suddenly, he frowned, took a step back and looked up at the dirty girders and corrugated metal roof beyond. I released the trigger of the compressed-air wheel-wrench and snapped at him to pay attention.

He ignored me and, before I could bollock him back into line, reached up to grab a handful of his scalp. His hair was Grade One short, no flowing locks to grip, only that tight, no-give skin that covers the top of our skulls. I thought he was having an epileptic fit, although he wasn't convulsing and he was still on his feet. He just stood there, a serious expression on his face, and pulled his own flesh. He had a handful of it. You can't do that. I've tried it since. You can't grab a handful of your scalp the way you can grab a handful of your belly.

He pulled.

And drew his face upwards so that the corners of his eyes were impossibly slanted, his mouth distorted into a nightmare clown grin and his nose yanked into a grotesque impression of a pig's snout.

I knew I should act. We had all passed our First Aid refresher about a month before, but they hadn't told us anything about self-flaying.

The skin slid up over his face. *Slid*, a word that doesn't begin to describe what I saw.

There was no blood. No tearing or crackling of ripped flesh.

424

Up it went, smooth as you like. What remained was no Nathan-shaped skull. No steaming red muscle. No bulging eyeballs and grinning teeth. This wasn't Nathan.

This wasn't human.

His new face, his under-face, was smooth and oddly innocent-looking. Its skin was white and veined in blue like marble. His eyes were small, blank and black, set on the surface rather than sunk into sockets. He had no nose or ears. His mouth was a hole that opened like a wound.

I couldn't move or even shout or swear. The wrench was in my hand and would have made a good weapon, but I simply could not grasp what had happened.

I noticed that Nathan (what else could I call this thing?) still held the skin of his head in his right hand. It was a floppy, rubbery membrane, complete with a sad, hole-eyed face and ears and a crop of bristly hair. It was, at that moment, more horrible than anything.

Then someone did shout. It was Unit, the exhaust specialist. He shouted a rude word, which was followed by the clang of a dropped tool. The noise broke my paralysis and I spun round to see Unit backing away. He repeated his expletive with each reverse step. Unit was a rough, tough, built-like-a-brick-shithouse, ex-submariner. I had never seen him scared before. He had scrambled from under the ramp on which was perched the Ford Ka he had been working on. Another figure emerged from its shadows. It should have been Stu. The figure wore red overalls and was as tall and lean as Stu. It even walked like Stu. But he didn't have Stu's head. He had a new head and it was identical to Nathan's.

There was more swearing, more dropped tools and shouting.

Livvy appeared from the far side of a battered old Micra (rear nearside puncture), repeating the word, "No," over and over again. Each *no* was louder than the one before. It took a few moments for me to locate the source of her shock. Then I saw that someone in a suit had entered the workshop. The suit looked expensive, dark blue, open-necked white shirt. Cufflinks visible. His head…

There was a sudden flight of red overalls, scrambling through the oily obstacle course of equipment and into the reception area,

425

where the thing that used to be Kahn was at his laptop, staring at the screen with his two, dead, black eyes. He looked up as we blundered in.

"Oooo," he said.

The sound echoed from the workshop. It was a sad, song-like noise, not at all threatening, but strange enough to drive us out into the cool March sunshine, where the first thing I saw was a woman pushing a baby tripper. She wore an expensive-looking parka with a luxuriously fur-edged hood. I recognised the coat and tripper as belonging to the owner of the Range Rover. She had been an attractive brunette when she entered the reception. But not anymore. Neither was her baby the cute, gurgling little beauty it had been when I first saw it.

The *Oooo* sound was coming from all over the industrial estate now. From the electrical retailer across the road, from the door specialists beside us, from the woman climbing from the delivery van parked in front of Auto-Parts.

We; that is Unit, Livvy and me stood in a frightened huddle in the parking area that fronted *Fast*Wheels and looked wildly around at the things who had been people until a few minutes ago. The aliens who had been our work mates, customers and neighbours.

We were outnumbered. We could see, and hear, more marble-heads (the name just slipped into my brain) than normal human beings.

"Bastards," Unit growled. He held a large spanner in his oil-grimed, bear-paw fist.

I was suddenly conscious that I had no weapon. Neither did Livvy.

We waited.

The woman in the parka continued to push her pram. The delivery driver went around to the back of her van and reappeared a moment later with several packages. Behind us, Kahn continued to enter data onto his computer. Tools and machines whirred and clattered from the adjacent squat and ugly industrial units. And from our own. Tyres were being changed and exhaust systems replaced.

It was as if the marble-heads were unaware of what had

happened.

A car raced past, gears grinding and I glimpsed its human driver and saw his fear. A couple of people hurried by, a woman in a blouse and skirt, a man in dark blue overalls. They held on to each other and glanced nervously about themselves as they walked. Normal people. People with faces. Frightened and trying not to run. They weren't alone. Humans poured from various industrial and commercial units all around us now. More and more cars had started-up and were trying to leave, jamming up the exits in their panic. Horns blared, windows were rolled down and the shouting and arguing began. I heard screams. I heard yells and cries of fear.

"Fuck this, I'm going home," Unit said and was making for his car before any of us could reply.

He was right. We had to get out of there. Home. That was the place to be. The marble-heads might be peaceable now, but their time was coming. Their moment.

The trouble was, I used the bus for work. Would they still be running, during an apocalypse? Only one way to find out. I set off for the entrance to the industrial estate. Yes, I left Livvy behind, but there seemed to be no imminent threat. She owned a car and neither she nor Unit had offered me a lift. Twenty-minutes into the End of the World and it was already every man and woman for themselves.

Groups of humans were gathered together on both sides of the scruffy street that fronted the industrial estate, the English need for personal space overridden by pack instinct. They were arguing, staring, and sometimes shouting at any marble-heads who passed by on foot, on bicycles, or in cars and vans.

I hurried towards the bus stop.

There was an outbreak of pushing and shoving ahead of me. A figure stumbled onto the road and fell heavily. He was a man in a leather jacket and tee-shirt, human but for his blank, vein-marbled head. He lay in an ungainly heap, struggling to get up. As I slid through the mob, a big, shaven-headed human broke free and kicked him in the ribs. The marble-head curled about his hurt. There were cheers that sounded like the baying of animals.

Cars swept past, many driven erratically by terrified-looking humans. I heard a crash, a thud, the tinkling of broken glass, the never-ending dirge of a jammed horn.

I walked on. Head down, unwilling to catch anyone's eye, whether normal iris-and-pupil, or black button.

As I took my place in the dirty glass shelter, I felt suddenly foolish. The world was ending and here I was waiting for a number seven bus.

I watched the chaos from my flimsy sanctuary. The street was already snarled with traffic, people ran in all directions. I glimpsed scuffles; human-on-human, and human-on- marble-head. Outside a mini-mart, which broke the uniform line of terrace houses opposite to where I stood, a middle-aged woman in a black business suit threw a punch at a male marble-head as he tried to walk past her. He too wore a suit and carried a briefcase. He ducked and danced to one side. The punch missed and he hurried by. Unbalanced by her wild southpaw, the woman fell against the shop's plate glass window. It held. Thank God.

The jammed horn blared on.

There was no fire yet, no looting, just confusion, fear and bewilderment, but I sensed that it was only a matter of time before things escalated to the next level.

Another car crash, directly in front of me. Head-on this time, in that familiar, startling detonation of shattered glass and bruised metal that made me flinch back. A large man with a shock of curly hair oozed out of the bigger of the two cars, a slight-built female marble-head climbed from the other. Curly's red-faced anger dissolved into abject fear. He spun about and fled as fast as his bulk would allow. The marble-head simply stood and watched him go.

Another marble-head appeared, draped in an expensive looking brown coat. She walked steadily, brief case in her hand. Another, followed close behind, a burly male in a bright orange high-viz, a tool case in his left fist. They both paused by the female driver. I heard their *Oooo* speech. The driver responded and they went their separate ways.

I saw it then. In that encounter.

The truth.

The marble-heads were carrying on with whatever business they had been engaged in at the instant of their change. I bet the compressed air tools at *Fast*Wheels still clattered and chattered. I bet delivery vans were still arriving at Auto-Parts and circular saws continued to whine at Finch Bespoke Doors and Windows (est: 1949). All the aggression, so far, all the panic and damage, was down to us normal-heads.

A police car raced by, lights on, siren blaring. Another jump-scare. Then as if to balance things, I saw a police officer striding down the other side of the street, minus his helmet, head featureless, white and marbled. His chest-holstered radio squawked and crackled. I wondered if his control realised that he wasn't human anymore.

Any*more*?

Was this a change or an unveiling?

To my amazement, a bus appeared and I did the only thing I knew to do and stepped out from the shelter, hand extended.

The bus glided to a halt. The doors hissed open. I stepped inside. The driver looked at me with featureless, black-pebble eyes and froze me in place. I glanced at the other passengers on the bus. Most of them were marble-heads, although there were a handful of humans, huddled near the back. They held onto one another or gripped the rails of the seats in front with white-knuckled desperation.

"Robin Street?" I said.

The driver nodded. He opened his circular lips and uttered a soft "Oooo".

Hand trembling, I passed him a five-pound note. I had nothing smaller. I didn't expect change, but the driver handed it to me as if nothing was wrong at all. The ticket chattered out of the machine. I tore it off and headed into the bus. I heard the doors close. I was entering the realm of the enemy. I was surrendering myself to their will. I sat, halfway down on the left. Away from any marble-head passengers and separate from the other humans. I trusted neither. I just wanted to get home.

The bus rattled, the engine revved and away we went.

The marble-head passengers were silent. Some looked my way

but there was no threat, just a sense of fleeting interest. The tension was brutal, however. The air crackled with the static of fear.

"No, God, please…" A young human suddenly rose from his seat and rushed through the bus. He stumbled, and staggered and bumped against a female marble-head. He recoiled, gibbering in terror and hurled himself to the front.

"Let me off, you bastards. *Let me off.*"

The driver ignored him. The man pounded at the door. It remained closed. The young man slid down to the floor, sitting with his back to the door, arms tight about himself. He wept. He shook his head and choked out great gasping sobs. He had messy, unnaturally black hair, tattoos and piercings. If he was supposed to be tough, he wasn't making a good job of it.

"What's the matter with you?" demanded a woman from the back. She was on her feet, striding down the aisle. She stopped and shouted at the marble-head passengers. "Let him off. Can't you see he's upset. Let. Him. Off."

One of the marble-heads *oooo*-ed to her, which seemed to incense her even more. "Who the hell are you? Why don't you go back to where you fucking came from and leave us alone?"

No response.

"Did you hear me? You fucking monsters, go away. Go *away*," she screamed.

Then she slapped one of them. A young male in a hoodie.

I was on my feet. I couldn't help myself. I wasn't sure if it was sympathy for the marble-head or fear of reprisal, but I rushed along the aisle to where she stood, shrieking saliva-speckled abuse. As I grabbed at her, the marble-heads opened their mouths and unleashed a different sound to their previous soft coo.

It was a cry. A choir. A soaring, tragic howl of what sounded like grief.

The woman yelped and fell back. I fell back too, arms flailing, scrabbling at the seats and other passengers for support. The woman collided with me and slithered down onto one knee. And all the time that song rang through my head and ripped tears from my eyes.

It stopped.

Silence fell, but for the growl and rattle of the bus.

I made to help the woman to her feet but she shrugged me off angrily, so I returned to my seat.

A lurch and the bus stopped. A hiss. The doors opened and the young man almost fell out. He scrambled free and disappeared. A couple of marble-heads and three of the human passengers got to their feet. The marble-heads made their way carefully to the door. The humans scrambled past, pushing the marble-heads aside in their haste.

We were at a bus stop. The marble-heads were keeping to the rules. *They* were keeping calm and carrying on. *They* were taking over from the humans who seemed, from what I had seen so far, to be losing their grip with terrifying speed.

Two more stops. No incidents. A handful more marble-heads got on the bus, a mother and child, an elderly woman, a teenage couple.

The bus stopped again. I looked up and was startled to see that I was home. I made for the front. It was important not to show panic. The door opened. I took a breath and stepped out.

Robin Road was a quiet little tree-lined avenue of pre-war, bay-windowed semis. A pleasant street inhabited by pleasant people. It was quiet this morning. Not unusual because most of the residents spent their days at work. There were, however, more cars parked than normal, indicating that I wasn't the only one who had headed home. I noticed fresh dents and scratches on some of the auto-paintwork.

The dull background traffic roar was punctuated by car horns and the emergency service sirens. Something was going to happen. Something was going to break.

My front door; light-stained oak. I'd bought it from Finches Bespoke Doors and Windows (est: 1948) a few months ago. I fumbled the key from my pocket and scrabbled it into the lock. I was shaking. No surprise there. The key turned and the door opened.

"Lisa?" I called out as I stepped into the hall.

And I knew.

Barely able to breathe, I moved through the house to the kitchen-diner. The door was open. I could see the sink unit and, above it, the window with its slatted wooden blind. I stepped through and looked to my right, to where Lisa sat at the dining room table. She was working at her laptop, her back to me. There were papers all about her, some stacked on the floor. She had stayed at home to mark GCSE English assignments.

I tried to say her name.

She turned to look at me.

Her skin was white and veined with grey. Her marble eyes were tiny, featureless black pebbles. Her mouth, when she spoke, was a hole that appeared in the plain featureless surface of the skin.

Then I saw the mask on the floor by her right foot; translucent flesh, long blonde hair.

She got to her feet and moved towards me. This was a monster who had stolen my wife's clothes, wore my wife's perfume and even walked like my wife. She reached out to touch my face with my wife's fingers.

I pushed her away. Violently. She staggered back and fell in the way my wife would have fallen. Her legs gave way. Her arms flew out. She made the same thudding sound as her bottom slammed onto the wooden floor. Then came the heavier crack of her back. She lay there for a moment then lifted her head – the monster's head – to look at me and she said "Oooo".

I fled the house.

*

Where to? I had family and friends. But...

They were all around us. Amongst us. Everywhere.

I found myself heading into the town centre. Why? Because there were people there? Because I believed that the authorities had taken control? They hadn't, of course. No one appeared to be in control. And the people I craved? They certainly provided no feeling of safety.

The traffic was snarled. People ran or milled around aimlessly. Police officers were trying to regain control, but no one was listening, especially as half the constables on the street were marble-heads. Glass shattered, looting already. I smelled smoke.

The first fire.

I walked because I didn't know what else to do. I still wore my overalls, hands in pockets. I tried to make myself as invisible as I could, but there were too many people and too many marble-heads to barge into.

A mob appeared, running along the street, dividing about the cars like the swirling water of a flash flood. Four marble-heads formed the crowd's vanguard. As they came closer, I realised that they were not the pack leaders. They were the quarry.

One of them fell, a young male, by the look of his clothes. He issued a plaintive "Oooo". Then he was swamped by the mob.

I walked on. Not wanting to see what happened next. I thought of Lisa.

I pushed her.

I saw her fall again. I saw her outstretched arms. I saw her legs give way.

I should go back to her.

No. It wasn't Lisa anymore. I owed that creature nothing.

The mob was getting closer. The first of its surviving prey raced past me. I felt the shockwave of her passing. I saw the tails of her coat flap the way the tails of anyone's coat would flap if they were running for their lives.

Now I felt the mob. I felt the vibration of its footfalls and the stink of its sweat. I was in its path. They wouldn't stop for me. They were not going to stop for anyone.

A café. People were in there. Proper people. Human people. I tried the door. It was locked. I banged on the glass. A woman in black and wearing an apron, came to the door and unbolted it. I was almost dragged inside. The door was slammed shut behind me.

The mob thundered by.

"What's happening out there?" the woman demanded. She had a husky smoker's voice. "Are they taking over?"

"I..." I shook my head. "My wife is...I don't know what's happening."

"Me too." This was an older man, hunched at a table near the counter, his hands wrapped about a mug of tea, which looked cold and untouched. "My Doreen..."

"It's an invasion. Aliens," said a middle-aged character at another table. He wore a hoodie and trainers, but looked nothing like a teenager and far from cool. He was round-faced, sweating. "It's like that film. You know, with Tom Cruise where the aliens were already here, waiting under the ground. Christ." He sounded as if he was about to cry then regained control. He held out a pudgy hand. "Don."

"Dave." We shook on it.

"Tea?" the husky-voiced woman asked.

I nodded. Nothing sounded better than tea at that moment. The electricity and gas were both on. Everything was working, but for how much longer?

As long as the marble-heads are allowed to carry on running things, while humans thrash around screaming?

"I heard that their ships have already started to appear, over cities, you know, New York and Delhi." Don again.

"They haven't bothered with London," I said. His certainties annoyed me. There were no ships. But surely this *was* an invasion. A deceit perpetrated on the people of Earth.

The tea arrived, along with a bacon sandwich. I sat on one of the café's plastic chairs, rested my arms on one of its melamine-topped tables and stared out of the window. People still ran, or clustered together. Comfort in numbers, I suppose. There was smoke now, drifting, fog-like down the street. Then I noticed the body. Glimpsed, in the road between the cars and vans that did their best to avoid it. Their erratic swerves added to the traffic snarl. There was blood. A glimpse of white flesh, marbled with blue-grey veins. I saw torn tights, one shoe on, the other missing, and a coat. Its tails weren't flapping now.

I stared at the body, transfixed. Out there on an ordinary day in an ordinary street on an ordinary planet.

Someone ran past the café; a young man, eyes wild, laughing. There were boxes under his arms. Loot. Things were getting out of hand quickly. He spun away and dropped a box on the pavement. It was a mobile phone. More looters stumbled past, burdened by their haul. The phone was crushed underfoot.

I watched, unable to eat or drink and no longer aware of the people in the café. The traffic stopped flowing. A van burned further down the road to my left. People scrambled over, and between, the stationery cars. Some carried goods I doubt they'd purchased.

The café radio blared excitedly about chaos, riots and fighting. The emergency services were unable to cope, not least because half of them had *unmasked*. The word punctuated the news report. Unmasked. The prime minister hadn't been heard from. It was assumed that she was in a COBRA meeting.

The alternative reason for her absence wasn't mentioned.

I watched because I couldn't stop watching.

"The army are going to sort this out," the husky-voiced woman said.

"We don't know that," the old man answered.

"Of course they will. You don't think the government is just going to sit there and do nothing."

I knew it was a lie, but the woman's certainty was oddly comforting. We were going to be rescued, regardless of what the breathless presenters were saying on the radio.

"They knew," Don muttered darkly. "The government, they knew."

Another cup of tea arrived, accompanied by toast this time. We drew together at one table, an unspoken need. The husky-voiced woman was Claire and the old man was Tom. There were two others, a couple who had kept themselves to themselves until now. Stefan and Anna. Stefan's English was good, Anna, struggled but was learning fast. Stefan was an intimidating character, but friendly and warm-hearted. I almost liked it in here with these people.

Outside, the world continued to break into pieces.

Lisa was gone now. She/it had lied to me ever since we had met. I owed her/it nothing. Even though she wore Lisa's clothes and perfume and fell to the floor the way Lisa would have fallen, if I had ever pushed her.

Which I hadn't, until a few hours ago.

Claire switched the lights on. It wasn't dark yet, although the afternoon was beginning to fade enough to make the interior gloomy. The lamps came on.

I tried to remember if there had been any clue. I first met Lisa in a conventional way, at a pub with some mates. There had been a band on, a covers outfit playing the usual, but loud enough to turn every conversation into a shouting competition. A group of young women had come in, laughing and obviously having a good time. I caught the eye of one of them, a blonde in cream blouse and black trousers. She was stunning. She looked back at me across the crowded, smoke-hazed room and I looked at her. Then we both turned away, embarrassed, I suppose. Shy maybe. It was glances after that, until one of my mates, it could have been Unit, elbowed me and told me to "get in there".

So, I sauntered over, legs shaking, mouth dry and somehow managed to ask her if she wanted to dance. My timing was perfect because the band slid neatly into *I've Been Waiting For a Girl Like You*, the old Foreigner song (it was a real ale pub for the middle-aged. My mates and I were there because the booze was cheap).

She was the most beautiful woman I had ever seen. She felt light and precious in my arms. I liked her smile and frown and voice. I liked the way she looked straight at me and I came to love her wisdom, kindness and spirit. Corny, I know, but I don't care. There was no clue that night, or on our first date in that Italian restaurant or when I proposed to her on one muddy knee on a rainy afternoon in the Lake District, or when she cried over the news that she, English teacher to the offspring of countless others, could never bear children of her own.

There was no clue or hint or sign that Lisa was anything or anyone but Lisa –

I started as a female marble-head bumped loudly against the café's window. She clung to the glass and looked at me with her tiny, black eyes. There was no expression in her face, yet I could tell that she was afraid. She wore a long cardigan and dark skirt. Her sleeve was torn at her right shoulder. Her blank face was smudged and dirty. Her breath steamed the glass. I heard her muffled and sorrowful "Oooo."

Suddenly a body slammed into her and she was thrown to the right and down onto the pavement. A gang piled onto her; men and women, some rough looking, others smart, a middle-aged man in a suit, an older man, a woman in a red coat. All of them screaming and kicking and stamping. I saw the marble-head raise her arm. Then I couldn't see her anymore.

Lisa...flying back from me. Hitting the floor...

I was out of the café before anyone could shout at me to stop. I grabbed at the nearest of the woman's attackers and hauled him back. He grunted in surprise, swung round and before I could defend myself, drove his fist into my belly. The impact doubled me over. The pain was shocking and reminded me, strangely, of childhood playground scraps. I staggered against the café window, coughing and gasping. The mob backed away from the marble-head and turned their attention towards me.

"Fucking alien lover," the woman in the fur coat shrieked. The stocky young man who had hit me the first time, lumbered in.

Pain turned to rage. I'm a big bloke. I was angry. I slammed into him and we both crashed down to the pavement. I punched his face, again, again. He struggled. Blood streamed from his nose and the sight of it enraged me even more. I pummelled his ugly, vile face until I was dragged clear. Someone kicked me in the ribs and I once more struggled to breathe. Pain seemed to burst all over me.

I was alone. On my side. The marble-head was only a few feet away. There was a widening pool of blood under her head. Her tiny, blank eyes were fixed on me.

I hauled myself up onto my hands and knees and crawled over to her. I held her hand. There was not much more that I could do. Her hand was warm and human. She gasped, then was still.

As I clambered back onto my feet, unsteady, nauseous and stiffening from pain, I wondered if I was the only one who felt the way I did. I looked around, disorientated by the jammed traffic, the running figures, the smoke, and the marble-heads who now seemed as confused and frightened as I was. Some carried tool bags, briefcases or handbags. One clutched a crying baby to himself. The baby was human.

Glass shattered somewhere. Shouts again, a scream. A shot. Jesus. A shot.

Lisa…

*

There was a fire in Robin Avenue. For a moment I was convinced…but no, it wasn't my house. I was relieved. Then guilty because it was *someone's* house. Flames spewed from the downstairs windows and from a huge hole that had been eaten into its roof. Its rib-cage of beams was visible amongst the writhing nest of flames. I hurried past, arm over my face in an effort to keep the smoke from my nose and mouth.

There might be people in there…

The heat was terrific. Even if there were people trapped inside, there was nothing I could do. I couldn't get near the place. I had to close my mind to the horror of it. I had to harden myself.

I made it to my front door and fumbled my key from my pocket. Inside. The smoke of the fire was so dense, it even tainted the air in here.

"Lisa! It's me."

No reply. I rushed into the kitchen diner. No sign of her. Still shouting I tried the sitting room and then the stairs. The smoke stink was stronger now. It made me cough. I ran up the steps, quickly out of breath. I crashed into our bedroom and there she was. Lisa, curled on the duvet,

I baulked at the sight of her for a moment. Then remembered the woman outside the café. The widening pool of blood spreading like a crimson halo about her ruined head…

"Lisa." I went over to her.

She flinched away from me.

"I…I'm sorry. I didn't understand…"

Carefully, I climbed onto the bed and reached for her. My hand came to rest on her shoulder. Lisa's shoulder; that familiar shape and feel. This was Lisa. And yet…not Lisa.

She lifted her head to look at me. I could see no thought or emotion in her blank, alien face. Yet, I sensed her sadness and her terror.

I pulled her to myself. Every instinct cried out for me to push her away. Her head came to rest on my chest. The same weight as my Lisa's head. But the feel of it was *wrong* under my hand; smooth,

438

hairless, softer than it should be.

I forced myself to hold her. I forced myself to kiss the pulsing, alien skin of her denuded scalp. She curled in more tightly to me and in that moment, I understood that, somehow, she really was Lisa.

"Who are you?" I asked, at last. A stupid question because as far as I was aware, the marble-heads spoke no English. I wasn't sure what they spoke, to be honest. Whether the sound they made were words, or a result of telepathy or just a cry of shock or pain.

I let go and drew away, suddenly unable to bear it. The fact that her body felt so normal and familiar and yet she was so utterly alien was too much. She looked up at me from the bed and it was impossible to tell if she was hurt, angry or uncaring.

"I can't...," I said. "Lisa —" It even felt wrong to call her by that name. "I have to know who you are."

Nothing.

I needed to get away from her again, if only to go downstairs and make a coffee. I couldn't look at her anymore, or speak. My only concession to her feelings (if she had any) was to not flee from the room, but force myself to exit at a decent pace. Once on the landing, I felt *in*decent relief. What the hell was I supposed to do?

Downstairs, I went into the kitchen, filled and switched-on the kettle.

Lisa.

For the first time for years, I felt like crying. Men don't cry, but I wanted to as I sat at the dining room table and sipped black, unsweetened Nescafe. It was horrible, but I needed horrible. I needed its bitterness and scorching heat.

It was night now, not dark, but a shifting blood red. Houses were on fire. Sounds filtered through, sirens, shouts. The usual theme music for an apocalypse. This was the strangest world-ending I had ever seen. Not that I'd seen any, other than on television or at the cinema.

I drank horrible coffee and burned my mouth and didn't care.

I was tired and I couldn't think right now. I needed to sleep then make some plan in the morning. Although what that plan was, I had no idea. Perhaps there was some sort of government sanctuary, a refugee camp. Or the army were being called in to take control of the situation. Well, half the army. The other half would be marble-heads.

Armed and highly trained marble-heads.

Was there no end to this?

Then I heard glass break and suddenly I stopped thinking.

It sounded as if it was the front of the house. I was on my feet and into the hall. I was unarmed and alone. I heard voices in the living room. Christ. I rushed the stairs and charged the landing. The living room door crashed open just as I reached the top few steps. I glanced back to see a big character wielding an iron pipe. He was on the stairs. I made it to the landing and spun round, aware now of two other intruders who must have followed him in through the broken window. One was a woman, that was all I registered, because my immediate problem was now right in front of me, red-faced and half-mad by the look of him.

I kicked out.

I've never had one martial arts lesson in my life, but that kick was perfect. His face was level with my work boot. I felt the shock of impact. I felt things crunch and give way. Then I heard his yell and the awful percussion of a human body tumbling downstairs. Not only an enemy felled, but an obstacle that hindered his comrades' assault. I didn't stay to watch the struggling and confusion, but hurried to the bedroom and back to the creature that had once been my wife. She was still curled on the bed, where I'd left her. Expressionless she might be, but I knew fear when I saw it.

The light was on, which reminded me that despite Armageddon, the electricity and water and other utilities still appeared to be working perfectly. I was convinced, now, that it was the marble-heads who maintained our civilisation while its creators were trying to burn it down. A fine army of invaders, these creatures had turned out to be; unarmed, persecuted and functioning as the human beings they had once been, while the race they sought to subjugate set fire to things and ran riot.

On second thoughts, not such a bad plan after all.

Without a word to Lisa, I grabbed the dressing table from under the bedroom window and hauled it in a rough, clumsy panic over to the door. Bottles of perfume and pots of jewellery crashed to the floor. Talcum powder exploded in a sweet-smelling plume as a flower-decorated tub fell to its doom. I jammed the table against the door as tightly as I was able.

A moment later, something, or someone, crashed against the door from the other side. I saw the door shudder and the dressing table slide a few inches across the wooden floor. I grasped its front edge and prepared to hold it in place. The pounding and shouting grew worse. I sensed someone beside me, glanced round and saw that it was Lisa.

I smelled not only her fear, but a hint of her perfume. An odd mix that confused me. I was repulsed and afraid of her, yet she *was* Lisa.

The pounding intensified. I was scared now. It was a level of fear I had never experienced before. It was intense and disorientating. It turned the real unreal. It sang through my head in great pulses of blood with each labouring heartbeat. I was about to die, yet my mind denied it. Not now, or here. I was supposed to be alive.

We couldn't hold them back for much longer. They were about to break in and when they did, there would be Hell to pay. I couldn't imagine the horror of their violence. Oh, I was in a pub fight or two in my younger days and I'm not afraid of a scrap, but this was different. This was desperate, hate and terror-driven violence that wouldn't be sated by a black-eye or bleeding nose. This violence demanded serious injury and even death.

The pounding rose to a crescendo. The dressing table bucked like an unbroken horse at a rodeo. The bottles and jars that had survived my panicked drag across the room, bounced onto the floor and the air was soon thick with a cloying scent of perfume and spilled creams and lotions. I strained into a final effort. Lisa too. She trembled, her formless, alien head lowered.

Wood cracked. Paint and splinters burst from a wound in the door.

This was it.

The end.

A horrible, painful, brutal end.

It stopped.

There were whispers. I waited, panting hard. Lisa uttered a soft *Oooo*. Then came the sound of people scuttling downstairs. They sounded excited. I'm sure I heard one of them laugh.

Gingerly, I withdrew from the dressing table and stepped back. If they had played the old-pretend-to-retreat-then-turn-back manoeuvre, we were done for. Lisa stayed where she was, hunched over the dressing table, ready to throw her weight back into the battle if necessary.

We waited. The table didn't move. There was no surprise attack.

I wanted to say something comforting to the being who dressed, smelled and acted like my wife, but I didn't know what to say to her. I didn't know if she even understood me. So, we stood there, pointlessly staring at the battered dressing table and the fractured door beyond.

I began to wonder if our attackers had given up and moved on. I allowed myself a little hope.

Until I smelled smoke.

Far from unusual today, but this was too strong and pungent to be from outside. This smoke-smell had an urgency about it. This smoke was close. Intimate.

No, surely not –

The smell intensified.

"Get back," I shouted. "Get away from the door."

Lisa did as I asked. The smell was growing stronger by the second.

I grabbed a dressing gown and put it over my head, with no idea if it would protect me, then wrenched the table back a few feet and carefully opened the door. I saw no flames, but the landing was misted by a thick haze.

There were crackling sounds. A rise in temperature. Fire was eating at my home. *Our* home. I moved out onto the landing. The smoke burned my throat and stung my eyes. I arrived at the top of the stairs and peered down to see the unguarded front door. Still no sign of any flames, but I knew that it was only a matter of time.

"Lisa," I called back into the bedroom. "We can get out if we're quick."

God knew what waited for us outside, but we couldn't stay in here. I slumped against the wall and crouched down onto my haunches. Weren't you supposed to stay near the floor? I discarded the dressing gown, which had become an encumbrance. It was getting hard to breathe. It was getting hard to see, as well.

Lisa appeared, a vague shape that crawled out of the fire-scented fog on her hands and knees. I set off down the stairs, crawling on my belly over the steps. The edges of the treads punched and burned my already sore stomach. The keeping-close-to-the-floor advice didn't seem to make much difference. The smoke was a black oily blanket that clogged my nose and scoured my eyes. I trusted that Lisa was behind me. I couldn't turn around to check. I had to keep moving.

There was a loud bang, somewhere ahead of me. Light flared into the gloom. And heat, brutal, skin-blistering heat that ripped animal terror out of my soul.

Fire.

Bringer of destruction and unspeakable pain. I saw that the living room door had been replaced by a twisting dance of bright orange flame. I scrambled to my feet, tried to hold my breath and threw myself downwards in a half tumble. I hit the front door, pushed myself back and wrestled with the handle, all the while, trying to ignore the searing heat that roiled out of the living room to my left. Other things burned now as the flames groped their way into the hallway.

The handle was hot. It burned my hand. I didn't care. The animal had taken over, screaming at me to get out.

I had to breathe.

One, big deep breath; that was all I wanted.

I felt my skin blister. I could barely see. There was nothing but darkness and flickering, restless light. I felt a body fall against my back. I felt a hand claw at me. I felt myself fade and burn. There was pain. There was suffocation.

Then the door opened and I staggered back, momentarily

throwing whoever it was behind me into a tangle of arms and feet. I didn't care. It was self at that moment. Me. My lungs. My skin. My life.

Out.

Where there was oxygen. I staggered down the short path and into the road. I was outside. I was in pain from the scorching flames. I was gasping for breath and wanting to vomit my lungs onto the tarmac.

I stood, doubled over, hands on knees, panting hard.

Lisa.

She, the alien, was there, a few yards to my right. On her knees.

Behind us, the house burned. I heard crashing noises and glass shatter. It didn't matter. We were alive. We were breathing and the air held currents of coolness that snaked through the heat.

A nearby garden fence collapsed. figures poured into the night-dark, smoke-fogged street. They were splashed orange by the fire. I saw their vile, hate-torn faces. I saw the weapons they carried, lengths of pipe, knives, lengths of wood. I saw old and young, men and women, smartly dressed and scruffy.

They formed an arc around us. We'd been smoked out. The ambush had been sprung.

I wanted them to get on with it. I was finished and frightened and broken.

Nothing happened. I could see their desire to launch themselves at us. I could see their loathing and fear, but there was hesitation. These were ordinary people, unused to violence. Setting fire to a house was impersonal. You're not looking anyone in the eye.

I had the advantage. Attack is the best defence.

I yelled at Lisa to get away then charged the mob. It felt like a good idea at the time. As I slammed into a man in a roll-neck jumper, I felt an explosion of pain erupt through my side and chest. An iron bar, wielded by a teenage girl with bunches that looked like Micky Mouse ears. Gasping for breath, I collapsed into a hell of kicking and pounding. I tried to fold myself into a protective foetus-curl. They were going to kill me. It hurt. Christ, how it hurt. Worse, they must be doing this to Lisa. God, I tried to save her. I tried –

The beating eased. The feet shuffled and stumbled out of my line of vision. Did they think I was dead? Were they gripped by a sudden crisis of conscience? Or had they stepped aside to allow my executioner access? What was it to be? Blunt instrument to the head? Cut throat? A bullet?

A sound filtered into the odd and sudden silence.

That choir sound I had heard on the bus. From close, Lisa perhaps, and answered from all around and from the far distance. The sound grew in volume. It drew goose bumps from my aching, bruised flesh. It was so plaintive it almost made me cry.

I struggled up onto my knees and saw, in the shifting orange light, the humans exchange uncertain glances. Perhaps this was the signal. The final hammer blow.

Lisa stepped forward and the mob cowered back. I noted that she carried something, which she lifted to her face. It was her skin-and-hair human mask. She reached up and drew it over her marbled scalp. There was no tugging or adjustments. The mask fitted smoothly and perfectly.

Lisa was back.

Yet not Lisa.

The mob looked about them and suddenly there were only humans. Confusion rippled outwards and broke the mob apart. Some of its members shambled off. Many simply stood, stripped of purpose and unable to find an enemy.

Or friend.

*

I didn't rush into the arms of my wife because I no longer knew if she was my wife. I might go to her, eventually, but not yet. Instead, I wandered away, as confused as those who had tried to kill us a moment ago. Burned, bruised and aching, I wandered into the shattered, smoke-choked streets of the town and stared fearfully at everyone I passed, just as they stared fearfully back at me.

Buildings and vehicles still burn. The dead and wounded still lay where they fell. They are the only ones whose identities we can be sure of. You see, we can no longer tell who are our own and who are strangers. The world stands still and it's doubtful that it will ever restart.

~

Terry Grimwood is an electrician, he teaches, sings (after a fashion), plays the harmonica, acts, Directs and sometimes writes. Terry is a jack -of-all-trades and master of...well he will let you decide for yourself. Author of numerous short stories, a handful of novellas and a few novels, Terry also edits, runs theEXAGGERATEDpress and writes occasional book reviews on his Exaggerated Review *site. His default position is horror and science fiction, but he has dabbled with thrillers, romance and the non-genre. He also writes non-fiction and has co-written a number of engineering and electrical text books. He is thrilled to have a story in* Strange Days.

WOMEN'S WORLD
Joseph Cusumano

I'm told that the prison population is about 1% of what it used to be. Gun sales have fallen precipitously, and the last school shooting was over 30 years ago. With women now comprising nearly all of the population, violent crime is rare and the death penalty isn't an issue. Military spending plummeted as extreme nationalism faded across the globe. As a result, we've been able to redirect resources so that everyone has a place to live, enough to eat, and access to medical care. And because tissue culture technology allows us to grow meat in incubators, the barbaric practice of animal slaughter will soon cease altogether.

Best of all, we aren't afraid anymore. Only the men are afraid; they're largely responsible for their own imminent extinction. In addition to their violent tendencies, they created the near catastrophic environmental factors which brought about The Change, heralded by the first asexual birth. We've long observed parthenogenic or asexual reproduction in animals, including vertebrates such as snakes, amphibians, fish, reptiles, and birds. But when an 18 year old high school virgin in Pennsylvania gave birth to a healthy baby girl on October 7, 2031, a new era began. No one believed her at first, but she insisted that she had neither engaged in sex with a male nor been artificially inseminated. Although the infant was not an actual clone of her mother, genetic testing confirmed that the child's cells contained only her mother's genes. She had no father. The decline in male births is not a mystery. When a woman becomes pregnant asexually, her child doesn't inherit a Y chromosome.

Christian fundamentalists never claimed that this virgin birth was the long-prophesied 2nd coming of Christ; they couldn't imagine Christ returning as a woman. But as it turned out, we women have become our own saviors; we don't need men to give birth. And for reasons not completely understood — one theory posits intracellular microplastics as endocrine disruptors — we've shed our desire for men. Of course there are exceptions in any biological paradigm, and I suspect that Dr. Kessel is one of them. I think she's taken up a physical relationship with a man, and it will be her undoing. I'm afraid for her.

*

"Lydia! So good to see you," Ms. Dowling greeted me. "Have a seat. Can I pour you some coffee? I just made some so it would be fresh when you arrived."

"Yes, Ms. Dowling," I replied. "Coffee sounds great." I glanced around her office and marveled at the clutter. Amazing that she can function in all this chaos.

"Please, call me Jane," she said. Ms. Dowling is at least 20 years my senior, I don't find her attractive, and she's still coming on to me. For my daughter Sara's sake, I try to stay on Dowling's good side while keeping her at arm's length.

She poured coffee for me, remembering to add a little cream and sugar, and asked about my family. I told her that all of us were fine, including Sara, who was applying to Harvard with Dowling's assurance that it would be taken care of.

I had come to her office in the federal building to make my monthly report on Dr. Jack Lindeman, the director of quality control at the facility where we grow meat for human consumption. All men in positions of responsibility are kept under surveillance for any indication of antisocial behavior. Lindeman is aware of this, so I keep a low profile among the other fifty-odd women working there.

"Lydia," Ms. Dowling said, "last month you reported that a variety of new supplies, reagents and equipment had been delivered to the facility. Has that continued?"

"Yes, ma'am. And I've discovered what the equipment is." Ms. Dowling prepared to take notes on her electronic assistant. "One piece is a mass spectrometer, which is used to identify the chemical structure of a compound. There is also a chromatograph. It can separate different compounds within a mixture. I thought these were odd acquisitions because we've been able to meet our federal production quotas at the facility for years without a chromatograph or a spectrometer."

448

"Did you ask what the new equipment was for?"

"I try to stay off Dr. Lindeman's radar, but I did ask our director, Dr. Kessel. She said they were trying to devise new growth factors to bolster meat production without increasing the incidence of tumor development."

"What do you think of her explanation?"

"I'm puzzled. We don't really need to increase the potency of our growth factors; we can boost meat production simply by adding more incubators. You may recall that one of my assignments at the facility is to identify incubators in which muscle tumors have developed and sterilize them. About 2 - 3% of the batches contain tumors, and they're somewhat difficult to detect and eliminate. Increasing the potency of the growth factors could increase the incidence of tumor development."

"So you think the two of them have other plans for the new equipment?"

"Possibly," I replied. "But I can't confirm it yet."

Ms. Dowling thought about this for a while and then asked an unrelated question. "Do you think there's anything amorous going on between Kessel and Lindeman?" I had previously reported that the two of them seemed to enjoy each other's company, but her question still caught me off-guard.

I hesitated, then lied. "No, ma'am. Nothing that I can see." A truthful response would have placed them squarely in the crosshairs, something I'm reluctant to do. In addition, I'm not at all confident about the nature of their relationship. There have only been subtle signs of anything illicit between them. How close they stand to each other, the tone of voice they use when conversing, little things like that. Men caught in love affairs with women are charged with rape and sent to concentration camps. Women undergo re-education. A second offense lands them in prison.

When I was in my late teens, I came across a photograph on the dark web that showed a man and woman having sex. He was standing behind and up against her while she leaned forward. It was shocking but I had trouble taking my eyes off it. I never told anyone what I'd seen, but the image was burned into my brain. If

Lindeman and Kessel are having a relationship like this, I have an obligation to report them.

*

My daughter Sara was in a terrible mood when I got home from work today. When I asked her what had happened, she shoved a letter into my face. The letterhead indicated it was from Harvard, and my heart sank as I read it. Sara had been rejected for the incoming class. It was a real gut punch.

"You told me I was a shoo-in!" she said.

"Sara, I thought you were. My contact is a long-time friend of the Director of Admissions, and she assured me you would be admitted."

"Well, it didn't happen!"

"I'm so sorry. I did everything possible." I resumed reading the letter looking for any clues as to why Sara hadn't been accepted, but there were no specifics. Only that *applications for the fall semester were at a record high* and *we didn't have space for many well qualified students*.

Crushed by the news, I dropped onto a chair in our kitchen. Had Jane Dowling been lying to me about her relationship with the Director of Admissions? I didn't think so. Did Dowling initially recommend Sara and then make a retraction? Why would she do that? I had detected the arrival of new equipment and discerned its functions, kept tabs on Drs. Kessel and Lindeman, recently reporting that I'd seen them drawing each other's blood, and never missed a monthly meeting at the federal building. Could she be angry at me for rebuffing her advances? Or is it that I haven't disclosed a possible illicit relationship between the two directors at our facility? Ms. Dowling would have no way of knowing this.

Or does she? What if Dowling has a second informant working at the facility, another woman who has reported that Kessel and Lindeman have a romantic interest in each other? My credibility as a reliable informant would be tarnished, and it might explain why Dowling had not helped Sara get into Harvard. There's no way to know unless Dowling comes right out and accuses me of negligence. Or worse, complicity.

*

Sara is in her first year at Oberlin, studying governmental administration, and I think she made a great choice. The federal government has nationalized all the major industries and is far and away the largest employer. We still have some small privately owned family businesses, what used to be called mom-and-pop operations, although pop is out of the picture.

Yesterday, I had my monthly meeting with Ms. Dowling, and I had several things to tell her. One of the young women at my facility took her own life. I didn't know Ellie all that well, but she appeared to be a loner. She worked in the division that started the meat cultures from living biopsy tissue, and our paths rarely crossed. When Ms. Dowling asked if Ellie might have been a closet heterosexual, I could only say that I didn't know. Suicides in that group are not uncommon.

I next reported that the incidence of tumors sprouting in the meat cultures had increased somewhat. Ms. Dowling, who is not a scientist, asked what would happen if some tumor tissue escaped my scrutiny and made its way into the final product we ship out. I told her several factors should preclude serious harm. When the meat leaves our facility, all the cells, normal or cancerous, are dead. Secondly, the meat will be cooked before anyone consumes it; proteins and DNA are denatured by heat. Lastly, any intact tumor cells in poorly cooked meat should be disrupted by stomach acid and pancreatic enzymes. That seemed to reassure her, but she then asked why the tumors were becoming more common in the incubated meat cultures.

Of course I had wondered about this too. The increase was not all that much, and some variation is expected from month to month. Maybe this will be a one month aberration and nothing more. But I stuck around late one night and got past the safeguards on Dr. Kessel's files. I was looking to see if she and Dr. Lindeman had strengthened the stimulatory effects of the growth factors we add to the nutrient broth, but a file labeled *Endocrine Disruptors* immediately caught my attention. I couldn't understand all of it, but I suspect they're using the new equipment to identify altered hormonal pathways responsible for asexual birth and the precipitous decline of heterosexuality. But even if Kessel and

Lindeman identified the specific changes which have occurred in our endocrine systems and devised ways to reverse them, they would never be allowed to disseminate their findings, let alone implement them. They probably believe it's the right thing to do, but they're on a fool's errand. The vast majority of women have no interest in returning to the past. This society of ours is no utopia, but it's far better than living with the violence and intimidation which past generations endured.

I waited to the end of my meeting with Ms. Dowling to report something that I expected would provoke her, and it certainly did. Dr. Kessel is pregnant.

*

A staggering amount of resources have been diverted over the last decade into moving our larger coastal cities inland. The buildings and infrastructure in the old locations were abandoned. New cities, unchanged in name and governance, were rebuilt inland. It's not just the melting of the polar icecaps; we get a lot more rain. In spite of massive changes in the way we produce electricity, it's still getting warmer. Warmer air holds more moisture. The added moisture gets returned to the ground as rain and then the cycle starts over. Flooding in nearly all regions of the country remains a big problem. We only have three seasons now. Summers last eight or nine months; winter is a luxury of the past. The bugs and the humidity are awful. We run the air conditioning at full blast from early March to late November.

The impact of microplastics remains controversial. Just as in the early stages of global warming, some reputable scientists are deniers. They say it's not really an issue even when the particles are intracellular, claiming that the plastics are inert and that our cells can handle the load they currently carry without significant disruption. They also point to the presence of microplastics in urine as proof that the human body is capable of disposing of them. Most importantly, they emphasize, we're giving birth to perfectly healthy babies. All girls of course.

Which brings me to Dr. Kessel. To be more precise, the gender of her fetus. Dr. Kessel and I were going over the tumor statistics one morning when Mattie, a rather androgynous middle aged

452

woman who works in human resources, approached us. She asked Dr. Kessel when she would like to begin her maternity leave. I could see this flustered Dr. Kessel, who finally stammered, "I'm … not sure."

"Well, what did they tell you when you had your ultrasound?" Mattie asked.

"I haven't had an ultrasound yet," Dr. Kessel said, her voice a little wary.

"You have one scheduled?"

"Well, no. But I'll do that soon."

"Okay, great. Please give me a date as soon as possible." Mattie smiled at both of us and headed back to her department. I could see that Dr. Kessel could use a little comforting but I didn't know what to say.

*

It wasn't until later that evening that I started putting things together. Lindeman, who has always been very kind and solicitous to Kessel, is even more so lately. What if he's the baby's father? He's dark-haired with brown eyes. Kessel is fair and blond with blue eyes. If the baby doesn't come out looking a lot like her mother, there could be trouble. Hell to pay if the baby is a boy.

Lindeman and Kessel have no way of knowing if her pregnancy is a result of their coupling or if it's a parthenogenic conception. I'm sure that's why Kessel hasn't had an ultrasound. She's not willing to take the chance that the fetus could be discovered to be male. They must be suffering an agony of worry. I understand what they're going through and wish there was some way to help them

*

Finally, a little good news. For reasons I can't fathom, Dr. Kessel went for an ultrasound, and she's going to have a healthy baby girl. Her maternity leave will begin in six weeks. I'm arranging a baby shower for her which will include family, friends and some coworkers. She's not completely out of danger, but at least she's carrying a girl. I'm keeping my fingers crossed that the baby will be fair and blonde like her mother.

In spite of the news, Ms. Dowling keeps pressing me for more information about Kessel and Lindeman. I've continued to shield them, stating that they have nothing more than a professional relationship. It's risky for me to do this, especially since Lindeman might be under the eye of a second observer. But I can't bring myself to accuse them of anything. Even were I to catch them in a passionate embrace, I would probably remain silent. We've all been raised in a society that regards heterosexuality as an abomination. But as I've had the opportunity to observe for some time now, it can be gentle, kind, and loving. Kessel and Lindeman are not hurting anyone, and it must be awful to have to hide their affection while everyone else can love freely and openly.

Fortunately, the increased incidence of tumor formation in the meat incubators has not persisted. What I had previously observed appears to be only a short-lived aberration. The facility continues to provide fresh, healthful meat for our dinner tables.

Another bit of good news: Sara is happy at Oberlin, doing well academically and has lots of friends. She sent me photos of a pretty girl named Allison who I suspect is her first real love. I'm very happy for Sara, but it's not fun coming home to an empty apartment after having her with me every day for 18 years. It's been a long time since I had a lover of my own.

*

"Do you call her Chrissy?" someone asked.

"No, just Chris," Dr. Kessel answered. There were so many of my coworkers surrounding her that I could barely see the new arrival. But after a few moments, I got a closer look. Chris was angelic; she melted my heart. But my delight was quickly tempered with concern. Chris had brown eyes and light brown hair; her skin looked a little darker than her mother's. I'm not sure if Dr. Kessel saw something cross my face, but I gave her a reassuring smile and told her how lucky she was.

I was a little surprised that she brought the baby in for everyone to see. She probably decided it would seem odd if she didn't. Everyone here has certainly been looking forward to greeting the new arrival. But if I noticed that Chris was not a fair, blue-eyed blonde, someone else might too.

Still unsure if Dr. Lindeman has been under scrutiny by a

second observer, I began watching the reactions of my coworkers as they came for a close look at Chris. No one seemed concerned until Mattie approached. At first, she was all smiles and appeared genuinely delighted that Dr. Kessel had brought her baby in. But when she focused her attention on Chris, her smile vanished. It was only for a moment, but it was unmistakable. I saw Dr. Kessel hold Chris a little closer to her chest; she must have noticed too. When everyone began to drift back to their work areas, Dr. Kessel departed with Chris. She wasn't smiling.

*

"I'm going to need your help," Mattie said to me. I was about to seed an incubator when she interrupted me. No one was within earshot.

"With what?" I asked.

"Dowling wants me to look at Dr. Kessel's files, but they're protected and I can't get in. Dowling told me to ask for your help. She says you know a lot about cybersecurity." Finally, confirmation that Mattie *was* a second observer! Of course I had to pretend I never suspected.

When I asked why she wanted to see the files, Mattie filled me in on what she had been up to. "Kessel's baby doesn't look enough like Kessel to suit me. So I did a little investigating. That ultrasound she told us about? It was a complete fabrication. She never had it; I checked every hospital and imaging center within a 50 mile radius."

I hadn't expected that, but it made sense. At the time, Dr. Kessel couldn't have known if the baby was male or female. Mattie went on to tell me that she had wondered if the baby was actually a Christopher dressed as a Christine. Her suspicion reached near-certainty when she discovered that Chris was delivered at home by a midwife who might have been willing to falsify the birth documents. This had never crossed my mind, but Mattie said that when authorities came to Dr. Kessel's home to examine the baby and take mouth swabs from both of them, she was proven wrong. Not only was the baby a girl, she had only her mother's DNA. Apparently, Dr. Kessel's genome also includes genes for darker hair, eyes and skin.

But Dowling and Mattie couldn't let things go, and I wanted to kick myself for telling Dowling that the chromatograph and mass spectrometer weren't really necessary to meet our production quotas. Dr. Kessel's files were to be examined within the week. It only took me a moment to decide that, if possible, I would protect Kessel and Lindeman even if they were subverting the established order.

*

Returning that evening after dark, I entered the facility and headed straight to Dr. Kessel's office. At her desk, I quickly broke through the security system and located the file on endocrine disruptors. After downloading the file onto my own microstorage device, I began to delete it from Dr. Kessel's system so it could not be discovered when Mattie and I came looking in a few days. Later on, I would give the file back to Kessel or Lindeman.

Just as the task was completed, I heard voices in the hallway leading to Dr. Kessel's office. My heart pounding, I slipped the small storage device into the flowerpot on Dr. Kessel's desk. A moment later, the office was flooded with light.

"Hold it right there! You're under arrest." I turned and saw Dowling standing in the doorway with two police officers right behind her. I was led away in handcuffs. They really didn't need to do that.

*

I had been under suspicion and fallen into a trap. Ms. Dowling and Mattie were way ahead of me, already aware of what was in Kessel's endocrine file and intent only in confirming my disloyalty. I stupidly obliged them and have been sent to prison. Arrogant of me to think they wouldn't have gotten access to the files without my help.

Dr. Kessel must be in a different prison because I've been here long enough to have seen her and haven't. None of the other inmates know of her. Lindeman is surely in a men's prison. Baby Chris will have been taken into the custody of the state; she'll be put up for adoption.

My prison sentence is relatively mild, only four years. That's because they never found the device onto which I had downloaded

Kessel's endocrine file. Had they found it on me, my punishment would have been considerably more severe. Maybe the device will be discovered by someone who will preserve it until the time is right. Nothing resists change indefinitely; someday we may need men again. If and when that time comes, I hope they aren't gone forever.

My re-education process has begun in earnest. This includes group and individual sessions. When I get out, they'll never let me return to my former job or work in any industry that requires a flawless record of conformity. I'll have to be retrained for a different type of work, but the state will pay for it. Fortunately, I'm a quick study and will eventually land on my feet. Everything is going to be just fine. Unless Dowling orders a mouth swab on Sara and me.

~

Joseph Cusumano is a physician living in St. Louis, Missouri, USA. When not writing, he enjoys designing, flying, and crashing radio controlled airplanes. His writing has been published by Crimson Streets, Pseudopod, Mystery Weekly, Silver Pen, Disturbed Digest, Flash Fiction Press, Scarlet Leaf Review, Heater, Agents and Spies *(a Flame Tree anthology),* Bards and Sages, Bewildering Stories, All World's Wayfarer, Soteira Press *and* Litmag *(University of Missouri).*

SPRITE
Andrew Darlington

Sirens. Red light pulsing.

Consumers glance warily across at each other.

We're in Costas, at the Services where the A1 crosses the M62. Simon and me, in mid-coffee. Regular white Americanos. When the siren wails, and the lights begin.

No-one seems quite sure what's going on. Then the staff are opening emergency doors and ushering people out. I scoop up my honey-oat biscuit, take a last slurp of my coffee, and we slouch up and out, smiling quizzically. He's tall and rangy, smiling in slow amusement. Now we are outside, standing around in small awkward groups on the Car Park perimeter. Clouds over the sun. My fingers move along the barrier rail. It is painted white, and a little rough to the touch. There's a pocket of corrosion beneath the cross-weld, where rust crumbles in flakes, particles stickle sharp up against the heel of my thumb.

I frame my fingers into a square, and squint through as though view-finding for a photo, and mentally click, storing the image away for future reference. "Probably burnt waffles in the kitchen set off the smoke-alarm?" I suggest.

"I remember the time you'd see a package abandoned on a train seat and you'd go 'I'll have that'!" says Simon, as he mimes reaching across to furtively seize lost property.

It's at that moment the Services explode outwards in blossoms of boiling flame. The heat impact blasts us into a protective crouch. Fragments of glass and a shrapnel of metal snipes with lethal intent. The very fabric of space-time trembles and buckles, slows and slithers into viscid tide, I see people time-frozen into its ripples as shockwaves radiate outwards. The very molecules of dust in its expanding roar are suspended. Memories in my head come apart in shimmers of lost time.

"Thank you, Melissa" I breathe low.

*

458

The time-ships arrive fifty years into the future, a fleet of them investigating the great extinction catastrophe. But, being time-ships, some of them spill further back, into the present, in order to seek out and glimpse pre-disaster symptoms. Because of their temporal fluidity they appear only as shimmering distortions that glide on the air. Most people in the town-centre Mall are too busy to even notice their fleeting presence. But I see them.

I take notes and compile lists in order to assist their research. I take mind-photographs that they can access and reference when they so choose. It's the only rational thing to do.

*

I am ten years old, and I write lists. That's what I do.

I start this list with "Melissa has pixie-ears".

Then I cross it out. That is a secret never to be told.

I like to touch things. That's what I do. Walking down twisting and twining Long Lane I touch the blades of grass. I touch the ripe juicy blackberry fruits on the brambles. I touch the nettles and savour the sweet stinging pain. I touch the water in the stream so softly I scarcely make a ripple. I touch the smooth moist sheen of the frog before it lollops back into the weed. And I touch Melissa's ears. They are warm velvet.

I watch the girls as they jump-rope to the skipping rhyme, "my Mother said, I never should, play with the gypsies in the wood". The gypsies appear overnight in their ornate caravans. Strewn beneath the overhanging elderberry and lilac trees along Long Lane, all the way to the hunchback bridge. I touch the big green painted wheels. I touch the aroma of cooking that hangs on the air. The tethered horses watch me warily as I go by. I touch their rough softness. They lick my hand, slurping me with their big rough wetness.

Long Lane goes all the way to the horizon and beyond. Melissa lives beside the bridge, in a hidden cottage by the stream. This is true, listen… she was my only real friend. And she was magical. When we walk side by side I get tongue-tied and clumsy. I say stupid things. But that makes her laugh in the way that small bells tinkle. And I love the way she laughs. We hold hands and spin each other faster and faster until our heads spin and we fall back onto the moist grass laughing as the sky and the world keeps spinning and swirling in giddy circles. It feels as though my eyes are twisting. Can eyes twist? Can a mind tremble? Or maybe it's more like watching the world through rippling water. Time slows and comes to a stop when we are together, so we have longer to play. She can do that. She has that ability.

Everything spins around something. Electrons around a neutron. The moon around the sun. The sun around the galaxy. Galaxies around each other. Me, around Melissa. Always.

"Frame yourself" says Mam. "You're living in your own little dream-world. Snap out of it. You've been playing with Melissa again, haven't you? That girl is no good for you. There's something not quite right about her. Why can't you play with some of the local boys instead? Why her?"

Sometimes words are sour fruit in your mouth. I try to do as she says. I don't see Melissa for a week. I ramble across Witty's field with Graham and Ian, riding pretend horses. We reach a point further down the stream, where we scramble down the embankment to flick stones into the swirling current. There are water-boatmen that scull across the surface on stickly legs. Listen to that. Listen to the silence. A silence you can touch. A clean silence, a drowsy beetle-drone sleepy-insect silence. A thousand bug-eyes watch us from the grass. I place that on a new list.

"Melissa? She's bad news. Her Mam's a mardy witch," says Graham. "Her Dad was Gypsy Dave who comes in the night, and vanishes in the daylight."

"That's not true. You're making it up," I protest, as defiantly as I can.

"They say she's the child of sin. She's heathen-born," adds Ian.

"I heard me Mam talking. She was saying as how Mrs Exeter couldn't have no baby, and that made her sad. So she goes to Melissa's cottage, all secret-like, and her Mam does some witchy pagan magic. I don't know what. Some spooky things with wild berries and herbs. A fox's skull. Some secret spells. And then, afterwards, she has a baby. I don't know. I'm not saying. But that's what I heard."

"Bollocks." I'm scared to argue back. Ian has copies of 'Tall

Tales Of The Spaceways' that he sometimes lets me read. And no-one likes Melissa. Except me.

There's a big rusty pipe that comes out the embankment in a spray of nettles and dock leaves. It extends out over the stream on a set of struts, to tunnel into the embankment on the far side. From there it's easy to imagine how it leads underground to Mr Pidd's ramshackle garage, where he repairs cars and broken-down farm machinery. There's a petrol pump outside the garage, just beneath the corrugated awning. He wears a greasy flat-cap with a thin ciggy-stub behind his ear, and he has gas-lights in his office and workshop. They give a warm glow that illuminates the grubby windows as evening draws in.

"Time for us teas," grins Graham. He likes to eat. He thinks there'll be sausages.

We ignore the rusted barbed-war spikes intended to discourage trespass, and climb up onto the fat pipe. There's a strong smell of gas. So rich you can touch it. There's a fissure where sections of pipe come together, where the gas leaks out. We inch like tightrope-walkers across the pipe, teetering from this side of the stream to the other. My nerves at work. Who knew?

When I get home I sit at the table and start a new list. Days without Melissa. One, two, three... all the way to five. Can it be true, that her Mam's a witch? That she believes in lunar months, tides and new moons. Melissa has pixie-ears, which she hides behind her long black hair. She wears a floppy knitted hat too, even when it's warm. Was her Dad really Gypsy Dave, who comes in the night? The Troll who lives in darkness beneath the hunchback bridge?

There are gypsies down Long Lane, beneath the white overhanging elderberry and lilac hedgerows. They weren't there yesterday, but they're here today. Romany, Diddycoy, Travellers who move from place to place, their homes on wheels. Gypos, all the way back to ancient Egypt. The swarthy men have tousled black hair and gold earrings. The women wear headscarves. Little naked children with supernaturally bright eyes peer out from where they hide behind the big carved caravan wheels. Skinny mongrels strain to the limits of fraying strings tied to those same wheels. Some housewives hide, crouch down beneath window-level when the women come house-to-house selling wood-carved clothes pegs from the depths of their wicker-baskets. They leave tinker's marks on gateposts. If you don't buy, they utter a gypsies curse. And no-one wants a gypsies curse. They turn milk sour in your scullery, cause cows to go dry, chickens to get egg-bound, and make pregnancies spontaneously miscarry.

Me and Graham pass their caravans on our way to school. A little way further down the lane there's a row of houses. On the step outside of no.10 there's a bottle of milk. He dares me. So I take it, and we run off sniggering. I depress the silver-foil cap in, and pries it off. We slurp the thick cream layer from the top, shoving the bottle back to each other as we gulp it down. They'll blame the gypsies. Of course they will. We sling the drained bottle into the stream where it floats and bobs its way down between weed and reeds.

Looking up, I can see Melissa's cottage on the far side of the hunchback bridge. I wonder if she's inside. I miss seeing her. She's bright and sharp in ways that Ian and Graham are dull and grubby. Ian bites his nails down until they bleed. Graham likes to pull his shorts down and wave his tassel at us. I see her in school, and we smile in a nervy awkward way. I like her smile.

On Sunday Mr Turnbull stands up in church to denounce the gypsies, and their familiars, who impose themselves on our decent god-fearing community. Someone should do something about them. Drive them away. Close down their sites so they can never return.

I know who he means. I'm frightened for Melissa.

*

The world is not a joined-up place.

Simian beast-brains lurk in the undermind, to erode away at logic and reason. We can go high. Yet more often we go lower. People see what's happening, then run and hide in soft illusions of safer yesterdays. Attack those who threaten the hive-mind of conformity. People hurt and maim each other over minor doctrinal details of pretend deities. As a species, we should have grown out of it by now. Yet here we are, in the twenty-first

462

century, blowing each other up in medieval conflicts.

And the others, the outsiders, the beings on the fringe of knowing, they watch us destroy each other so they can inherit the world once we're gone. I know they're there. I've seen the ripples they leave in their wake. This is far too unbelievable a story for me to tell. But I have to tell it somehow, to someone. So I'm doing it here in the Sci-Fi zone. Maybe you – the reader, will understand. Maybe you will see beneath the surface of things, and see what I see?

*

I am ten years old. I think I've always been ten years old.

This is true, listen… it was Miss Jackson's class. She's drawing earthworm diagrams in chalk on the blackboard. We sit at our desks and fidget. There are coils of worms in a jam-jar on Miss Jackson's table. There are books on the shelf behind her. I've read some of them, Rosemary Sutcliff and Henry Treece. There are paintings on the wall. We do artwork on Friday afternoons. Sometimes I draw ships, Roman triremes or Viking dragonships. I gaze out the window across the playground to the fields and trees beyond. I can see the souls of all the dead cows that ever grazed the grass in that field, and the jackdaws circling the wall, who peck eyeballs out of eye-sockets.

Miss Jackson has three scalpels. She unscrews the jam-jar, and uses tweezers to extract three wiggly earthworms, placing them on three white saucers on the table, beside the three scalpels. Then she tells three of us, Ian, Paul… and Melissa, to come forward.

"No, I don't want to," says Melissa. "I don't want to cut them."

"Don't be silly," snaps Miss Jackson impatiently. "They're only worms."

Melissa sits tight. I want to help. I want to get up in her place. But it's not necessary.

There's a pause. Then Graham yells, and starts to his feet. Something wet and wriggly on his bare leg. He flicks the worm away. One girl screams, then another. They leap to their feet, others jump up onto their desks. There are earthworms. Ten. A dozen. Twenty. Swarms of them in a wriggling tide slithering across the floor, like a platter of dropped spaghetti, twining up the chair and desk legs, squidging beneath panicky children's feet. Shoes slick with mashed worm goo.

Miss Jackson strides down between the aisles of desks brandishing her ruler, then backs off. "Come here children, in orderly fashion…" opening the classroom door, ushering us out into the corridor. But in the rush Miss Jackson's table gets shoved hard, it tipples over backwards, the jam-jar smashes, the worms wriggle free.

Only Melissa is smiling. She knows.

*

Sprites. Faeries. They appear only as shimmering distortions that glide on the air, due to their psychic fluidity. They create mushroom circles in glades beneath the trees, gateways to enchanted Devic realms, into the Wobbly Worlds that lie at the interstices between dimensions. Their circles resemble the stone sites the Druids made. I research them. Arthur Conan Doyle knew the Cottingley Fairies were real; he'd seen the photographs taken by the girls beside the beck falls. Mam knew, as she tucks us in at night, singing a creepy song about: "up the airy mountain, down the rushy glen, we daren't go a-hunting, for fear of little men". She knew to fear those wee folk who watch us from behind haunted trees in Arthur Rackham prints. I research how, in 1895, in remote Tipperary, Michael Cleary and the villagers of Ballyvadlea ritually murder his wife, Bridget, to free her of fairy ensorcellment, burn her until her skin melts, beat her, deluge her in urine. The children know as they recite the skipping-rhyme: "are you a witch? Are you a fairy? Are you the wife of Michael Cleary?" as the skipping rope goes whip-whip-whip.

I compile these lists. Melissa has pixie-ears.

*

There's a fight in 'The Cross Keys', which spills out into the car-park. I hear the sounds from my bedroom. I go to the window. I can see.

Later it seems there were three gypsy men who come into the barroom. And some of the villagers object to their presence. They start making taunting accusations. There's been thieving, milk-bottles disappearing from front doorsteps. It gets violent. I only learn about this later on. I can see across the moonlight field. The pub is next to the schoolhouse. The pub-sign lit by the streetlight around which bats flit. I can see figures in the car-park. Mr Turnbull is there, gesticulating wildly, urging them on. They're angry. An angry mob. They're milling about and yelling, although I can't hear what they're saying. They start to move out onto the road. Straggling towards Long Lane.

I've seen the angry mobs in the 'Hammer Horror' films. I know what they're doing. I know what's going to happen.

Melissa is in danger. I'm frightened for her. The linoleum is cold on my bare feet. At first I'm scared. Then I know exactly what to do. I get dressed. I go down to the kitchen – Mam's not there, must have gone next door, so I get what I need. Then scarper out into the night. I know the way. I can hear voices raised, yelling and angry. They're heading for the Gypsy camp. There's going to be trouble. But I can hare across Witty's field, squelching through the night, to reach the point further down the stream, and scramble down the embankment. The moon makes a huge white night rainbow. The field is frozen. I climb across the rusted barbed-war spikes, and up onto the fat pipe. I can smell the gas. So rich I can feel it. There's a fissure where two ill-fitting sections of pipe come together, where the gas leaks out. Looking across the stream, I can see how the pipe leads underground to Mr Pidd's ramshackle garage. There's no glow in the grubby windows. He's probably at 'The Cross Keys', wearing his flat-cap, with his raggy ciggy-stub behind his ear.

I know what I must do. I fumble the duster from my pocket. Use the cigarette lighter, holding it with trembling fingers. At first it just blackens along the lower hem, then there's the ghost of a flame that smoulders and dances upwards. I wait for as long as I dare, until its flare burns up to scorch my fingers, the hairs on the back of my hand crinkle. I smell the crinkle. Then I stuff the flare down into the fissure where the pipes join, jamming it down with a knifeblade. At first there's nothing. Nothing. Nothing. Everything is still and moon-frozen. Then there's a sucking roar that seems to ripple along the pipe. I feel it tremble beneath my feet. There's a pause, then a dull whumping sound from across the stream. A sudden brilliant flare that flashes around the dark windows of the garage. A mutter of flame, that gathers and flickers.

I jump down off the pipe and scrabble back up the embankment. As I reach the top, the flames reach the petrol pump outside the garage, just beneath the corrugated awning. It explodes outwards in blossoms of boiling flame. I feel the heat blast on my skin, forcing me down into a protective crouch. Fragments of glass and metal shrapnel spins into the night, carried on the breath of Hades. The very fabric of space-time trembles and buckles, slows and slithers into an oily tide, as the shockwave radiates outwards. The very molecules of dust caught in its expanding roar are suspended in silver moonlight.

Breath roars in my throat. Terrified at what I've done. There are voices. The figures of running men, distracted from the angry mob by the greater urgency. I watch for as long as I dare. Frame my fingers into a square, and mentally click the photo, storing the image away for future reference. They are forming a human chain passing buckets of water from the beck to the conflagration, deluging the flames that devour what's left of the garage building. The gypsy encampment forgotten.

Later, lying in bed, the memories in my head come apart in shimmers of lost time. Sirens. Red lights pulsing. I see them now. As the Service Station detonates. Reverberations ripping through space-time, coming loose, destabilizing reality, then and now, playing backwards and forwards in giddy circles.

The following morning is dull, with steady drizzle soaking everything. And the gypsy caravans are gone. Melissa and her Mam have gone with them. I never see her again. Except in dreams. She speaks to me in dreams. She still does. What was left of the garage is charred black, the ash soaking down into an unhealthy mulch. I touch the black slush, rub it into a paste between my fingers. The ruins of Dresden, fused into slag. The ruins of Chernobyl. The surreal debris of a science fiction war. After the great extinction catastrophe, the time-ships know that all the world will be this way.

The unfortunate explosion is blamed on a gas-leak. Mr Pidd is so ancient he's close to retiring age anyway, and never really resumes the business, just tinkers at odd jobs here and there on farm equipment or servicing cars. Melissa's cottage has a 'For Sale' sign planted outside it soon after. It stands empty for around six months, the roses and thistles in the garden getting tangled and unkempt. Until Mr and Mrs Campbell move in, a quiet elderly couple, dull and boring. I resent them living there in her cottage.

I fail my exams and move up to the Secondary Modern School, travelling from the village in the school bus, with Graham and Ian. But Melissa was magical. A sprite. I miss her, I still do. She's out there somewhere. She helps me when I'm in trouble. She helped me today. She's here beside me now. Thank you, Melissa.

Melissa is the girl with pixie-ears.

~

Andrew Darlington has walked the magma crust of the Nisyros volcano. James Lowe of the Electric Prunes is his Facebook friend. And Kink Dave Davies answered his Tweet. He writes about music for R'N'R' (Rock 'n' Reel), *and counter-culture for* IT: International Times. *His latest poetry collection is* Tweak Vision: The Word-Play Solution To Modern-Angst Confusion *and his Scientifiction Novel,* In The Time Of The Breaking *are both from Alien Buddha Press, USA. His writing can be found at* Eight Miles Higher: *http://andrewdarlington.blogspot.co.uk/*

NEST
Stephen Laws

"Oh no, not *again*!"

"What?"

"Not again, for God's sake!"

"What, not again?"

"I can't believe this is happening again..."

"What?"

"Wasps!" exclaimed Don Wilson in exasperation, as if it should be self-evident.

"Oh no!" His wife Trudy's hands flew to her cheeks in that theatrical, tragic manner that could be so infuriating. "Not again!"

"I just *said* that!"

Trudy joined Don at the conservatory window, the flats of her palms still on her cheeks so that when she spoke again, her voice was muffled:

"Where?"

"There!" Don rapped on the window pane in front of him. "Same place."

The conservatory had been added to the house seven years ago; mostly glass with PVC framing to form full length floor-to-ceiling windows. The sliding door that had once led directly to the back garden from the living room now gave entrance from the house to that conservatory; with a new conservatory door in the far corner of that extension now leading out into the garden. It had been a good investment. Six summers of glorious sunshine where sitting in the centre of so much glass still felt, in a strange way, like sitting in the garden. Six winters of swirling snow around the conservatory gave a cocooned feeling of warmth; like sitting in a snowdrift, but completely protected and warm as toast.

The seventh summer hadn't been so nice, and that was because of the wasps.

Trudy followed Don's pointing finger to the leylandii hedge facing the conservatory at the bottom of the garden. It grew to a height of forty feet and from behind a four foot fence, where grass cuttings were dumped after the lawn had been mowed. There was a small hole and a crack in the planking smack dab in the centre of the fence – exactly the same place where the problem had occurred last year – and there they were again, swirling around it. Bloody wasps!

"The *same* nest?" Trudy's words were still muffled.

"Can't be," said Don, now standing back with his hands on his hips, like the stern parent he thought he should be. "The exterminators blitzed that one with the white powder. I watched them do it. They went crazy. The wasps, I mean. Not the exterminators."

A ragged ribbon of wasps swirled in the air around the crack and the hole. And now they were gone, not a wasp in sight. None emerging from the fence, or flitting around in the hedge. Don and Trudy held their breath unconsciously in hopeful expectation – then expelled together in irritation when the wasps reappeared just as suddenly, as if deliberately taunting them.

"Bugger," said Don.

"You think they've just moved back into the old nest?"

"Trudy – it's not like they get evicted or something. That white powder is lethal to them. They go in and out, all frenzied up 'cause something's attacking the nest when that stuff gets squirted in. They get it on themselves, spread it all around. Go crazy. Die. That nest would be like a big poison trap. They're not going to go back to..."

"That poison lasts more than a *year*? They didn't tell us that."

"They're not going to go back to..."

"You mean we've got poison at the bottom of the garden we can't get rid of?"

"They're not going to go back..."

"What about the kids? We can't have it getting on the kids, Don!"

"Trudy! I went behind that fence after we got rid of the wasps last year. Pulled it out. Burned it."

"But the poison...?" Trudy was horrified, words no longer blurred now that she had removed her hands from her face. "Did you get any of it on you?"

"No I didn't. I knew you'd make a bloody fuss if I told you what I was going to do. Never mind about the poison. There's no poison. And there's no bloody nest. I mean, there's no *old* nest. So that means this must be a *new* nest."

"But Don, that exterminator stuff is..."

"I'm still here, aren't I? Anyway, I finished the job. So that's a new nest, not an old nest." He put his arm around his wife's shoulders and wished he hadn't said anything. For a while, they stood in silence, watching the wasps come and go. To Don, it was as if the little bastards were making a point by building a nest in the same place as the old one.

Somewhere upstairs, a door slammed; followed by the muffled thunder of thirteen-year old feet on the carpeted stairs as their son Jimmy descended, shouting: "Wasps in the garden again!"

"We know," called Don and Trudy in unison, as Jimmy exploded into the conservatory, running to the windows for a better view.

"Saw them upstairs," continued Jimmy breathlessly. "Millions of 'em! Like last time."

"Mum..." Their 15 year old daughter – Trish – began to call from somewhere upstairs.

"We *know!*" Don and Trudy replied, in further exasperation. "Wasps again!"

Jimmy changed position at the window, trying to get a better look. "Think they'll get under the floorboards like last time?" Now he began an exaggerated stamping experiment on the carpet to see if anything would happen.

"No, they won't!" snapped Trudy. "And stop doing that. Dad sealed the airbricks up at the front of the house."

"Not supposed to do that," said Jimmy, gaze still concentrated on the carpet for emergent flying insects. "House gets damp or something."

"Everyone's an expert," muttered Don.

Trish joined them in the conservatory, towelling her damp hair. "Get rid of them, Dad. I hate wasps." She craned forwards, looking to right and left.

"Are the windows closed upstairs?" asked Trudy. "Don't want them getting in up there."

"Yes," Trish put her face close to the nearest window, looking up to where her bedroom window would be. "Little buggers..."

"Don't swear," said Don. "And don't..."

His words were cut off as Trish yelped and recoiled from the window, startling everyone else in the room.

Several wasps had appeared on the other side of the glass, flying close in tight, concentrated circles, making chitinous clicks and scratching on the window pane.

"Did you *see* that?" cried Trish in outrage. "They came for me! The little buggers *came* for me!"

"No they didn't." Don strode to the window, rapping on the pane as if they were the respectful children that he deserved and would fly off, duly chastised. They did not. "You think all the wasps and bees in the world are out to get you – and only you. They're not."

"Buggers!" snapped Trish, fiercely towelling her hair again as if to rid it of any potentially entangled wasps. She stamped out of the conservatory.

"Language!" Don snapped.

Trudy moved to join him, shooing Jimmy out of the way when he began swatting at the window with a rolled-up comic book. To Don, she said: "You going to get someone out to deal with it?"

"Of course," replied Don. "But not on a Sunday. We won't get the Council to come out on a Sunday."

"Why the Council? Ring one of those private companies, like Blastobug or someone."

"You're joking. They cost a fortune last time – and they didn't do the job properly. That's why I had to burn the nest afterwards."

"So we've got to put up with them for the rest of the day?"

"Keep the windows closed and don't go out in the back garden."

"That's nice, isn't it? Like being a prisoner in your own home."

The wasps at the window had gone.

Don turned to Trudy, hands apart in a *'So what's the fuss?'* gesture.

But she had already left the room in disgust.

*

The Daily Telegraph: 21ˢᵗ April (Science Editor Column) - Could the mild Spring mean that a new breed of wasp is coming to the UK? Experts have warned that a previously unidentified species of wasp that eats bees and has caused the deaths of six people in France is heading to Britain because of the warm spring. Very like the Asian hornet in appearance, which can grow to over an inch long, the wasps are much more aggressive and carry a more toxic sting. Experts say the UK's recent hot summers provide the perfect climate for the creatures to thrive should they arrive.

*

When Trudy called Don at the office on the Monday morning, it was not at a good time – from a professional point of view. The Management Team meeting had not gone well for him. Nor had Trudy's telephone call to the local Council's Environmental Services Department.

"Have you any idea how long I had to wait to speak to someone?" Trudy snapped, as if she was still on the telephone to a Council employee. "It took all morning before I got through..."

"Trudy, this is not a good time. Did you get someone to come out, or what?"

"Yes and no..."

"What's that supposed to mean?"

"Yes, I got through to someone but no, they're not coming out."

"What the *hell...*?"

"After I'd been passed from pillar to post, I got this jobs-worth demanding to know if I was sure that they were wasps, not bees..."

"*Trudy!*" hissed Don impatiently, trying to speed her up.

"Because if they're bees, they're a protected – *protected, for God's sake!* – species! So they can't – *won't* – send out the exterminators. So I said..."

"But you told them they were definitely wasps?"

"Of *course* I told them they were *wasps*. Not bloody bees. Wasps are thinner, and they're not hairy!"

"You don't have to tell me the difference! I spent the entire Sunday yesterday with you and the kids trapped in the ruddy house while they buzzed at the windows."

"You don't have to raise your voice to me, Don! I'm just as upset as you are."

"I *know* that..." And then, forcing himself to be calm: "I know that – darling. I'm the one who had to run to the car this morning, waving a newspaper around my head, remember?"

"And I had to do the same, Don! I ran the kids into school in the other car. Didn't want them standing at the bus stop outside. And when I got back, the newsagent rang to say that the newspaper boy couldn't deliver this morning. Couldn't get to the front door because of the wasps."

"Trudy – the Council?" continued Don through clenched teeth. "So how did you leave it with them? I mean, how did they leave it with you? I mean – with us..."

"They're too stretched to come out today. That's the word they used. Stretched! But if they come out tomorrow – or the day after – it'll only be to check to see if they're wasps or bees. And then – and then – even if they've established that they're wasps (and we *know* they're wasps) they can't do an extermination there and then. They'll have to come out on *another* day!"

"Bloody hell"

"I know, I know..."

"You'll have to ring up a private extermination firm. Check the internet for a local company. Or use Yellow Pages – if you can find one in the house."

"Don! We're trapped in this house with a back garden full of wasps! You're going to come home and sort it out."

"Trudy, darling. I'm at *work*. It's not going well here this morning... sweetheart. I shouldn't be on the phone to you now."

"Don – sweetheart – if you don't get someone out here straight away, I'm collecting the kids from school and taking them straight to my mother's house."

Christ, thought Don. *Your mother. A woman who stings worse than a nest full of wasps.*

"I mean it, Don. We can't stay here with this going on."

"I'll... see... what... I can do..."

*

The Guardian: 29ᵗʰ April (Science Today Column) - The Department for Environment's National Bee Unit is to meet in Suffolk for an emergency seminar to tackle the potential arrival of Vespa Furiosa - a previously unidentified species of wasp which can devour up t0 50 honey bees a day. The Department for Environment, Food and Rural Affairs (Defra) has sent email alerts to UK beekeepers asking them to be on the look-out for the species. Members of the public are being urged not to approach nests, which are usually found high in trees or on the sides of buildings. The insects seem to have been spotted in Kent, Devon, Surrey and Sussex over the past week and pose a threat to our bee population – they are known to kill up to 50 bees a day to feed their larvae.

*

When Don got home, Trudy's car was still parked out front of the house – so he knew that she hadn't carried out her threat. Tyres crunching on gravel as he drove down the front drive, the sound made him think uneasily that the tyres might make the same sound driving over thousands of wasps' bodies. As well as the back garden accessed from the conservatory, the house had its own front garden set back from the road, with the same kind of leylandii bushes that contained the wasps' nest in the back garden; providing a once-comfortable barrier of seclusion and privacy that had always been so comforting in the past but which now made him feel uneasy, and somehow hemmed in.

The front door did not open as it usually did, even when – as now – he was home early from the office; and Trudy was not framed in that doorway with a welcoming smile.

Striding through the house, front door banging behind him with loud and unnecessary force, Don found his family in the conservatory; standing in front of the windows and looking out into the garden.

"Are they...?" he began, sliding out of his jacket.

"Yes," said Trudy tearfully as she turned at last to greet him and, despite his frustration, he took her into a comforting embrace. "They're still there. And there are lots more of them. Did you...?"

"Yes, I got through to the exterminators. A firm called Langelaan. They'll be here soon."

"Cool," said Jimmy, eyes wide, chewing on a sandwich and watching the roiling swarm in the leylandii hedge.

"Gross," said Trish, yet again towelling her hair. But she was not looking at the wasps.

*

The Sun: 1ˢᵗ May ("Ouch! That has GOT to sting!") -The Animal Health and Veterinary Laboratories Agency is officially on standby to kill the Vespa Furiosa – a new species of wasp - using special chemicals. A Defra spokesman said: "We are aware of the potential impact this wasp could have on honey bees and there are plans in place to remove them if they are identified. This includes comprehensive monitoring with teams ready to destroy any confirmed nests." The Chairperson of the Norfolk Beekeepers' Association has also confirmed the arrival of the wasp, which is thought to have arrived in France on a consignment of pottery imported from China in 2005, but which has now found its way across the English Channel to the UK. Multiple stings have been known to cause a heart attack or multiple organ failure; even for those who are not allergic to the predators. One victim was a 54 year old farmer who died after he disturbed a nest and was attacked by a swarm in the Loire Valley.

*

Langelaan, the exterminator firm, had promised that they'd be there in an hour. Three hours, and many telephone calls, later – two sheepish individuals pulled up in the drive, in a white van.

The taller of the two was already out of the van and pulling on white overalls when Don yanked the front door open in an act of pre-emptive anger. He didn't have to say anything. The taller man's frozen smile acknowledged that they were late. The second exterminator, a sullen teenager, kept his head down and pulled out a cylinder and hose from the van.

Don looked at his watch meaningfully.

"Soon have you sorted out," said the tall man. As if Don himself was the problem. "Wasps get lazier and easier to deal with later in the day."

The younger man scrambled into his overalls while the taller stood with his hands on his hips, making a silent but exaggerated appreciation of his client's surroundings. No eye contact. When the younger was fully fitted-up and hefting his equipment, the older man looked up to see his client barring the doorway and pointing off to a side gate in the garden at the left of the house. No access through the house then.

"Okie-dokie," the taller man said cheerfully.

Both men headed for the gate, and the front door slammed.

*

The Times: 2ⁿᵈ May- "Potent Predator - A hunter of bees with a toxic sting." Vespa Furiosa – a new species of wasp that has arrived on the English mainland from France (or accidentally imported in plot plants, cut flowers, fruit or timber) is a highly effective predator of insects, including honey bees, and can cause significant losses to bee colonies. It has also attracted intense curiosity from scientists, who have observed aspects in its behaviour, reproduction and feeding techniques that cannot be properly explained. Dr William Castle of DEFRA has said that: "There appears to be a curious morphing aspect to Vespa Furiosa which requires critical analysis and study. In addition to the consumption of its prey, Vespa Furiosa seems to have the ability to acquire and develop genetic changes from its food sources that can radically affect its own organic structure; a development which passes on through successive generations. This is very exciting and requires considerable further examination and analysis."

*

In the living room, Don chided Jimmy for making more exploratory stamping on the floor and impatiently joined everyone in the conservatory at the picture windows.

"They know," said Trudy as the two white clad figures came into view and stood in front of the leylandii hedge.

"Who knows what?" asked Jimmy.

"The wasps know they're in for it. Look. They've stopped swarming."

Don moved to get a better view.

It was true. There were none at the windows and the dense cloud at the hedge had shrunk to no more than half a dozen flitting in and out of the foliage.

Isn't that just the way? Don thought angrily. Just like the time that Jimmy banged his head on the sideboard. Got a lump the size of a duck egg on his forehead. Spent all day in the Accident and Emergency department of the local hospital before being seen by anyone; by which stage the swelling had gone down to the extent that the bump had almost vanished. It made Don feel like a fraud or something. Made him feel as if he should poke where Jimmy's lump had been with a finger, just so that it would pop up a little again and prove that they weren't wasting the hospital staff's time.

"No, look!" exclaimed Trish. "There they go."

The two white-clad men were moving purposefully forward – the younger man now raising the nozzle as they reached the leylandii. A white cloud sprayed into the leaves; once, twice – three times.

The men stood back to watch as the Wilsons also moved eagerly closer to the picture window to watch what happened next.

At first, Don thought that the sun had suddenly dropped behind the skyline. Much too early for that, surely? And much too swiftly. And surely a cloud covering the sun couldn't have resulted in the great darkness that had suddenly descended on the garden?

But it was nevertheless suddenly dark when it had been sunny before.

And in a disorientating moment, it seemed that everything out there in the garden had turned into the negative of a photograph. In this negative, two white-clad figures in a silent storm of wind-whipped black pellets had suddenly become two black-clad figures in a frenzied snowstorm.

"Oh my God," said Trudy in a small voice.

"Mum?" said Trish in a voice that seemed even smaller.

"Awesome," said Jimmy, filled with wonder.

The two originally white-clad men were now both a smothered and squirming mass of small glittering yellow-black bodies that leaped and ran, stumbled and fell. The canister and hose fell to the grass, emitting another gush of white powder. Far from dispersing the thick and swirling black cloud that had emerged from the hedge into the garden, that whiteness was instantly engulfed and obliterated by the swarming blackness. The two glistening-black figures still danced and thrashed, hopped and stumbled, whirled and flailed.

The air was filled with a throbbing vibration of sound that could only barely be described as 'buzzing'; more like an underground dynamo or the grumbling roar of an approaching underground train.

Bu now, there was another unmistakeable sound coming from the garden.

The two figures were whooping and screaming in fear and agony.

The Wilsons recoiled in terror from the picture window as the blackness swept in a sudden and enveloping surge to the windows on all sides. The view of the garden disappeared. Now the blackness resolved in a mass of squirming movement to become an entire floor-to-ceiling tapestry stitched from a million angry wasps.

The Wilsons recoiled further from the windows in one reflexive group-step.

Don looked at his family. Trish had both hands to her face in that familiar gesture of horror, veins now somehow pre-eminent in those hands. This time she was responding not to a minor domestic issue that represented 'horror' in her life but to a real and overwhelming horror that defied belief.

Jimmy's initial response of 'awesome' had now become an immobile, slack-jawed and white-faced expression of shock. The towel hung from Trish's head like a veil, obscuring her face. She whirled, eyes wide, and blundered past him; running from the conservatory through the living room and into the kitchen. Don turned in a confused circle, gaping in shock from the confused hive of activity covering the conservatory's windows to his wife and son – and now stumbled towards the kitchen when he heard the sound of his daughter retching in the sink.

"Trish... Trudy... it'll be..."

But no, it wasn't all right.

Because now Trish screamed, gossamer thin streamers of spittle flying from her lips as the kitchen window above the sink was suddenly covered with a smothering blanket of angry wasps. Trish made a *glugging* sound, and with a full two-handed shove away from the sink, staggered backwards into her father's arms. The impetus carried them out of the kitchen in a ragged-breath embrace, just as Trudy gave another cry of fear.

Somehow they were now, all three of them, father, mother, son and daughter – in a clutching tangle of each other's arms in the centre of the living room.

Staring wide-eyed, back and forth at the impossible buzzing chaos of wasps swarming over every downstairs window on the ground floor of the house.

Window, to window, to window...

"Upstairs," said Trudy, at last.

"The windows," said Don.

And suddenly, still clutching at each other, they were out of the living room; now bustling up the stairs.

There was something wrong with the light on the staircase and the landing above.

The main and spare bedroom doors, and the study door, were usually open (as they were now) and the lowering sun would send bright shafts of sunlight into that space. But there was no sunlight now. Just the same swarming and leprously dappled swarm-shadow on the walls and ceiling as that in the downstairs rooms. Don could feel a panicked little-boy voice inside wanting to repeat *"No, no, no"* over and over again, but he kept his already tightened throat closed as they huddled together again at the top of the stairs.

Up here, the air was also filled with the vibrant *thrum* and hideously organised vibration that had invaded the house downstairs.

The outside of the bedroom windows and the overhead skylight was covered in a blanket of wasps.

"Ch... ch... ch..."

Don looked at Trudy, wanted to shake her out of the terror that enveloped her.

"Chimneys," she managed to say at last – and Don understood. "They're fake, remember? All blocked. They can't get in that way."

"Dad?" Jimmy's wide eyes prompted him to focus.

"Nine, nine, nine," said Don grimly, and now – still in a tight family knot – they descended again to the hall.

Breaking away and striding to the telephone on the radiator stand, Don glanced quickly past the hall door to the small window panes in the top section of the front door, already knowing that they would be covered in wasps, and tried not to let Trudy and Trish's frightened gasps send further shards of glass into his heart. Don snatched up the telephone, dialled quickly. Trudy saw him prepare to speak, and then watched the colour drain from his face.

"What is it?"

When Don looked at her, his eyes were dull. Before he could replace the receiver, she lunged forward and snatched it from him. He tried to resist, but was already rethinking and knew that if he resisted too hard it would escalate everyone's terror.

"Hello, hello!" Trudy's eyes remained fixed on Don as she held the receiver to her ear.

There was only the sound of buzzing.

And not, somehow, the buzzing of a disconnected or faulty telephone line.

"Mobile!" snapped Don, also snapping his fingers.

Jimmy fumbled in his jeans pocket. "What's happened, Dad?" When he produced his mobile phone, Don snatched it from him, stabbing with his finger; as if finally taking control of the situation.

"Nine, nine, nine?"

"*Which service, please?*" asked a calm female voice on the other end of the line.

"Thank God! Police? Yes – police!"

"*Connecting you. Please hold.*"

"Are you through?" Trudy's voice was higher than normal by an octave. "Are you through?"

Don nodded impatiently, and then held his hand up for quiet when a male voice asked: "*You're through to West Enfield Police. How can we help?*"

"My name is Donald Wilson. I live at Number 4 Druridge Road, West Enfield. My family and I are trapped in our house."

"*You're trapped in your house, sir? By whom?*"

"Wasps."

"*I'm sorry, sir. Please repeat. Who has trapped you in your house?*"

"Not who! Them, it – wasps!"

"*Sir – you're telling me that you're trapped in your house by wasps? Is that right?*"

"That's right. They're all over the windows and we can't get out."

"If you have a pest control problem, then you need to be ringing your local Council services or a private extermination firm. This number is reserved for emergency services and there are serious penalties for its misuse."

"You don't *understand*. There are two men in our garden, covered in wasps – and they might be dead."

The operator made Don start again, and this time his responses were tight and measured, every phrase carefully chosen; not only to allay the fear and anxiety on the faces of his wife and children, but to ensure that someone should come out – and come out *now*. When he handed the phone back to Jimmy, Trudy's eyes demanded an answer that would put everything right and put the world back together again.

"Yes," said Don, sighing deeply and pulling everyone close to him. "They're coming out immediately. We just have to sit tight."

"I don't think they believed you Dad," said Jimmy, eyes wide.

"Of *course* they..." Don maintained control. "Of course they believed me. Believed us. Just sounds weird, doesn't it?" His throat was now terribly dry and his words were sticking. "They're coming to sort everything out."

"Those men in the garden..." said Trish weakly.

"They came to do a job," mumbled Trudy, and didn't believe she had said the words that came out of her mouth; her bewilderment renewed when she saw the expression on the faces of her husband and children.

"All right, okay" said Don in a voice that was far from all right and okay. "Let's all sit down here. On this sofa."

Still keeping tight, arms around each other like learners stranded in the middle of a swimming pool, they shuffled to the living room sofa and sat together in a tight knot of limbs.

They tried to ignore the buzzing that was also somehow a howling; tried to ignore the swarming of light and shade from the windows, reflecting on the pale pastel living room walls.

"Wished we'd gone for wallpaper now," said Don, and wished dearly that he had not said the words. "Right," he continued. "Right."

They waited.

And then, he went on: "Right, okay. We need to be *practical*, don't we? We need to be doing sensible things while we're waiting for the police or the fire service or... whoever... to come and sort things out. So, you're all going to stay right here on the sofa, and I'm carefully and quietly – *quietly*, mind – going to go around the house again and make sure that everything's all sealed up."

"Sealed up?" asked Trudy, flatly.

"Yes," continued Don. "We know that they're not under the floorboards, because they haven't come up through them like last time."

"Oh God," whimpered Trish. "They *still* might come up, though..."

"They *haven't* come up because they're *not* under the floorboards. Right? And we know that the upstairs windows are closed, and the chimneys are all blocked up. Fakes, I mean."

Trudy winced at the word *fake* as Don went on, glad that she'd kept her mouth shut.

"All the downstairs windows are closed, or they would have... got in. But they haven't and they won't. So we're all okay. So I'm just going to go round the house and check *everything*. Okay."

Trish and Jimmy nodded in unison. Don saw that Trudy's eyes were closed, her mouth set firmly as if she was going to stay that way for a very long time.

"So. Right. I'm going to double-check. Yes. Double-check. That's what I'll do. And you all stay here and... stay here."

And so Don, carefully and quietly – stealthily even – moved from the sofa and checked the downstairs windows; looking back to check the frozen tableau of his family, still sitting together with arms clasped as scrawling shadows crawled over them; those same shadows crawling over the walls and the floor and the ceiling. The low howling and buzzing continued.

Ascending the stairs, and always looking back at them, he realised that he had forgotten to breathe. He paused, steeled himself, breathed deeply – and continued.

The upstairs windows were all still fastened securely. Every pane was covered with a mass of seething yellow and black. Surely they'd give up and go? Surely at least *one* of those windows would be clear by now? And if there was one – just *one* – no matter how far from the ground; well then, he'd hurry downstairs, gather them up, get them up here – and they'd all climb out and jump. Yes, they'd *jump*. All of them – and it didn't matter if any one of them sprained an ankle or broke a bone, they'd be clear and they'd run, God how they'd run – until they were free and clear of this... this suffocating nightmare that shouldn't be happening.

But none of the windows was clear – and the angry swarm of wasps (the impossibly *huge* swarm of wasps) was not going away.

Don leaned against the landing wall, remembering to breathe again.

On the way down to rejoin his family, a stair cracked underfoot, somehow as loud as a pistol shot. Don froze. It felt like something had stung him inside.

Trudy's eyes were still closed tight in a denial of what was happening Trish's eyes remained wide, darting around the room at the crawling shadows, waiting for small shapes to emerge, fizzing and furious. When Don sat with them, Trudy flinched – eyes still closed – but Jimmy grabbed one of his hands.

"It's all right, son."

"Dad..." Jimmy's face was white; his eyes not on his father, but on a fixed point somewhere beyond and behind Don.

"Really, we'll be okay. Everything's sealed up."

"No Dad." Jimmy was struggling to speak.

"We've just got to..."

"*Dad!*"

Don gripped his son's hands in both of his own, leaning down into Jimmy's face and trying to project some sense of security that he didn't feel at all. And saw – so close now – that there were flecks of movement in there; speckles that were reflecting something that was going on behind Don.

"The k-keyhole."

A droplet of sweat ran down Jimmy's white and furrowed brow.

"They're getting in... through the front door... *keyhole!*"

Don whirled in fear.

Wasps were buzzing and flitting in the hallway, between the main front door and the interior glass living-room door.

Trudy and Trish and Jimmy were all screaming now as Don leapt from the sofa, yelling: "Don't scream! Don't *scream!*" – and realised that he was screaming, trying to drown their own out as he catapulted to the living room door and slammed it shut. Instantly, wasps were dancing at the glass on the other side. Fumbling for the door handle now...

No keyhole in this one! Of course, there's no keyhole!

Frantically checking around the frame.

Rubber seal! They can't get in! There's a rubber seal!

Fingers frantically at the glass panes; every one intact.

No cracks! God, no cracks!

And all the time screaming: *"Stop screaming! Stop screaming!"*

Don turned back to them again, arms wide, as if he was going to charge them in anger.

They stopped screaming.

Drawing deep breaths, now holding out hands to placate and somehow do his family's own deep breathing, reaching out to them, Don implored: "Calm down... calm down...calm... that's it... good, calm, calmer..." Don swallowed hard and said: "Someone... *someone...* is coming.

And then the mobile phone in his pocket rang shrilly, and everyone started screaming again.

"Stop SCREAMING!" screamed Don, tearing the mobile phone from his pocket and jabbing at the buttons. *"Yes, yes, YES!"* into the phone – and then, *'STOP SCREAMING!"* at his family. Their screaming stopped. Now there was only the sound of Trish's sobs and Trudy hyper-ventilating. Jimmy continued to stare at his father, wide eyes and glassy. Don took a deep breath, squeezed his eyes shut and answered again. "Yes?"

'That's the residence of Mr and Mrs Wilson? 4 Druridge Road?" The voice at the other end was female, stiff and clipped.

"Yes," replied Don.

"You are Mr Donald Wilson?"

"Yes."

"And your wife, Mrs Trudy Wilson. Your son James and your daughter

Patricia – they're there with you now?"
"Yes."
"And they're safe?"
"Yes, but we're..."
"Are they safe, Mr Wilson?"
"Well, we're trapped in here, but we're..."
"And has anyone been stung?"
"Stung? No."
"Are there any wasps in the house with you now? Are they getting in anywhere?"
"No. The windows and doors are all shut. Some got into the hall through the keyhole, but they're trapped in there and they can't get to us. Now, listen! Who *are* you? What's *happening* out there...?"
"My name is Lieutenant Colonel Marion Davies of the Territorial Army, Division E."
"The army?!"
"Yes, sir. We have a detachment here and the police are also with us. There's no need to panic. We have a situation involving a dangerous infestation and it will be resolved very quickly. For the moment, Mr Wilson, you and your family should remain calm and stay where you are. Where exactly in the house are you?"
Don found that he could not swallow. "In the... living room."
"Very good, sir. Remain in the living room. You may hear sounds of some organised activity out here. Please do not be alarmed. We are taking measures to remove the source of the infestation and we will advise you in a very short time when it is safe to come out. Can you do that for me, sir?"
"The *army's* been called out to deal with *wasps?*"
"Can you do that for me, sir?"
"Yes, but I don't understand."
"Can you remain calm – and can you keep your family calm, sir?"
"Yes!" declared Don, manning-up and feeling far from manly.
"Good. Then I can confirm with you, Mr Wilson that we're dealing here with a new and aggressive species of African/Asian wasp. And can I ask you again sir, are you sure that no one has been stung?"
"Stung? No – no one's been stung. Why are you emphasising...?"

"Stay where you are, Mr Wilson. And keep the family there with you. I repeat – there will be some activity outside as we proceed with extermination. But don't worry about that. We'll have you out of there very soon."

"Yes, but..."

"Stay calm, Mr Wilson," said the measured voice at the other end, and then the line went dead.

Don looked up at his wide-eyed family. Now it seemed that the crawling light and shadows on the windows and walls were also crawling on their faces and reflecting in their eyes. The unspoken pleas in those eyes demanded that he respond with a confidence that he did not feel.

"We're okay," said Don. "There'll be some noise and stuff while they're clearing the wasps. But they're getting us out very soon."

They moved back to sit on the living room sofa. There was no way of telling how long they sat in silence, with the buzzing and droning in their ears and the hideous patterned swarming of light and shadow all around. Perhaps minutes, perhaps hours. Fidgeting, wide-eyed and terrified. Without realising that he'd done it, Don dialled 1471 on his mobile phone to get the number of the military person who had called back. His stomach lurched when he received a monotone 'No Service' sound. When he looked up to see his family's fragile and desperate eagerness for good news, his frozen smile remained rigid and he tried to keep despair out of his eyes as he looked down and dialled again.

This time there was no tone.

Only the sound of buzzing from the phone.

Don almost dropped it.

Fumbling, he put it in his lap and kept his head down.

"Engaged."

His voice was flat, deliberately devoid of the fear that threatened to overwhelm him.

Something *cracked!*

The tight knot of limbs that were Trish, Trudy and Jimmy spasmed as one but made no sound, breath held tight. Don sat bolt upright, the mobile phone flying from his lap and skittering across the floor. He leapt to his feet and snatched it up as if he'd made a terrible mistake, quickly jerking back to the sofa and sitting ramrod-straight.

The sound came again; flat, but sharp and shocking.

This time, Trish whimpered. When Don exclaimed again, they flinched.

"Outside! The noise came from outside, not inside."

There were several more sharp reports, and then silence.

"Are they gunshots, Dad?" quavered Jimmy.

"Yes, no," replied Don. "Probably. I don't know."

"What, they're shooting wasps, one by one?"

"I don't know, son. Really. I don't *know*."

Now, above the sounds of the buzzing and droning, there was a different noise. At first, it sounded like a distant rush of street traffic; an erratic susurration, a displacement of air that was suggestive of movement. Don's ears pricked up and his air of alertness and frayed optimism instantly communicated to the others.

The sound came again.

A rush, a rumble.

Now more frequently.

And when it became a low, rumbling short-burst 'roar' – the tumbling cascade of light and shadow on the living room windows and walls suddenly became a flare of orange-red light.

Don jumped to his feet and hurried to join his family in another group-embrace.

Again, the low-grumbling throaty roar, like some kind of approaching jungle beast, and again the room was suffused with that billowing orange-red light that now turned their faces momentarily into carnival masks.

"Flame throwers," hissed Don. "They're using *flame-throwers!*"

"Yay!" exclaimed Jimmy in a voice of boyhood enthusiasm that was at odds with the glittering fear in his eyes.

The living room window momentarily *hissed*, the yellow-and-black squirming movement there became a crackling, black and sooty mess. A cloud of myriad pin pricks of light flurried at that window as the charred remains of wasps fell away and new yellow-black bodies tried to fill the gaps on the glass.

"It's okay!" gasped Don. "It's going to be okay!"

He left them on the sofa, walking gingerly towards that window with his hands at either side of himself as if he was walking on a tightrope and only now as if completely aware that there had once been a wasp problem under the floorboards; a problem that he had blatantly averred could never happen again.

The encrusted, scrabbling black mass on the living room window was gradually becoming a living yellow-black mass again. "Come on, then!" hissed Don. "Come on. Let's have some more of that *fire*, you bastards."

"They know what they're doing," said Trudy in a small voice. It was the first time that she had spoken in a long while, and it angered Don for a reason he couldn't understand. Helpless, angry and struggling to keep his inner turmoil from exploding outwards and causing more panic, he turned back to storm from the living room, footsteps heavy on the carpet in defiance of any bastard wasps that might be under the floorboards after all. In the kitchen now, he stared at the same writhing mass on the window there.

Where were the flame-throwers now?

Why had they stopped?

Why weren't they still using them on the windows?

He walked in a tight circle, fists bunched at his sides – then strode to the kitchen sink beneath the window, bracing his hands there to stare at the seething mass. And then the thought came to him.

What if the glass can't take it? Maybe they can't keep spraying fire on the window because the glass or the wooden frame can't take it? If the glass cracks or breaks or melts, then the wasps are in!

The possibility made his stomach roll and he remained braced there, fighting the urge to retch.

"It's like being inside a hive." The words hissed out through Don's clenched teeth. "We're the ones *inside* the hive – and they're on the *outside!*" Angrily, Don snatched at the first thing within reach on the kitchen bench, his anger now overwhelming as he tensed to fling it across the kitchen.

It was a jar of honey.

Idiot! Wasps don't make honey. Only bees!

488

Don checked his anger and fear, trying to extinguish it by slamming the jar down on the kitchen bench; an instant mistake when he heard the startled gasps of his family next door.

"Dad!" cried Jimmy.

"It's all right, son. It's just me."

"Dad. Come and look."

Don turned quickly back to the living room.

Trudy and Trish were still on the sofa, but Jimmy had moved to the living room window again, keeping a wary distance from the now fully reformed squirming mass on the other side – but craning his head forward to stare intently at something else there that had caught his attention.

"Don't get too close," said Don as he strode across to join him.

"There's something wrong with those wasps, Dad."

"What do you mean?"

"There's something wrong with their heads."

Jimmy stepped closer, eyes squinting as he tried to make more sense of what he was seeing.

"Their heads...?"

The window pane *cracked!*

A zigzag fracture suddenly crazed from the top left of the window and sped like frozen lightning to the centre of the pane. Jimmy recoiled into Don's arms as the crack halted, like a living thing; now deciding which direction to take next.

Don heard whimpering behind him, but did not know if it was Trish, Trudy or both as he and Jimmy held their breath; waiting for the crack to continue, or the window to implode – smothering them in a living, stinging cloud of yellow-black horror.

But the gigantic crack had ceased to move, even though there was still a terrifying and dangerous crackling sound. Don and Jimmy remained frozen. Don recognised that sound from his youth: a tentative foot placed on what seemed to be a shallow but heavily iced-over pond in winter. The now too-heavy weight of his boot on that now-clearly very deep water on what was now clearly very thin ice – as glass-webbed fractures began to crunch and craze outwards from the outline of his foot and, oh God... had he taken a step too far?

The sound continued, but there were no smaller cracks appearing around that one dark bolt in the pane, no sign that the fracture was spreading. But the noise – what was the noise?

At last, Don realised that the sound they were now hearing was not the continued sound of cracking glass at all. As the yellow-black horde on the other side of the window-glass began to surge and undulate in even more frenzy, he could see and *hear* now that they were somehow moving and making noise in a completely *different* way. As needles of faint light began to stab and flicker into the room, Don could see that knots of squirming wasps were clumping themselves in different convoluted masses – to allow *gaps* to appear between them on the window.

"Dad... Dad..."

Now, in the briefly cleared spaces of cleared glass – smaller, wriggling clumps were forming specific and somehow familiar shapes'.

"No, son. It's not possible. They're not..."

But, somehow, they were.

The wasps were swarming and rearranging themselves on the glass to make familiar, clustered patterns with their bodies.

"They're making..." stammered Jimmy.

"They're *not*..." stated Don emphatically.

"Letters and words," finished Jimmy.

And Don could not finish his statement, for the wasps were indeed making letters and words on the window with their bodies. There was something even shriller in the change to the buzzing, droning sound that filled the living room – as if the mass hive-mind of this rapacious horde was insanely eager for those trapped inside to understand what they – what it – wanted them to know.

Girl

Boy

Girl

Boy

And then all the gaps in the window were filled in again as the window became a complete seething mass as before. The squirming activity there seemed somehow even more intense, as if the wasp-swarm was frantically deciding on a different course of

490

action; perhaps a different series of images. Yes, now it was impossible not to know. The maddening and deafening buzzing had changed *tone*.

Gaps appeared again as words began to appear once more.

Boy

Girl

Boy

Girl

Boy

"What does it mean, Dad?"

Don could not bring himself to turn when he heard Trish's words from behind as he drew near from the living room, unable to stay on the sofa any longer.

"What does it *mean?*"

The seething activity on the window seemed somehow to react to Jimmy's question, the wasps altering their frenzied, mass configuration as they continually repeated two words:

Boy

Girl

Boy

Girl

"They want me and you, Jimmy." Trish had appeared behind them soundlessly to watch. "Oh God, Mum. I think I'm going to be sick..." Her hand flew to her mouth as Trudy launched from the sofa to embrace her, white-faced, incapable of speech but instinctively protective. She moved her staggering daughter towards the shower room and toilet across from the hall, where wasps still danced on the outside of the interior entranceway doors.

Don stabbed at the mobile phone again.

"For Christ's sake!" He'd started the telephone message before he'd finished dialling. "Why aren't you doing anything? Why have you stopped...?" He couldn't bring himself to mention the crazy 'words' that the wasps were making on the window, because his mind simply could not take in what he had seen, and some strange inner part of him wanted to believe with every iota of self-conviction that he still possessed, that if he simply didn't mention it, then it hadn't happened and perhaps it had gone away.

But it had not gone away.

And the only other noise on the other end of the mobile phone – was buzzing.

Something flashed past Don in a blur of motion, making him recoil and almost drop the phone. It was Jimmy – heading for the kitchen, snatching up a tea towel from a bench and hurling himself at the kitchen sink.

Don spun on his heels, heart hammering, looking for any new source of threat.

"What...?"

"The tap, Dad! The tap in the sink. They can get through the pipes that way!"

"Christ! Did you see any?"

"No – but I just thought."

"God – yes!" Don yanked open a kitchen drawer and pulled out a roll of parcel tape as Jimmy wound the towel tightly around the tap head, his father joining him to rip a length of tape from the roll, biting off the end with his teeth. Jimmy seized the length of it, quickly wrapping the sticky tape around the towel and sealing it in place.

Were the wasps on the kitchen window somehow *angrier* now?

Both Don and Jimmy couldn't bring themselves to look, in case these wasps too had begun forming those same two words on the window as they worked.

"The taps in the upstairs toilet," said Jimmy tightly and in a matter of fact way that was uncanny in its calm.

"Yes..." Don grabbed for another tea towel, but had barely turned from the kitchen when Trish's scream froze him in his tracks.

Trudy was shouting for him over and over, with Trish's shrill cries of panic in counterpoint – and with the bubbling, scrabbling buzz that filled the room – and with Jimmy now at his side, sobbing for air, the room tilted and swerved so that Don's senses whirled in horror as he lost all sense of direction and balance. Expecting to see the carpet looming up at him just before his face made contact with it just before he lost consciousness, Don suddenly found himself braced in the downstairs toilet/shower room door, hands gripping the doorframe at right and left as it holding the fabric of his world together.

Trudy was kneeling on the tiled floor beside the lavatory bowl, cradling Trish with one arm as she clung to her, still giving vent to those terrible cries as Trish. With the other arm, Trudy was flapping a towel wildly towards the blue-tiled shower stall.

"What?" Don's voice was hoarse. "*What?*"

"She's been stung!" gasped Trudy. "Don, she's been *stung!*"

"Where?"

"On her arm!"

"No! Where's the wasp?"

"There, *there,* for Chrisakes!"

And as Trudy flapped the towel again, Don saw the wasp at last, droning and circling against the tiles and somehow much too large at close quarters to be any kind of wasp he'd ever seen before.

"This is a new and aggressive species of African/Asian wasp", the female voice on the other end of the telephone line had said. And then: *"Are you sure that no one has been stung?"*

Jimmy suddenly snatched the tea towel from Don's hand, slapping past him into the shower stall as he looped the towel into a rope and ferociously *thwacked* at the wasp.

"Jimmy!" shouted Trudy.

The wasp evaded the towel, circled high in the stall when the towel hit the tiled wall and Jimmy's heels squeaked on the tiled floor as he slipped and pivoted, crouched low, looked up – and then straightened and whiplashed with the towel again. The wasp dropped into the stall.

"Bastard!"

Jimmy stamped it flat; once, twice, three times – leaving a black-yellow stain as large as a trampled kiwi fruit.

Don put a restraining hand on his son's shoulder as he sucked in air, chest heaving with anger and exertion.

Much too big to be a wasp, said that voice in his head again.

"Oh God," said Trudy. "Get rid of it!"

Don pulled out a length of roll from the toilet holder, scraped up the splattered insect with disgust and threw it down the toilet bowl. Trudy hurried to him, elbowed the flush and returned to draw Trish to her feet. Their daughter had stopped screaming now and was sobbing low and soft. Don thought that his heart might break as he hurried to them.

"Where? Where's she stung?"

Trudy pointed vaguely to the top of her arm as Don helped to usher them out of the shower room. When there was further movement from the shower stall, Don looked back to see that Jimmy was hastily wrapping the other tea towel around the shower head and gesturing to his father for the roll of tape that Don still held limply by his side. He rushed back to hand it to him and as Jimmy quickly yanked out another length and secured the towel, Don stumbled back to the kitchen. Jimmy began stuffing toilet paper into the plug holes of the bath and sink.

"Medicine..." The words choked in Trudy's throat. "...kit. In the cupboard."

Don fumbled in the kitchen cabinet, looking anxiously back. Trish's sobs had diminished, but her eyes were closed as her mother held her, and her body was trembling. Don had never seen his wife's face look so white. He found the kit – and a 'Wasp Aid' spray beside it, looking horribly useless on the shelf. He grabbed them both and hurried to his wife and daughter.

Has anyone been stung? The voice had said.

What did that *mean*?

Trudy pulled back the top of Trish's sleeve, furiously scrutinising for any sign of a sting, now spraying so hard that a cloud surrounded their heads, making her cough.

"Why aren't they *DOING* anything?" Don suddenly exploded.

"The phone," snapped Trudy. "Try the phone again."

"I tried the phone!"

"Try it again!"

Don stabbed at the mobile again.

This time, it seemed that there might be a connection. There was a noise, a slight suggestion of ringing and then, Don recoiled when he realised that the sound he could now hear on his phone was the same rasping and buzzing sounds of the wasps at the windows. Jimmy had joined Trudy to help with the spray and now with a salve that she had found in the medical kit and – thank God, they were not looking back at the kitchen window where, as if waiting for Don to notice, the wasps were even now forming new words on the window.

And Don could only look from those newly forming words to his wife and son as they tended to Trish, not wanting *them* to see as the swarm scrabbled and droned on the window, that same noise emanating from his mobile phone, hissing over the flat-line bleeping of an unavailable connection.

Don't look up, Don projected at his family. *For Christ's sake, don't look up at the window.* And then, to the window: *Go away. For Christ's sake, please go away.*

The new words continued to form and sweep away, form and sweep away – like magnetised iron filings on those old games that he so loved as a child. And God, oh God, how he wanted to be a child again and so very far away from here. But the wasps continued with their relentless messages:

Want Girl
Want Boy
Want Girl
Want Boy
Want Girl...

"Trish, darling." Trudy's voice sounded cracked and broken. "Come on, love. Wake up..."

Was there some way he could cover that window?

"Don!"

His attention jerked from the glass.

"She won't wake up, Don."

Don knelt to stroke his daughter's damp hair away from her face. It was white and clammy. Her eyes were semi-closed; he could see her pupils moving rapidly behind her eyelids.

"Oh God," gasped Trudy. "It's – what do you call it – anaphylactic shock? Is that what it is?"

"I don't know. Wake up, Trish. Wake up!"

"Do something, Don. We've got to do something!"

"What the hell *can* we do? They're not answering the fucking phone and..."

But Don was talking to empty air as Trudy laid her daughter down into his lap and dashed to the main telephone. Before he could tell her that it was no good, she had plucked it up and stabbed 999. By the look of anxiety and then horror on her face he knew without asking that she could hear the same manic buzzing that was on the mobile phone and within the house itself.

"Computer!" Trudy whirled from the telephone table.

"What?"

"Where's your laptop, Jimmy?"

"In my room..." Jimmy was walking in circles now, not knowing what to do.

"Get it!"

Jimmy sprinted up the stairs to the first floor, feet thudding on the carpet as Trudy returned to Trish, now cradling her head and trying to make her open her eyes.

Robbed of strength, Don could only ask: "Laptop?"

"If we can't get a line, we can send email or text or Google 'wasp sting' or something..."

"But if we can't get a phone signal then we won't get a..."

"We've *GOT TO DO SOMETHING, DON! Don't-you-SEE...?*"

"What was that?"

"*What?*"

Don was staring at the living room windows, now stupidly relieved that the words there had gone and that the wasps had continued in their undulating, formless, massed covering of the glass. "Did you hear that? I heard something."

"*WHAT?*"

"Something. I heard people shouting. I did! They're still out there, Trudy! They're still trying to help us. Listen!"

"I can't hear anything."

"Listen!"

As they both strained to listen, Jimmy's feet thundered on the stairs again.

"Mum, Dad! The laptop's not working. It's just all static or something."

Waving the laptop, he jumped that last few stairs into the living room. Don was already on his way into the study when Trudy instructed Jimmy: "Stay with your sister. Keep her head up off the floor." As Jimmy cradled Trish's head, Trudy hurried after her husband.

"But Mum, I don't know how to..."

"Just keep her head up!"

Don had already switched the computer on earlier that morning and as Trudy joined him in front of the static filled screen, they both tried to avoid looking at the drawn venetian blinds and the swirling mass on the window glass beyond; casting its own slatted swirling shadows on the study furniture. Don furiously swivelled the computer 'mouse' again. "How can the telephone and the computer reception be affected like this? These are wasps, for Christ's sake. They're just *wasps*." Don looked furiously around the study. "Maybe books – encyclopaedias – anything..."

When Trudy screamed into his ear, Don almost catapulted across the room, his thigh colliding with the desk and rocking the computer on its table stand. A tray loaded with pens and pencils skittered across the desk, its contents rattling to the floor.

"Trudy!"

Heart hammering, Don whirled to see that his wife was braced in the study doorway, looking back out into the living room. Something was happening in there now; something that had stabbed pure terror into his wife's heart – and even though he struggled to push past her and get back to the kids, she seemed wedged in that door frame. At last, he dragged one of her arms free and could see Jimmy and Trish in there. But somehow, there was something wrong with what was happening to them; something so terribly *wrong* that it made no sense – no logical sense, at all – and some strangely skewed part of Don simply refused to accept it.

"Trish...?"

His daughter was no longer prone on the floor, with Jimmy bending over her. Their positions had been strangely – and quickly – reversed. Jimmy was now lying on the floor, on his back and with his arms spread wide in cruciform, and Trish was now kneeling over him – and with her face bent closely over her

497

brother's face so that it was mostly obscured by her dangling hair.

Her face was *very* close to her brother's.

And now, Don could see that his daughter's face was somehow *much too close* to Jimmy's face as he lay completely motionless beneath her.

Was she *kissing* him?

Her head was moving rapidly. Tight and rapid and *busy* and oh God, something here was all *wrong* – as Don pushed past his wife and shouted: *"Trish!"*

Oh Good God, is she eating *him?*

In that moment, Don had two powerful and sickening images that threatened to overwhelm him.

The mandibles of a wasp, eating a piece of fruit.

The mandibles of a praying mantis working on the ruined head of its mate as it devoured its partner.

"TRISH!"

But when Don's daughter reared back to stare in hate and defiance, there were no mandibles, no desiccated and bloody flesh. The pure hatred in Trish's expression was so ferocious and so alien that it stopped Don in his tracks and drew a frightened gasp from Trudy at his side. For a moment, he did not recognise Trish as his daughter. Jimmy remained unconscious and apparently unmarked, his face blank and peaceful as if he was asleep upstairs in bed.

"Stay away!" hissed Trish, grabbing Jimmy's arm and suddenly rising to drag him away from them across the living room floor.

Trudy lunged forward.

"What are you *DOING?*"

She strode quickly forward to grab her daughter's arm and Don came up quickly behind to grab them both when Trish suddenly flew at her mother, as if trying to scratch her face with both clawed hands. And as he struggled to separate the thrashing mother and daughter, a voice in Don's head was screaming: *"Why is Trish making those sounds? Why is she HISSING like that?"*

Trudy succeeded in grabbing her daughter's arms as they wrestled over Jimmy on the floor. Don saw Trudy stand on her son's chest, yelled aloud and tried to grab Jimmy's leg so that he could drag him from under the affray. Jimmy's head lolled from side to side as Don tugged again – and Trudy was suddenly pitched headlong into him. Don staggered back, felt his ankle twist, cried out in pain and alarm – and Trudy was suddenly in his arms. His centre of balance was gone; the world tilting, and he had to hang on to his wife for dear life or she would be flung off this spinning world. He had no sense of falling, so that when the floor slammed into his back, the impact and pain felt as if he had somehow stepped into the path of a ten ton truck. All air inside his lungs was instantly expelled in a painful rush, and Trudy's hair was in his face, his eyes and his mouth.

His teeth felt as if they had been jarred loose, and he could taste blood.

"Trudy, get *OFF* me..."

"What...?"

Don could hear a *slithering* sound above the ringing in his ears and the omnipresent buzzing and rustling of the things on the windows. The ringing was bad, and the droning buzz was hideous – but there was something *terrible* about this new slithering sound – which now came again – and Don knew that he had to get out from under his stunned wife and do something to stop that slithering, because if he didn't something even more terrible than the terrible things that had happened that afternoon might finally overwhelm them all.

"Trudy! Get up – I can't move..."

Don shoved at the dead weight of his wife.

And the slithering began again.

"Trudy! Please!"

And yet more slithering.

Trudy groaned and rolled, giving Don just enough space to slide out from under her to see the source of the slithering sound.

Trish had recommended dragging Jimmy across the carpet. Now, her tongue was sticking out in the way that Don remembered from when she was a little girl, concentrating on a puzzle or working on one of her paintings. But with her suddenly white face and the impossibly large and black irises of her eyes (when he knew those eyes to be a brilliant blue), the gesture was somehow obscene in its intensity and its hidden intent.

"Trish? What are you doing...?"

Don squirmed and shoved; now stupidly cursing his semi-conscious wife for deciding to give up on her self-imposed diet because its lack of effect had been making her depressed.

"You're not well. That sting... Trish..."

Now at last, he realised where she was dragging Jimmy, and the realisation both filled him with horror and gave him the strength to redouble his efforts to disentangle himself from his wife.

"Trish! Don't..."

Trish snatched at the interior door leading to the front door, caught the handle, but wasn't near enough to twist it open.

"For Christ's sake, Trish! What are you *DOING?*"

Don kicked with both feet and Trudy rolled away from him, groaning.

But it was too late.

Trish jumped from Jimmy to the interior door, twisted the handle again – and suddenly it was open. The wasps trapped in the hallway were instantly into the living room.

"TRISH!"

Don blundered to his feet as Trish returned quickly to his son, now grabbing with both arms and yanking him into the hallway as Don staggered, head down, towards them – waving his arms.

The wasps that had been hovering and fluttering on the other side of the glass door but were now in the room, seemed suddenly filled with one quicksilver and determined purpose. Bunching together quickly into a fist sized mass with a trailing 'tail', they came directly at Don's face – making a high-pitched whirring sound that he had never heard before; arrowing en masse and with such sudden velocity that he could only throw himself to one side, colliding with the sofa – now grabbing at a sofa cushion and flapping it wildly around his head while that bloody woman's voice rang in his head: *Has anyone been stung? Has anyone been stung?*

Don heard the latch on the front door click, felt the draft of a hot wind and saw light from the drive at the front of the house as Trish yanked the door open – was aware that Trudy had recovered and was weaving beside him now and shouting Trish's name over and over as she too flailed in the air with a sofa cushion in either hand.

Oh Christ, the door is open! THE DOOR IS OPEN!

And suddenly, a chaotic black-yellow storm of wasps erupted en masse through that open front door and filled the room.

Don continued to flail in panic, shouting hoarsely and feeling furred, prickly and squirming shapes in his mouth and waiting for the stings that would surely make his tongue swell and choke him. They filled his eye sockets, hunting for the soft jelly behind his eyelids. He could feel them on his face and in his hair, massing on his hands in great squirming lumps that surged under the cuffs of his shirt sleeves. He fell to his knees, spat and coughed and waited for the pain that would be as enveloping as being lowered into some terrible acid bath. The awful droning and buzzing seemed to reach a new intensity; the all-consuming and invasive noise seemed suddenly to *swell*, making Dons ears *pop!* And at that precise moment, just as Don felt he would disappear into agony – the invasive noise seemed somehow to suddenly *shrink* to a buzz-saw, a whistling squeal of sound that pierced his brain and made him scream.

And then the suffocating, swirling, engulfing noise – was gone.

Instantly, it seemed, the wasps all over his body had disappeared.

The shock of it made Don leap to his feet, hunched and staring at the front door. And he knew then that the wasps had got into his ears; pierced his ear drums with their stingers, and that he was deaf. Because there should be noise. There should be some sort of sound to accompany the horror of what he was seeing right before his eyes.

The buzzing had gone, the infernal swarming droning sound had gone, but the wasps were still here – still in the living room, not on his body now, not on Trudy – but still swirling in a vortex around Trish as she stood in the opened doorway, dragging her brother out of the house as the now impossibly silent swarm enshrouded both of their figures to the extent that they were now only silhouettes.

Don tried to shout, but could not – and flung his hand out when his daughter and son disappeared from sight in that swirling and silent mass. Trudy was clawing at his legs, trying to rise, and he pulled her up onto her feet. And suddenly, as if that doorway was somehow the frame of a film camera aperture and the film in that frame had suddenly gone into reverse, the all-encompassing wasp cloud boiled backwards and away out of the doorway with impossible speed. Bright white light flooded the room, blinding Don and Trudy as they staggered towards it.

The door slammed viciously shut.

Don collided with the interior door, shattering glass as he lunged to the front door now, wrenching at the handle as Trudy collided with his back. The door remained steadfastly shut, as if locked. In a frenzy, yelling obscenities and screaming for his children, Don yanked at the handle with both hands to no avail; now throwing himself at the door, pounding and punching at the wood panels, tearing fingernails as he clawed at the frame and Trudy wept at his back.

When he at last collapsed exhausted to his knees in front of the door, Trudy continued to hold him from behind.

They wept.

And did not realise, until much later – that the hissing and swarming movement at the windows – had gone.

*

"Do you feel it?"

Don seemed to recognise that voice but couldn't put a face to it. When he looked up from where he knelt, he realised that he knew the tear-streaked face of the woman kneeling next to him, but couldn't bring her name to mind.

"Do you feel it?" the woman asked again, and now Don realised that this was his wife – and knew what she meant.

"Yes." His voice was raw and his throat seemed full of gravel.

"Have we been asleep?"

"No. Yes. I don't know..."

"I don't know how long we've been kneeling here."

"We have to find them." Don began to struggle to his feet, his arms and legs heavy and clumsy.

"I think we've been drugged," said Trudy.

"Drugged? How can we be drugged...?" Don staggered across

the glass strewn floor to the main door and began tugging at the handle, just as he'd done before... before what?

"The wasps," Trudy also began to rise unsteadily to her feet. "Could they do that? Phero – phero... "

"Pheromones." The word came drunkenly out of Don's mouth. "No – they can't do that." He tugged again at the door, which remained unyielding – and now he could see why.

The door frame was packed solidly with a compacted and crushed mass of dead wasps. The lintel and frame had been sealed with a hideous wasp jelly. Staggering back, drunk and unsteady, Don clumsily picked up a sliver of glass from the floor. Now with one hand braced on the door, he began to drag the sharpened end down between the door frame and the door. Dead wasps crackled and crumbled around him as he worked. For a long while, Trudy watched him in apparent stupefaction and then – slowly and painfully, also picked up a sliver and staggered to join him, copying Don's action in the other door jamb with zombie arms.

Both wanted to call out for Trish and Jimmy beyond the door. But somehow, neither had the strength to summon the words.

With a final crack and judder, Don tugged at the door handle and it began to open grudgingly, a black and yellow crackle of dead wasps tumbling around him from the edge and overhead lintel of the door. The sliver of glass in his hand fell with a silvery tinkle at his feet.

Several weak tugs later and with a continual thin screech of tortured wood, the door was halfway open and grey light stabbed the hallway, somehow rendering everything in black and white. A car horn was sounding, somewhere far off.

Wisps of – something – crept around the edges of the door as Don edged himself outside, a carpet of dead wasps and glass crackling around his feet. Mist? Fog? Don retched and coughed, holding his forearms across his face and mouth as Trudy staggered to join him.

It was smoke.

They both stood at the top of the steps outside their house, holding each other and looking at the scene of devastation before them.

The smoke was drifting through the hedges on either side of their front garden in tattered wisps, and the drone of the car horn went on and on.

There were dark and blackened shapes on the garden lawn. Streaks of flattened ash that had clearly been caused by blasts of fire, and crumpled bundles of blackness that at first were indeterminate but as the wisps of smoke curled around them and were scattered by the wind, some of them now clearly and horribly recognisable as formerly human bodies. One of the more flattened outlines had a ruptured cylinder still fastened to what had been its back – a flame thrower canister, with a semi-disintegrated hose and blackened nozzle lying beside it.

Don and Trudy became aware of another sound now. Like the continuous car alarm, somewhere distant and the source of the noise not visible. But clearly, the *whup-whup-whup* of a helicopter rotor blade.

And everywhere on the lawn around the blackened smudges and ragged mounds of semi-ash silhouettes of what had once been human – thousands upon thousands of dead wasps, carpeting the green and festooning the garden hedges and shrubbery in crumpled clusters of yellow-and-black.

Trudy staggered down the three small concrete steps that led from the door to the garden. Don watched, still stupefied, as she stepped tentatively onto the lawn trying to avoid the clusters of crushed and burned insects. Something about a particular mound of yellow-and-black seemed to be drawing her dimmed curiosity and Don could only stand and watch as – slowly and awkwardly – she descended to one knee. She turned in his direction as she knelt and now Don could see that not only were her movements not only stiff and juddering, but that her face was also changing in expression as she rested on her second knee, now placing one hand and then a second carefully on the grass as she stared downwards, lowering herself still further to stare at the mound of wasps that had so drawn her attention.

With each marionette move, Trudy's face was contorting to a white mask of fascination, horror and revulsion. Her horror seemed to also have something of growing awareness as she lowered herself now to her forearms, staring intently at the crumbled pile.

Don stumbled down the steps towards her with no conscious realisation that he had decided to do so. When Trudy looked up, her terrified and staring eyes froze him where he stood.

"Don! *Don!* Why have they got little heads? Why have they got little *faces?*"

When she screamed, it was like an electric shock coursing instantaneously through every nerve end of his body. It acted like shears, slicing through his own marionette strings, so that all he could do now was to slump to his knees beside his wife and the black and yellow pile between them.

When Trudy looked down at that pile again, his own gaze was dragged with hers to the jumbled mess and now he too was leaning further down to gaze and inspect as his wife's words hissed in his ears.

"They've got faces, Don! They've got *faces!*"

Down, down – and further down.

Staring.

And gazing.

And yes, now he could see that –

My God they didn't have the heads of wasps, they didn't have those jet black marbled eyes or the mandibles. They had – faces, yes faces...

And when he was so close that he could see clearly for the first time – Don screamed and leapt to his feet, kicking that crumbled pile into scattered fragments.

Trudy was screaming somewhere too as reason left Don and he ran staggering around in circles, kicking at the black-and-yellow piles; skidding on the blackened and crumbling human remains as ash and debris and shoals of dead wasp husks exploded all around him in a choking and horrifying cloud. In his whirling, out of control madness, Don collided with the small metal garden seat beside the nearest hedge with a hollow clang that sent a thin mist of soot shivering from its pitted grey metal frame. A forgotten watering can beneath the seat spun out from beneath, tangling with his legs. Don kicked it madly away and was only barely aware that someone or something had grabbed his forearms and was now shouting directly into his face. With his throat hoarse and his breath now in shuddering gasps as he finally staggered to a halt, the other sounds in the garden came back to his ears as his wild dance subsided, the *whup-whup-whup* of the close-by but still invisible helicopter, the drone of the invisible car alarm and the thudding of his own heart in his ears. When his eyes refocused, he could see that it was Trudy holding his arms; her white face thrust into his own as she hissed continually into his face: "Look, Don! Look – over there! Over *THERE*!"

Stupidly he followed her gaze to the area just beneath the garden seat, and to the place where the watering can had lain before he kicked it away.

Something was moving there on the small unscorched section of grass.

Something very small that wriggled in the spare stalks of grass.

Don allowed himself to be dragged to the bench.

"Look, Don! *Look*!"

Trudy was on her knees again now, dragging Don to kneel beside her. When she hunched right down eagerly, fiercely scrutinising what wriggled there, Don joined her; face thrust next to hers, both intently staring.

There was a wasp there.

Unburned, somehow stunned or ailing or drugged – and somehow entangled in that grass.

No – not one wasp.

Two wasps.

Both with something different about their heads.

Trudy sobbed.

When Don and Trudy's faces were pushed down close to those struggling insects, they could now see – with infinite horror – what they so terribly yet instinctively knew was so 'different' about those wasp heads, and of all the wasps' heads in that garden.

"Save them!" hissed Trudy. "Save them, Don!"

Don looked frantically around for something – anything. He could find nothing. He slapped his trouser pockets, his shirt pockets. Nothing. Now frantically hunkering backwards, he clambered to his feet and ran back up the garden steps, crunching through crackling piles of dead wasps and dashing back into the house and into the kitchen. Re-emerging from the house, gasping for breath, he hurried back to his wife and hurriedly prayed that the two surviving wasps had not recovered and flown away in that short period of time. Gibbering, sweat now streaking his dirtied face, Don squatted down next to Trudy and carefully – ever so carefully – he tenderly nudged each of the wasps into the opened matchbox that he had snatched from one of the kitchen cupboards.

When they were inside the box, Don slid it carefully closed and slumped back into a sitting position with a relieved and idiot grin on his face.

He looked up at Trudy.

She was staring at the matchbox in his hands, and smiling.

But to Don, she seemed to have gone to another place inside her head.

As he watched her, the sounds of the helicopter and the car alarm carried on, and it seemed that there were voices now. Men, shouting in a way that soldiers might shout orders to each other.

Trudy began to hum.

And to rock on her knees, from side to side.

Don recognised the tune.

It was an old Abba song: 'The Winner Takes it All'.

Now he remembered a lyric from that song, as Trudy continued to hum. Something about building a nest or a home and being strong there.

Now there was the sound of distant gunfire, more urgent shouting and the faraway *whoosh* of more scorching but unseen flame.

The smoke thickened as it drifted over them on the lawn; coiling, enshrouding and then scattering away in ragged tatters. Fascinated, Don's gaze followed those tattered ribbons of smoke upwards and away – just as something else moved in the sky, far away.

A dark, roiling cloud was coming in across the city.

No – not a cloud.

This was moving in a different way. It was swirling and undulating like a cloud, with breakaway coils and ribbons that reminded Don of the way that starlings massed together in the sky. What was it called? A murmuration. Yes, that was it – it moved like a murmuration of starlings.

But these were not starlings.

This was something else.

Trudy's hand was on his arm.

She had stopped humming.

"Let me see again..." she said, staring at the match box.

"I don't want them to fly away," answered a little boy's voice that Don suddenly realised was his own.

"Please."

They both hunkered over the box as Don prised it open by a minimum, finger ready to slide it shut. There was wriggling movement. Enough to keep Trudy happy. She sat back again, smiling as he slid the matchbox shut.

"We haven't lost them, then?"

"No," said Don. "They'll always be here."

Above and far away, but getting closer, the 'cloud' was making a noise.

The men's' shouting was now more intense. There was more gunfire and the sounds of flame throwers. More smoke rose and swirled from somewhere beyond the hedges.

The noise of the approaching, enveloping cloud drowned out the sound of the helicopter and car alarm, now drowning the sounds of the men and the guns and the fire.

Not so much buzzing, as howling.

Louder and hungrier and howling, howling, howling...

The sky began to darken.

Don and Trudy sat, cradling the matchbox, and began to hum Abba together.

~

Stephen Laws *is a full-time novelist, living in Newcastle upon Tyne in England. His award winning novels include* GHOST TRAIN, SPECTRE, THE WYRM, THE FRIGHTENERS, DARKFALL, GIDEON, MACABRE, DAEMONIC, SOMEWHERE SOUTH OF MIDNIGHT, CHASM *and* FEROCITY. *His short stories can be found in the collection,* THE MIDNIGHT MAN.

His novels have been published in America, Canada, Germany, France, Spain, Japan, Norway, Denmark, The Netherlands, and Italy. His short stories have won BBC Radio and 'Sunday Sun' awards. He is also the recipient of the British Fantasy Society Award, the Count Dracula Society Award and the SOFFIA.

His website is: www.stephenlaws.com

———

* Roger Keen *was born in London and attended art colleges in Plymouth and Bournemouth before pursuing a career in television. He began publishing fiction and non-fiction in the 1990s, specialising in noir short stories and articles and reviews concerning genre film and literature. He has a particular interest in the Surrealists, the Beat writers, 1960s psychedelia, cyberpunk and weird cinema.*

He has written a counterculture memoir, The Mad Artist: Psychonautic Adventures in the 1970s, *and a psychological horror/crime novel,* Literary Stalker. *His other work has appeared in numerous magazines, anthologies and webzines, including* International Times, Out of the Shadows, *the* PsypressUK Journal, Reality Sandwich, The Digital Fix *and* The Oak Tree Review; *and he also writes booklet essays for Blu-ray releases of classic weird and psychedelic films for* Arrow Video.

THE OTHER MIDNIGHT STREET ANTHOLOGIES

RAMSEY CAMPBELL
PETER STRAUB
SIMON CLARK
STEPHEN LAWS
NINA ALLEN
THANA NIVEAU
RALPH ROBERT MOORE
JOEL LANE
PAUL FINCH
ALLEN ASHLEY
GARY COUZENS
RHYS HUGHES
TONY RICHARDS
DAVID TURNBULL
KEN GOLDMAN
ROSANNE RABINOWITZ
STEPHEN GALLAGHER
ANDREW DARLINGTON
SUSAN YORK
ANDREW HOOK
MICHAEL WASHBURN
& MANY MORE....

FIND OUT MORE AT:
www.midnightstreetpress.com

Printed in Poland
by Amazon Fulfillment
Poland Sp. z o.o., Wrocław